T0312516

MICHELLE KENNEY is a firm believer in magic, and that ancient doorways to other worlds can still be found if we look hard enough. She is also a hopeless scribbleaholic and, when left to her own devices, likes nothing better than to dream up mystical, fantasy worlds in a dog-eared notebook. Doctors say they're unlikely to find a cure any time soon.

In between scribbling, she loves reading, running, attempting to play gypsy-folk music and treasure-hunting on deserted beaches with her young dreamers-in-training.

Michelle is a graduate of the Curtis Brown Writing for Children Novel Course. She also holds an LLB (Hons) Degree and is currently an Accredited Practitioner with the CIPR, with whom she has won several national awards for her magazine and media/PR-related work.

Michelle is currently represented by Chloe Seager of Northbank Talent Management and can be found at:

facebook.com/BookofFireMK
@mkenneypr
@michken01
Website: michellekenney.co.uk

Also by Michelle Kenney

Book of Fire

City of Dust

MICHELLE KENNEY

ONE PLACE. MANY STORIES

This novel is entirely a work of fiction. The names, characters
and incidents portrayed in it are the work of the author's
imagination. Any resemblance to actual persons, living or
dead, events or localities is entirely coincidental.

HQ
An imprint of HarperCollins*Publishers* Ltd
1 London Bridge Street
London SE1 9GF

This paperback edition 2018

1
First published in Great Britain by
HQ, an imprint of HarperCollins*Publishers* Ltd 2018

Michelle Kenney asserts the moral right to be
identified as the author of this work.
A catalogue record for this book is
available from the British Library.

ISBN: 9780008322984

For more information visit: www.harpercollins.co.uk/green

For Nick,
and our journey around the words.

Et in Arcadia Ego

Chapter 1

When a black aquila falls from the golden sky, it will spark a winter of a thousand fires. Or so Grandpa used to say. Yet this day was iris blue in bud. Colour enough to steal a girl's thoughts. And the ground was green with the sweetenings of spring as the bird fell. It was noiseless at first, before the hollow barrelling of wind, like a meteorite powering directly towards Arafel's forest. And as though it was Pantheon's ice-bitch herself, I ran.

'Tal?'

Max's whisper steadied me, like the steadfast branches of the Great Oak in the middle of monsoon season. And I strained through the nightmare towards the voice that could take me away from the fear, the watching forest, and the distended white faces that loomed and receded, jeering. Always jeering.

'Tal?'

The second whisper pulled me back. It was the way it worked. The first reached through the haze of distorted images; the second caught and pulled me home.

I rolled in to his chest, burying my face in his outdoor scent as my room loomed into focus. Everything was just as it should be. The wizened branches of our white oak were still entwined above my simple reed mattress, mirroring our bodies. I drew

1

a steadying breath, and forced my tight limbs to relax. I was home.

'The same?'

His gentle question said everything, and I nodded before turning away to stare out at the kind night sky. It blinked its forgiveness. Somehow it knew Max's care was bittersweet. That, after Pantheon, I'd understood three things:

One, that for some inexplicable, never-to-be-understood reason, Max loved me; two, that I loved him back, fiercely; and three, that his forest-green eyes were entirely the wrong colour.

I'd nearly whispered it once, after a dream, but managed to stop myself just in time.

Commander General Augustus Aquila. It helped to think of him as Pantheon's new leader, untouchable and distant somehow. It kept him at bay from my everyday thoughts, even if it didn't work in my dreams. And yet somewhere deep inside, Max knew. I saw it in the way he glanced at me when he thought I was distracted. And the guilt was suffocating. Which was why I kissed Max, why I wanted his body to warm mine before the dawn shift, why I listened when he talked about the future – our future – ignoring the twisting deep inside.

And according to the seasonal crop chart, it had been twelve months. Twelve sunlit months since I'd escaped the Lifedomes; fifty-two grey weeks since Grandpa had left; three hundred and sixty-five fragile dawns since he'd touched my skin.

August.

I closed my eyes, and this time my oblivion was like the fathomless sky.

***

'Brace of pheasant! Enjoy 'em now before the monsoon! Coming early this year so Mags says … Enjoy nice fattened birds, two for a good price!'

2

I grinned at Eli, ignoring Bereg's overloud prediction that the late summer rains would wash the wildfowl clean out of Arafel. He said the same every year, even though everyone knew he and Mags, the village fortune-teller, had a long-standing arrangement. And despite his gloomy warnings, I'd never once eaten squirrel all winter.

'Split shifts this week,' Eli signed as I traded two of Mum's woven garlic and shallots chains for a loaf of sunflower bread. It was her favourite.

There was a buzz about the market this morning. The warm spring sunshine glinted off the ripened beef tomatoes, and early corn-ears were piled high like edible gold. One of the perks of wholesale climate change was the chance for two harvests if we farmed carefully, though the monsoon rain always threatened the last. This year the first crop was good though, and that took pressure off us all.

I nodded, stifling a yawn.

'My best lychee source for your morning shifts?' I signed, watching my twin's face break into a mischievous smile.

Now twenty, Eli had changed the most over the last twelve months. Isca Pantheon had scarred us all in more ways than one, but when Max, August and I thought Octavia had beaten us, Eli had found strength in his extraordinary gift. And that day had bred a new quiet air of authority in him.

He'd left the shy boy behind, along with his dependence on his sister to communicate with the world. And while I found it disquieting at first, it was also oddly freeing. I'd always loved with him a protective intensity, but he'd forced me to see the man he'd grown into. And he was a man who'd saved us all from a barbaric death; a man who looked after those he loved; and a man who understood animals better than anyone else I knew.

'Your best lychee source – and you muck out Celia for a week!' Eli bartered, winking.

'What? She's in season, isn't she?!' I protested, alarmed at the thought of going anywhere close to Eli's heavy boar sow at her most unpredictable.

'Think I'd rather snooze in the Great Oak,' I added, watching his smile fade.

'Still not sleeping then?' he signed.

We made our way out of the busy marketplace towards the wizened wisteria tree at the edge of the forest. Its aged branches and lavender fronds created a natural canopy under which hunters gathered on days like today – the last day of our working week, celebrated with traditional tree-running trials.

I shook my head lightly, shifting the woven basket of traded goods on my arm. My disturbed nights weren't exactly a secret, but I was wary of talking about them with Eli. Because of Max.

The tension between them was so real, and yet I couldn't have survived the last twelve months without my best friend. A brief glance over the village fire, and Max and I were both back in the dark clawing tunnels, trying to breathe through the swirling dust of the Flavium. Those memories often clung to the edges of my consciousness until dawn crept through the woven roof of our treehouse, or Max's warm arms chased them away.

Mum had turned a blind eye to his dusk arrivals and dawn exits through my window. She recognized we were no longer two people, as much as two parts of a story that only made sense together. But Eli had been less enthusiastic. Max had always represented an intrusion to our twin bond, and our new arrangement had only compounded that feeling. I tried to reassure my brother, but he only shrank from conversation, isolating himself from me. The truth was, Max and I were closer than any other friends I knew. And although the line was blurred, there had been one night of torrential rain two months before when the nightmares wouldn't stop, no matter how tightly Max held me.

We were both guilty of needing to leave it all behind – Pantheon, its cruel perversions and terrifying creations – and somehow that desire had turned into a fire we couldn't quench.

4

And there was an irrevocable feeling of needing to know whether it could mend us.

So, he'd stepped inside my world completely and when he gripped my hand that night, our bodies fused, we unlocked a door we couldn't quite close.

It hadn't happened again, despite the burn in Max's eyes, but the memory was there now, binding us, dividing us.

And Eli didn't like it one bit.

'At least my dreams are tamer than the rumours!' I winked.

Eli grinned. The whispers about the Inside flourished despite our attempts to quash them, and were more exaggerated every time I went into the village school. Most of them were fireside stories, embellished to entertain. But an echo of the truth was always there, despite our pact to say as little as possible about what we'd actually seen.

'Kai asked whether Insiders breathe fire yesterday!' I signed.

'Ha! Hope you told him only his schoolteacher can do that!'

I smirked and shoved him.

'Time to run,' he challenged.

I smiled as he grabbed my basket and passed it to Mathilda, one of the Elders who invigilated the trials with members of Arafel's Council. The trials were an important village event, honoured every ten days, and we raced according to our age and ability. Eli and I both competed as adult hunters; although Max and I often ended up leading the field, much to Eli's irritation. Today, though, I wanted to run with my brother.

'Time to fly,' I corrected, pushing my tongue into my cheek. He grinned his response, and just for a moment it was just like old times.

'Hey, foraging queen! Hope you weren't expecting me to go easy today!'

Max's strong arms lifted me clean off my feet and swung me round, despite my protest. He put me down rapidly, but the damage had been done. Eli's sunny expression dissolved as he turned his back to watch the young tree-runners line up. And with his tight shoulders and folded arms, he might as well be a million miles away now.

I glared at Max who only held up his hands a little guiltily. We'd discussed keeping things low on the village radar. For Mum and Eli's sake. But I also knew Max suspected me of an ulterior motive, and that he wanted Eli to know about us. He was saved by the sound of a sonorous ibex horn, followed swiftly by a whole cacophony of whoops and cries as the youngest tree-runners set off. Dressed in small trial tunics, with their faces painted the colours of the forest, they looked every inch a feral, tree-living tribe – worthy inheritors of Arafel.

'Come what may, nature finds a way,' I whispered under my breath. My ancestor Thomas's legacy looked to be alive and kicking. Seconds later, they had been completely enveloped by the thick mass of trees and bushes, their presence only evidenced by the occasional rustle or flurry of surprised birds.

'We're up?' Max tested.

'Great,' I responded in a way that told him he wasn't off the hook.

But I knew my brother too well to attempt a clumsy retrieval of the situation just now, and the three of us made our way across to the hunters' start point in silence.

Rief, Saba and Fynn, old school friends, were already waiting by the maple and I nodded briefly. There was always an air of anticipation at the tree-running trials. Learning to move and live within the trees had saved our ancestors from extinction, and the trials served to remind us of the survival skills that brought us through the dust.

'Chalk?' Rief asked.

Eli accepted the piece of dusty rock, and rubbed his hands ceremoniously, before passing it to me. The white powder helped with grip, but also focused our thoughts before the race began. Although most of the hunters knew the flying routes well, the

6

Council occasionally added special challenges. The intention was to replicate the unpredictability of the outside forest as much as possible. This week Max, Bereg and a few of the older hunters had helped construct a sticky net between three acacias to challenge the younger runners.

I took the chalk from Eli, and whitened the palms of my hands methodically. The older trials were usually judged by speed, our acumen as hunters not expected to be in any doubt. But the Council weren't above throwing in wild-card obstacles for us occasionally either. Either way, it paid to be prepared.

'Hunter … Positions!'

Art's command hung in the air and the majority of Arafel's most skilled hunters suddenly melted out from the trees, as though it were the most natural thing in the world. I stepped between Eli and Max, casting a swift glance down the starting line. There had to be more than eighty of us this morning. And with long, lean limbs, faces streaked with dirt and waists hung with seasoned weapons, the hunters were an impressive sight to behold.

A pregnant hush descended, before the pulse of the ceremonial chant thickened the air. It was a simple repetitive beat, low and rhythmic, supposed to replicate the drum of a hunter's heart. A feral heart. I inhaled deeply. It was time. I focused my gaze on my leather-soled feet, and silently repeated the words that had come to feel like a prayer.

'Why run when you can fly?'

I reached out to squeeze Eli's cool hand, and he returned the pressure without looking. Then the ibex horn sounded again and it was just me, the forest and the sun at my back.

We flew like birds, running through trees as though we were animals that had always belonged there. Occasionally I caught the flash of a green tunic or brown hand, dirtied with dust to make it less visible, but no greetings were exchanged. Tree trials were sacrosanct, and no serious hunter would compromise their time with mischief or chat.

7

At first I hung back for Eli, hoping he might still run with me, but when I finally caught sight of him, he'd paired with Fynn. I swallowed my disappointment and flew on, Grandpa's advice lulling me into a swift rhythm:

'Remember what Thomas taught us. An Arafel hunter believes in natural order, respect for his place in the forest, and takes only what he needs to survive.'

His words were as good as imprinted in my mind, and it was several minutes later when I finally dropped to the floor to pause beside a drinking hole. This part of Arafel's forest was lush and dark, and the water came from a deep underground spring, which made it reliably fresh and cool to drink.

I leaned over the water, and watched two hazel eyes gaze back from an earth-stained face. I stared back, trying to read them before I bent to drink. August had always seemed to find it so easy, but right now they seemed as closed and secretive as the dark pond water in which they danced.

I glanced over my shoulder. All was still. Max and Rief had run into a nest of fire ants, which had left me out in front. Fire ant nests were more usually found at the base of trees, but this particular nest had somehow managed to find a home in the centre of one of the well-used tree forks. I frowned. Art's Council were clearly upping the stakes, and I had a suspicion it wasn't just to keep things interesting. Art was nervous, and he had every reason to be.

We'd all but razed Pantheon to the ground, and then taken off. August had been left in charge, but who knew how that had gone down in the twisted, archaic world of Isca Pantheon. And now our existence wasn't a secret. Cassius might be dead, but the Insiders couldn't deny our existence any longer. I thought about the message I'd left: the photograph of Cassius striding through the forest, smiling and helmet-free. It was a message about betrayal on a momentous scale.

I stared back into my own jaded eyes. Our idyllic forest life looked cocooned and protected, but in truth it all balanced on the edge of a harvest scythe. Its continuity depended on political stability inside the domes, and that was so dangerous to assume.

The faint crackle of weighted branches filled the air, and I didn't need a second warning. Rising swiftly, I darted up the nearby kapok tree.

A good hunter never gave up her lead, not for all the apricots in Arafel.

Chapter 2

It was falling fast now. I shimmied down a fallen trunk and leapt up into a thick willow, keeping my eyes trained on the sky above the trees. Max followed agilely, sensing my need for urgency, and only paused when I reached the swaying branches near the top. I held up a hand, knowing the thinner, reedy branches wouldn't support his weight. And it only took one of us to look past Arafel's silvery waterfall into the canopied clearing beyond.

It had been two days since the hunter tree trials, and we were on the outer perimeter of Arafel's forest, the last thicket before the gently sloping pastures we'd cultivated for our rotational crop supplies.

I scanned the busy fields swiftly. I could just spy Kela, today's shift leader, checking the green shoots of the second barley crop, which once only grew in the old-world Middle East. It was another newcomer since the change in climate, and we were grateful for the flour that provided our village with barley bread throughout the volatile monsoon months.

Beyond the long pastures were the gentle, arid slopes that signalled the start of the mountainous terrain. They were used mainly for grazing the village goats, and the occasional wild caribou kill. The slopes were also where Eli had found Jas, our snow leopard watch-cat, when we were just children. As far as I was aware, she was still the only living creature I knew to have wound a precipitous route from the North Mountains' snowy peaks into our hidden paradise.

Today though, Jas's Herculean feat was not foremost in my mind.

I'd followed the tiny falling speck from the roof of our tree-house, feeling suspiciously like I'd fallen into one of my nightmares. Yet this speck was real, I was sure of that. It was also big with a predatory shape, like one of the birds of prey circling way up in the mountains. And its direct, urgent flight marked it out from the rest.

I craned my neck, trying to peer through the dense foliage into a clearing a few tree jumps away. The bird had merged with the trees here several minutes ago.

'What was it?' Max's whisper was barely discernible above the rustle of the willow. 'Boar?' he added hopefully.

I shook my head, drawing mixed comfort from the warmth of his breath against my calf. The fallout was forgotten. I never could stay mad with him anyway, he was simply too Max. And he never suffocated me with words; everything that needed to be said was conveyed with a look or a touch. Apart from that one night, when he'd rolled onto his side to look at me. Really look at me. And I'd never felt more naked. The moon painted his Outsider skin in runes when he whispered the three words that terrified me most. And it was the best and worst moment of my life.

My own words had dried at the back of my throat, and it was part of the reason we hadn't stopped. Because I couldn't wrap words around my own feelings. They wouldn't fit no matter how much I tried to force them. And now the nights were so much harder. The question was always there, hanging between us in the darkness. I really tried to bury my memories, to leave it all behind like we had that night, but the same confusion that stopped

11

my words, stopped everything else. His frustration was tangible. And I could only hope that it overshadowed my guilt, which gnawed like a hunger at the pit of my stomach.

The sun glinted through the trees the way it always did, but today felt different somehow. I lifted my head and sniffed. It was too early for the rains, but the breeze was sharper.

I craned again, and then I glimpsed it, several trees away. The tip of an outstretched wing, a burnished gold-edged wing, and then something else that made my fingers clench the willow until the whites of my knuckles gleamed.

I shinnied back down the branch to face Max.

'Hey, what's up?' he asked, weaving his fingers into mine. 'You look like you spied a strix!'

'Golden plumage,' I whispered, loosening my hand before leaping again into a strong maple, and scurrying down into its thickened fork.

'Griffin?'

Max was right behind me in a heartbeat.

He meant Friskers of course, our much-loved village pet griffin, who now roamed the outside forest. Although the outside forest inhabitants had been disgruntled, I'd no choice but to leave Octavia's engineered beast there when I made it back from Pantheon. I knew it stood the best chance of survival among the wilder animals and vegetation, rather than within our farming community. But instead of embracing its new-found freedom, it had taken to waiting patiently in the outside forest for Arafel hunters to appear, when it would appear like an over-enthusiastic dog, its pink tongue lolling over its carnivorous beak. Even genetically modified mythical beasts had the potential for domestication, it seemed.

One of the village children had since named it after its unique mix of bushy feathers and whiskers, and somehow the name had stuck.

I shook my head.

'Two heads,' I mouthed, watching the teasing light fade from his eyes.

This time his pace matched my own. We both understood the implication of what I'd glimpsed. And as far as we were aware, the only two-headed creatures in existence were Octavia's genetically enhanced haga, supposedly incarcerated inside Pantheon's Lifedomes. Not flying free over the North Mountains.

We took a wide, circuitous route around the clearing, and leapt through the trees like spider monkeys, before dropping into a grove of large banana trees. A newcomer to the western world, they grew in abundance here. Today, I was grateful for their thickened corms and blades, which obscured us from whatever was shuffling around the forest floor just ahead.

I stole forward, pausing only at a light touch on my shoulder. I shook my head abruptly before returning my gaze to my path. Max had always struggled to accept my need to look after myself, but it was one thing I couldn't compromise on. Like those words.

The pounding in my ears steadily increased as we crept forward beneath the swollen leaves, and each careful footstep seemed to sound as loudly as a felled tree branch. But as the interwoven leaves thinned I glimpsed bright colours that made my hairs strain to attention, until finally as I pulled aside the last fronds, there was a sharp gasp. It took a couple of seconds for me to realize it was my own.

I'd seen nothing and no one from Pantheon in a year and yet, somehow, I was staring straight into the archaic eyes of one of Octavia's flying watchdogs of the night.

A haga.

It threw back its crested heads as our eyes connected, one microsecond before it crowed its aggression to a group of red pandas above. They scattered while we stared, mesmerized by the impressive newcomer, which was as alien to its forest surroundings as ever a creature could be.

It reached head and shoulders above any man or woman in

Arafel, and had a wingspan that extended beyond twice that of a natural eagle. It was also one of the creatures August had sworn to keep within the world of Pantheon, despite my protest that the natural world would survive if he threw open the doors. Its containment was one of the fundamental reasons August had stayed behind; so what, in the name of Arafel, was it doing out here?

But I had no time to think. The question was crushed by a sudden leaden weight around my shoulders, sending me careering forward into the lush green grass as a muffled exclamation filled the air. Blindly, I wrestled against my assassin. He was small and lithe, but uncannily fierce, and it took all my strength to thrust him backwards. I was on my feet and spinning around in a heartbeat; just in time to witness Max force his attacker to his knees. He had autumn skin, and curious inked drawings all over his arms and neck. He wasn't from Arafel.

I shot a look at my own combatant, who was drawing himself up to his feet. *Her feet.* I caught my breath again. Our eyes locked, and the forest melted away until there was only the heated rush of recognition. Then there was a brief stunned silence, before I forged forward to wrap myself fiercely around her slight frame.

'Ow! You still have a ridiculously strong grip for a girl!' she complained, detangling herself.

I chuckled, releasing her.

'Like you can talk, General!' I shot back, recovering myself.

The grin illuminating Aelia's elfin face faded a little, and I was suddenly acutely aware of her jaded appearance. Her clothing was even more tattered and stained than I remembered, and she looked tired, deathly tired.

'Are you hurt? How did you find us? Are we really to believe you somehow made it over the mountains on a haga?' I fired incredulously.

Everyone knew the North Mountains were precipitous and unforgiving; their dangerous peaks and terrains had always been

14

our protection. That a girl on a mythical bird could navigate her way over them seemed impossible. Yet here Aelia stood. A miracle, and an ominous threat.

Her eyes gleamed with adventure, and a sleepy dragonfly flapped its wings against the inside of my ribcage. I couldn't imagine how it had taken me so long to work out Aelia was August's Prolet-born sister. They shared the same shrewd wit, and eyes the colour of an Arafel dawn. And right now, they were more unsettling than I cared to admit.

'Max! Let Rajid go. He's got the most awesome Cerberus ink you've ever seen!' she admonished, stepping across to them.

I watched Max relinquish his prize, before catching her up in an affectionate, slightly awkward hug.

'Hey, Lia, wish you'd said you were popping in. I would have gone all out for a brace of rabbits instead of fresh trout!' He winked, holding out a conciliatory hand.

The inked man shook his head and jumped to his feet in one agile move, rubbing his neck.

'And if I'd known you were cooking, I'd have worn my best Prolet dress and booked the sky train instead of an oversized pigeon with no sense of direction!' she retorted.

They grinned, and not for the first time I acknowledged just how suited they were. In another time and space they would have been perfect for one another.

'Tal, there's a lot to say. But probably … not here?' She frowned, shooting a look at Rajid. 'And this big pigeon over here needs some attention. It was cold up there. His flight feathers took a little frosting from the northerly winds.' She ran her hands over the exhausted haga.

I nodded briefly, collecting my wayward thoughts. Aelia was here, and she had to have a burning reason to risk her life over the mountains on the back of a haga.

'Yes, of course! And Eli will take a look at the … bird. Will it follow? We can take it straight to the animal infirmary.'

15

Over the past year, Eli's animal whispering had matured into full-time veterinary care in a purpose-built hut he and Max had built near Arafel's centre. All the villagers trusted him with their livestock, and he never seemed to be at a loss for a diagnosis or treatment, despite being entirely self-taught.

I shot a look at Max, his grin saying it all.

'And then I think Max has promised you trout,' I added.

A golden pheasant peeped among the crickets as we followed the quickest path back through the forest, silenced only by a pair of amorous rainbow lorikeets. Aelia broke off our conversation to better watch their dance against the cornflower sky, unfettered by cavern or dome ceilings. Clearly, the array of wildlife running freely through the trees entranced and bewildered her. And I understood more than she realized.

Completely cut off from the outside world for nearly two hundred years, Arafel was a paradise compared with the brown grit of Isca Prolet. I recalled my own astonishment when Unus and I had emerged out of the tunnels into the Prolet world – Pantheon's genetic rubbish tip, and Aelia's natural home. Life there was so engineered, disparate and exploited. It couldn't in any way compare with life on the outside, which had recovered far faster than anyone had expected.

I stole a glance across at the slight, elfin girl who had been so full of secrets in Pantheon. And now my mind was spinning with more questions, like one of Max's water wheels, but I kept my lips pressed firmly together until we'd delivered the haga into the wide-eyed keeping of one of Eli's volunteer helpers. It was only when we'd pulled the willow ladder back up inside our treehouse, that I allowed my curiosity to show. And Aelia's nerves were as clear as Jas's objection to the sudden intrusion.

'Is this the actual cipher? Thomas's cipher?' she whispered, crouching to inspect the freshly swept floor of our small living space.

Cursing silently, I nudged Mum's handmade reed mat over the

crude drawing with the heel of my foot. I'd thought so many times about erasing the charcoaled markings Thomas had painstakingly drawn out on our living-room floor, but it had always seemed sacrilegious, especially with Octavia and Cassius gone.

Now, though, my inaction seemed foolish. Although Aelia had proven her real loyalty to the outside, I'd always sensed her scientific weakness for Thomas's research and Octavia's obsession with the Voynich Manuscript.

'Its existence still isn't well known in the village.' I smiled apologetically.

It would have been so much easier if Thomas hadn't recorded the cipher to decode the only known genetic blueprint for mythical creatures.

'And Art felt it was for the best – to protect the other villagers.'

'Doesn't seem entirely open, in such an open society?' she commented, her eyes narrowed and suspicious.

'Would have been far better to burn it – for the firewood it is!'

Rajid's low mutter cut across the small circle, and this was swiftly followed by another round of low growling. I shot a look at Jas's sleek white body curled up in her bed, her yellow eyes watching our guests unwaveringly. She looked every inch the content treehouse cat, although her beautiful white jowls twitched unusually. I tried to assess her mood briefly, before returning my attention to our guests.

We were sitting in a makeshift circle, around Mum's clay cooking pot of fresh trout stew. The aroma was making my stomach grumble, and by the looks on their faces, it had been a good while since our guests had eaten too.

Rajid was crouching, warming his hands by our fire. I shot him a careful look. Everything about him was at odds with Arafel. His manner was so cool and indifferent, and the mythical Cerberus snarling up his neck couldn't brand him more a product of Pantheon, and yet he was here. In our forest home. I followed

17

the purplish line of the ugly, salivating hounds, mesmerized by the reddened tongues hanging from their jowls, and wondered at the artistry that brought their bulbous eyes to life every time he swallowed.

Who would choose such a mark?

'So, tell us everything,' I invited, as my mother ladled the steaming food into wooden bowls.

She looked particularly tired and drawn tonight, and I could sense she was anxious. Eli had taken a shift foraging and hadn't returned yet. And even though hunting in the outside forest was now deemed a lot safer, she never smiled until we were all back in the same room.

'You mean, why am I here, disturbing your little corner of paradise?' Aelia responded, her delicate features twisting up into a grimace. 'Well, let's see, where to begin?'

'How is August?'

The question was out of my mouth before I could stop it. And although it was just three words, lightly spoken, it felt as though they carried the entire weight of the treehouse on their back. I tried to ignore Max's eyes boring into the side of my head, telling myself it was perfectly normal to ask about her brother, especially given everything we'd all been through.

But a brief shake of her head undid every good intention.

I stared at her, an uncomfortable flush crawling up my neck. 'What do you mean? He's … everything's OK, isn't it?'

Max's frown deepened into a scowl.

'August hasn't been seen for three months. Not since the Director General took his seat back in the Senate,' Rajid interjected, staring into the fire embers beneath the cooking pot.

I glanced at Max, my skin starting to crawl like I'd fallen into the fire ant nest myself.

'The Director General? Cassius? He's …?'

'Alive? Yes,' Aelia confirmed.

A stunned silence pervaded the small rounded room.

18

'The head wound Unus inflicted in the Flavium would have killed any ordinary Pantheonite, but as one of Octavia's original fighting elite … well it turns out Cassius was pretty strong,' she continued.

'When the Flavium was cleared, the Scientific Generals had him transferred to the infirmary, where he remained in a comatose state until last month.'

'But if Cassius is alive, August …?' I whispered, feeling all my old nightmares start to stir.

'… was instantly compromised,' Rajid drawled with a glance at Aelia.

'It turns out Cassius still commanded a loyal following among the elite Pantheonites, despite what happened in the Flavium,' Rajid continued, his tone at odds with the gravity of his words.

'And as soon as news of Cassius's recovery began to spread, August's new legislation was frozen by the Senate. Cassius played the game cleverly,' he continued. 'He didn't immediately pull rank. Instead, he offered to work together with August, to bring about a fairer, more open Isca Pantheon that pursued the more … useful elements of the Biotechnology Programme.

'He recruited old friends, like Livia, as his Empress-Consort Deputy.'

My brain whirled as I tried to recall what I knew about the original mother of the Holy Roman Empire, though Aelia's scowl already spoke a thousand words.

'Livia … as in Livia Drusilla? Wasn't she the real wife of Emperor Augustus?'

'The wicked witch of Rome?' Aelia responded, her top lip curling. 'Yeah, she was a real shining beacon of womanly virtue … apart from the power games, treachery and systematic murder, of course.'

I stared, feeling my world grey.

'And Cassius was convincing,' she continued, the dark circles beneath her eyes suddenly more noticeable. 'His speeches in the

Senate were persuasive, especially among the newly elected Prolet representatives. He nearly had me believing in his integrated school for every Prolet and Pantheon child, irrespective of genetic coding. He always was a powerful orator.

'Besides, the Senatore were weak. Octavia's sudden death left them fractured. She wasn't loved, but she'd always been there, at the helm. Her poison was still trickling through their veins, and Cassius was a direct link with the old way of life.'

The room went quiet and Aelia and Rajid exchanged another glance, almost as though they were deciding exactly how much more to share.

'The Senatore decided Cassius's seniority demanded he be given a chance.' Rajid shrugged. 'And that August should lead a new important mission – the investigation into habitable life.'

'On the outside.' Aelia's whisper seemed to merge with the faded forest pictures I'd painted on the walls as a child.

I glanced at Max. It was the first time we'd heard of any deliberate move by Pantheon to investigate the outside world.

'Despite his repeated request they send someone else, he was dispatched with the elite Equite force on an exploratory mission. Across Europa,' Aelia confirmed bluntly.

I grew colder. August was somewhere, on the outside. And he hadn't come to Arafel.

'His key objective was to gather scientific evidence for sustainable community living across Europa,' Rajid clarified.

Aelia nodded, swallowing hard.

'It was Cassius's idea, that the Senate explore opportunities for satellite Lifedomes, which would help start a re-familiarization programme. The Senate were impressed, heralding it as a new era, an opportunity to combine the best of the old with the future.

'And August, with his background in fieldwork, was the obvious choice to lead the investigation.'

'The mission was expected to take six weeks. It's been three months,' Aelia offered, her eyes flitting past Rajid's.

'Rumours spread swiftly after that. Now most Pantheonites believe August planned his desertion, and that the group of young Prolet Freedom Fighters abandoned the new Civitas to go looking,' Rajid added.

'Anyway, Cassius has since denounced them all as deserters.'

He paused to draw breath, while I stared, already knowing the answer to my question, but I needed to ask anyway.

'Looking for what?' I whispered.

'For you, Tal,' Aelia returned, like a challenge.

Chapter 3

'In the name of Arafel ...? Why!?' Max interjected, his golden skin darkening with a scowl.

We'd finished the trout stew, and Mum was silently cutting up a fresh pineapple into hand-sized chunks. I wasn't deceived though. I could assess her mood by the tight compression of her lips.

'They want to join you, Talia, all of you, here in Arafel. While Cassius has restarted the propaganda machinery, most of the free thinkers believe an outside community thrives. The truth is, Arafel ... Max ... you ... you've all become rather legendary.'

Silently, Rajid got up from his cross-legged position by the fire and walked over towards Jas. She lifted her head, growling her warning softly, but he didn't falter. Instead, he slowly lowered to his knees beside her. She eyed him coldly for a beat, before yawning and rolling over. I stared in surprise. An invitation to tickle her snow-white belly was a real sign of trust. Aelia shot us a satisfied look, her elfin cheeks tinged with spots of colour and I wondered, briefly, what had passed between her and Rajid. They were both Prolet Freedom Fighters, and she obviously trusted him. So why did he unnerve me?

'The day after the Senate reported August as missing, a group

22

of Prolets took off – through the old Roman tunnels beneath the ruined city of Isca,' Rajid offered in a low voice, still stroking Jas. His voice was almost hypnotic, and I suppressed a frown. Jas had a pretty sharp instinct with people, yet she'd clearly accepted him.

'Beneath the city?' I repeated, recalling my own journey beneath the domes. 'The Roman tunnel only leads to the Lifedome exterior wall. I had to fly the griffin over the mined land.'

Only once in the last twelve months had I crept to the edge of the forest to stare out at the domed rise of Isca Pantheon; and the dirt-land separating the two worlds looked just the same as it always had: barren, impenetrable and terrifying. It had claimed so many Arafel lives in the beginning, and their memory rested there with their bones, in the blackened soil.

Rajid broke off grooming Jas to look up, his face creased with disdain. 'The Prolets are, among other things, resourceful archaeologists,' he responded.

'Your exit tunnel was just the beginning of the secret excavation work. Since then, we've uncovered a whole network of ancient Roman tunnels that lead out and interconnect beneath the old city of Isca Dumnoniorum … or Exeter as it was known before the Great War.'

'Rajid led the excavation work. It was dangerous but incredible, like rediscovering a forgotten underground maze,' Aelia added.

'Does Cassius know?' I asked, trying to keep up with all the revelations.

I recalled his face the day he thought I was at his mercy – just minutes before Unus arrived. It was a look that had hard-wired itself into my brain. Cold venom. Like a death adder.

'He didn't, but he does now, of course. And the first thing he and Livia did was freeze the new freedom of movement powers August brought in to support the Integration Agenda. Cassius said it was just to retain balance until August returned. But there are those …'

'… who know better?' I muttered.

She nodded.

'And he's sending out search parties on a daily basis to bring back the missing Prolets. Armed search parties.'

Max looked from me to Aelia, his frown deepening.

'She can't help.'

I'd been listening so intently, I'd forgotten Mum was at the back of the circular room, shelling beans. I gazed at her familiar face, brown and seasoned from her years spent working in Arafel's fields. Eli and I took on her load as much as possible, but Grandpa's death had hit her hard, especially since he'd filled the breach Dad had left eleven years before.

'It's OK, I'm not going anywhere,' I reassured her.

'Aren't you also on the Senate, Aelia? As General in Command of the PFF?' I asked, trying to understand how so much could have been undone so quickly.

She smiled in a way that said everything.

'You mean ex General in Command. Cassius voided my position within the first week August was missing,' she relayed, her brow puckering.

'He said there was no need for the PFF any longer, since we were working together with a new vision for Isca Pantheon. Made a big deal about all positions on the Senatore needing to be earned through the popular vote, although the prejudiced voting system hasn't been replaced, and so guess what? The only people currently entitled to vote live within … Pantheon.'

Max scowled. 'But then the Senate vote is never gonna reflect Prolet will.'

She smiled again, her teeth just visible, and I could tell her nerves were frayed.

'Eat,' I urged, pushing her refilled bowl back towards her.

Jas stirred from her comatose position beside Rajid, and my gaze shot back to the trapdoor, though I knew exactly what had made her beautiful flocked ears perk up. Jas was the most intuitive watch-cat in the world. Whenever Eli took an early hunting

24

shift in the outside forest, she waited for his return intently, and always seemed to know when he was back on Arafel soil. I strained my ears and, sure enough, a few moments later detected a scuffle at the bottom of our tree.

Mum was up in a breath, flying across the floor towards the trapdoor, to let down our woven willow ladder. Seconds later, an earth-streaked hand pushed aside the rough netting we hooked over the exit, and a mop of sandy-brown hair appeared.

I drew a breath as his grey-blue eyes followed, his expression quickly changing as he acknowledged the newcomers. He vaulted through the trapdoor like a forest cat, and Jas stretched out her sleek hunting body in response, bypassing Rajid as though he'd never existed. She padded up to Eli, purring like a queen bee in the height of summer, as he bent to reassure her, a bundle of cloth cradled beneath his arm.

He held the small wrap out to Jas, who sniffed with her usual casual interest, before he let a tiny, doleful little owl peep out of the top. A murmur of interest whispered around the room as he straightened, placing the newcomer inside one of the egg-shaped woven baskets suspended from the ceiling. We were very used to our treehouse being an impromptu animal hospital, and immediately Mum started warming some thinned milk.

'Orphaned?' I signed.

'Yes, and this little guy was the last in his nest,' Eli signed swiftly before walking across to Aelia and giving her an affectionate hug.

None of us missed the question in his eyes. The entry tunnel into the village was a long-kept secret, and revealing it was punishable by expulsion. Clearly, he hadn't been to the animal infirmary on his way back.

'She and Rajid caught the overnight haga to Arafel,' Max interjected, a gleam in his eye.

There was a ripple of laughter as Eli held his hand out to Rajid. He gripped it with respect. There was something in Eli's unflustered air that calmed even the hormone-fuelled bucks at rucking

25

time, and as Rajid inclined his head respectfully, I noticed the Cerberus climbing his neck doing the same.

'Haga?' Eli signed incredulously. 'Where on earth is this intrepid bird? And how did they know how to find us?' he added to me directly.

I raised my eyes at Max. Only Eli would ask after a bird before enquiring about Aelia's daring journey.

I signed quickly, bringing him up to date, as he gently removed the little owl from its basket cocoon and pipetted thinned, warm milk into its open beak. Watching him sustain such a tiny fragment of life as though it were the last helped to calm my jumbled thoughts.

'So, where are the group that escaped now? How many Prolets made it out?' Max asked in a low voice.

I was still signing, but my ears pricked up. Max was always the underdog champion – no matter the stakes. He wouldn't leave a rabbit alone to face a fox. But this rabbit could be anywhere, and I was still reeling with the news that Cassius was still alive. There could be no crueller fox.

'Prolet Levels Thirteen and Fourteen emptied overnight. So, a party of around sixty is unaccounted for,' Rajid offered, sauntering back to join Aelia by the fire.

'Livia spared no time in offering her services to help flush them out, should they fail to return within three days,' she added with a grimace.

'And she doesn't mean round up.'

My stomach twisted like one of Max's trap knots. At last Aelia's urgency was clearer. But Arafel was already in the region of three hundred heads. How could it support another sixty? And wouldn't a rescue mission just bring Cassius directly here to Arafel?

'Care for the seed, and it will care for you.'

I had no idea where Grandpa's whisper came from. It was just there, hanging in the oaken breeze, as though he was beside me now.

I straightened my shoulders and cleared my throat. I had to think like Grandpa.

'It's a matter for Art and the Council,' I said decisively and quickly, 'but I don't think we have any choice.'

I was conscious of all eyes in the room swinging my way, including my mother's.

'Grandpa taught us to value life above everything else. All life. We can't sit here in our safe idyll of a valley, while others scour the Dead City sewers searching for us!'

'Talia, think!' My mother looked ashen as she rose to her feet, the beans she was shelling spilling onto the wooden floor.

'We just about manage to feed everyone as it is. We can't support sixty extra mouths through the winter months. What if bringing them here also brings that ... that monster to our home? And how do we know *she* wasn't followed?'

Mum pointed towards Aelia, her face twisted with fear. My chest contracted. Mum had been through enough, but how could I justify putting her above the needs of sixty desperate Insiders?

Jas whined above the chatter of a capuchin in a nearby tree. My little apricot monkey ran through my head, and I bit my lip, tasting the tiny trickle of salty blood. Freedom always came at a cost, which was what made it so precious.

'We take it to Art,' I repeated grittily, watching Mum close her eyes as though I'd just committed us all to certain death.

***

A chevrotain was grazing by the yew and I approached slowly, trying not to startle it. They were shy animals and this one had to be a little confused to be out at late afternoon. Grandpa used to call them mouse deer, or deer bewitched by the fairy folk; either way they were unusual enough to be considered good fortune in Arafel.

I allowed myself a small smile as I crouched silently, watching it. I could do with some good fortune just now. It had been an hour since the discussion in the treehouse, and I'd stepped out for some fresh air before seeing Art. The Council members took their shifts in the fields like everyone else, which meant all Council matters were dealt with after working hours. It was a tradition that protected our primary resource: food.

But as I extended my hand, I sensed it. A threatening presence. I was on my feet and spinning in a heartbeat, arm raised high to deflect the incoming missile. There was sharp pain as it found a target, the fleshy underside of my arm. I winced. The stone would have killed the mouse deer outright, but the nervous creature was already gone, the bushes rustling their relief.

'In Arafel, the mouse deer is considered sacred,' I challenged the lurking shadows.

'In Isca Prolet, the mouse deer would feed a family for a week,' came the acerbic response.

'Last time I checked you were staying in Arafel, at our invitation!' I retorted.

Rajid sidled into view, an indecipherable look on his swarthy face. He seemed taller and leaner in the open air, and for the first time I noticed a large white-handled blade dangling from his waistband.

'*Prolets can take care of themselves.*'

Max's words echoed through my head although I didn't doubt it for one second. I flexed my fingers. Didn't he know Outsiders invented the rule book?

'What are you doing out here?'

I was suddenly conscious he must have followed me to find me in this quiet part of the forest.

'Just getting some fresh air, and exploring the local animal species. Interestingly, they seem to have a uniform number of legs.'

He drawled rather than spoke, elongating all the s's in any word. I stared at him intently. Despite Jas's acceptance, this man could get under my skin, and the reddened jaws of his Cerberus were glinting in the evening sun, like some sort of portent of ill luck.

'How long have you known Aelia?' I asked.

'For about as long as she's been a Prolet.' He leaned casually against a convenient oak, as though it was the most natural thing in the world for us to be standing here, discussing Aelia.

'We grew up in the same corner of town. Then, when she won the funded medical place with Isca Pantheon, I joined the mineral miners. As you can probably imagine, it's a rather popular choice in the wonderful metropolis of Isca Prolet!'

He grinned at his own joke, revealing a blackened tooth near the front of his mouth. The neglect reminded me how different our paths had been. The sight of a lush, green forest had to be one of the most arresting he'd ever seen. And yet, he seemed so detached.

'And then the PFF?' I pushed.

'And then the PFF,' he closed.

His head dropped to one side, as though he was assessing a laboratory specimen. And for a second we stood there, engaged in some sort of unspoken combat, before he sauntered across and paused closely enough to me to feel slightly uncomfortable. I held my ground, even while his slightly soured breath filled my face.

'Just what is it that makes you so special?'

I wasn't even sure he'd whispered the words; they were spoken so quietly.

'Rajid! Why are you out here? I wanted to talk to Tal before we head over to Art!' Aelia's sharp tone cut through the air. 'The sun's on the horizon; it's time.'

I glanced across at Aelia's shadow, tense and agitated. Beneath the bough of a twisted hazel, she had clearly been counting the seconds until we could see Art.

Rajid stepped back, inane smile resurrected, before sauntering after Aelia. And as I followed, I wondered again whether the Cerberus was more than a tattoo.

***

'I'll have to call an Extraordinary Council of the Elders, and a village-wide Ring to tally support after that. This is not something I can decide on behalf of Arafel, Talia. Should we choose to send a task force and then take these people under Arafel's wing, we will undoubtedly compromise the safety of every man, woman and child living here. That action must not be taken lightly or without full, open acceptance of the possible consequences.'

I stared at Art's wizened face in the dim light of his study. His treehouse was tucked between the branches of the oldest ash in the village, and the closely knotted pale branches created a twilight space, even though it was only just dusk. It was the colour between day and night, and usually that soothed me, but today I was conscious only of Aelia's anxiety.

'I don't think we have that sort of time, do we, Aelia?' I asked, her twitching foot belying her calm expression.

She shook her head swiftly. We'd been through it all in detail, and the more we talked, the more I felt her apprehension.

'They've been gone for weeks. We think they're hiding out in the tunnels beneath the city, but they must have run out of food by now, and they have no means of cooking whatever they may catch among the ruins. My fear is that they're living off sewer rats and unclean water, with no access to light. Their prognosis is pretty grim, unless we get help in there quickly.'

She spoke rapidly, her clinical training giving her strength although I knew she had to know most of the renegade Prolet families personally. As leader of the Prolet effort to integrate with Pantheon, she had to feel responsibility for their protection too. It was clear that whether Arafel helped or not, she would do everything she could to find them.

30

'If they are in a weakened state, and Cassius releases his personal battalion of molossers or even strix, they won't have the strength to fight or escape. And Cassius likes to make an example of those who challenge the system. I can't imagine he will be content simply to parade sixty insurgent prisoners. He will want something in return – and I don't mean their white flag.'

I turned back to Art, hoping he would make an exception, just this once. He was Grandpa's successor as leader of the Council, and infamous for his strong sense of fairness. He was also a stickler for the rules.

Art stared at us both, his astute eyes getting the measure of Aelia swiftly. Then he drew a deep breath.

'I'm sorry, Talia, but on this my hands are tied. The only thing I can offer you for certain is an extraordinary meeting of the Ring, followed by a vote. It will take a little longer than you will like, but perhaps that time is usefully spent considering the path that may lie ahead? None of Arafel's hunters will know the ruined city tunnels, and if we are forced to engage with Cassius, there will be injury and loss of life.

'I understand your urgency,' he added gently, 'but this decision needs thorough debate. We are hunters, farmers, survivors … not warriors.'

I glanced at Aelia. She was pale and completely still.

'I will call a Ring, but I cannot promise you the decision you want.'

I nodded, knowing better than to push. We'd secured a meeting, and that had to be enough for now. Moments later we were dropping down through Art's aged trapdoor to the forest floor beneath.

I looked at Aelia, her face in shadows, her agitation tangible.

'I know it's not exactly the outcome we wanted. But just let Art talk to the village … I'm sure they'll—'

'I understand,' she cut in shortly. 'It's a big ask, and Arafel is your home. You are all safe, while the insurgents … my people …

Look, I get it, OK? I just need a few minutes to compose my thoughts before the meeting. And I need to speak with Rajid. I'll listen for the Ring alarm and meet you there.'

I nodded silently, wanting to say so many things but unable to find the right words. Aelia was my feisty friend who was as unpredictable as she was loyal, but this time we weren't facing the manticore or some other beast of Pantheon. This time the stakes were so much higher. She spun on her heel and headed off into the darkness.

Reluctantly, I started in the opposite direction, intending to find Mum and Eli before the alarm. The last of the afternoon light was receding and Pacha, the village lantern-bearer had begun lighting the beeswax candles suspended in willow rope jars from our treehouses. They illuminated a path through the forest at night, but the effect was to cast our homes into an ethereal half-light. Mum called it fairy-tale, but tonight their glow did little to soothe my nerves.

'Tal?'

Max's voice stopped me in my tracks and when I followed its direction, I could just make out his healthy face among the dusky branches of a dense red cedar. Instinctively, I gripped the strong arm that followed. His proximity was usually the only thing that enabled me to think straight.

I leveraged myself using the tree's thick, nodulous bark but there was no real need. Max led Arafel's treehouse construction team, and I was sharing his bough within seconds. I gazed through the feathery leaves that fringed his brown skin. He had three fresh rabbits attached to his leather waistband, and a forced smile pinned to his face.

For a moment neither of us said anything. It had been like this for a while now. The weighted silence. Like he was slowly building towards something methodically, the way he built tree-houses. Only this subject wasn't approachable with sheer logic, and there was no previous design for him to copy or adapt. It wasn't a conversation I was anticipating in any way either, which made me the biggest coward, and him more than confused.

I loved Max fiercely, but there was a dam somewhere in my throat, one that blocked up all emotional pathways between my heart and mouth. And no matter how close we were, there was still a void between us, preventing those final words.

'I made something for you,' he murmured.

There was an underlying question in his voice, and I knew he wanted to ask how the conversation with Art had gone, that in his head he was already racing across the forest. *Max to the rescue.* He was always so damned busy trying to rescue everyone, he rarely stopped to ask if they wanted rescuing in the first place.

My stomach pitched as he held out a small wooden object. Anticipating, always anticipating. I stared incomprehensibly at first. In the twilight it looked a little like a wooden mushroom with a short fat stalk and a bigger, carefully whittled cap. Then, as I gazed, the fine markings of his determined wood-carving knife became clearer. I reached out and picked it up in wonder; it was no bigger than a whistle, but the craftsmanship was superb.

Lost for words, I turned it over and around in the palm of my hand. It was all there – the thick trunk, the veined knotted branches, the tiny indentations of a willow rope ladder and trap-door.

'It's a treehouse,' I whispered, my words slowing as the significance of his gift began to sink in.

He nodded shyly, waiting for the right reaction. A reaction that gave him the light he needed, a reaction that patched the need for real words – and real, honest conversation.

'Not just any old treehouse,' he returned, reaching across to pick it up gently and perform a swift manoeuvre. I gasped, as with a swift twist of his deft fingers, the small tip came away revealing a small, perfectly formed dart tube.

'It's one of the most accurate blow tubes I've designed.' He frowned in concentration. 'The aperture is just large enough to take one of our darts, and the narrow circumference maximizes direction and speed … Like this, see?'

He plucked a fresh cedar leaf, rolled it up into a tiny scroll and inserted it carefully into the tube. Then he raised it to his lips, and aimed at the floor beneath our feet. Two seconds later it was lying next to a small grey stone, slowly unfurling.

I stared at him in wonder.

'You really are the most incredible craftsman,' I murmured with real awe, hoping it would be enough, for now.

'It's perfectly balanced … the treehouse dart tube I mean,' he added, his eyes shining uncertainly.

I nodded, knowing it wasn't what he meant at all, that he hadn't intended just to give me this. That it was his door into a conversation.

'Max, I …' I intervened, my head racing with a thousand inadequate words.

'Sssh!'

He pressed a work-worn finger against my lips; and an expression flickered across his face, something between frustration and stubborn hope. It made me want to reach up and cradle his honest face in my shallow hands.

'I thought you could wear it, like a necklace? So it rests here … my favourite spot.'

He dropped his fingers to gently brush the hollow of my neck, and I felt a flush steal up my neck. They were the same words he'd whispered that night, and he knew it.

'Here, I could kiss here all night … I can see your blood pulsing, alive and vibrant. It's such a gift, after everything.'

My world wobbled.

We'd already sealed our caring the most intimate way possible so why was I still holding him at arm's length? And, if he wanted it all so much, why in the name of Arafel wasn't that enough?

Perhaps if I just closed my eyes and pretended, I could lose myself long enough for it to become the truth.

'It's a practical keepsake … for while I'm gone,' he whispered.

'What do you mean?' I frowned. 'Art will need to send Arafel's best hunters. I'm one!'

'I know. But you can't leave your family, not again. Your mum's right – you've risked enough already. It's your turn to take a back seat, Tal. If Cassius came across you …' He paused, a ferocious scowl suddenly contorting his face.

I looked away. The moon wound only a milky light through the cedar's branches, but right then it felt as though I were standing in the full glare of the sun. I pressed my nails into my hands, suppressing the feelings running wild beneath my skin. I couldn't let Max see how I felt about Cassius. That I knew he would like nothing more than to have his vengeance on the Outsider who brought Pantheon crashing down around his ears. And probably in the most sadistic way. Because Max would make it his own war. And I couldn't have that.

'I understand the risks,' I whispered, watching light diamonds flicker in his eyes, 'but he'd still have to catch me first.'

A brief silence hung in the air. The moment had gone and we both knew it. And although it was only a temporary reprieve, for one insane moment I felt disappointed. Gritting my teeth, I pushed myself onto the balls of my feet, readying myself to leap. Just as Max's fingers brushed my forearm.

'Has Art even agreed to it?' he asked intently, his breath warming my cheek.

I shook my head. 'There's going to be a meeting and a vote in the Ring. Art said he has to put it to the Council. Aelia was …'

'Angry?'

'Terrified.' Our whispers coincided as Aelia's strained face spun into my mind.

The cedar leaves rustled with the breeze, and the tiny hairs on the backs of my arms prickled. Where would this all lead?

'She thinks we're hesitating because we don't want to help. She says time is running out.'

I started as he reached forward and silenced my words with a swift, determined kiss. It was the briefest of gestures, but one that burned as though he had scored his initials there.

'She's not the only one,' he whispered. 'And at some point in the not too distant future, that fragile branch you're clinging to is going to break. And then you're going to have to decide if you'll let someone real catch you … Let them build a life with you.'

I breathed through the sudden vice in my chest, chased by a vivid memory. It was the image of us both in the dusty Flavium, surrounded by mounted Equites, waiting to die. I'd burned then for the power to heal his wounds, for the chance to make him well and happy. And finally, here I was holding that very same precious power, and balking.

And all because of a faded face, looming out of the swirling dust. I closed my eyes as Aelia's words echoed like a ghost through my head.

'August was chosen to lead the investigation into habitable life. He was dispatched with the elite Equite force on an exploratory mission. Across Europa.'

He hadn't come to find me. It didn't matter how many times I told myself, it still sucked the breath from my body every time the words echoed through my head. And why should he, after all? We'd known each other a matter of a few short days, barely enough time to like someone, let alone anything else.

I ground my teeth. August might as well have died back in the Flavium, among the blood-coloured dust and crowing griffins. While Max was alive, here, trying to love me. And I couldn't ask him to wait for ever. Something clicked over inside.

I pulled open my eyes and looked straight at Max.

'I want you to catch me,' I whispered, 'after we've helped Aelia.'

Just as the words left my mouth, the night air thickened with the sound of the Ring alarm. It was a stark, invasive sound among the everyday hum of the forest, and a shiver stole through me, even though I knew its purpose. It was only ever sounded in emergencies or rare situations that couldn't be resolved by Art and the elected Council, and most of my twenty years had passed without the need for it to disturb regular forest life.

Max didn't answer me, but the diamonds in his eyes brightened as they caught the glint of the moon. And as I dropped onto the forest floor, my promise felt loaded with more conviction than I'd felt in a very long time.

Chapter 4

The rustle of the trees seemed to echo my promise, as I trod the short distance towards the torch-lit cavern we called the Ring. I couldn't understand myself, or my impulsiveness, only that my aversion to hurting him had become suddenly and painfully overwhelming. He'd risked his life so many times in Pantheon, just so he could protect me. And it was reason enough. *Wasn't it?*

Why run when you can fly?

I bit my lip. Our childhood tree-running mantra had come to mean so much more following Isca Pantheon. We'd won a victory of nature over the most advanced biotechnological world, a world I hated with every fibre of my being. It had stained my hands with deceit and desire, and yet it still wasn't a stain I wanted to fade. Not completely. So why had I just promised Max everything?

My pace slowed as I approached the cavern; it looked as though the alarm had done its work and the entire village had turned out. I could tell by their pallid faces most were panicked about the sudden roll call, and I felt more than a little guilty as I scanned the queue for Aelia.

I cursed softly. What I was about to ask fell into one of the most difficult and challenging questions ever asked of the Arafel community, and Aelia was nowhere to be seen.

Seconds later, I spotted Eli and Mum, and wound my way through the crowds to take Mum's arm before filtering inside, like everyone else.

There was already a formal semicircle gathered around the wide, raised boulder that served as a platform, and once we were inside Art gave the signal for the thick woollen hangings to be let down. It was part of the procedure that usually made me smile, as though he expected the trees and animals themselves to be capable of spying on us. Tonight though, I didn't feel like smiling.

'Friends, I apologize for the intrusion to your evening; but we are called together as a matter of urgency.'

There was a murmur around the crowd.

'We have received a plea for help. And it doesn't come from within Arafel, but instead from people – our kind of people – outside this mountainous valley.'

This time there was a stony silence. And I understood why completely. Whispers about the Insiders had been told, and retold, since my childhood. And now they were fleshed out by the story that had accompanied our return from Pantheon a year ago, like a noxious cloud.

We'd relayed a scant version of the truth at Art's request, but Grandpa's murder had been felt by each and every member of Arafel. He'd been a much-loved, trusted leader of the Arafel community for many years, as well as the last direct link to Thomas's original Council through his own grandfather.

When news of his death at Octavia's own hand had broken, many had wanted a task force to storm Pantheon to demand justice. Only Art's diplomatic tongue had persuaded them it would be tantamount to taking a torch to Arafel.

And now, we were asking them to look on a party of Insiders kindly, with pity even. I doubted there was room in their hearts.

I scanned the crowd covertly. Aelia was still nowhere to be seen.

'Insiders can never be our kind of people!' Bereg, one of the head butchers, jeered from the back of the cave.

There was a noisy outbreak of support for the thickset, respected hunter before Art held up his hand. A slow hush swept across the space. Art had never commanded the same love as Grandpa, but he was still Arafel's experienced and trusted leader.

'My friends, I feel the same doubt, but let me beg your indulgence a little longer while I present one of the Insiders who asks for our help. A young Prolet who has risked her life on a hazardous journey over Arafel's very own North Mountains, to find us … Aelia? And Talia? Where are you both?' Art's venerable voice echoed oddly around the cavernous space.

I stood up, feeling the weight of my mother's anxiety as I weaved through the crowd towards the dais. Art smiled, but my own facial muscles felt stiff, and I knew this was going to be hard. I turned slowly and surveyed my friends, their usual affable expressions replaced with suspicion and fear. They already bore a hatred of Pantheon.

What would Aelia say if we turned her down?

I glanced at Max, who'd taken one of the watch guard's posts beside the Ring entrance. He shook his head and I tried not to frown.

Where on earth was she?

'I don't stand here with any … expectation,' I began haltingly. 'We all know what's at stake every time we leave the valley … every time we cross paths with a Sweeper or Insider – and have to run for our lives.'

The silence was heavy and oppressive. I surveyed the crowd; it was so quiet I could almost hear the lemurs in the outside forest.

'But we run because … because we have somewhere to run to …'

Someone coughed, and I swallowed. This was so much harder than I expected.

'A home that I know *we* have created and nurtured, but also one that has nurtured us right back … Grandpa used to say: "care for the seed and it will care for you."'

I paused, surprised by the sudden heat behind my eyes. A soft murmur of recognition swept through the listening crowd, and I inhaled, suddenly feeling stronger. Grandpa's wisdom and legacy lived on within us all. I just needed to harness it.

'When I was a child, I thought he meant the seeds blown into the valley of Arafel. But now I'm older, I realize he was talking about seeds far closer to home. He was talking about us.'

I stared back at their solemn faces. Watching me. I had their full attention now.

'He meant for us to take care of one another, and I don't think he meant just the people living here, in Arafel. Grandpa knew the day was coming when the tables would be turned, when the Insiders needed us. And maybe, just maybe, that day is here.

'The people who have asked for our help *are like us*. They come from a world inside Isca Pantheon that is made up of the discarded and rejected, a world where living beings are designed to work until they drop, and a world where they are always ...'

I scanned the faces, feeling their fear. Feeling Max watching me, willing me through.

'... afraid. And now they've done the single most brave thing of their lives, and escaped their prison – Pantheon. They are hiding – men, women and children, just like our own – in the ruins of the Dead City with barely enough to eat because of the myth of an Eden – here – on the outside.'

A sudden gust of wind echoed down the connecting rocky corridor, almost as though it was adding its own objection.

'They are desperate, and will die without our help. And two of them risked their lives crossing the North Mountains just to find us ... and ask for help.'

My voice trembled as the full force of my own words began to sink in, and the very worst possible explanation for Aelia's absence reared its head. My throat dried and I tried to swallow, scanning the crowd once again. Every face but Aelia's looked back.

And in a breath, I knew it wasn't just my fanciful imagination; that my fear was a materialization of the worst kind; the type of knowledge that comes with really knowing a person's spirit and capabilities. Aelia hadn't come to the meeting because a better idea altogether had presented itself – and in Arafel the choice was pretty limited.

I didn't make the decision to run, I was just conscious of a sea of bemused faces as I leapt from the platform. My suspicions rang as loudly as the Ring alarm, although I was aware of Max's voice reaching through the clamour of my anxiety. I shook my head fiercely, before flying through the entrance archway and down the narrow stone corridor leading outside. And I didn't hesitate as my light feet left the bamboo market huts and store-houses for the obscurity of the candle-lit trees. My only thought was to reach home as fast as I could, praying Jas had been her reliable, unsociable self.

The forest reached out like an old friend as a few errant chickens flew up in fright. Then I was flying like my life depended on it, ducking between thick, twisted tree roots and swinging through a banyan, not even pausing beside the meat-curing huts to hiss at an inquisitive honey badger. I barely allowed myself to breathe. All of our fates would hang in the balance if my suspicion was correct. How could I have been so stupid?

Finally, I reached a length of pecan tree that entwined with our white oak treehouse, and froze, listening intently. The tree-house was lit only by Pacha's beeswax candle jars, and a small outdoor lantern Eli had fashioned from some dry willow. It creaked stiffly every time the wind rustled through the leaves. Usually the noise was friendly and welcoming, but tonight it grated like a rusty saw.

With pounding ears, I leapt to the floor and scaled our twisted rope ladder, willing Jas to greet me as usual at the trapdoor entrance. The familiar cosiness reached out, but Jas was ominously absent, while her bed was dishevelled and empty.

My chest tightened as I flew across the floor, telling myself there was no way Aelia or Rajid could have known where the

42

Book of Arafel was hidden, and that Jas would never have let them move her bed, let alone root around in the empty space beneath. Then the small hiding hole at the back of Aelia's cave in the Prolet world materialized in my head.

Aelia knew how to hide. Hadn't she hidden her true identity from most people from the day she was born?

The special fuss Rajid made of Jas at dinner crowded my brain, as the remainder of my calm evaporated. Had it all been for a purpose should Arafel not be able to help? I yanked aside Jas's bed to prise up the old wooden floor plank beneath. It was worn and slotted together in a way that didn't require old-world metal nails, but tonight I wished I'd had the foresight to add some of the pine sap glue Max used in his building work.

'Do you want some help?' Max's whisper in the dark made me jump. I'd tuned out the telltale creaks of the floor.

I flashed him a look. His face was full of shadows – and questions.

I'd never told Max the whole: that the Book of Arafel contained Thomas's secret research into the Voynich Manuscript; a genetic blueprint for mythological creatures, though I'd often wondered if he'd worked it out anyway. He'd listened to Aelia and August's excitement about Thomas's cipher. But as far as I knew, he'd never connected the Book of Arafel, the sacred book charting Arafel's emergence from the dust clouds of the Great War, with the Voynich Manuscript. At least, not openly.

'It's OK. I guessed you'd hidden the Book of Arafel in here somewhere, after your grandpa …'

I nodded swiftly, not wanting him to say the words, even now.

He reached forward and with one deft movement, prised up one of the uneven floorboards. I peered inside, and immediately felt my world contract to the size of a corn kernel. The space was dark and empty.

'They've stolen it!' I whispered, struggling to force the words over my lips.

'But why? What can they possibly want with it?' Max responded in confusion.

I stared at him, dread creeping through me like a mountain mist.

'Cassius! She's taken the Book to Cassius … to negotiate for the insurgents! Perhaps even August?'

Even in the dusky light I was aware of the sudden anger in Max's eyes. I'd deliberately avoided speaking August's name for twelve whole months, and now I'd managed it twice in the same day. But it was a farce anyway; Max knew me inside out. And he'd sensed the charge from the start.

'But why? What possible interest could our village book hold for Cassius? And what makes you think Aelia wants to negotiate for *him* at all? Perhaps he's not missing,' he added. 'Perhaps he made it outside and decided to disappear! Who could blame him? He had the perfect opportunity – you knew he always wanted more. Maybe Cassius gave him the opportunity to change it all, an opportunity too good to resist!'

I stiffened. It suited Max for this to be August's choice. It made it reasonable for him to hate him.

'He saved us, Max,' I snapped, 'in the Flavium, remember? You may have forgotten that, but I definitely haven't. He rode out alone when—'

'I know, I know – like a knight in frickin' futuristic armour and defied the might of Pantheon!' he scathed. 'I was there, beside you, remember? And how does a forest builder ever compare with that?' he continued, his eyes narrowing. 'Isn't that what it comes down to? And while we're being honest, how about you share with me exactly *why* the Book of Arafel is so precious to everyone else? This isn't just about the cipher on the floor, is it?'

I stared at him, knowing the situation was spiralling out of control, that I needed to rein it in somehow, and say the right thing. But I was too scared and furious to think straight.

'I'm not just a dumb treehouse builder, Tal! I know Octavia

44

wanted the Book, and it wasn't just because of some old feud between her and Thomas. And I know you've avoided telling me, and for the love of Arafel, I've not pushed you – though I've wanted to. But it seems I'm the only one *not* in the circle now. *Despite everything we've shared.* Even Aelia places some special value on the Book, and I'm still left guessing, because presumably, I'm just not him – that's it, isn't it?! I'm just not him!'

The words cut the still air between us, like a knife descaling a fish, removing twelve months of armour with just a few short strikes. And I could tell by the look on his face how much it had cost to deliver them, and that he was fighting himself even now. I knew exactly what he needed me to do. And so much of me wanted to throw my arms around him, tell him it was all his imagination, that August meant nothing to me. That I only wanted him. Especially since that night.

But I couldn't, no matter how much I wanted to push back the tidal wave of guilt. Because it was a downright lie. And while suffocating my feelings was one thing, outright denial would be like prising them out at the root.

The whole damned world is waiting … August's last words fell through my thoughts like tiny sharp hailstones. If, by the whole world, he meant a daily trajectory of denial and distraction, followed by the slow burn of reality, he just about had it summed up.

How could he have left Isca Pantheon without looking for Arafel? And for me? Were his memories not slowly eroding his sanity?

'If that's what you really think, you can keep this!' I ground out, whipping off the hand-carved treehouse dart tube and throwing it at him. 'I haven't got time to stand around listening to a neurotic fairy tale. Someone has to stop Aelia before she leaves Arafel!'

Spinning around, I flew towards the window. I was flying before Max could answer and I didn't look back.

Anger always put the devil into my tree-running, and tonight was no exception. Aelia and Rajid had stolen the village's most prized possession, something Grandpa had charged me to protect with my life. And now there was a very real chance it could end up in Cassius's hands.

Cold fear gripped my stomach as I paused at the end of a thick ash branch. What could they possibly hope to achieve by giving Cassius the final means to decrypt the Voynich? They might buy the escaped Prolets and August time, but Cassius would be able to accurately re-create beasts from myth and legend on an unthinkable scale – beasts that were extinct for a reason.

'Come what may, nature finds a way.'

It was one of Grandpa's favourite mottos, but I wasn't sure the recovering world would ever be ready for that dark day. My feet flew as though they had grown wings. I grasped a low-hanging pepper tree branch, and ignored the way a pair of bush babies cried out as I disturbed the last of their sleep. I had no time to waste, and my frantic thoughts kept pace with my feet.

Aelia couldn't physically take the Book through the tunnel, even if she knew where it was located, which meant she either had decided to navigate the North Mountains on foot – suicide, but plausible – or make her way to the animal infirmary and take a certain mythical two-headed haga back to Pantheon. My acorns were on the latter, and that meant there was a very real chance she could be gone before I even reached the infirmary.

I took my running and leaping as high as I dared into the topmost branches of the trees I knew like the back of my hand, but it was still too long before I dropped down near Eli's veterinary hut, where we'd left the exhausted two-headed Roman eagle a little earlier.

With a pounding chest, I pushed through the thick fringe of banana trees, and out into the grazing paddock. It was a communal grassy community space, where hens, pigs and Eli's injured menagerie roamed during the day. But tonight it was deserted.

I made my way silently across to one of the dozen oak timber and willow huts that lined the field. They were emergency shelters should a monsoon storm hit our treehouse community, but also served as an indoor space for wet market days, grain storage and my favourite: Arafel story nights.

Cautiously, I pushed open the grass door to the animal infirmary, and was immediately greeted by a cacophony of sounds and dubious smells. The hut was Eli's special project when we returned from Pantheon, and together with Max, he'd painstakingly designed it to meet the needs of all kinds of sick and injured animals. I'd often thought it was his way of coping with what had happened; Max and I had turned to each other, while Eli had thrown himself into his work.

'Eli?' I whispered.

There was no answer and then I remembered. Eli wasn't here. He was in the Ring with every other member of Arafel debating the issue of the day, and probably my sudden departure too.

Holding my breath, I sprinted down towards the end stall he reserved for the larger animals, willing the haga to be there, willing Aelia to have had second thoughts. But when I reached the stall and peered over at the sawdust floor, only a lone golden feather the size of a cedar leaf gleamed back at me.

I bent down to pick the feather up, as the moon slipped behind a cloud, and for a moment the air thickened with meaning. I inhaled slowly, feeling a shadow creep over my home. Knowing the stark truth. Arafel was standing in the eye of a cold, dark storm, one that was whispering names.

I lifted the feather to my lips. It was still warm. And when I cast a look out of the small netted window on the back wall, the last of the dusk was receding in to the horizon. It was bleeding the colour of Arafel's ruby orchids, the deepest shade of their brief exotic season, and staining the sky blood red.

Chapter 5

'Rye bread?'

I shook my head at Max, and glanced around our makeshift camp for Eli.

'Seen Friskers?' he signed as I made my way towards him on the opposite side of the clearing.

'Max said he was here earlier,' I reassured him, 'testing the porridge for us before he slunk off. He's more cat than anything else, I reckon.'

Eli grinned, clearly more concerned about an AWOL griffin than his own skin.

I scanned the jungle bushes, already glistening with the day's heat. We'd left Arafel at dawn with enough provisions for a couple of days. After that we would survive on hunting skills and luck – Outsider basics.

My mind returned to the previous evening, when I'd discovered the haga was missing. I'd sprinted back to the Ring, but the meeting was already over, and the majority of villagers had voted to reject. And I couldn't blame them, not really. Protecting Arafel rather than a group of Prolet rebels who could bring the wrath of Pantheon directly on our heads was logical. But, of course, none of them understood the real value of the Book of Arafel, which was why I hadn't told them about its theft either.

It had been my idea to go rogue. There was no other choice for me, and Max and Eli were in from the start. Aelia had come to us in desperation. And if we mounted a rescue now, we would win the loyalty of a group of Prolets who knew a covert, underground route back into Pantheon. It was far from perfect, but our best chance of retrieving the Book. And I couldn't help but feel Grandpa would want us to help the insurgents, come what may.

'Grandpa used to say the Dead City is a day's hike north-east,' I signed. 'We should be there by dusk, and most of the journey will be forested.'

Eli nodded. 'It'll be the farthest east we've ever been,' he responded, frowning, 'and the closest to the Lifedomes – without actually going inside.'

I nodded.

'Although that's not your plan is it?' he added.

I grabbed his arm, and pushed him into the thicker bushes. The last thing I needed was Max guessing at my real intentions. It was only when the bushes opened out into a small scrub clearing, that I looked up into Eli's guarded face, and felt a surge of guilt. The distance between us was hurting him. I'd been so wrapped up in my own frustration, I wasn't doing anything to make it any better for my clever twin. My complex, insightful, sensitive twin who'd guessed Max's feelings long before I had. And lately his closed nature and preferred solitary lifestyle had prompted a few more questions in my head.

I sat down on a banyan root, as Eli stooped beside the knotted tree, tightening a trouser binding. Seconds later, I felt a handful of leaves and grass being pushed down the neck of my tunic. Stifling laughter, I shook the foliage from my forest tunic and elbowed him affectionately.

'I know Grandpa entrusted you directly with the Book's safekeeping,' he signed, taking a seat beside me, 'but I know he wouldn't want you to go back in there, not for anything or anyone.'

I frowned, feeling the lighter mood dissipate swiftly.

'I also know Octavia wanted the cipher Thomas drew out on the treehouse floor. And that you figured out *how* the cipher worked … But you never shared anything else?'

He paused to run his fingers through his sandy-brown hair.

'No wonder you and August had a thing,' he signed, eyeballing me carefully. 'You're the same – neither of you trust anyone.'

I suppressed a retort. I'd never discussed my feelings with Eli, and his insight felt unusually cynical.

'So what else aren't you telling me? Does Max know more?' he added.

I shook my head emphatically, knowing how much it had cost Eli to let Max come between us over the past few months, to relinquish some of our special twin bond.

He seemed momentarily satisfied.

'Don't you think Grandpa would want me to help you? That he'd want you to share the burden, especially now that he's gone?'

A slow dread started creeping through my bones, as the promise I'd made Grandpa echoed inside my head. I'd given my word I wouldn't tell another soul about Thomas's research hidden within the Book of Arafel until the day I died. I'd already compromised that secret by trading information about the cipher's existence with Aelia and August in return for their knowledge of Roman symbology. And now both Eli and Max knew about the cipher on the treehouse floor. But the fact that the Book of Arafel actually contained Thomas's research notes was still a secret – well, it was until Aelia stole the Book.

I glanced down at my interlocked fingers, recalling the yellowed pages of nonsense lettering and interconnecting circles that always looked so like the scribbling of an imaginative child to me. The knowledge that it coded one of the best-kept secrets of the modern world; and that mythological creatures had actually existed, back in the aeons of time, had seemed so fantastical – but not any more. Since Pantheon, nothing surprised me.

And then there was that one particular faded pencil drawing, buried within Thomas's notes. Its charcoaled lines had first spun out of the dust clouds in the Flavium when I thought all was lost. It was the moment I'd realized Thomas's notes concealed a clue about an ancient burial ground for the unique creatures that had once walked the earth, information Cassius would probably trade his entire Roman battalion to own.

I squeezed Eli's hand.

'Isn't the fact that Aelia has stolen the story of Arafel's emergence from the dust clouds enough?' I whispered.

I could tell by the slight lowering of his eyelids that I'd failed. I looked down at my leather-soled feet, knowing my loyalty to a promise was dividing us. Pulling us apart. Was it always going to be like this now?

A rustle of branches and raucous cawing saved the moment.

'Friskers?' Eli signed before rising to his feet and striding off in the direction of the call. Seconds later, the dense greenery parted and he re-emerged with the tip of an oversized hook beak just visible over his head. I smiled, despite myself.

The griffin always made me stare. Standing around two and a half metres high, its powerful lion forepaws were around the size of my mother's cooking pot, while its blood-red eyes and vibrant gold plumage were brighter than any exotic bird of prey. But it was its hard, calcified beak, filled with a double set of serrated canines that magnetized me.

They were sharp enough to shred a human arm in seconds, but that was before Eli discovered griffins were living in a world of silence. He'd saved us all from the brink of death by using rudimentary sign language to communicate with the modified beasts and now, this particular creature could understand and respond freely.

Though it still skulked around like a moody, domestic cat.

'If you were less conspicuous, we could have taken you with us!' Eli signed to Friskers affectionately. 'But I'll tell you the same thing I told my beautiful, wilful Jas. If I'm not back in three days' time, feel free to come and rescue me.'

He soothed the beast's burnished neck feathers, which were gleaming in the morning sun, as it lifted its angular head to proclaim its loyalty. A couple of capuchins chimed in, and the griffin eyed the foliage with fresh interest. There was no doubt it had taken to forest life with ease.

'It's OK,' Eli added with a smile. 'I don't really expect either of you to play the hero, not a lot for a handsome griffin to do in a city of dust.'

He dug around in his pocket for a couple of sweet hazelnuts. A natural carnivore, the griffin also seemed to have a taste for herbivore treats, and Eli made sure its diet was well supplemented.

'Sun's up, it's time we got going!' Max interrupted.

He disappeared as abruptly as he'd appeared, back in the direction of our small breakfast camp. Eli threw me a look that cut through every defence like an invisible Diasord.

'Boyfriend got the hump?' he signed, raising an eyebrow.

I flushed and stood up. 'You know it's not like that!' I scowled.

Right now, I'd never been less sure of what we were, only that I'd made a promise that was haunting me.

***

'We believe in natural order, respect for our place in the forest, and taking only what we need to survive.'

Grandpa's principles rang in my ears as we hiked through the unknown forest in an easterly direction, and I wondered what he would say if he could see us now. Hunting in this area of the outside forest had always been strictly prohibited; it was too close to the Dead City and wall of the Lifedomes.

The dense, untouched foliage made for slow progress, but our hunting machetes sliced where our feet and hands struggled, and we were in good spirits, reaching the fringe of the forest by the end of the day's hike. We trod cautiously as the trees began to thin, picking our route through a thicket of wild hawthorn with care. And although Friskers had followed us for some time, he'd chosen to retreat while the sun was still high. It seemed even a displaced griffin had better sense than to get within striking distance of the Dead City.

It was only when we finally glimpsed our first view across the landscape of the monolithic domes that we paused to agree final tactics.

'We try for the city when the sun touches the horizon and regroup here, dawn tomorrow morning. Prolets or no Prolets.'

Max drew a white cross on a royal poinciana with a piece of natural chalk, his voice brusque.

I looked from him to my brother. A similar unease was etched into both their faces. No one from Arafel had ever been close to the perimeter of the Dead City ruins, let alone explored them. And yet we'd all heard the stories, and stared at Arafel's scant pre-war pictures of impossibly tall stone trees that stretched on and up.

Less well known was the fact that a few of the more agile hunters, including Max and myself, had occasionally glimpsed the City from the highest branches of Grandpa's Great Oak. The tree's age meant its thinnest branches extended beyond the rest of the others, and it was from these reedier lengths that you could make out the north-westerly tip of the ruins. But it was only ever a glimpse, and from such a distance there was no sense of the layers of dust and ash – the remnants of the people who'd once lived there.

The years had done their work, and now the ruins were fighting a different enemy, the forest herself. I recalled the moment I'd stepped out onto Octavia's balcony, and witnessed the endless broken landscape stretching out before me like a nest of grey vipers. Sleeping and waiting.

I repressed a shudder. Being fanciful about the Dead City wasn't going to help at all. Our first aim was to locate the Prolets and bring them back to Arafel. We wouldn't be popular, but burying our heads in the sand would buy only time, not a reprieve. And Eli didn't need any further reason to think I was planning on a different course of action – at least not yet.

'I suggest we eat up and rest while we can. Tonight we're going to need our wit, energy, and all the luck of Arafel,' Max muttered, turning away to make a small camp.

***

It was the absence of distinct birdsong I noticed at first. Almost as though they too sensed this was a place where life had sung its last song, where anything natural had been obliterated leaving only a hollow echo in its place. It was both mesmerizing and terrifying, making all the tiny hairs on the back of my neck lift in the breeze.

For a moment we stood there, the three of us, staring out at the distant charred landscape interspersed with the creeping determination of the hardiest plants, fighting to reclaim their birthright. It had taken decades before any life had been spotted from a distance, the effect of cataclysmic biochemical warfare having rendered this part of the landscape scarred beyond recognition. But slowly nature was showing herself to be the victor.

'We stick together, no solo heroics!' Max spoke softly just behind me.

He still hadn't really forgiven me, but there was no misunderstanding him, and I felt the oddest sense of déjà vu. It was exactly what I remembered him saying in Pantheon, just before we faced Octavia's guards and were separated.

I nodded at Eli who was slowly surveying the dusky ruins. My brother had never been suited to combat of any kind, and it was a wrench to leave the care of his injured animals to a trusted friend in order to secretly help his sister trawl morbid, ruined cities. I touched his arm.

'You don't have to come. Max and I can cope. Camp here?' I signed.

He frowned, arching his eyebrows. 'And wait for you two to run headlong into trouble because you're too busy arguing? I don't think so!'

He crouched to release an injured salamander he'd been carrying up his sleeve for most of the journey.

I glanced up and down the edge of darkening trees, like age-old sentries watching the landscape.

Light was disappearing quickly now, although it was only around suppertime in Arafel. I pictured Mum sitting by the cooking pot by herself, and hoped Raoul had gone to keep her company as he often did when we were hunting in the outside forest. I'd left Mum a note. She'd never have agreed to the plan, and probably wouldn't sleep until we got back. *If we got back.* I pushed the thought firmly from my mind.

A barn owl hooted twice through the waiting quiet, like a siren. It felt significant in some way. And there was no reason to delay any more.

We took our places beside each other, and as I narrowed my eyes against the glare of the dying sun, I muttered a silent prayer. There were a good couple of kilometres of lumpy arid dirt separating us from the start of the Dead City sprawl. Three of us to bring sixty souls back.

It seemed a good return should we make it.

There were no guarantees, of course; no one knew what the ruined city of Isca Pantheon was really like. But we were better equipped than the last time I left Arafel. Although there were no Diasords between us, we'd brought weapons that we'd grown skilled at using every day of our lives: machetes, daggers, axes, bows and in my particular case, a certain well-used slingshot.

We started out together, and I noticed the cool dirt crumbling beneath my leather-soled feet straight away. This was a thin, recovering topsoil, seemingly like the one Grandpa and his forebears had to coax back to rich life. It made for quick, stealthy progress, and the three of us broke into an easy hunting sprint across the amber landscape, towards the ruins.

It was deceiving at first, the way the ground shifted, almost as though it could have been merely the impact of our running feet against the dehydrated earth; earth that hadn't seen human feet for more than two hundred years. But then a pained cry razed the empty landscape, and the enemy was so close as to be laughable. The ground was moving. The cry belonged to Eli. And when I glanced in his direction, he was no long running.

I froze instantly, my eyes straining against the fading light until I could make out his crumpled form on the ground. My heart rate doubled instantly. We were tree-runners; we never fell.

'Eli?'

My whisper died on my lips as Max caught my wrist.

'Look at your feet,' he forced through gritted teeth.

And there was something in his voice that froze me to the spot. I levelled my gaze, and fixed on the earth beneath my feet. The earth that moved. And now that we were stationary, I couldn't understand how I hadn't felt it before. The earth wasn't just moving; it was writhing.

I peered harder. My mouth was as dry as the arid soil beneath my feet, and my blood echoed like a waterfall in my ears, but I was unable to break my gaze. Not until I made out the heaving mass of giant, overlapping pincers, just visible beneath the lumpy dirt; and their segmented tails, poised and ready to paralyse their ignorant prey at any given moment.

'For the love of Arafel, fly!' Max growled, as we lunged together, grabbing Eli and pulling him to his feet.

Then, between us, we propelled him over the remaining barren land at breakneck speed. I bit down hard as our feet flew, now fully aware of the heaving mass of scorpion topsoil crunching beneath our thin-soled shoes. We gave no thought to the noise we were making, or obvious profile we were cutting across the barren landscape. Our only thought was to reach safety as quickly as possible. I clenched my fist around Eli's lower back. At this rate we could expect a personal welcome from Cassius himself.

It was only when the broken silhouette of the city outskirts loomed up out of the gloom that I allowed myself to hope. The ruin seemed quiet and still, but taking no chances, we made straight towards a large concrete boulder resting in the shadows. With one final effort, we half carried, half pushed Eli on top, before scrambling up ourselves. Then it was only us and the vast oppressive night.

'Eli,' I whispered, reaching across to my brother. He was curled up, motionless, and for a second blind panic clawed up my dry throat. Was he dead?

Then he rolled over and lifted an eyelid to consider me carefully.

'First time I've ever considered de-friending *Hottentotta tamulus*.' He winced, his breath slightly laboured.

'You're stung?' I scolded, reaching into my rations bag for some of the medical herbs we carried on us.

'Yes, I'm also winded,' he complained. 'My feet barely touched the ground in the last part of that run.'

Cursing, I scrambled in my leather bag. Two hundred years of living in a jungle climate meant we'd developed some natural antibodies against snake and spider bites, much stronger anti-venoms than our ancestors used to possess. All the same, the *Hottentotta tamulus* was one of the most venomous scorpions around.

I pulled out my water bottle. 'Where?' I demanded.

Eli rolled up his right trouser leg, revealing a raised red welt on the front of his calf. I tipped some cool water on a small rag, pressed some fresh meadowsweet into the wet patch and then placed it over the injury. He smiled gratefully, and squeezed my hand before taking over.

'It's not stinging so much already,' he consoled. 'Think I may have got lucky with a small one.'

'Not sure any sized scorpion sting counts as luck!' Max retorted. 'And if this is just a warm-up for the Dead City, we're gonna need so much more than luck.'

I nodded grimly. Max was right. This wasn't a good start. Eli's leg wasn't life-threatening, and so long as there were no other visible signs of shock, his body was coping. But the effect on his leg would probably slow us for a day or two – time we could ill afford to lose. And then there was a prophetic feeling I couldn't shake. If this had happened to Eli, just about the most popular human in the animal kingdom I knew, what chance did Max and I stand if there were more of them?

'We move slowly and as a team,' I said, trying to control my spiralling fear.

I hadn't risked the wrath of Art just to become scorpion food. My head filled with his wise face. I hadn't even told him about the theft of the Book of Arafel. There hadn't been time, and I doubted it would change much, although he would have been sad and angry. But mostly I hadn't told him because it would be like shining a light on my own ineptitude. I'd already broken my promise to Grandpa by letting others understand some of the legacy of the Book. Admitting to its loss felt like exacerbating my own sense of failure. Far better I put the situation right. Or at least tried to.

For a few minutes we remained seated in the shadows, recovering our breath while the voice of the Dead City reached through the shadows. It moaned. Not in the biblical sense, although in some ways I wouldn't have been surprised; it was so much bigger and more oppressive now it loomed up in front of us. Instead, the eerie groan was of nature herself, creaking through the rubble alleyways and broken roofs, and whistling through every decrepit gutter. As if she was warning that nothing should ever breathe or live here again.

Silently, we examined the leather soles of our shoes, but somehow our slim goat-hide soles had protected us.

I threw a glance at Eli. His face was filled with the same quiet foreboding I was feeling. We all understood the dangers of the forest, and had learned how to combat the most cunning cats, ferocious boar and shrewd snakes. But a sea of scorpions was new to me. It had to be nature's response to the arid conditions in this part of the landscape, and might explain why the Prolet insurgents had become landlocked in this crumbling shell of a city.

Silently, we bowed our heads together, an old Arafel custom to offer thanks for the sparing of a soul. There was no going back that way – that much was certain – and I couldn't help but feel that this was the precise moment we were leaving Arafel behind. Was it for good? I pulled my trusted catapult from my leather pouch, and fought the sudden burning behind my eyes.

'You think you can walk on it?' I asked, as much to distract myself as anything else.

He nodded. 'And if not, Max can give me a shoulder ride!'

I smiled as Max grimaced.

'Yeah, right after you,' he jibed. 'Time to go?' he added, crooking his neck to look into the darkness, while withdrawing a short, gleaming blade from his hunting belt.

I frowned. Like most hunters in Arafel, Max could handle a knife, bow and fishing spear with practised ease. But he was particularly gifted when it came to knives, often dispatching prey from as far as fifty metres away. His precision and brute strength also made him a formidable adversary in combat, but this was different.

I shot out a hand to pause his course, before loading a stone in my slingshot. Swiftly, I took aim and released so the stone flew through the broken archway into the darkness beyond. The hollow echo of the stone's tumble filled the tense air, before it came to an abrupt standstill. My skin felt like a thousand scorpions were crawling across it, in some giant arachnid march. But there was no answer – nothing but the same chilling whistle of wind through the broken streets.

There was no more reason to hesitate.

Supporting Eli between us, we slipped off the stone and stole forward together. And as we passed beneath the crumbling Gothic arch and into the shadowed ruin beyond, I was immediately struck by a cloud of grey oppression, despite the green moss and hardy creepers.

The whistling moan of the wind was louder here, as though it belonged in the way life had once, whispering memories. Warning us. We stared around the ruined space in silent wonder. We'd made it; we were inside the Dead City. We were the first Outsiders from Arafel to have trodden here since the Great War, and we didn't belong at all.

Swallowing, I tried to get my bearings. This first building was large and rectangular, with several broken pillars splayed across the debris-strewn floor. They must have once supported a high-vaulted roof, at least twenty times the height of our treehouse.

Briefly I wondered what purpose the space might have served, and then I spotted the parallel lines sunk into the floor a little way off. They were beyond rusted, and almost obscured by overgrowth, but I'd studied the old world enough to know I was looking at what our ancestors would have called a railway station.

'*Toxic boxes on wheels … They choked the earth and burned precious resources, making men fat and lazy …*'

I could hear Grandpa as though he was standing next to me, and his words seemed to resonate eerily in this overgrown crypt. The space rang with the echo of a thousand impatient footsteps that no longer bore any connection to our forest community. I felt my hands grow clammy. Our ancestors' obsession with speed

60

and technology hadn't brought them freedom; it had trapped them for all eternity.

'Let's move,' I whispered to Max. 'There's no living soul here.'

Eli's wan face gleamed in the thin moonlight, and I knew without asking that he, too, could hear the dead voices clamouring in this place.

Max threw us both a cursory glance before stepping out in front, his sure feet cutting across the echoes, and pushing back the ghosts. He cut a diagonal line across the floor towards another crumbling stone arch, before beckoning that we should follow. We traced his path across the cracked, overgrown concrete to pass beneath another wide, intact arch with some kind of long oblong set into the wall. Up above, there was a series of smaller oblong boxes attached to the ceiling, some broken and dangling. I guessed them to be old-world computers of some sort, but to me they looked like nameless gravestones.

We hurried beneath the thick arch, and I breathed a sigh of relief when the crumbling railway façade opened out onto what must have once been a long wide pavement, scattered with creeper-clad broken stones.

Concrete city foundations had prevented a lot of thick, upright growth; and a surprisingly clear old road ran parallel with the railway, lined with blackened, toothless buildings. Further up the road there was a circular juncture with several similar-looking routes extending from it like a spider's web.

I glanced at Max in disbelief. It looked as though there was far more of a city skeleton remaining than any of us had ever expected, and the Prolets could be anywhere.

'OK, steady progress, that's all we need!' he reassured, his gaze lingering on Eli.

I smiled tightly, conscious of how our footsteps seemed so intrusive here, a city that had once known the pounding of so many feet. And the sheer scale of the structured ruins meant there were countless roads and decaying buildings to scour. Even if we split up it would still be an impossible task to achieve in one night.

And yet we were here, and there was no going back.

The three of us started up the middle of the crumbling, over-grown road. Although the sun had long disappeared, everything was draped in a lazy veil of moonlight and clinging cloud. I fought a shiver. Even though the darkness was our friend, I felt more exposed now than I ever had in the outside forest at night.

My ears were straining and senses on high alert. There were enough walls remaining to differentiate between the buildings where people had once traded food and goods, and those that had offered shelter and a home. But there was a something else too, a feeling that the shells weren't quite as lifeless as we first thought. There was a scuffle here, a rustle there, and always the sense that we were intruding, trespassing on hallowed, sacred ground.

Gritting my teeth, I focused on the sound of our feet on the cracked concrete, pushing all fanciful notions to the back of my mind. But Eli getting hurt so soon had sent a fracture haring through my confidence. *Eli.* I'd already come too close to losing him in Pantheon. There was no way I could risk either him or Max getting hurt again because of me. It would be worse than getting hurt myself. Which was why I knew that when the right moment came, I was headed to Pantheon. Alone.

We stole on, alert to every new noise. Eli was managing to walk unaided, but I could tell his leg was throbbing, despite the meadowsweet. I fumbled for my rations bag, intent on finding some willow bark for him to chew to dull the pain, only to graze my own shin against a dark object protruding between two broken slabs of concrete.

I yelped and reached down.

'What's the matter?' Max whispered, turning to see why I'd paused.

I scowled down at the offending object, still rubbing. It was made from metal, and layered with years of grime and dirt, but with a little effort I could just make out black lettering running along its length.

'Queen St,' I read, frowning.

'Queen … sting? Queen … strop?!' Max tested carefully.

I pulled a face to cover my relief. It was the first real reference to our fight since leaving Arafel. I'd hurt him, I knew that, and in some ways I'd understand if he never spoke to me again. At least not like that. Humour was always a good, safe place for us.

But just as I opened my mouth to retort, Eli started signing frantically.

'Something up there! Inside!' he gesticulated rapidly, pointing up at the charred remains of a blackened second-floor window, just above us.

It was Max's turn to scowl. 'What kind of something?' he signed awkwardly.

'Not sure,' Eli signed, 'but it moved … a shadow?'

'This place is full of shadows!' Max exploded.

I glared at him. 'If Eli says he saw something, we ought to check it out!'

We all stared up at the concrete hole that had once been a large formal window. It looked as black and uninviting as any of the charcoaled, deserted buildings.

'Protect it with your life, Talia, come what may.'

I tried to pretend I hadn't heard, but he was there, echoing around the edge of the cool February breeze. Cursing softly, I sprinted up the cluttered stone steps that must have once been a formal entranceway, before I could change my mind.

And as soon as I passed beneath the large grey entrance arch, I knew this building could never have been any ordinary shop or house. Even dressed in murky shadows, it was big, with a white, formal staircase that gleamed and stretched upwards in front of me. Everything was covered in years of dust and scorched debris, and half the ceiling was completely missing exposing a finely balanced balustrade. At the top of the first white flight, watching over years of debris and dust, was a single lonely sculpture. Its athletic silhouette shone in the darkness like an angel of war, and it was only when I finally made out its name that I allowed myself a smile.

'Prince Albert … and about time,' I whispered to myself.

'Huh?' Max whispered, stepping up beside me.

'Nothing,' I dismissed, carefully eyeing the curve of the balustrade from the first flight to a precarious second flight with the central rises missing. I flexed my fingers; I had my route.

Without hesitating, I ran lightly towards the staircase, took hold of the cool stone and leapt, knowing Max would have to follow much more gingerly given the fragility of the structure. It wobbled, and a shower of debris fell from the landing above us, but I didn't pause. It was a tree-runner's number one rule: never doubt. *Doubt and you fall,* Grandpa would say.

Within seconds, I was standing opposite the heroic Prince Albert, and I held my breath as I followed the shaky bannister around. The second run was much steeper, and the middle of the stone rises were missing, which meant no second chances. I narrowed my eyes, and tiptoed up until I reached a point close enough to leap. Then I was flying like a squirrel monkey, claws outstretched, until they grazed the old wooden first floor.

I drew myself up to standing, letting my eyes adjust to the dingy gloom. This part of the building seemed to have survived quite well, and there was a large open corridor leading in both directions.

After only a moment's consideration, I turned down the left corridor. Both walls were lined with large glass cases that had somehow, by the luck of Arafel, escaped the effects of the Great War. Curiously, I peered into a cabinet labelled *Gladiatorial Artefacts*, only to recoil as a spiked head with black, eyeless holes in the centre leered back at me.

'Boo!' a voice whispered.

I gasped before rounding on Max with a glare. He grinned mischievously while rubbing the glass to remove two centuries of dust.

'We're in one of those places they used to display old stuff – a museum, isn't it … Miss?' he teased.

I turned back to the display. I didn't want to give him the satisfaction of knowing he'd rescued me from the memory of Cassius riding out into the Flavium; a monster on a black mount wearing similar headwear. And as I gazed, a tiny black sign at the bottom of the glass case caught my attention: *Roman Gladiatorial Helmet – worn by Rome's elite gladiators.* I grimaced.

Of course we were in a museum. Exeter Museum. Or the shell of it anyway. It would also explain the sculpted figure halfway up the steps. It seemed incredible that anything like these silent exhibitions had survived the most cataclysmic war the earth had ever seen. They were like treasures left beside a grave.

'The room's up ahead.'

Eli suddenly hobbled out of the grey, his signing jerky and stressed.

I sighed. So far my attempts at protection were proving futile.

'The back stairs were complete,' he offered simply.

Inwardly I cursed for not having the foresight to check for another set myself.

'You should have waited below,' I hissed. 'Thought we agreed no heroics?'

Two sets of eyes danced ironically, and I spun on my heels, swallowing my retort.

There was less natural light in this part of the corridor, and the air was rank. Something with a thick tail and muffled squeak ran in front of me, making the hairs on the back of my neck strain. There were plenty of nocturnal rodents in the forest, but the shapes that moved in this ruin somehow felt much less animal than at home. I swallowed, and forced my feet forward towards the large closed door at the top of the corridor. It was the room we'd pinpointed from the street outside, where Eli had seen a shadow move.

Max leaned forward to listen, and for a moment all I could hear were three hearts pumping so hard I was sure anyone inside had to know of our presence instantly. He shook his head, and the strange tingle spread across the back of my shoulders and down my arms. Slowly, he reached out and turned the door handle. His knuckles gleamed, despite the lack of light, and afterwards I realized it was because he was gripping so tightly. Then it swung inwards to reveal a huge, shadowy room, half open to the stars. Full of eyes.

'Get back,' Max whispered hoarsely but not before several huge black, bulbous shapes inclined their skinny heads towards us. The stench hit us like a wall. It was putrid rotting faeces and my world closed in, taking me back to Pantheon's tunnels in a heartbeat.

We stumbled backwards through the doorway, my thoughts running wild. Had Cassius already unleashed monsters from the tunnels? Could we have happened upon a pack of sleeping strix?

Nausea reached up my throat, as my clumsy movement sent a loose stone scuttling across the floor. There was a moment's poignant silence, and then the air was filled with opal hunting eyes, threatening hissing, and the deafening beat of large, heavy wings.

Pandemonium ensued, but somehow I was conscious of Eli forging forward in the opposite direction. I made a grab for him, but clutched only thin air as he disappeared into the murky whirlwind inside.

'Eli,' I yelled, holding my arms high in front of my eyes to protect them from the thick, swirling dust.

Eli was the most gifted animal whisperer I knew, but what if these new creatures were of Pantheon's design? I recalled the effort it had taken to calm the manticore and molossers, and felt my panic swell.

Then, just as suddenly as the chaos had erupted, it fell unnaturally quiet.

'Eli?' I whispered again, my chest thumping so hard I thought it might explode.

Although my brother couldn't hear me, he usually sensed when I called him. But there was no response, and the still black was more than I could bear. So, swallowing my panic, I crept inside.

For a moment, I was conscious only of breath, of living bodies other than our own sharing the same dark space. Then as the moon moved out from behind the gunmetal clouds, and the shadows became low-lit pools, my gaze was drawn to the centre. Towards Eli.

He was seated cross-legged on a central, raised dais that must have originally been some sort of displaying table; while a pack of waist-height, hairless birds scavenged around him. They were huge, skinny, and beyond ugly.

But they weren't strix.

Holding my breath, I edged closer. The birds clattered around the floor, occasionally raising their heads to sniff the rank air. With featherless blue-grey heads, brown ruffed necks and tapered wings, they were clearly birds of prey; and at more than a metre tall each, they were also birds to respect. But no creature on our free-living planet could resist Eli, and right now they appeared calm enough.

'What are they?' I signed.

'Cinereous vulture,' he responded studiously. 'One of the two largest, vulturous species of birds on earth.'

A brief memory of the giant, clawing strix flickered through my head, but I knew he was talking about birds outside Pantheon. Apex predators of the natural world.

'Have been known to eat flesh, but much prefer their dinner deceased.' He smirked as Max stepped up beside me.

'Yeah, well … when you're done having tea with the local wildlife, we've a job to do,' Max forced out, scanning the room.

I followed his gaze and scowled as more silhouettes of stuffed, old-world creatures took shape within the gloomy darkness. A towering elephant and giraffe made the vultures look little more than pecking chickens; while their glassy, yellowed irises gleamed lifelessly from their mottled skins.

I dragged my eyes away. The stuffed creatures' stare was almost worse than the vultures' clear suspicion that Max and I were a potential threat to their new king. I glared at my brother, who sighed before standing up to address the unsavoury group with a series of crude gestures. Then he slowly backed away, taking care to push us through the doorway first.

'So, what did you say to them?' I signed, once we were back on the road outside.

'I told them my friends were a little chewy; but if they stuck around I knew of a few others who were rotten to the core,' he responded blithely.

And right on cue, a dozen dark shapes soared effortlessly out of the window and into the smoky sky above.

I scowled. Ravenous, cinereous vultures weren't exactly my idea of the perfect cavalry.

Chapter 6

The grey air was oppressive in this part of town, the memory of the Great War clinging to the buildings like a shroud. We picked our way down the old road, avoiding the shelled buildings which felt like tombs after nearly two hundred years of desolation. Their scale could only mean we'd arrived in the city centre and we walked soberly, the way we might through Arafel's graveyard. And although there were no visible human remains here, I could feel anguished faces staring out of every crumbling window and burned-out metal box Grandpa used to call cars and lorries.

Never before had I been quite so aware of the erasing effect of the Great War. A hundred thousand people had once lived in the bustling city of Exeter, and now it seemed even the scurrying ants avoided this place.

'We haven't come across any large life whatsoever, let alone the Prolet insurgents,' Max muttered, voicing my thoughts.

I threw a glance at the sky, where a silent flock of vultures shadowed our progress.

'Aside from baldies anonymous of course,' he conceded with a quick grin.

I grinned back, grateful for our new ease, and immediately

noticed the new bronze-edged angular weapon hanging over Max's right shoulder.

I nodded. 'What's that?'

'This old thing?' he repeated airily. 'Oh, just something I picked up back there.'

'Back there, where?'

'Er … in the museum,' he muttered, faint colour creeping up his neck.

'Max Thorn!' I exclaimed, trying to prevent a laugh from escaping. 'What on earth can a respected Arafel hunter pick up at a wreck of a museum that could possibly be of use in the Dead City?'

'It's just a keepsake – nothing to get excited about.' He flushed, shifting the stolen item further down his back.

I made a grab for it.

'OK, OK, it's a cheiroballistra,' he admitted, sidestepping deftly.

'A cheiro-what? What in the name of Arafel is one of those?' I asked.

'A cheiroballistra. Y'know, a … Roman … crossbow,' he answered as though it was the most natural item in the world to loot.

'You stole a Roman crossbow from the museum?' I repeated, this time unable to keep from laughing.

'No! Well, not exactly … This has got to be a reproduction. A real one definitely wouldn't be worth stealing! But this one is made of some other hard-wearing material I can't really identify and … Look, it's not like anyone was using it, or looking at it even!' he defended. 'I just thought it might come in useful, and, well, I've always wanted one.'

'And now we get to the truth!'

'Cool!' Eli signed. 'Get me one?'

Max shook his head teasingly as I smiled, aware it was the first time the three of us had shared a joke in ages. And maybe he was right. Its addition could hardly hurt, and besides which, it looked as though the ice between Max and I had finally thawed, which was worth all the looted crossbows in the world.

'Just so long as your pockets aren't stuffed with little tin soldiers too!' I winked.

We walked for a while in an easier silence, our footsteps interspersed by the groaning breeze. Eli had dropped a little way behind to observe the vultures, or so he said.

'Do you think there's any chance Aelia could have got it wrong? About the Prolet insurgents hiding out here?' Max asked after a few minutes. 'I've seen no fresh water, let alone anything a group of sixty people could survive on for more than a day or two.'

'Not sure.' I glanced around, unable to deny the truth of what he was saying. The buildings felt as dead as the people who'd once lived in them.

And Aelia. What was her real motivation for stealing the Book? I recalled the glint in her eye when she talked about the Voynich, how I'd tried to navigate the maze of conversation about the Book of Arafel, without revealing the whole of Grandpa's precious secret. And finally, there was August. And his stolen kiss.

I inhaled softly, trying to order my wayward thoughts.

I'd told Aelia about the cipher, even drawn it out for her, because I needed her specialist symbolic knowledge. And I knew the cipher was useless without the keyword. I also told her Thomas's original research was destroyed. But I was obviously the worst actress in the world because she guessed it still existed, as well as where it was most likely to be hidden. Had she worked out the keyword already? She had a much better understanding of Latin and genetics than anyone I'd met before.

And finally, there was the question that spun harder than all the rest: how long did I have before she traded the Book for the Prolets? Or August? Or both? If any of them were still alive.

'Look, just because Aelia drops into Arafel and steals the one thing she knows will create a reaction, doesn't mean anything's changed between us, OK?' Max offered a little roughly. 'And that

71

goes for arguments too. It doesn't change the fundamentals … At least not for me.'

He smiled at me and I nodded, painfully aware he was a much better human being than I could ever be. Then the full force of his words hit home. I grabbed his forearm.

The one thing she knows will create a reaction.

'Actually, I don't think Aelia has ever been wrong about much. Max, what if she didn't steal the Book of Arafel to trade with Cassius, but as an act of deliberate provocation?'

He looked down at me in confusion.

'A deliberate act of provocation? To who? To what end?'

A sudden chill, like winter ivy, coiled around my core. August had forbidden Aelia to use me as proof of an outside world, but now he was gone, and she was desperate to mobilize her threatened Prolet world. Perhaps Aelia wasn't thinking of negotiation at all. Perhaps she needed a spark to start her Prolet revolution.

I stared up into Max's darkening scowl. He suspected it too, I could tell.

'To draw me,' I whispered, as a heavy thud filled the silent night.

**

I turned as though in slow motion. The silhouetted road was empty. My breath was patchy and jagged. *Eli had completely disappeared.*

'No!' I gasped, my voice sounding oddly disembodied.

I forced my legs into a sprint back to the place I'd last seen him and whirled around, real panic clawing up my throat.

'Eli! Eli! Max! Where is he?'

Max started running towards me.

'He was there just a second ago, where in the name of Araf … Aarrgh!'

His shocked yell tore through the night as a large pale limb suddenly twisted up out of the ground, and wrapped itself around his right leg.

'Aarrgh! Get off me! You son of a bastard …! Get off!'

The whole street started to shrink, as Max buckled under the sudden pressure of assault, half of his right leg disappearing into a gaping hole I'd not noticed before.

'Max!'

I pelted forward, not caring about the noise I was making, just as a second thick limb reached up and wound around Max's other leg. He slammed to the ground, grappling for one of his hunting knives, but whatever had gripped him was far too strong. And in one raw breath, half of Max's body disappeared into a black hole, leaving only his chest and head exposed.

'Tal,' he yelled hoarsely, his face paling to ashen as it squeezed the breath from his body, 'whatever happens … I …'

But what he was going to say was lost as he disappeared from sight, leaving me completely and utterly alone in the City of Dust.

'No! No! No!'

I flew over the last few metres, my feet barely touching the ground, and threw myself down beside the hole.

'Take me too!' I screamed furiously into the black. 'You can't take them and leave me here! You underground son of a cave bitch! Take me too!'

The edges of my voice grated like sandpaper, while my chest felt like it was being anchored to my feet with a vice. I hadn't told him. He was gone and I hadn't told him.

And then nothing. The desolate street was quiet, save for the faint hissing of the vultures, watching from a nearby rooftop, and the wind. Moaning. Always moaning.

'*This isn't how it's meant to be,*' I whispered into the dust.

Then the pale limb reached up, and took me too.

***

I was dimly aware of a metallic object being dragged, extinguishing any remaining light through the sour-smelling tunnel. Then I was set on my feet, and as I fought a momentary dizziness, my eyes were drawn by a tiny flicker of light.

It was only a small lantern, but enough to illuminate the glistening rock walls weakly. I swallowed my panic, knowing I needed to stay calm. To think. But my new companions stole all my attention anyway, and I gazed in wonder at a towering snow-white satyr and a small grubby child in a headscarf and smoke-grey tunic.

To my intense relief, both Eli and Max were seated behind the satyr, their hands bound and mouths gagged, but otherwise unharmed. Instinctively, my hand closed over my catapult, as we all stared at one another in some doubtful sort of stand-off. Then I peeled my tongue from the roof of my mouth.

'Prolets, by any chance?'

'I'm Lake, and this is Pan – as in the god, not the dish!'

The small girl laughed at her own joke, before clamping a white hand over her mouth.

'We're not supposed to laugh. Sound travels a looooong way underground,' she whispered, her eyes wide and dramatic.

I smiled cautiously. Her cheekbones gleamed tightly in the half-light, while her arms looked pitifully thin, lending weight to Max's theory about survival in this barren place. Then I looked from her to the imposing white satyr, its broad muscular chest defined by the hollows between its ribs, and inspiration struck.

'Untie my brother and friend, and we'll give you all the food we have.'

There was a poignant silence while the satyr looked meaningfully at the child, starvation written all over its broad white face. After a beat she relented, sighing.

'OK, but not a word to the others.'

I reached into my leather ration pack and withdrew a wrap

74

of cape gooseberries, two bananas, a round of goat's cheese and a wedge of rye bread. It was everything I had, but I could see they needed it more than I did.

Lake turned the proffered food over in awe, before nodding at her pale companion who in turn reached to pull off Max and Eli's gags. Then, withdrawing an ugly-looking blade from a sling, he freed them of their bindings with a single upwards slice.

'Well of all the jungle ways to introduce yourselves. I thought you wanted to eat us!' Max joked.

Lake was across the tunnel in a heartbeat, a short stubby knife from the rope around her waist pressed forcefully against Max's throat.

'And we might still if you don't learn some respect! We've not eaten in a long while, and Pan here is pretty hungry!'

She spoke fiercely, her short curly brown hair escaping her dirty headscarf and black circles accentuating her fine green eyes. And all at once I was filled with awe for this steely child who'd managed to survive beneath this eerie shell of a city against all the odds.

Max drew back in confusion, while Pan's thick white eyebrows forked sharply. He looked down at his snow-white hoof-feet, clearly not wishing to undermine his small, fiery friend.

'We're friends, Lake,' I intervened gently. 'We've come to help you. At Aelia's request.'

Aelia's name bought us the instant credit we needed.

'What do you mean?' she asked, her brow puckering as she lowered her knife and stepped closer.

Now she was within a hair's breadth, I could see she was even younger than I first thought, no more than about ten or eleven years old. She was also a true child of Pantheon, and regarded me suspiciously from beneath double eyelids. They gave her a narrow, serpentine expression that somehow suited her emerald eye colour. What experimental genetic creation was she?

I smiled gently. A tiny bloom had crept into her cheeks as a result of the food, betraying her need.

'Lake, I think your people may be looking for me. I'm Talia.'

***

The claustrophobic rock corridor took me back to Pantheon's underground tunnels in a breath. And to the desiccating dread I only recalled in my dreams. I told myself these tunnels were friendly, that the strix and Cerberus were many kilometres away, but in truth they were closer than any of us cared to think about. And Aelia had already mentioned Cassius's threat to flush the Prolets out.

I forced myself to focus straight ahead, on the dim silhouette of our guides' backs. And the first thing to strike me was that Pan wasn't a satyr at all. His ears were too elongated and covered in white fur; while a long tail swung rhythmically from his behind as his tufted feet padded along the stone floor.

Racking my memory, I recalled a mythical ancestor of the satyr. It was one of the oldest creatures classical writers had recorded, but I was sure the physiology of this creature was related. It was also legendary for its guardianship of the young and weak; although this particular individual looked no older than Max or me.

'Silenus?' I asked as he turned to gesticulate before disappearing around a dark corner.

A cursory nod was all the answer I received, although his eyes were laden with care when they rested on the child. I suppressed a frown. They seemed such unlikely companions.

Lake was clearly on high alert as she led us through the damp, mouldy walls. These tunnels were much colder and tighter than those beneath Pantheon, and it wasn't long before I was missing even the Dead City above our heads. At least it looked at the sky.

I flicked a cautionary look at her pallid skin. Born underground, she was accustomed to a lack of sun, but the Prolet underworld was warm and dry. The dank atmosphere of this new underground maze had to be a breeding ground for disease.

'Old Roman tunnels?' Eli signed by the light of Lake's flickering lantern.

I nodded. It was the only plausible explanation, and it made absolute sense that the Prolet people, forced to live underground in Pantheon, would take refuge in the environment they knew best. Even so, as Pan led the way down a red earthen slope, I found myself fighting a sense of impending doom, a feeling that we were descending right into the heart of hell.

Max's athletic step echoed behind me, and a new cocktail of relief and guilt infused my cold limbs afresh. Even when I'd come so close to losing Max, I couldn't stop myself from thinking about him.

'That's it, isn't it? I'm just not him.'

His furious words echoed in my head, and somewhere in the walled-up tissues of my heart, a drop of water formed and froze. An ice tear. Because the worst part of all was that he was one hundred per cent right. It was absolutely nothing to do with him, and absolutely everything to do with him not being *August*. And how could I explain that?

Or my promise.

Was it too much? Could he tell? Would he even want me still?

An image of us lying naked and entwined on my reed mattress at home flickered through my head, making me grateful for the meagre light thrown out by the lantern. We'd managed to forget the world that night. Could we do it again? For ever? Could I finally leave the ghost girl behind: the imposter who looked and acted like me, but who'd actually left her real self behind in Pantheon? And if not, would a ghost girl be enough for a boy who deserved the sun, the moon and the stars? Because it couldn't get more real than that.

We progressed through the tunnels swiftly, only just keeping up with our seasoned guides. Briefly, I wondered at the choice of such a young member as lookout, and whether Pan was the real authority, or if they'd formed a small breakaway group from the main rebellious party.

Somehow, I couldn't shake the feeling it was none of the above.

After a good twenty minutes hard walking, Lake's pace slowed, and I sensed we were finally approaching the Prolets' base camp. She held a thin white finger to her lips, and then gesticulated swiftly for Pan to go ahead and check the way. He was as dutiful as any foot soldier; and his pale, muscular frame disappeared around the mouldy corner without question, only to reappear seconds later. His brief nod, pricked ears and relaxed facial expression cleared the way, and I drew a deep breath. This was it.

'Ready?' Eli signed with a brief rise of his bushy eyebrows.

I nodded, confident we now stood a chance.

Then we rounded the corner.

And I couldn't have been more unprepared for the view that rose up to greet us. The claustrophobic tunnel ballooned out into some sort of crumbling underground ruin. The central forum was large, about the size of Arafel's market square, and peppered with small stone rises that looked like the remains of some sort of ancient water or heating system. Patchy, ancient frescoed mosaics adorned the top half of each mottled wall, and there were numerous doorways beneath decaying archways.

But it was the curious eyes that stole my breath. I scanned the room, my suspicions racing like wildfire. There were small hammocks hanging inside every arched inset, corroborating Aelia's approximation of the insurgent numbers. And the group were together, and seemingly intact.

She'd just failed to mention they were all children.

Slowly the fog concealing the rebel group's motivation began to lift. Aelia's urgency to find them, Cassius's fury that they were missing – even their reputed idealistic belief that a girl on the outside could be found if you looked long enough – became suddenly, terrifyingly clear. They were all too young to know any better. Or worse.

Max stepped up beside me, his golden skin paling as he surveyed the scene before us.

'What in the name of Arafel?'

A strange silence descended as sixty pairs of hollowed, inquisitive eyes assessed our friendliness. Then a cheer erupted throughout the room, and we were surrounded.

'Hey, take a chill pill! Told you I'd bring home the goods, didn't I? You can't eat them, but trust me, they're useful.'

I glanced down at Lake, who was flushed with triumph and now seemed quite old in comparison to some of the others.

'Lake, where ...? Who is your leader?' Max asked, in a troubled voice.

Rapid thoughts cross-fired through my head. This young Prolet group had to represent a good proportion of Cassius's future workforce, which meant our assistance was going to reap the worst possible vengeance upon Arafel. Cassius would never let such a valuable commodity go without a fight.

Where were their parents? And why hadn't Aelia told us the full story?

My head whirled as I frowned at Eli. This was complicated beyond everything.

'Atticus!' Lake called, seemingly unaware of any tension.

She scanned the chamber until a young adolescent boy, around fifteen years of age, skulked out from beneath one of the arched antechambers set into the wall.

He surveyed us all with a faint scowl before making his way towards us, the young excited crowd parting to let him through. And as they moved I noticed there was far more variety of life than I first realized. These weren't just a group of young human Prolets, there was a pretty good cross-representation of all Prolet life gathered here. Just very juvenile in years.

Five young satyrs, one holding a three-legged dog with a pig snout, stared at us with wonder etched on their gaunt faces. To their left was an elfin boy with a pair of gold-brown feathered wings stretching and retracting rhythmically. And when he reached down to pet a tiny, perfectly proportioned griffin, I noticed his entire back was covered in the same burnished down. Towards the back of the crowd, two young girls with white hair held hands together, while a monkey with bright cerulean eyes chattered effusively, as it leapt around the towers of flat stones.

I thought at once of Isca Pantheon's laboratories, of their cruel experimental purpose, and my stomach lurched. These children and creatures were the product of Octavia's reign. What horrors had they endured already through their short lives? And how had they ended up here, all alone, at the mercy of whatever nightmare Cassius chose to dispatch through the tunnels?

'Welcome to our humble abode.' Atticus bowed with an exaggerated flourish, his eyes sharp and questioning.

He was easily the tallest after Pan, with opal-black eyes and short raven hair fashioned into two spiky horns at the front. It gave him a bold look, which together with his calculating smile, felt oddly familiar. I wondered if he'd orchestrated the whole escape; the whole group seemed to hold him in such respect.

'Good to meet you, Atticus.' Max stepped forward to hold out his broad, brown hand. 'We've come here, at Aelia's request, to bring you safe escort to your new home … Arafel?'

There was a low mutter of excitement around the young crowd. Clearly, the name of our village carried mysterious promise, and my heart sank a little further. Atticus raised a slim white hand, exposing a fine Pantheon dagger dangling at his side, before settling his gaze on Max. I stared, trying not to frown. If a Prolet boy had seized the chance to steal an expensive Pantheon dagger and lead a band of renegade children this far, he deserved respect.

There was a moment of silence as each considered the other. Max was by far the older and heavier, but the spiky boy held his nerve, running his eye over Max critically, before offering his own hand. I watched as a curious light crept into his coal eyes, a new doubt firing through my own veins. His manner was altogether too casual, his mood indifferent, and when he finally spoke, his voice was surprisingly authoritative.

'We thank you for your trouble, but I'm afraid you've wasted your time. You see, we're already home.'

Chapter 7

I pondered over a tin dish of chewy snail and nettle broth, washed down with boiled water from the run-off at the base of the mouldy walls.

Aelia hadn't told us the whole story, and perhaps she'd guessed a party of child insurgents would have been far harder to welcome into Arafel. Not because we wouldn't want to help, but because of the trouble that would surely follow them. If there weren't any biological parents, Cassius was hardly like to sign off his future workforce without a fight.

My brain whirred like Arafel's grain crusher at harvest time. How had sixty young Prolets managed to escape the detection of greater Pantheon, make it all the way here to this graveyard, and survive these past few weeks? And how could Atticus possibly call it home? I cast my mind back to the heart of the underground Prolet world, the genetic rubbish tip of Pantheon and most vibrant array of life I'd ever come across. It wasn't a free world, but there was food, warmth and decent shelter at the very least.

And what would August make of so many Prolet children being stranded beneath the Dead City, alone?

'*There are so many possible recriminations: people who won't welcome the change, those who will hold us – you – responsible for every good and bad consequence. We have to face facts. It might just be that the safest thing I can do is to leave Arafel, and the outside … alone.'*

Even the dim memory of his voice set off the ache in the pit of my stomach. He'd been so insistent the people of Pantheon needed a gradual reintroduction to the idea of an outside world, that Octavia's creations could endanger it all. And I'd accused him of being arrogant, of denying them a chance. Now he was gone, and it looked as though the only people who believed there could be more to life, were those who'd experienced the least of it.

I was sandwiched between Eli and Lake, around a long dirt trough serving as a makeshift dinner table. And as a succession of small fires were kindled inside its length using old sticks and dry grass, I suspected the main event would not be standard Arafel fayre.

'How long have you been living down here, like this?' Max asked as a young satyr presented four lifeless adult rats to Atticus.

I stared distastefully at their thick tails hanging lifelessly over the edge of the rusted platter. An attempt had been made to lay them out ceremoniously on a bed of yet more nettles, but that only made their appearance more grotesque. I swallowed hard. The young insurgents had to be surviving on something, and rodent was technically meat, but one glance at the mangy fur and weeping eyes was enough to know these specimens weren't in their own best health.

I thought rapidly. 'Of course rat is always a … delicacy, but Arafel farms chicken, lamb, pork – and enough bread and fresh vegetables for you all.'

My words hung like choice, ripe fruit upon the air, as sixty pairs of hollowed, hungry eyes swung my way.

'We live in a treehouse community,' I continued, taking care to keep my voice emotion-free, 'but there are no leaders growing fat while others work. Instead everyone takes their turn in the village fields, to ensure there is enough grain for the harvest. For everyone. And there is a village school, where children like you can learn about our ancestors, about life before the war.'

'What use is that?' Atticus scorned, picking up a wooden stake and driving it straight through the first rat, rump to brain.

'Life before the Great War was broken. People worshipped money, images, everything that distracted them from real life – it led to nothing but violence and death.'

A pregnant silence hung in the air while the vein in Atticus's neck pulsed visibly. He was fierce, and I guessed these were words he'd learned from another. The hard way.

I glanced around at the sea of young faces willing me on, urging me to challenge Atticus's leadership and his decision to stay here.

'How do you see the stars, if you don't first know darkness?'

It was one of Grandpa's favourite mottos. He used to reinforce the richness of our simple lives compared with before the Great War.

There was another silence as Atticus pulled out a large knife, hacked off one of the rat tails, and threw it into one of the small crackling fires in the trough. It writhed and twisted in the sudden heat, making me shudder.

'The past is ugly. Why do we want to waste time learning about that? Far better we spend our time building something new and far better. Building our own new world where no one works from dawn 'til dusk, where respect is earned and where no one is forced to be anyone they don't want to be!'

Atticus's voice rose suddenly, betraying his youth and anxiety. He scowled and hacked off the other two rat tails with machete-style blows. There was an uncomfortable silence.

'You don't have to be alone, Atticus,' Max responded gently. 'In Arafel, you would be part of a big community. A community that knows how to survive on the outside, in the real world. This …' He looked slowly around the sea of white faces. 'This

84

isn't living. This is existing, like one of those rotten creatures you're about to roast!'

He pointed distastefully at the rat platter.

All eyes swung back to Atticus, and there was a guilty mutter around the trench. His group were far from settled, and yet he clearly held great influence.

'It's OK to change your mind and want something else. In Arafel, you could share the work and responsibility,' I urged, watching a flush creep up his neck as he lifted one of the vermin to his mouth.

'For the love of … wait …!' Max intervened, guessing what he was about to do.

But his horror only goaded Atticus further, who after only a second's deliberation, clamped down hard with his teeth and tore off one of the mangy rodent's ears. A muffled gasp echoed through the chamber, as he chewed swiftly and intently, before swallowing.

'Maybe I'm not afraid of responsibility, the same way I'm not afraid of raw rat or Cassius … maybe I don't need anyone else to tell me what to do!' he ground out, running his tongue around his mouth deliberately as though to tease out any remaining gristle.

'That's gross!' the elfin boy blurted, before hiding his face beneath his burnished wings.

A black scowl twisted Atticus's face, just as Eli started signing rapidly.

'My brother wants to say something,' I interrupted, putting out a hand to prevent Atticus from rising.

His scowl intensified.

Eli gesticulated again. I nodded. Yet again my insightful twin was doing a far better job of reading the room than anyone else.

'He says … I'll translate as he signs … He says … In Arafel, people are all treated the same, no matter how many fingers, toes, wings or friends they have – and no matter where they've come from.'

85

Atticus's eyes narrowed and he opened his mouth to interrupt, but I ploughed on, translating Eli's thoughts as swiftly as they came.

'Our grandpa would have said: "Come what may, nature finds a way." And Arafel is as rich a mosaic of life as you would want. There are many imperfections among us, some visible like my own, and some invisible – like Max's inability to share his food.'

I paused as Max threw his eyes to the cavernous ceiling, and a giggle trickled through the room.

'But one thing is constant,' Eli continued. 'We all believe that life on the outside is worth living, and dying, for. After all, what point is there in escaping one sewer, only to trap yourself in another?'

I gazed at Eli in admiration. Sometimes he reminded me so much of Grandpa.

'And raw rat runs the risk of Lassa fever, hantavirus, salmonellosis and hemorrhagic fevers among other unattractive options, by the way.'

He shrugged unapologetically, as my words echoed around the cold space. I smiled. He was nothing, if not brutally honest.

Tension swallowed the room, as Atticus placed the speared rats over the smouldering fire. Then he looked up.

'We looked for you,' he began, his voice sounding suddenly younger, 'but we found nothing but deserted, charred buildings. Then we lost three of the youngest trying to cross the plain to the forest.'

'The scorpions?' Max asked gently.

Atticus nodded, his face schooled but his eyes full.

'But I always had a back-up plan,' he added, lifting his chin, 'and we started making a new home a few weeks ago … It's here in the Dead City – New Arfel!'

'Why don't you show us?' I urged, conscious of the scrutiny around the cavern, 'and in turn we can tell you more about Arafel.

86

Then you can choose whether you might prefer to live somewhere Cassius can't hunt and find you.'

'I'll show you,' Atticus returned defiantly, 'but we're not leaving. We want Cassius to find us. How can we prove to the older Prolets there's a real world outside if we disappear? How will they find us when they come?'

'Your parents?' I asked after a beat.

There was a pause before he shook his head.

'We have no biological parents. Most of us are Octavia's Type A3 workforce, genetically designed to meet a specific objective.'

His eyes barely moved, but I could sense the test behind his words.

'Designed? Objective?' I repeated, feeling my bile rise. She was dead, but her legacy was here, in this room. Still trying to throw off her shackles.

'August, the commander general, told us about you,' he clarified after a beat, 'before he went missing. He said no matter our Pantheon grading or laboratory number, we all still contain Outsider DNA. He said that inside each of us a free heart was beating – just like yours.'

I gazed into Atticus's questioning eyes, willing the glass veneer that had been my friend these past months not to break. I was so conscious of Max's scrutiny, but the words ran on repeat through my head anyway.

He'd not forgotten me.

***

We pooled the remainder of Eli and Max's food provisions; and accepted three folded hammocks that were stacked neatly inside an empty inset archway. It was warm enough with the trough fires burning, but the air was rank and stale despite the number of dark arch exits. I viewed each in turn before dragging my eyes away. No one mentioned the children who'd lost their lives on

Scorpion Plain, but it was obvious the hanging beds had once belonged to them.

And there was no prospect of visiting New Arfel tonight – that much was clear. But I could tell we'd rattled Atticus, and there was a hushed excitement among the group who seemed to view us as some sort of providential sign.

'Did it hurt?'

The soft whisper was barely perceptible, but I turned anyway, and found two large doleful brown eyes peeping around the edge of our arch. It was the small boy with the burnished wings, and now he was closer, I could see the feathery down extended all over his head.

I smiled. He had a vulnerability that was hard to resist.

'Did what hurt?' I repeated quizzically.

'That.'

He pointed to a scar that ran up my brown calf, which kept shining in the flickering light of the cavern. It was an old injury resulting from a tangle with a field scythe when I was eight. It had taken two of Arafel's best medics to clean and stitch the wound, and the pain was still etched in my memory.

'Not too bad,' I lied with a smile, 'but you should have seen the tiger!'

The boy crept around the corner and sat cross-legged on the floor, his eyes as round as grapes.

'You fought a tiger?' he breathed.

'Yes, and she strung his teeth around her neck as a warning to any others!' Max teased from the shadows of the archway where he'd been hanging up his hammock.

I lifted my hand instinctively to the handful of snow leopard teeth strung around my neck. They were Jas's baby teeth Eli had fashioned into a necklace when I was much younger. I rarely took it off.

'A tiger is only half the size of a molossus, Therry,' Lake interjected from the shadows before taking a seat beside the boy. 'There are far greater creatures in Pantheon!'

'Well, that depends on the measure,' Eli signed. 'Technically, if weight and size were the only relevant factors then Pantheon could indeed make that claim, but as complexity of nature and purity of gene pool could argue for equal, if not greater, weighting … you could be on thin ice there, as Dad used to say.'

I grinned as Lake stared, confused.

'What did he say?' she asked suspiciously.

'Nothing,' I reassured her. 'Obviously a tiger is small fry compared with most Pantheonite creatures.' I watched her pull a handful of small stones from her pocket and scatter them around Therry's feet.

He made a grab for them and shook his small fist. It was clearly a game they played here, something similar to pick-up sticks, a favourite of the children in Arafel. Their complete distraction was poignant, it echoed their age and vulnerability in a way words couldn't.

Lake smiled, her eyes widening in childish delight as Therry's stones failed to beat hers.

'In Isca Prolet, we used to place bets,' she offered tossing the stones again, 'on fights in the market square. Sileni never lose.'

She grinned into the shadows, and when I followed the direction of her gaze I realized Pan was there, watching. His presence was oddly reassuring, though their precise relationship was still a mystery, and I felt sure his care was solely for Lake's wellbeing.

'Not completely true,' Atticus interjected from the floor where he was whittling dubious-looking arrows. 'When Brutus was sent to quiet the satyr rebellion, no one saw a silenus stepping in to help.'

'Brutus doesn't count!' Lake fired, her cheeks flushed with sudden anger. 'And neither does the black aquila! They are more Cassius than creature!'

My ears pricked up.

When a black aquila falls from the golden sky, it will spark a winter of a thousand fires.

'Black aquila?' I repeated swiftly, looking from Lake to Atticus.

He stood up and after making a big play of brushing himself down, sauntered forward. And there was something in his gait right there and then that took me back to the asphyxiating fear when we were trapped in the Flavium, faced with a crowd of jeering Pantheonite faces.

I flexed my fingers. He was young and arrogant, but he wasn't one of them. He was here, beneath the Dead City, leading the Prolets. And I was letting my emotions get the better of me.

'Haven't you met Cassius's newest pet?' He smiled sardonically.

'Well, we've had the pleasure of rattling monkeys, monster hounds and manticores,' Max levelled, stepping in beside me, 'so there's not too much that'll surprise us. Has he got a new toy?'

'Cassius is always working on something new,' Therry moaned, tucking his head inside his wings.

Instantly Lake slid across and put her stick thin arms around the smaller boy, hugging him tightly. I bit my lip, feeling as though my chest was caught in one of Bereg's forest traps. They were no older than the schoolchildren I taught in Arafel, some even younger. They'd already lived a hundred lifetimes, and bore the scars to prove it.

'We can help you, Therry,' I tried. 'Arafel is a hidden valley, surrounded by mountains. You'd be safer there from Cassius … and Livia.'

I crouched down and placed a hand on his bony, down-covered back. He flinched as my fingers brushed the fleshy ravines barely hidden by his feathery down, and sank a little lower.

Lake looked up at me, her eyelids narrowed so much I could barely see the emeralds glinting beneath.

'They are the ones who need to be afraid!' she hissed, making a grab for the scattered stones.

'We are getting bigger and stronger all the time,' she continued, 'so we just watch and wait for the right moment. Then we strike them down … and watch them burn.'

She threw the stones again so fiercely a few of them ricocheted off the back wall. Max winced and rubbed the back of his calf, as Pan slid out from the shadows, his snow-white skin glowing in the lantern light.

'Nice arm!' Max joked ruefully. 'In Arafel you'd be very welcome in the construction team, not to mention the wrestlers!'

There was a tense moment as Lake eyeballed Max, then Pan placed a hand on her shoulder and she relaxed. She reached up to place her own small white hand over his and smiled, the strain gone.

I moved off to give them space. Pan was gentle I was sure, but I still couldn't decide if he was more guardian or guard.

'You see, why do we need your help, when we have a savage eleven-year-old promising hellfire and damnation,' Atticus drawled, exiting into the shadows.

***

It was hard to tell night from day in the cave in the Prolet camp, and if it wasn't for the arrival of fresh rat and boiled water for breakfast, I could have been persuaded it was still the middle of the night.

Max eyed the morning offerings with distaste.

'There is no way I'm eating that rank rodent again for anyone. Who's for an al fresco?'

He gesticulated above our heads to the Dead City. I caught his arm, watching Atticus address a small group across the cavern.

'I think a morning shift may be in talks,' I whispered, as Atticus trod swiftly towards one of the black arches with two small satyrs, a human boy and the pig-dog trailing behind. They all looked distinctly unhappy about whatever lay ahead.

'Atticus!' Max's voice echoed around the cavern, making a group playing fetch with a tiny griffin, look up.

'Need another hunter?'

Atticus nodded once, scowling and, not needing any further invitation, Max joined the grateful team.

An hour later we were feasting on fresh rat and nettle tea, a distinct improvement on the run-off we'd drunk the evening before.

'Well at least it's seen grass and sunshine,' Eli signed, hardly able to repress his delight at Max returning with a sackful of above-ground rats and proclaiming it was the worst hunting ground he'd ever seen.

I shook my head faintly, trying not to grin.

Max maintained a proud hunting record, but his ego was fragile, and Eli knew it. It was funny, but hardly the time.

'So, did you get to see New Arfel?' Eli signed, as we helped clear away the broken miscellany of foraged pots and plates.

'Not a hint.' Max shook his head. 'We followed tunnels for a good half-kilometre and came up in a road I didn't recognize. No wonder Atticus is confident they have time – it's a complete maze down here!'

'The molossers would still sniff them out in seconds,' I muttered.

Eli shot me a concerned frown. I glanced over my shoulder and cursed under my breath. A young girl with red plaits and a bag full of freckles was standing close by. I'd heard the others call her Faro, and she looked no more than eight or nine years of age. She had the cerulean-eyed monkey perched on her shoulder. It was chewing nettle leaves, and darting its gaze around inquisitively.

'Are we going to die here?'

Her question was just loud enough to stop the cavern, and all eyes looked our way, including Atticus.

'We all die in the end,' Lake intervened, 'but not without a fight. And not here, not today.'

Faro beamed and, accepting a handful of pick-up rat bones, scuttled away. Content, for now.

92

I stared down at wise little Lake, an unofficial mother figure with the world on her young shoulders. She returned my look with a defiant smile. As though she was ready, and my questions were a game.

'Who were your parents, Lake?' I asked.

Her top lip curled like a snake, as though she was fighting the impulse to burst out laughing.

'The stars and moon, the gods and goddesses, and every last genetic dreg of Isca Prolet!' Atticus drawled, reclining beside the fire trough. 'We've been trying to work that one out for years, haven't we?'

He grinned at her, and then I saw it, the affection that had somehow bound them together in this mess. It was a most unlikely camaraderie, a faith fired by the chaos that had brought them this far together.

'And yours, Atticus?' I quizzed playfully. 'Are yours also to be found among the genetic wonders of Prolet life?'

I knew I'd trespassed immediately.

'Mine are dead.' He scowled and looked away.

Chapter 8

There was a blind monotony to the hours beneath the Dead City. Days seemed to be about foraging and surviving until the next meal, with little planning in between. The truth was the Prolets were too inexperienced to bring many good habits from their old life, and too hungry to invent anything new.

Eli became an instant favourite, setting up an impromptu health checkpoint beneath one of the archways. Each time I looked, his menagerie had grown, the children taking great delight from his easy communication with the small griffin and other ad hoc animal life accompanying them. And he looked happier than he had in a long time, pulling faces and chatting with the aid of basic signing and gestures. I often thought he would have made a fine schoolteacher, like Dad, had he had the confidence to pursue it. But the world of silence had taken him a long time to conquer, and those who judged least were still his preferred company.

'At least someone's having fun!' I remarked, watching Faro's monkey leap from Eli's head to the floor, and make off with the stones they were scattering.

There was a burst of spontaneous laughter and Atticus glanced up from the opposite side of the cavern.

'Yeah, shame they're not all of an age. Would have been easier,' Max responded.

'If they'd all been of an age, I doubt they would have been here at all!' I mused. 'And yet there is Pan …'

I glanced across at his familiar sentry position beside one of the darkest arches. His expression was neutral, but his demeanour was alert, watchful.

'How does an adult silenus wind up here with a pack of Prolet kids?' Max asked.

'I don't know,' I responded.

The exact same thought had been troubling me. Friendship with Lake or not, Pan's presence was an anomaly, and Max had given me an idea.

***

'Can I sit with you?'

Pan barely flinched, and the only sign he acquiesced was the slight lowering of his white eyelids. He had to stand over two metres tall, and his muscular frame bulged impressively, despite his emaciated ribcage.

'Do sileni eat meat?'

I'd noticed he'd given his share of rat to Lake at lunch.

He stared at me before shaking his head slowly.

'You eat fruit and vegetables, like apples and carrots?' I pursued, thinking of the horses that ran in the outside forest occasionally.

This time he turned his head completely, and regarded me with his lucid, pale eyes.

His starvation was evident.

'A … pul,' he whispered thickly, making my heart lurch.

'Arafel has an orchard that is full of the ripest, juiciest apples – and as many carrots as you can eat.'

He stared at me, his white lips moistening.

'Pan, you know this is suicide, right?' I asked. 'I know Atticus and Lake mean well, but we're sitting ducks right here. No matter how fortified this New Arfel is, we're too close to Cassius, to Livia … to Pantheon.'

He seemed to blanch, despite his white skin.

'If you're willing to work with us, to persuade Lake that you all need to come with us, we may stand a chance.'

His head was shaking before I had chance to finish. And the fear in his eyes left me with no hope of persuasion. Pan was wise, strong and loyal. But he wasn't in charge. And it looked as though no amount of promised treats or encouraging words would change his mindset. There was something absolute about it, almost as though he had no choice but to obey and defend Lake until the day he died.

I tried to contain my frustration. It was yet another brick wall, and as my eyes drifted back to Faro and Therry playing pick-ups, I knew there was only one route left.

***

It was nearing our third round of dinner rat, and neither Max nor I could justify another night without some sort of progress.

'I'll ask him,' I muttered in a low voice, 'and if he doesn't agree, we'll ask Lake to take us – tell her Atticus thought she was too young to lead a visit.'

Max grinned. 'Canny! I like.'

'Downright manipulation,' I corrected.

In the end it didn't matter. Because Atticus agreed anyway. I tried not to look too surprised and wondered silently if he too was thinking about Faro's question. Either way it was a lead. But he made us wait until well into the evening, when most of the rest of the group were settling down for the night.

And as we made our way across the floor towards him, there was something about his bearing that unnerved me again. He

96

had a proud stance and common brows I told myself. Nothing distinctive in any way.

I suppressed a frown and turned briefly to wave to Eli. A sea of hopeful young faces peered back at me from their makeshift hammocks, and for the first time I saw just how much they wanted to go with us to Arafel. It was a feeling that weighed like an anchor, no matter what Atticus was saying about his plans for New Arfel. Eli smiled pensively and I nodded. We were reluctant to split up, even for the shortest time, but it made sense for him to remain behind. He clearly had the best rapport with the young Prolets, and he was still limping from his *Hottentotta* sting although the swelling had receded.

As he settled down, the tiny griffin clucked contentedly around his feet. He reached out to stroke it thoughtfully, his face saying everything. He was as anxious as me to get the renegade group moving. And none of us could imagine Arafel closing its doors when they saw how young and vulnerable they actually were.

'We'll persuade Atticus it won't work,' I signed, with more conviction than I felt.

I wasn't sure a boy who willingly bit a rat's ear off was going to be easy to persuade of anything. I turned before Eli could respond. In truth, it was impossible to promise anything right now.

***

'We found this stairwell by accident,' Atticus announced proudly.

He was just ahead, staring up into slightly less murky darkness after several minutes of claustrophobic tunnels. I scanned our surroundings. We'd reached a basic juncture and two dark tunnels led off in opposite directions.

'What's down there?' I asked, pointing in the opposite direction to the way in which we were headed.

Lake's expression tightened in the flickering torchlight.

97

'That way leads back to the prison!' came the acerbic response.

I stared into the gloom, my ears straining and head conjuring up a myriad of images and sounds: the drumbeat of a thousand booted feet, the scratching of ravenous rat-owls, the laboured breath of a demonic three-headed dog … and the lightest of touches in the small of my back.

I jumped, and threw a look over my shoulder. I could read the question in Max's shadowed face several oak trees away. It was the same promise Eli wanted to extract before we left, and I smiled tightly, knowing I could stall for only so long.

'Let's keep moving,' he murmured.

My anticipation grew with every roughly hewn stone step. They were steep and uneven, but the air filtering down from the outside was as intoxicating as the forest after a monsoon rain.

Finally, Atticus held up a hand.

'At night, there are eyes,' he whispered, 'in the sky.'

I nodded. It made sense Cassius would be sending out scouts of some nature, and it was good to see Atticus was cautious. Still, by the time Pan gave us the all clear, I was desperate.

We climbed out behind a fallen gargoyle into the opaque moonlight, and for a moment we remained there, filling our lungs with the cool night air and absorbing our new surroundings.

'It's complete?' Max asked in wonder, staring at a ruined grey Gothic cathedral that stretched up into the sky before us.

'No, but we don't need it to be.' Atticus grinned for the first time since we'd arrived. 'Welcome to New Arfel!'

He executed another mock flourish, as my breath quickened with recognition. I knew this place. And as I stared, the months rolled back until I was standing on Octavia's balcony staring out at the ruined city. With August next to me. Octavia had deceived everyone, basking in the glow of the sun while the rest of the Insiders believed the outside world to be toxic. And it had come as no surprise that her preferred view was of the ruined city, where so many had lost their lives.

Yet even that day, when everything had been so shadowed, the cathedral tower had stood tall with the ghost of an ancient grace. It had withstood the worst moment mankind had ever seen, and survived while the rest of the city decayed into the ground with its inhabitants. Its unique structure made it the best lookout position in the Dead City. And the worst.

'We need to move this along,' Max whispered as Atticus waved us towards a stone archway that led inside the cathedral.

'I know,' I muttered, scanning the sleeping city.

Although there was no glimmer of dawn yet, time was moving swiftly. And every minute that passed was another minute closer to Cassius or Livia deploying something unspeakable through the tunnels. The sooner we persuaded Atticus to come with us, the better.

As soon as we entered the ruined cathedral, the scale of its destruction became apparent. Four broken walls led only to the sky, while a further tower lay collapsed in a heap of rubble the size of our treehouse home.

'Only one tower survives,' Lake explained as we veered off the vaulted nave towards another stone archway, nearly obscured by fallen debris.

I nodded, watching Pan. His long ears were twitching, on full alert to every new noise around us.

We climbed a few lone stone steps to a wooden door, which Atticus opened with a hard shove, and then we trod down a dark corridor towards another stairwell. These stairs were tighter than the last set, and wound around in a circular fashion for what seemed for ever. Atticus set a fast pace, but thankfully our tree-running legs stood us in good stead, and before long we were watching him force open another wedged door right at the top of the tower.

We looked around in silence at the large circular room, lined with a dozen huge brass bells.

'The old bell tower!' Max exclaimed, walking over to brush one of the gigantic structures.

'Perfect isn't it?' Atticus announced proudly. 'We need to strengthen the walls at the bottom of the tower before I move everyone, but it's the best view in the city!'

He walked over to gaze out of one of the medieval archer windows.

'Come see our sleeping area!' Lake insisted excitedly, grabbing my hand and pulling me towards a tatty old curtain screening off one part of the room. She pulled it aside to reveal crudely made beds stacked on top of one another, reminding me of the beehive caves in Isca Prolet.

'Right now we sleep among the rats, but in New Arfel we will wake up among the birds,' she said, her unique eyes dilating at the thought.

I gazed at her gaunt face, at the way her brown shoulder-length hair fell limply around her bony shoulders, and bit my tongue.

'And what's this?' I asked, walking towards a collection of what looked to be old junk piled high, in one corner.

As I drew close, I realized the junk had been separated into piles of similar objects, and there were mottled knives, axes, tubes, darts and all sorts of rusted ironmongery that looked as old as the tower surrounding us.

'It's the start of our armoury,' Atticus muttered defensively. 'We've foraged it from the city so we can defend ourselves – before we strike a deal with Cassius to let the rest of the Prolets go. So we can all start again, here!'

He withdrew his knife, and thrust it sharply through the air as if to make the point.

They believed their own fairy tale so much it hurt.

'And what if he comes before you're ready?' I asked.

He scowled.

'Cassius can come when he wants. We'll be ready and waiting!'

'Aelia said she needed a party to go ahead,' Lake interjected keenly, 'to be pioneers, like Thomas! We just need to keep working

100

on New Arfel, and then when the other Prolets join us, we'll be just like you. Like Arafel.'

Her tone was so wistful, her face pleading with us to understand – and for just a moment, as she stood silhouetted against one of the windows, I fancied a whisper of her dream escaping her mouth like a tiny spiral of smoke. I shivered – it really was quite cold up here.

'Did Aelia encourage your party to be her pioneers and escape through the tunnels?' I asked incredulously, conscious of Max's growing impatience.

'Not directly,' Atticus admitted, 'but Lake … the other Prolets … they're done being told what to do. They needed a better reason to live.

'I overheard Aelia at a meeting of the Prolet Freedom Fighters, a secret meeting,' Atticus continued. 'She was so certain a new life was waiting on the outside, she made it sound … perfect.'

'All the older Prolets were cowards!' Lake interjected. 'So, we decided it was time to take matters into our own hands, to show them it was possible to leave Pantheon, and start again. In Arafel! Or somewhere like it.'

I drew a deep breath, my thoughts reeling. No wonder Aelia was so desperate – she couldn't have intended to have been interpreted so literally. And now all the young Prolets were stranded here in the Dead City, because of a random overheard conversation.

'Atticus, this isn't like Ara …' I began, only to feel my words freeze on my tongue as the air was filled with a discordant, high-pitched cry. It wasn't human, or any animal I recognized, and the scowl creeping across Atticus's face confirmed my worst suspicions.

I ran towards a window, and scanned the dark, ruined city. My skin prickled with fear, but the sky was veiled and the city as lifeless as ever. Max was beside me, just as a second raucous cry filled the air. This time the strident sound was louder, and coming from directly behind the stone tower. We spun in time to witness Pan's schooled features twist into the most unlikely grimace, as he traced the sound through the stone ceiling to the opposite side of the tower. Then the room was filled with an oppressive silence, before he threw his head back in an agonized cry and bolted from the room.

For a second no one moved.

'We have to go after him! Atticus!' Lake hissed, her emeralds glittering in the low light.

She dashed across the room, and spun Atticus around with impressive strength for a girl of her size. He scowled, but I could tell by the pale tightening around his lips that he, too, was scared. Whatever creature the cry belonged to, it had stolen his swagger and confidence.

'Fine! I'll handle it myself!' she snapped, before bolting across the room after her friend.

'We need to move,' I threw out at Max, feeling my world begin to spiral as Lake's slight frame disappeared from view. 'Now!'

'Tal! Wait!' Max called, but I was already through the old wooden door and sprinting down the timeworn steps.

There was no sign of Lake as I sped downwards, the only light the occasional sliver of moonlight through random turret windows. I could hear Max and Atticus behind me, but tonight I flew as though I had a pack of strix on my tail.

I couldn't fathom what had suddenly made Pan so furious, especially since he'd seemed so gentle and protective. Protective. Unless what was out there posed a threat to Lake? I sucked in a tight breath. I was no closer to understanding all the relationships, and now there was another threat. And I couldn't shake the feeling it had nothing to do with the Dead City, and everything to do with Pantheon.

I reached the last few steps, and flew along the passageway, only pausing when I reached the arched doorway that led out into the ruined nave. I held my breath as I surveyed the eerie

102

scene. There was something wrong. It was too quiet. Too watchful.

Hesitantly, I stepped through the broken, moonlit church towards the archway that led out into the open wasteland. The fallen gargoyle was still there, concealing the entrance to the tunnel, and everything looked peaceful enough except for one big fat anomaly. Lake and Pan were nowhere to be seen.

'Have you seen anything? Where are they? Did they go back into the tunnels?' Max panted, catching up with me.

I scowled holding a finger to my mouth. Sometimes it felt like he was the loudest person in the whole world.

Silently, I assessed the distance to the fallen gargoyle, deliberately avoiding its grotesque, laughing face. It seemed allegorical somehow, and not in a good way.

'They might have – they're both pretty fast.'

Another grating cry filled the air. I pressed back against the ancient cold stone. It wasn't a cinereous vulture, I was sure, but it was the cry of a big predator, and it was approaching from the dark sky behind us.

We swung our gaze around and upwards, craning our necks to see past the broken walls of the cathedral, and then it was there. Slowly staining the sky. We ducked simultaneously as the angular black shadow soared low over our heads, its powerful design creating a rush similar to that of a hundred birds.

At first, I thought it an eagle, the prominent symbol of Octavia's Equite. But its fire-feathered underbelly, and gleaming golden eyes forced me to think again. It was some kind of crested double-headed eagle, only twice the size of a griffin.

I stared speechlessly before the view crystallized. My hand flew to my mouth, but I was too slow to prevent a cry; for dangling lifelessly between its razor-sharp claws was a small, limp body.

'Lake!' I screamed, my fear emptying into the night, and reaching into every corner of the ashen city.

But the monster bird was already halfway towards the domes

dwarfing the horizon. I stared after its silhouette as though trapped in a nightmare, my mind crowding with images: the creature landing on Octavia's balcony, delivering Lake to Cassius and Livia, and then the torture they would surely inflict for daring to believe in something different. If she wasn't already dead.

Anger doused my veins, replacing the horror with something far more purposeful. *Grandpa, Eli ... now Lake.* It never stopped. Well, Cassius wanted a fight, he was going to get a fight. And this wasn't just about Lake or the Book – the future of every last Prolet depended on what happened next. On what I did next.

Cut us, we all bleed.

It was something Grandpa used to say.

'Some more than others,' I whispered as though he could hear me.

Max shot me a troubled look. He knew; of course he knew.

'We should think about ... No! Wait! Tal!' he yelled as I took off across the courtyard towards the fallen gargoyle.

'Atticus, find Eli!' he barked, flying after me. 'Move everyone to the tower. Tonight! And for the love of Arafel, don't wait for us!'

Chapter 9

I didn't notice the suffocating air this time. My head was full of Lake's gaunt smile when she'd shown me their crude beds; and the way her hooded eyes had exuded real, painful hope. I couldn't believe that smile was crushed between the claws of a monster. It didn't make any sense, I raged, for her to come this far, only to be dragged back inside the mouth of hell. The injustice of it all provided the grim determination I needed not to flinch, even when I reached the tunnel fork.

And as I sprinted directly into the gloomy unknown, I felt Max close his distance.

'For the love of … Tal, please! Let's just do this a little more covertly,' he reasoned, accelerating to draw level with me between the narrow rock faces.

There was just enough room in this new tunnel, and the rhythm of our synchronized pace soothed me, taking me back to Arafel and the whisper of the forest.

'We're probably running straight into a trap, and what about Eli and the rest of the Prolets? What about the nightmares we might be facing down this wormhole any second now?' he hissed.

I slowed as his reason pierced my fury like tiny darts. Eli's cool anger flickered through my mind, chased swiftly by a blood-sniffing Cerberus. We wouldn't stand a chance against either the strix or Isca Pantheon's favourite pet dog in this space. Furious or not. Then there was the fact that a certain violent Roman Director General wanted my head on a stake. But all the reasoning in the world couldn't outweigh the damned hope in Lake's eyes.

'You don't need to come!' I seethed, angry I'd already broken a promise to myself to do this alone.

I was more agile than Max; I could jump and flip quickly if needed. I just couldn't risk him getting hurt again, not for me. Not if I could help it.

He glowered, and right then, I knew it was non-negotiable.

Whatever lay ahead, we would face it together.

'Every second counts,' I muttered, accelerating into the murky darkness again.

It was a few minutes later that I sensed we weren't alone. It was the same feeling I got in the forest at night, when I knew an animal was nearby. Not a sixth sense exactly, but something more arcane, a feral instinct our Great War ancestors had almost forgotten.

We ran on until the feeling became so intense, I wasn't at all surprised when I made out the hunched shape of an animal just ahead, amid the gloom. We both slowed to a halt.

'Pan?' I whispered after a beat, squinting to get a clear view.

The shape shifted, and stared back through the darkness. It startled me at first, but then I gleaned its pained expression. And eyes, which stole all my attention. Not so much for their lucid blue colour, as for their tiny new radial black lines, rhythmically contracting and expanding.

'You can see in the dark?' I whispered in wonder, as he crept towards us.

It was so clearly a Pantheonite signature, the type of genetic enhancement I'd come to loathe, and yet I couldn't help but welcome whatever advantages it brought now.

Pan nodded. He made no sound, but his hurt was tangible. I

still longed to ask what act of fate had entwined him and Lake so closely. But there was no time, and I doubted he'd tell me anyway.

'We find Lake ... together.'

It was more a statement than a question. He wasn't turning back. He studied us both carefully, and I wondered whether he might consider us more hindrance than support. But he nodded briefly, and turning on his hoof-feet, forged into the darkness ahead.

***

I thought of Unus so often as we sped through the endless tunnel beneath the arid dust, I could almost hear his ponderous footsteps behind us. I'd only survived the hazardous underground tunnels in Pantheon because of his companionship, and humble heroism. And although there was no fetid scent or overt clattering of claws yet, I could sense Pantheon's nightmares were inching closer. The thought made my skin crawl. And yet, there was no choice to be made.

Cassius had Lake, Aelia had the Book of Arafel, and I'd made Grandpa a promise. No matter Aelia's exact motivation, she'd taken the one thing I'd sworn my life to protect, and couldn't pretend didn't exist. I recalled Grandpa's words as though he'd uttered them yesterday:

The Book of Arafel is the responsibility of one of our line only. You must only share it when it is time.

I grimaced. There was so fine a line between a legacy and a curse. But one thing was for sure. Thomas had bequeathed fire the day he hid his Voynich research inside the Book of Arafel.

'Just like the old days!' Max forced through gritted teeth, as we loomed up towards a solid rock face in the narrow passage.

But instead of turning around, Pan indicated a rough dark circle carved into the thick rock ceiling. We took a pace back as he stepped beneath and started heaving upwards with his thick, muscular arms, his tapered equine ears brushing the glistening surface. I longed to ask him so many questions: why had he run from the tower? Why had Lake considered she could take on the black aquila by herself? What secret did they share?

But there was no time.

Instead, we pressed back to avoid the earth and small particles of debris raining down as the rock groaned and gave way to Pan's strength. I inhaled the sweet night-time air briefly, but my relief was short-lived. The great white expanse of Isca Pantheon's south wall stretched above our heads like a formidable fortress. We were within touching distance of hell. And it was terrifying.

Memories loomed from the recesses of my mind as Pan heaved himself out through the hole, and I inhaled raggedly, trying to control my racing pulse.

'You OK?' Max whispered.

I nodded. This was just the beginning, and there was no room for weakness. At least, not openly. I grasped Pan's white outstretched arm, and let him pull me into the cold night air.

Despite his raw-boned state, Pan was still far stronger than Max and I put together. The thought gave me some comfort as we slipped around the monolithic structure, staying well within its shadow. And as we left the southern wall behind, I allowed myself a final glimpse back at the distant, silhouetted city of Exeter. It stood bleakly in the starlight, a shelled monument to its previous glory. And yet somewhere beneath its dust, my brother and a party of young Prolets inadvertently carried the hopes of an enslaved underclass. Outsiders in their own natural world.

The thought stilled me.

'We'll make it back,' Max whispered.

I nodded before realizing he was staring in a very different direction, out at the dark whispering forest fringe just visible on the western hills. I reached to slip my fingers inside his, drawing strength from their familiar contours and warmth.

'I know, there's a whole summer yet,' I answered, the bleak wind lifting the hair from around the nape of my neck.

'A summer to remember.'

He turned to look at me, and I could hear the quickening in his breath.

I flushed, despite everything.

'I'm sorry …' I tried awkwardly, 'for bringing you here … again.'

'Tal,' he responded, pulling me to him gently, 'do you honestly think I'd let you come alone? That I wouldn't want to rescue Lake and the Book of Arafel? That I'd let you face that monster without me? I knew what you were planning to do, and what's at stake. I always have. But I'd rather die trying with you, than watch you leave knowing you weren't coming back.'

I closed my eyes. I could feel his fear like my own, but I knew it wasn't because he was afraid of Cassius or Pantheon. He was afraid of losing us, and that crippled me.

I reached up and drew his face down to mine. I needed to taste the forest, to make him see I cared more than I could ever put into ordinary small words. He met me unquestioningly, pulling me inside his warmth, and for a few seconds, it was just us beneath the inky sky, saying what is best said silently. Moments later, there was only a hint of the truth still shadowing his eyes.

'I don't care,' he whispered. 'He might have cut a hole in your heart. But I've got the rest, and it's right here, with me.'

I tried to answer, but couldn't force the sounds over my lips. And after all, what was there left to say when he was the one being brave?

'The little treehouse,' was all I managed. 'Have you still got it?'

He grinned then, a lopsided grin that took me straight back to the forest games we would play as kids. Tree-tag was a favourite, as it honed our skills faster than all the tree-running trials in the world. I'd hide, curled up inside one of the baobab forks, until he spooked me enough into a run. But he was always there, just a few paces behind.

He reached into his pocket, pulled out the little hand-carved treehouse, and rehung it around my neck.

'I also made you these,' he added, digging into his leather rations bag and withdrawing a handful of hand-carved, aerodynamic darts, 'from your white oak ... for luck.'

'You're all the luck I need.' I smiled, instantly seeing the time and care each one must have taken.

'Then we'll build the rest,' he responded, tucking an errant hair behind my ear, 'when we get back.'

'When we get back,' I echoed silently, turning back towards Pan.

And as we slipped down into the last tunnel connecting the outside world with Pantheon's Prolet underworld, I meant every word.

***

I looked around at the rock walls and gritted my teeth.

'Single file; be ready,' I whispered to Pan, gripping my slingshot.

I could see by the way the radial lines in his bright eyes were contracting vigorously that he was already very aware of the nightmares lurking in Pantheon's tunnels. I put out a hand, and he flinched at my touch. I thought of Unus again. Despite their strength and size, they were both the gentlest creatures.

'Pan ... back in the tower, you ran out. Why?'

There was a moment's silence while he eyed me nervously.

'Pro-tect ... Lake,' he managed finally in a difficult, thick voice before turning and creeping forward again.

We followed as swiftly as we dared, sensing the growing threat of the encroaching world, step by step. This last tunnel was much shorter than I remembered. And while Pan led the way my chest pounded, not with fear, but with injustice. The Voynich might be a Book of Fire, but nothing could compare with the rage burning in the pit of my stomach. Grandpa had spent the last moments of his life fighting. He'd died believing he had bequeathed a more hopeful world. And now it looked as though it was all for nothing.

I frowned at Pan's tall white figure, hunched over to prevent the tips of his ears scraping the rock ceiling.

'*Pro-tect … Lake.*'

What exactly had he meant? There were plenty of other young Prolets to protect, so why was one child so special? And why did I feel he would protect Lake above everyone else?

I'd faced so many monsters at Pantheon's hand, but I still couldn't shake the feeling there was a darker shadow to come. And why had August abandoned them all? Abandoned us all? *Why did you disappear when we needed you most?* I forced my feet onwards, burying the hurt that lurked just beneath my veneer of calm, like a serpent biding its time.

By some quirk of luck, this tunnel also appeared unoccupied and we found ourselves approaching the Prolet domestic quarters before the hour was done. The walls started taking on a drier, more amber hue and we followed their downward gradient, alert to any new sound of Prolet life.

It was only when we rounded the last rock corner that I sensed the change.

One of the redeeming factors of the Prolet underworld had been its warmth, courtesy of a huge fire pit sunk into the centre of the cave floor. But the temperature tonight was different, much colder, and the light travelling down from the silhouetted entrance was oddly reduced. I strained my eyes and focused on the entrance. From what little I could see, the huge vaulted chamber was filled with a strange tomb-like twilight. Shivering, I fastened my softened leather tunic top. At least we were better equipped than last time.

Moments later, Pan drew to an abrupt standstill, holding up

a large white hand. Silently, we watched as the tall silhouettes of three Pantheonite sentries came into view, before pressing back against the rock walls to agree a plan. This exit was guarded by Prolet satyrs when I left. It made sense that Cassius would increase the Pantheonite guard on all exits after the insurgents' escape; his pride had taken a direct hit and now he had a point to prove. I narrowed my eyes; he wasn't alone in that.

'Why run when you can fly?' I mouthed to Max, who winked and nodded.

'Keep count, Pan?' he whispered.

Pan stared. I reached out to touch his arm, and he flinched before inclining his head.

There was no time to lose. Max and I crept forward in parallel until we were within a few metres of the tunnel exit. And as I focused, the rock walls melted away until we were just two Arafel hunters, doing what came naturally. He loosened the coil of rope wound around his shoulders and back, and passed a length across to me. I ran the well-worn, strong rope through my hands. Our well-practised assault made a great return rate on rabbit, boar and deer; we'd just never tried it on Pantheonite guards.

Max stepped forward a couple more paces, pulling a dagger and blindfold from his leather belt. The guards were clearly visible now and seemed very distracted among themselves, playing some sort of game that involved a handful of crudely shaped die.

'Five, four ...?' I signed, starting to throw a small loop.

He nodded before creeping forward a final few steps. Then the air stilled just as it always did before a kill in the forest, and I let the rope fly. My aim was true, dropping over the shoulders of the two rear guards, before I yanked back hard.

The element of surprise is more valuable than brute strength, Talia.

Grandpa's wisdom echoed in my ears as the two heavy Pantheonites sprawled onto the rock floor, too winded to call out a warning.

Max was as swift and precise as he always was in the forest, jumping on the looped guards and stunning them before they had chance to call out. Leaving the third. Who clambered to his feet and started to run.

'Max!' I hissed, taking aim with my catapult, just as Pan bolted past me.

He reached the third guard in a heartbeat, and leaping high over his head, planted a thick hoof squarely in his chest, sending him sprawling back towards the mouth of the tunnel. The sheer velocity of his kick meant the guard slid nearly as far as my feet.

Quick as a flash, I jumped on his chest, and ran what was left of the rope around the guard's mouth, hands and ankles, trussing him like a chicken for roasting. I repeated the manoeuvre on the concussed duo, and only looked up when I was satisfied none of them could move or call out.

It was only then that I noticed Max and Pan were watching.

'What? Girls can't do rope?' I glared, returning my small paring knife to its sheath.

'Just admiring the origami!' Max teased.

And for a second, I thought I detected a glimmer of a smile on Pan's face too.

'Cameras?' I whispered, raising my eyebrows.

Max grimaced. Neither of us had forgotten the screens in the Flavium. Octavia had shown moving images of us, edited in a way that made us look like Prolet insurgents to the baying crowd. I had no idea if Cassius was using the same equipment, but had no desire to shine a spotlight on our arrival either.

With the three bemused guards bound and trussed in the shadows of the rock face, I cast a long look around at the all-too-familiar surroundings.

'It looks empty,' Max muttered.

He was right. The old, rickety interconnecting walkways were silent, and the individual sleeping caves mined into the rock wall seemed completely devoid of life. In the old Prolet world, there had always been a buzzing undercurrent of life, repressed or not. Now there seemed to be only a cold, empty waiting. It didn't make any sense. I ran my eyes over the dank walls again. There was the rickety walkway, the glowing fire pit, and vaulted cavernous ceiling, speckled with tiny glowing lights.

I paused, frowning.

There hadn't been so many individual lights before, I was sure of it, which meant they were a new addition. Perhaps it was one of the changes August had implemented, an improvement to Prolet sleeping quarters. Tiny star lights, which moved.

I thrust an arm across Max's chest, certain one of the lights had just slid across the ceiling. But we were too far away to be sure. Pan sidled up beside me, his attention snagged too. There was a faint click as his eyes focused, followed by a swift intake of breath as he shrank back against the wall.

'What is it?' Max whispered from the other side.

'I'm not completely sure,' I scowled, 'but I think the ceiling might just be a little … alive.'

Chapter 10

Pan's silent dread was worse than all the shrieking in the world.

We crept along the cavern wall watching the ceiling, which flickered and blurred intermittently. It looked innocent enough from our distance, but this was Pantheon, where science and nightmares knew no natural boundaries; and we held our breath until we were crouching beneath the decrepit stairwells.

I gazed up through the broken rises, recalling the last time I'd climbed them, searching for Aelia and August. I'd just arrived in the noisy, bizarre Prolet underworld, desperate to know if August had survived surgery. And now I was here again, with even less conviction he was still breathing. Or whether I should care. The irony wasn't lost on me, and yet as I gazed at the empty worm-ridden wooden beams, I would have happily stepped inside a time machine. The whole cavern felt dead. Where was everyone? Where was Aelia?

An uncomfortable suspicion began to seep through my bones. Aelia had said Cassius had removed all privileges after the insurgents' escape. And it was the middle of the night, which meant the rest of the Prolet population should be here now. Under curfew.

'I'm going up,' I whispered to the others. 'Wait here and keep watch!'

'I'll come too,' Max interjected.

'It doesn't look strong enough,' I hissed.

Pan shot a panicked look upwards as my whisper ricocheted around the cavern. We followed his gaze and, for a second, no one moved as several of the lights grew brighter, before fading again. He finally looked back at me, his elongated ears twitching and face paler than ever. There was no mistaking his warning.

I turned abruptly, and scaled the first section before anyone could offer any more objections. Despite its appearance the walkway frame seemed firm enough, and as long as I trod a central path, the wooden beams supported my weight without objection. I flew up the rest as quickly as I dared and was outside Aelia's snug cave entrance within a couple of minutes. Her tatty old woven blanket still concealed the entrance, and I hesitated only for a moment before drawing it aside. Steadying my nerve for what might lie ahead.

Cautiously, I scanned the threadbare cave-room, my eyes adjusting to the gloom. There was no sign of Aelia, although her tiny cave looked as though she had just popped out for a moment. A small book rested on her tiny tabletop, alongside a half-eaten cob of bread. My eyes narrowed. Aelia would never willingly leave food behind.

I walked across to the tiny snug at the back of the cave, into which we'd all crammed to examine Aelia's hidden research. The same research that had turned out to be missing pages from the Book of Arafel, the rest of Thomas's research into the Voynich. *It was also where August had kissed me.* But those memories were suffocated today. The small curtain was drawn aside, and the tiny hiding hole completely exposed. My anxiety intensified.

What had happened here? There was no way of knowing, and yet I couldn't shake the feeling that she had left in a big hurry, not long before. I turned swiftly, feeling oddly exposed, but as I made my way back towards the entrance, the slim book on the table drew my eye again.

'GENETICA: *A short analysis of advantageous genetic modifications 2204–2205.*'

It had to be a Pantheonite publication, published inside Octavia's reign of terror and propaganda. I frowned. It was also a most unlikely, dubious book for Aelia to possess, let alone leave lying around.

Impulsively, I crossed to the table, and opened the well-thumbed text. There were a lot of annotated diagrams throughout and, as I flicked through, my attention was drawn by a bulbous section towards the back.

After a swift glance at the still entrance, I turned to the thickened section and discovered a small piece of paper, triple-folded, between two pages headed:

Genus: Rhinolophus; Species: ferrumequinum

Directly beneath the bold title there was a drawing of a large grey-brown bat, labelled *Original Greater Horseshoe*, together with a series of scientific drawings describing its key genetic modifications. Most of the bold arrows were concentrated around the enlarged head of the creature, which had extended vampiric fangs, the annotation *Batrachotoxin* underscored three times, and white, dilated eyes.

On the right-hand side of the double page, there was also a box of text outlined in red, which read:

Experiment: Rhinolophus ferrumequinum

1) Species remodelled with Batrachotoxin poison sacs behind protruding premolar on the upper jaw and distinctive noseleaf*

*Batrachotoxin trialled from *Phyllobates terribilis, poison dart frog.*

2) Species remodelled with 20/20 Night Owl Vision optics with processing technology. Warning: modified LED lights will burn through a human retina, effecting long-term damage if exposure is extended.

I scowled, pocketing Aelia's triple-folded note. That would have to wait. So much for a moving starlit ceiling. It seemed Cassius had replaced Octavia's CCTV system with something a little more biological. A ceiling full of crawling, venomous bats with enhanced night vision. A fitting Pantheonite welcome!

I sprinted from the cave, only pausing at the top of the wooden walkway to glance upwards. At this height, I could just make out the silhouette of hundreds of furry bodies, some the size of large rats, hanging and crawling across the pitted stone ceiling. I shuddered as a set of piercing white eye-lights passed across my face, partially dazzling me.

Grabbing the wooden balustrade, I forced my eyes to the ground. No wonder Pan had looked so terrified. These modified rodents were the worst type of Trojan horse, hiding their real nature behind the appearance of their original species.

I assessed the floor rapidly. I could just make out Pan and Max beneath the walkway, and there were two exits from the cavern – one led home and the other led to the heart of Isca Prolet, via putrid tunnels inhabited by flesh-eating strix. There was no real choice to be made.

Without further hesitation, I flew down the first precarious flight, barely allowing myself to breathe. But just as I made the second landing, a sinister crack divided the air. I shot out a hand to catch hold of the horizontal beam, but the damage was done, and I could only watch as the bottom two flights of stairs collapsed to the floor amid a huge cloud of dust and bat guano. Instinctively, I swung a leg over one of the remaining staircase props, dangling there as a heavy silence claimed the void. And for one insane moment, I wondered if I'd got away with it.

Then the air was alive with angry, squeaking bodies.

'Tal!'

But Max's roar was muffled by the swarm of rodents already flapping furiously around my face and hair, lighting up the cavern walls in micro-detail with a mist of tiny LED light beams.

It might have looked fairy-tale, had I not known it was the effect of thousands of genetically modified bats being rudely awakened.

Refusing to acknowledge the panic climbing my throat, I pulled out my leather slingshot. Then I unhooked one end rapidly, and slinging the smooth side over the remaining diagonal beam, I pushed off with all my strength.

I was unprepared for the speed of my descent, or for the barrage of bodies that impacted like small rocks. And their anatomical detail loomed large as I flew. *Vampiric fangs Batrachotoxin trialled from Phyllobates terribilis, poison dart frog.* I gritted my teeth. There would be no second chances should one of us get bitten.

'They're poisonous!' I yelled, as my feet touched the solid floor. 'And their eyes can burn – don't look at them!'

I felt them then, a heaving mass of vampiric bodies, swirling and descending upon us. Someone screamed – it could have been me, but my panic was so intense I couldn't be sure. I groped blindly for Max, every muscle of my body tense, waiting for the inevitable sharp bite that would mark the end, before we'd even begun. Just then a strong arm grabbed mine, and started propelling me through the swarm as surely as though it were broad daylight. I thought initially it was Max, until I realized the hand shape was all wrong. And then I recalled Pan's radial eyes, and knocking away a bat with a suspicious interest in my shoulder, I gripped back with all my strength.

We stumbled across the cavern floor together, the colony following us, but by some miracle we made it to the opposite wall, which we followed until we fell into the cool air of the tunnel.

I leaned back against the craggy wall, trying to catch my breath. Somehow, we'd made it to the tunnel connecting the domestic cavern with the rest of the Prolet commercial underworld.

'Thank you,' I whispered, reaching out to grip Pan's anxious hand. And this time he didn't flinch or pull away, he simply gripped back, his pale face full of shy kindness.

'Was anyone … bitten?' I added, panting, while peering into the tunnel gloom.

Had we run from one nightmare into the wake of another?

'How did you know about those flying … rats?' Max asked, leaning forward over his knees.

'Aelia left a warning, in her cave,' I responded.

'They're greater horseshoe bats modified with poisonous frog venom and 20/20 night owl vision technology.'

Max stared at me.

'Friendly little critters then! Special welcoming committee just for us?'

'Yes, or a new control over the rest of the Prolet community. Either way, it looks as though Aelia was interrupted,' I added, 'and forced to leave in a hurry.'

As though to corroborate, one of the larger bats chose that exact moment to spiral into the tunnel and crash-land at our feet. I stifled a shudder as Pan turned it up and closed its fading eyes.

'Wait!' I interjected, as he made to throw it back out into the frenzy.

I pulled out Max's carefully shaped darts.

'You think we could squeeze a little of the bat's venom onto these?'

'Poison-tipped darts!' Max whispered with real admiration. 'You really are the most incredible girl.'

'Oh, I'm just borrowing the idea from the Trojans,' I muttered, with a swift look up the tunnel.

Max looked blank.

'And a bit of paralysis and asphyxiation might come in useful,' I added.

He nodded, reaching inside his own leather rations bag and withdrew a fistful of crossbow arrows, each one the length of my forearm.

'More keepsakes?' I quipped, feeling mildly envious. 'Do they actually work?'

Max winked before holding out the clutch of arrows, bar one, in front of Pan who carefully depressed the dead bat's fangs, releasing a stream of warm venom all over their tips. Max then pulled the crossbow off his shoulder, levelled his remaining arrow, and released it into the cloud of bats still circulating in the open cave. There was a squeak and a thud, as it made swift contact with an unsuspecting victim.

I smirked as he flexed his arm, withdrawing the piece of paper Aelia had left inside the book.

'Did you find that in her cave? What does it say?' Max quizzed, making room in his weapons belt to accommodate his newly tipped arrows.

I unfolded it, and studied it in the small pool of light inside the entrance of the tunnel.

'It's not a note,' I responded, puzzled, 'it's part of the Book of Arafel. She's torn a page out of our own village book!'

I folded it again swiftly, suddenly conscious Max still didn't know about Thomas's research hidden inside the Book of Arafel.

But I'd seen enough to know Aelia's note was a torn page. I recognized it immediately – chunks of nonsense Voynich lettering in his spidery handwriting, together with a faded drawing. Just about visible. I'd never singled it out for special attention as it looked like everything else in his research. The nonsense scribbles and sketches of a child. But here in Pantheon, torn out by Aelia, the drawing seemed to take on a much more sinister significance.

It was the sketch of a creature with multiple animal parts: the front quarters of a large lion, the tail of a serpent, and a goat rising bizarrely from its back. The result wasn't any natural creature I recognized, although I recalled Grandpa describing some creatures in mythology comprising mixed animal parts. He said classical writers had considered them indulgent, dazzling, imaginary creatures. And an omen for disaster.

There were also faint, hand-drawn lines labelling various parts of the creature with more nonsense lettering. Finally, across the top of the page there were three roughly sketched capital letters I'd not noticed before, a faint: REQ.

There were so many bizarre and unusual drawings among Thomas's painstaking research, but for some reason Aelia had seen fit to single this page out and, judging by the jagged tear through the page, she'd done it in a hurry.

I stared at the dim rock wall, willing myself to understand. This was a specific mythical creature Thomas had seen fit to draw out and annotate. And now Aelia was trying to tell me something about it. Did it have something to do with her disappearance? Why had she brought me all this way just to give me another puzzle? I thought of all the gaunt, hollow-eyed faces of the young Prolet insurgents hiding beneath the Dead City. She had to know time was running out.

I clenched my fingers. Cryptic clue or not, Aelia and the entire Prolet population couldn't have vanished into thin air. The sooner we found them, the sooner I could hope to rescue Lake, the Book of Arafel and find out the significance of this drawing.

'Does it matter?'

I shot Max a glance.

'What do you mean?' I returned.

'About the Book. Does it matter if Aelia trades the Book with Cassius to buy a reprieve for the Prolets – or August?'

'Yes … I mean … no,' I stumbled, uncertain of the direction he was taking.

'I mean Cassius has the Book – does it really matter?' he clarified after a beat. 'OK, so he will have the story of our community's survival, but is it worth our lives?'

I squeezed the folded note in my hand, glanced back at Max's face, and read the real question there.

Why couldn't I trust him after everything we'd shared?

Intended to share. And I longed to blurt out the truth about what I was really protecting. But I'd made a promise.

'Yes,' I answered decisively, turning into the gloom, 'it's worth the whole damned world.'

***

The connecting tunnel was no less suffocating. The scent of rotting faeces mixed with something else, something animalistic, pervaded the air. Or perhaps it was the scent of fear. Deadly, vampiric bats could only be a warm-up to Octavia's mythological strix.

We pushed on into the murky darkness, our hearts beating faster than usual. But although a suspicious echo stalled us in our tracks every so often, we failed to encounter the underground rat-owls that had haunted my dreams for nearly a year. Carefully, I shielded one of the beeswax candles I'd brought from Arafel and, as the shadow of the small flame danced, I tried not to stare at the pitted grainy walls where Octavia's watchdogs of the underworld had scored their territory.

Pan led the way, his large frame blocking what little other light was filtering through, but the events of the last cavern had forged a new trust, and recalling how the satyrs had proven fair adversaries for strix, we stayed close. Max brought up the rear, crossbow at his shoulder, cursing readily.

Thankfully, Pan moved fast, his elongated ears alert and twitching at any slight sound. And I wondered again at the tall, silent creature whose enduring love for a child meant he'd willingly re-enter a world he so obviously detested. It was so moving, and beyond perplexing. They couldn't be related, and yet he was quite clearly prepared to do anything to find her.

I wiped another bead of cold sweat from my clammy forehead. My skin felt like I'd run three kilometres in the dead of winter, and several times I fancied a clawing behind us, only to find Max's tense face amid endless darkness when I glanced back.

Still we pushed on and much to my amazement, before too long the dim light of the commercial Prolet centre reached down the tunnel, confirming we'd made it unscathed. I relaxed back against the cool stone of the tunnel exit in momentary relief, letting my eyes run over the familiar earthen silhouette of Isca Prolet.

And then I caught my breath. Because I might as well have been staring at the ruined Dead City for all the life we could see. Isca Prolet was completely and utterly empty.

We gazed out on the deserted underground city, our fragile hopes spiralling. The machinery that had pounded incessantly at the back of the gigantic cavern lay dangling and useless. The dirt streets that had exploded with Isca Pantheon's diverse, genetic rubbish tip of life were hollow and lifeless. And the segmented tower, which had once housed Aelia and Tullius's surgery, rose silently above the scattered miscellany of empty buildings and streets I'd found so charming after the white, surgical lines of Pantheon.

I took a few tentative steps forward, unwilling to believe my eyes.

'Where is everyone?' I whispered, my hair on the back of my arms starting to strain. This place was quickly losing its appeal as a good trade for the tunnel.

'*I have nothing to tell you. I destroyed the Book many years ago. It brought nothing but pain and violence.*'

I froze in violent confusion, watching Max's face wash stone grey.

'*Do not underestimate my granddaughter. Talia will never cede to you. She is a Hanway, and as a descendant of Thomas, she is as free and feral as we are made on the outside.*'

This time the voice was clearer and stronger. It was a voice that carried memories of warm evenings around the Arafel village fire; of hours curled up in the treehouse library discovering new myths and legends – and of that last night beneath the Great

Oak, when I held his hand until the angels stole him away. Grandpa.

And as I turned, the world slowed as though some unseen pressure was clinging to my feet, holding them in a quagmire. I was aware of Max's mouth moving, but I was no longer in control. There was an instinct, a rush of emotion, an eruption of memories – combined into one spontaneous act of wilful motion. And I didn't run, I flew.

The streets became a blur of market stall fronts and mud-brown hovels. Where before I'd admired the colourful array of disordered living, now I was only aware of one long homogenized streak as I headed towards his voice.

'You and Cassius are a disgrace to humankind, if I can even call you that. You have forfeited the chance to experience real life, outside life, and now you are denying others the same? It is worse than the most heinous crime; it is a massacre of free will!'

I was dimly aware of passing the tall metal tower, of heading out towards the outlying streets, an area of the Prolet world I'd not visited before. If I'd just stopped to think for just one second, if I'd allowed myself to listen to Max's hoarse voice a few paces behind, I'd have rationalized that it just couldn't be. But instead I made stubborn sense of the impossible, and sprinted towards the frail brave tones that had existed only in my memory for nine long months.

Right until a firm wrestle brought the ground up to meet me, filling my nose and mouth with pungent, red iron dirt.

'Get off! Max!' I seethed as his solid weight propelled me under the metal awning of a dingy trading hut. I rolled over to face him and paused. It wasn't Max at all. It was Pan, terror etched all over his face, his long white ears flat against his head as Max dived in next to us.

Furiously, I brought my feet up beneath me, just as Pan pressed a shaky finger against my lips and pointed outwards. And something in his eyes made me look past the broken shop façades, past the roughly fashioned tools and scattered, wizened vegetables – right to the end of the street. Where grim reality returned with a crash.

From this vantage, I could just see the square beyond. It was derelict and ramshackle, like everywhere else in this squalid Prolet world. But it was the centre of the square that held all my attention. There was an elongated stone plinth, flickering with intermittent blue light, a moving image, exactly like the one we saw in Pantheon the day we emerged from the Prolet work trams.

And he was there, a lone figure on top of the stone. It was just a projected image, but him all the same. Grandpa. Lying on the bed, a metal plate attached to his head and tight restraints securing his thin, weakened body. And a second blue figure, Octavia, was crowing over him, the epitome of an evil huntress from the bleakest of fairy tales. Except this was a real memory.

In a flash I was back there, in Octavia's personal experimentation room, face to face with the ice-bitch herself. Grandpa had been so physically weak, and still the most seasoned warrior for the outside; a warrior who'd used his last strength to save my life. And even though it was just a cruel image, his passion reached deep inside me like a clawed fist, dragging me back into reality.

This wasn't just about rescuing Lake or protecting the Book of Arafel; it was about being true to the feral will he'd nurtured inside me. It was about remembering all he'd taught us about Thomas's vision for Arafel: about respecting the forest, knowing our place, and taking only what we needed to survive. *It was about being an Outsider.*

And as I listened, I felt his wisdom course through my limbs like white water, steeling my nerve. Whoever was playing this knew we were here, that I was here. And it was being played directly to torture me. To weaken me.

The picture crackled again, and when it cleared it had changed. Now it was time for the other ghost in my life. And I gazed, feeling my world crumble all over again. He was dressed in full

Roman General regalia, his aquila insignia emblazoned across his military tunic and his helmet held firmly within the cusp of his arm. His tall, proud figure was standing alone in the square. Defying the world. The air felt thin, and I struggled to breathe as his swarthy face loomed and filled my vision. *August.*

It's not him. It's not him, I repeated silently.

It was just a detached, three-dimensional echo. A moment caught in a vast vaulted assembly room, which had to be Pantheon's Senate.

'Isca Pantheon needs to change.'

His authoritative tone washed over the lifeless market stalls and streets like a warning given too late. The pictured fizzled and cleared again, revealing August standing in a different room, much like his own private quarters. He was talking to someone beyond the picture, and his face had changed. It was closed and guarded, the exact expression he'd worn for most of the time I'd known him before the Flavium.

'I accept I may have acted hastily. Change and integration need to be introduced slowly.'

I frowned as he nodded to whomever was standing beyond the pool of light.

'The early integration analysis indicates a common stress symptom among the Prolet class, which may be a reaction to the existing vaccine to suppress independent will. Of course, the recent rioting cannot be tolerated.

'Because of this, and the new investigation required, I would recommend a temporary suspension of all new Prolet privileges and reinstatement of the existing Pantheonite system.'

I stared with mounting horror as this new August I didn't recognize smiled and saluted. Had the Prolets also seen this?

Then another voice.

'And do you accept the mission from the Senate, Commander General Augustus Aquila?'

August appeared not to hesitate.

'Yes. I accept the mission to carry Isca Pantheon's banner and find a sister site for our growing population. I do so in the hope that it will further the Biotechnology Programme's Objectives; developing new experimental facilities, and pursuing existing Genetic Modification Programme aims.'

I stared at the red, earthen ground staining my hands, like the blood of the Prolets.

This rigid commander, flickering before me, was a complete stranger. A traitor. And yet the August I'd known had seen the outside and everything it could be. He'd promised he was going to find a new way for Isca Pantheon. He knew the lives of every Prolet man, woman and child depended on him, and now I was to believe he'd cast them all onto the pyre. For what? A secret ambition he'd been nurturing all along? Was this the real reason he'd remained behind?

The picture fizzled out leaving only the murkiness of the Prolet underworld, and the heat of Max's stare. He'd always suspected August capable of deceit. And he knew I'd refused to believe it. I'd brought us back to this place, shone a spotlight above our heads even, all to discover that August was a traitor of the worst order. A pretender and a coward. It couldn't be worse.

Everything was eerily quiet now. The moving image had disappeared completely, leaving a dusky veil that clung to every contour of the underworld. And it was so still I could hear Pan's jagged breath as loudly as though it were my own.

I surveyed our surroundings with a slow, sickening suspicion. There was no doubt Cassius knew we were here. Which meant there was only one certainty left. This was a trap.

Chapter 11

'Don't move.' Max's whisper was low and steely.

It was one of the few occasions I'd heard real fear in his voice, like the final few moments in the Flavium, before Eli calmed the griffin.

I scanned the square again. It was completely empty. And then I saw them – distorted shadows, staring out of every crevice and gutter. Thick, hooded shadows, watching us.

'Bas-i-lis-cus,' Pan hissed under his breath.

And in a breath I was seated cross-legged in Grandpa's tree-house room, poring over the book of mythology and legend, staring at the king of serpent snakes, fabled to have a deadly touch and poisonous breath.

'The basilisk reminds me of you, Talia – small but deadly!' Grandpa had whispered. *'It dripped venom in its wake, and could kill with just one look!'*

He'd hunched his shoulders and twisted up his face comically, while I'd burst out laughing. It was such a game back then, little more than a shared passion for the classics and mythology. But he'd been equipping me with a whole armoury. And I'd just made the stupidest decision of my life because of a weak, emotional reaction. I shot a glance at Max's stoic face. He'd been so suspicious of August all along. How could I have got so much so wrong? Had he been watching me, watching August?

'Ab-ove.'

Pan's stilted warning came just as a drop of something warm and viscous fell onto a pair of iron tongs lying discarded beside me. There was an acidic, bubbling noise as the liquid made contact with the forked end, and then the metal disappeared altogether. The tiny drop dissolved the thick, solid iron in less than a second.

We were up and flying back down the street within a heartbeat, August's deceit clinging to me like raw shame.

The entire Prolet population, including Aelia, were missing. Cassius's Biotechnology Programme was already developing entirely new species. And most disturbingly of all, he knew a few images from the past would be enough to trap a stupid girl from the outside. I shot a look at Max's grim profile, and was flooded with the worst kind of guilt.

Then I looked behind us, and wished I hadn't.

The dirt track was completely awash with writhing black serpentine bodies, each with a thickened crested neck, much like a cobra. They were short, no longer than the length of my calf muscle, and possessed solid, muscular bodies and black eyes that shone like mirrors in the twilight. And they were gaining on us.

I had no idea if their stare was venomous. How could such a thing even be possible? But this was Pantheon, and I couldn't put anything past Cassius.

'We need to get up high!' I yelled, grabbing both Pan and Max and pushing them towards the iron-metal tower stretching up towards the cavernous ceiling. Max and I were scaling the giant ant-like structure within seconds. We were used to tree-running in Arafel, and the thick metal beams of the tower made for swift progress. I only paused to glance down once we reached the mid-level housing Tullius's surgery.

Which was when I realized Pan wasn't with us at all.

'Max!' I yelled, reaching out to grip his arm. 'Pan?!'

I scanned the floor, before inhaling sharply.

No wonder our climb had been so easy and unhindered. Pan was still at the bottom of the tower, using his muscular equine legs to kick the swarming basilisk back across the track as soon as they got close. He was strong, but the swarm was thickening every second. My mind flew back to the bat-infested cave. He'd saved us, despite his own palpable fear. And he had to be terrified now, and yet he was still putting us first. We had to do something.

'Oh for the love of Arafel!' Max groaned, turning and anchoring himself on a thick metal beam. He snatched up his crossbow, and began loading up the Roman arrows he'd filched.

'Go on! Find Aelia!' he yelled at me, without one iota of expectation.

I didn't even bother to answer. I'd already witnessed one noble-hearted Prolet sacrifice near everything for the sake of two Outsiders, and Pan reminded me of Unus in so many ways. My chest contracted. I couldn't let myself wonder what fate had befallen the kind-hearted Cyclops who defied everything he was designed to be. But here and now, we could help Pan.

'Why run when you can fly?' I muttered to myself, reaching for a fraying rope that stretched end to end across the dirt street, before flipping myself over in a backwards somersault. Then pulling a foot up, I teetered there for a moment, finding my balance through my supple leather soles. I gritted my teeth, and in the next breath I was up and wobbling at least forty metres above the ground. It was high and unstable, but I'd walked worse in search of the best honey in the forest.

'Just like a forage,' I told myself, putting one foot in front of the other before throwing caution to the wind and running to the centre of the rope.

It jerked and swayed like a restless snake, but somehow I found the centre and dropped down as though I were in a giant swing. Then, I let myself fall backwards so I was dangling upside down directly above the writhing creatures. From here I could see their shapes more clearly, and was awed by how thick and muscular their bodies were. They could undoubtedly climb the metallic tower given the chance. And there were also far more of them than we could hope to kill with our poisoned darts and arrows.

'Pan! Max and I will hold them off – get climbing!' I yelled, shoving the tiny treehouse dart tube between my lips and loading up a dart. I blew and it made contact with a basilisk rearing up close to Pan's legs. It fell sideways with a thud.

'Climb!' I yelled again.

But the tall silenus only shook his head with the saddest smile. It was a smile that reached through my ribcage and slowly squeezed my heart. My mind flew back to his watchful care of Lake, to his suffering on such meagre rations, to his horror when she was taken, and consequent determination that he had to rescue her. He'd turned into the most unlikely hero and friend, and now … why wasn't he trying?

I opened my mouth to yell again, but as he lifted his leg to kick another basilisk away, I caught a clear glimpse of the underside. Of a hoof protruding through thickened skin. An ice-cold realization flooded my veins instantly, leaving my skin cold and clammy.

'Max!' I yelled. Why hadn't I thought of it before?

'Pan can't climb! He has hooves!'

Max paled, and began descending swiftly, but before he could make any headway, Pan looked up and shook his head, mouthing two words.

'Pro-tect Lake.'

Then he smiled, in the most carefree way he'd ever smiled. And it was a smile that told me exactly what he was going to do. I opened my mouth, but there was no time and the scream clawing up my throat suffocated as he stepped quietly inside the swarm of serpents. They were all over him in a heartbeat, his muscular form remaining distinct as the heaving mass of basilisk coiled their strong leech-like bodies around his and sank their jaws into his pale flesh.

For a few seconds, Max and I were too frozen to do anything but stare. The excited mound had attracted other basilisk swarming down the street, and swiftly the writhing mass grew. Like giant parasites celebrating an unexpected feast.

'Tal, Tal!' Max yelled hoarsely, collecting himself first. 'We have to move. For Pan's sake. He's done this to give us a chance. So we can escape and find Lake!'

I looked across at Max's earnest face, my chest vibrant with pain, and knew he was right. To hesitate now would be to undo Pan's bravery. And yet I'd never felt less like flying in my whole life.

I swallowed. My mouth felt like sandpaper and there were no words.

'For Lake, Tal?' he urged.

And somewhere, I found the will to move.

This time, we didn't stop climbing until we'd fallen through a rusty window onto the dark corridor floor that connected with Tullius's rooms.

Max slammed closed the small casement, and we sank down against the dank walls to catch our breath.

'He just ... walked into them,' I whispered.

Max's eyes were dark and unreadable, his body language distant.

'He knew,' he muttered, after a beat.

He stepped swiftly across the dark room, and I read the fresh uncertainty in his body.

'Knew what?' I asked, though I already knew I wasn't going to like the answer.

'That caring for someone screws you over!'

I recoiled from his sudden anger, the flame between us guttering. And I was suddenly so mad. Mad because I couldn't go back to those few days when I'd let myself be deceived by the worst kind of pretender. Mad because the August I'd fallen for didn't actually exist. And mad because I'd known Max a lifetime, and he'd never made me feel the way August had in just a few days.

'So we're back here,' Max added furiously, 'chasing Aelia who has gone AWOL with the Book of Arafel because of her so-called strix-shit of a brother … who has as good as abandoned everyone! And now the good guys are dying … again! August was nothing but another Cassius, waiting in the wings, and now we're running through this … this cesspit … being chased by creatures that have no place on this earth, and for what?

'To help a population who've also disappeared off the face of the world! A community who've watched their own children do the only decent thing anyone in Isca Pantheon has done for centuries, and yet who would rather let them die of rat disease … than set foot outside the place in which they've coaxed out some chicken-crap excuse of an existence!'

Silence hung in the slim corridor. I'd never heard Max so furious.

And it hurt.

'Fine!' I forced out finally, my voice sounding tinny in the oppressive silence. 'It's my fault we're here again. But you weren't forced to come! And what about Aelia, Lake and the Book? What about the fact an entire population has completely disappeared? What about the look on Pan's face when he ran from the tower? Didn't you see it? There's something else, Max! Something we're not getting yet. Pan couldn't tell us, but it involves Lake.

'If you're done, fine! Go home! I'm going to find Aelia and Lake, and then I'll do what August started before he …'

'… deserted Pantheon and everyone else he ever knew?' Max cut in.

I glanced at him brokenly, unable to deny anything, or control my own guilt. I pushed myself back up to standing, and the piece of paper Aelia tore from Thomas's research rustled softly in my leather rations bag. I was sure it was some sort of message, but how could I share it with Max without breaking my promise?

Maybe Grandpa was wrong to entrust the secret to a feral girl, who'd always acted far too rashly. Maybe it was just too big.

'Max, I …'

'Perhaps the Commander is strix-shit, though I think strix-breakfast might be more accurate by the time I'm done … But calling our home a cesspit? Now some might call that a little rude.'

The voice was whimsical, and oddly recognizable.

We turned slowly, and I was suddenly acutely aware of just how careless I'd almost been; of forgetting where we were and nearly blurting out a two-hundred-year-old secret. And now we had company.

We pulled our weapons simultaneously, and levelled them at the shadows, just as the figure of a man emerged. An autumn-skinned, lithe man; with a Cerberus tattoo snaking up his neck.

'Rajid!' Max exclaimed, lowering his dagger while I kept my slingshot trained at his forehead.

I still had no idea whether this man was friend or foe. Nothing in Pantheon was ever as it seemed. He'd helped Aelia steal the Book of Arafel, and I hadn't forgotten our conversation in the forest. Had he already sold Arafel's location to Cassius?

'We've been looking for you,' Max added darkly. 'All of you!'

'Where's Aelia?' I kept my voice steady and slingshot high. At this range I could kill him, and Rajid knew it.

He turned his head slowly to stare with panther-black eyes. In the shadows his bright blue Cerberus gleamed like a moonlit map, its three twisted necks reaching out like rivers.

Our last encounter in the forest replayed through my head.

Just what is it that makes you so special?

I gritted my teeth.

'Where is Aelia?' I demanded again, my voice unwavering.

'Well, your guess is as good as mine, but this isn't the place

135

for chat. Cassius and his guard will be here within seconds. If you like looking at the insides of your own eyelids, take your chances. Otherwise, this way – and best be quick.'

Rajid disappeared back into the corner of the oblong room, and there was a discordant grating noise. Moments later his shadow was gone.

I ran across to discover a rectangular hole in the metal floor, and a thick plate lying next to it. I scowled at Max. The choice was between Rajid or Cassius and his molossers. It could be a trap, but if Rajid was trying to help, he could be our last chance of finding Aelia. And perhaps Lake.

Moments later I was easing myself through the exit onto the metallic support beam below.

We were about fifty metres from the ground, balancing on one of the thick rusted tower beams that stretched all the way to the ground. The basilisk were still swarming all over Pan's obscured form directly below us, and I forced hot bile back down my parched throat. He'd given himself to buy us precious time, and now it looked as though we were returning to the floor.

Rajid was already halfway, climbing as nimbly as though he were an Outsider, and my head rang with a distant echo. It was something Max had said before we'd faced the guards and molossers in the laboratory.

'Prolets take care of themselves.'

I set off at sprint pace, despite the drop.

The support was thin but sturdy, and the soft padding of Max's footsteps gave me a sense of rhythm. Before long, we were approaching the ground floor at the rear of the Prolet market centre.

'Basilisk,' Max whispered as we came to a skidding halt at the base of the beam.

I looked at Rajid, waiting nonchalantly, the way he might wait in a market bread queue. And yet, we needed to trust this man with the snake ink.

His answer was a smirking grin, revealing his missing front tooth.

'Basilisk fast ... but we're faster, yes?'

His tone was mocking, as the air filled with the faint hiss of excited basilisk. And then there was something else, the echo of a howl. Molossers. Which meant Cassius.

'This is madness; we're trapped against the rock wall this way!' Max exclaimed, panic-stricken.

I glanced from him to Rajid's smirking face. There had to be a reason why he was still here while everyone else had disappeared.

'Lead on,' I growled, 'and let's see how fast a Prolet can run!'

Rajid's eyes glittered and narrowed. He spun on his heel and sprinted directly towards the rock wall at the back of the cavern. Max drew level with me, gesticulating madly. I scowled, unable to provide reassurance. If Rajid had no back-up plan, we would be entirely trapped against the back wall, with no means of escape.

We reached the grainy, red-ravined rock face breathlessly, and looked up. It had to be nearly two hundred metres high, and almost sheer. But Rajid seemed more interested in the wall itself, while the combined chorus of the basilisk and molossers was building, like the clamour of a nightmare just before dawn. A shudder passed through me as I recalled Pan's submerged figure. We were running out of time.

'We need to move!' Max seethed through gritted teeth. I shot out a hand to stay him as Rajid ran his hands along the rock face at chest height, following the ravines as if they were old friends.

Instinctively, we glanced back down the eerie deserted street. The first of the basilisk were just visible now, thick black bodies writhing with a thirst for fresh blood. My chest hurt with the effort of controlling my jagged breath, and just as I was beginning to wonder if I'd made the stupidest decision of my life, I turned to find Rajid had completely disappeared.

'Where did he go?!' Max exclaimed furiously.

I ran my hands across the rock, my forehead clammy, only to

exclaim when they disappeared completely behind a thick, concealed shelf of rock. Carefully I followed the camouflaged edge diagonally down to the ground and, stooping, peered behind. There was a slim dark void, just wide enough for a person to squeeze through.

Was it an escape tunnel? Or a trap?

I glanced back into the cavern. The basilisk were fully visible now, a thick wave of hissing black lava, headed our way. Max nodded urgently, the whites of his eyes gleaming in the low light. There was time left and no other way.

So, I closed my eyes, and crawled inside.

Chapter 12

I knew I was falling, just not how far. If I die, let it be as swift as Max's hunting blade, I prayed. Let it be so fast that I am back in Arafel's forest in a heartbeat, with the lazy sun in my eyes and whispering leaves at my back. Let Grandpa and Dad be there, in the wheat fields, waiting.

But then I landed in something soft, something that felt and smelled remarkably like soiled animal straw. And the impact confirmed I was irrefutably alive.

'Apologies for the used compost, I'm just rather partial to my bones,' Rajid commented whimsically, as though falling ten metres into a latrine was an everyday occurrence.

It was murky black, and a distant light shone down another dimly lit passage. I scrambled towards his languid hand, conscious Max was following. And sure enough, as soon as I hauled myself onto solid ground, Max landed amid a stream of blurred cursing.

'For the love of Arafel, what is this stuff?' he croaked, picking up a handful of the crumbling matter and sniffing it.

'Excrement!' Rajid called glibly, as he scaled a crude wooden ladder back up to the void above our heads.

At the top he unwound a thick rope, and swiftly inserted a slim stone into the entrance until no light remained. Then, wrapping his feet around the ladder, he slid back down to the ground.

'Old excrement, but excrement all the same,' he clarified, as Max slid out of the pit faster than his tree-running personal best. At any other time, I would have laughed my forest soles off.

'They can't get through?' I asked.

'They haven't so far.'

Relieved, I looked around. We were in some sort of drainage tunnel.

'It's not much, but it's home,' Rajid quipped, his eyes mocking.

Briefly I wondered if we'd simply followed a lonely madman into the Prolet latrines. Surely there had to be no lower metaphor, the toilets of the Prolet underworld. There was a delicious dark comedy to the moment, and Max's pained expression said it all. I stifled a bubble of hysterical laughter.

'Where does this lead, Rajid?' I managed with some effort. 'Where is Aelia?'

'Soon!' he called, walking away down the tunnel.

'Rajid!' I called, determined not to be put off any longer. 'We know where the Prolet insurgents are … We know about the children!'

This time he stopped abruptly, turned and began walking back towards us with an odd expression twisting his passive face. Was it hope?

'They made it? To Arafel?' he repeated incredulously.

And it was all there in his tone. Arafel was a Garden of Paradise, a distant sanctuary offering a life in the sun, and protection. A blade twisted deep inside. These people had turned our valley home into a Mecca, a promised land, and Arafel had bolted the door before they'd even had chance to knock.

I thought of Atticus willingly chewing the ear off a rat, and then of the tower the young ones were preparing as their substitute New Arfel home. And guilt bled through me like a river of lead.

'My brother Eli is with them,' I added. 'They're surviving in the passages beneath the ruined city at the moment. They're all safe – well, nearly all …'

Rajid fixed me with a stare.

'Lake, Pan?' he whispered, and even though it was dark I could tell his face was full of new shadows.

I nodded.

'Atticus?' he questioned, frowning.

'Is happily feasting on raw rat!' Max chipped in, now finally satisfied he'd removed every particle of human excrement from his person.

Rajid chuckled drily, pursing his lips.

'Then we can safely assume we have even less time,' he muttered, before turning and striding into the darkness.

I shot Max a tight grimace before setting off after him.

***

There were dirty mesh-sealed jars, set at intervals, filled with strange moving lights. After a time, I worked out they were eyes. Somehow, strange resourceful Rajid had managed to capture a few of the deadly vampiric bats, and use them to illuminate the rough tunnel. It was genius in a way, but every time we passed one of the light stations a fresh revulsion washed through me. This tunnel was also oddly strix-free, although it created a feeling of waiting too. Somewhere in this dank, lightless world, a flock of hungry strix were lurking, and I couldn't imagine it was too far away.

From the gradient and direction of the slope, I could tell we were travelling north-west in the direction of the main Isca Pantheonite dome. I fought my dread by trying to work out how many hours had passed since we left the Dead City. The morning had to be well advanced by now, which meant the city of Isca Pantheon was fully awake. It wasn't a good thought.

Finally, after what seemed like an age, the narrow, putrid walls opened out into some sort of small square chamber. There was sackcloth in the corner and the remains of some half-eaten provisions; but it was the small rope ladder in the corner that drew my attention. It was fixed to the rock wall, and disappeared up what looked to be a narrow ventilation chimney. Any new hopes I'd begun to cherish, guttered instantly. Narrow corridors were one thing, but this chimney barely looked big enough to squeeze into, let alone climb.

'Don't tell me we're going up there!' I protested, my stomach turning over.

'Where are we, Rajid? How is this getting us closer to Aelia and Lake?' Max demanded, glancing at me.

He understood, even though it was many years ago. He'd helped the search party when I went missing. I'd crept into the Arafel log store during tree-tag, and the door had become wedged, leaving me to shout 'til I was hoarse. It had started out a game, but ended a nightmare, and left me with a lifelong fear of small spaces.

'It is the only way,' Rajid responded, holding a finger to his lips.

I opened my mouth to protest, and then I heard it. At first I told myself I was panicking, but one glance at Max's ashen face told me he could hear it too. It was a sound laden with muted, repeated nightmares; and a sound I had grown to equate with nothing but carnage and blood. *It was the sound of the Flavium, filling with people.*

My mind filled with images I thought I'd buried, bloodied images of limbs strewn all over the Flavium amphitheatre. And suddenly I could smell and taste the dusty air as vividly as though I was standing inside the arena itself.

Cassius couldn't have resurrected the Games so swiftly, could he?

My head started to race, finding a million different reasons why the torturous arena couldn't possibly be in use again, and yet with Cassius in control it could explain so much. The absence of the Prolets, perhaps the absence of the strix, and the curious excitement on Rajid's face as he stared at us.

Was he the only one to have escaped?

I thought of the miscellany of people and creatures I'd first encountered in the Prolet commercial world, and my stomach dived. It was Octavia's genetic rubbish dump, filled with the most curious mix of creatures, people and rejected genetic experiments. And yet, they were a people who had stolen my heart with kindness and intelligence. My head suddenly filled with Unus's great pudgy face, and I struggled for breath momentarily.

Max whistled softly under his breath, still looking a little pale.

'So that's his game is it?' he muttered, striding over to the dirty rope ladder in the corner.

'How far does this contraption reach then?'

Rajid held his finger to his lips again.

'Keep your voices low. The ventilation tunnel runs the entire length of Isca Pantheon. Basilisk have an acute sense of hearing and I, for one, have no wish to meet our hungry friends again.'

I nodded, and forced my legs across the low cavern to join Max. The entrance to the chimney was no more than half a metre square, and went up much further than the bat lanterns would show.

'But first we rest!' Rajid announced jovially, almost as though we were waiting for a party. It was maddening.

I looked at Max uncertainly.

We hadn't stopped since leaving Isca, but how could we even think about sleeping now?

'The celebratory Ludi Games are this evening, and Aelia will be there,' Rajid added as a rider, before settling down on his sackcloth bed. 'Which beats her current position inside a fortified Flavium cell, guarded by a battalion of guards and molossers, in case you were wondering ... Now rest. You'll need all your strength and wits before this day is done.'

I could tell he was serious.

'What about Lake?'

A silence pervaded the room.

***

It was several hours later that we were shaken awake.

'Is it time?' I asked groggily.

Sleep had come unexpectedly, and the uneven floor had somehow wedged Max and I closely together, our exhausted arms strewn loosely over one another. It wasn't the first time, but a new frost had crept in since watching the projected image of August, and we detached ourselves awkwardly.

'Nearly, yes. But first I show you something. Something to help you understand.'

I nodded at the wiry, inked man and wondered how it had come to this: standing with the last Prolet to escape detection, and having to trust everything he said.

Two minutes later we were travelling along a tunnel adjacent to Rajid's hideout, that smelled suspiciously like another latrine drain. The narrow rocky path, built on a gradual gradient, stretched on for what seemed like for ever and I thanked the distant stars for whatever luck was holing up the strix, however temporarily. Finally, the tunnel forked and Rajid walked towards another worn ladder clinging to the mouldy walls.

'Does that thing even work?' Max asked suspiciously.

Rajid grinned. 'Maybe … and maybe there's only one way to find out!'

He stepped forward and scurried up the ladder as swiftly as though he were a squirrel monkey, barely pausing when he reached a small hole at the top.

'Just like home?' I muttered, glancing at Max.

'I'll go first,' I added, before I could change my mind.

I scrambled up as quickly as I dared and pulled myself into

the black box at the top. There wasn't much room, and I fought my instincts as Max's athletic bulk squeezed in beside me, pushing me up tight against Rajid.

'Not all that keen on sardines, mate!' Max grumbled, just as a vertical shaft of light pulled our gaze through a tiny window into a bright, sterile world.

We were crammed into a metal unit no bigger than Jas's bed.

Silently, Rajid slid the thin door back, extending the vertical shaft into a fully open window. For a moment we stared in blank confusion at the grey sterile units and sinister-looking equipment. And then I realized. I sucked in a hoarse breath and shrank back against the metallic back wall of the unit. We'd climbed right into the heart of the scientific laboratories!

I scanned the room. There was no one around but it had to be noon at least. Was it a trick? Surely it was the worst time of day to come here? I turned, eyeballing Rajid furiously.

'Hey, ease up on the wildcat … Pantheonites take a siesta on Ludi,' Rajid crooned. 'It's a day of celebration, for them.'

'Let's get this over with then,' Max said, pushing through and out of the unit so he could stretch his cramped limbs.

'The cameras?' I hissed, reaching out to pull him back.

'No surveillance in siesta,' Rajid responded, climbing out languidly. 'No one to man them.'

I stared at him. His skin glistened under the bright lights, but it didn't make much sense for him to lie. Much.

I forced my legs out and stood up, grateful to be out of the dark tunnels and cramped space, even if the trade-off was standing in Pantheon's macabre experimental heart.

Rajid gesticulated towards a shimmering screen in front of an exit door. I recalled the last time I'd encountered one, and August's amusement.

'It's an infection screen, perfectly harmless … unless you're a virus or bacteria.'

It was just after he kissed me, to protect me from Cassius, he said. I stiffened at the memory. At the time I'd believed it all an act, and now? Who knew? Perhaps he didn't even know himself.

Rajid took the lead, stepping through the fluid, gelatinous screen, and I followed. It was just as I remembered, an ice-cold mist of adrenaline, barely perceptible to the eye yet capable of setting every nerve ending haring. I gasped at the sudden tingling across my skin, and then once again when I opened my eyes. It was just as my nightmares painted it. The laboratory stretching away up towards a distant domed ceiling, with every space between filled with scientific tanks and suspended cages.

I looked around, and memories of the manticore scattering molossus hounds as easily as skimming stones reached back through the formaldehyde-thick space.

Max pulled his forest tunic up over his nose. 'This place smells like a three-day-old breakfast.'

A bubble of hysteria crept up my throat and I forced it back down. Now was not the time to lose it. Rajid scurried over to a large container on the right-hand wall. And, within a breath, he'd scaled the side and was climbing the wall of the laboratory, using the containers and tanks as foot and hand holds.

'Third floor, move!' he hissed back at us.

I frowned and sprinted after him, recalling the floating walkways August had activated. Pantheonite birthright bought so much privilege in this distorted, hierarchical world. Within seconds we were all scurrying up the wall as though we were spiders created there.

Rajid set a good pace, and paused only when he reached a door set into the wall about a third of the way up. It bore the outline of a white figure overlaid with a bold black cross.

'Recombinant DNA: Transgenic and Molecular Species Unit. Classified personnel only,' I read, before staring suspiciously at the flashing red box beside the door.

Rajid reached out and typed a series of digits so swiftly I couldn't follow.

'How?' Max began, only to be silenced as the door slid open revealing a sterile laboratory stretching out like a new labyrinth.

I stared down the parallel banks of bleeping tanks and cages, and felt the fear I'd been suppressing start to leak through my veins. It was hard to stay detached when Pantheon's regard for life was so oppressively clear. It was a possession to be assaulted, manipulated and erased, all according to the whim of one man.

Rajid started forward first, his wiry form stalking down through the technology while Max and I followed, unable to drag our eyes from Pantheon's obsessive game of genetic roulette.

'There are no rules,' I muttered after I'd passed a few tanks.

I'd been trying to assess the small rodents objectively, to work out Cassius's key experimental aim and as far as I could see, each group were differentiated by some small physical abnormality. Some had clearly shaped animal limbs protruding through their skin; while others simply looked like smaller, unhealthier examples of their species.

There were rats with tiny tapering horns extending from their foreheads; mice that jumped around the tank floor like frogs; and a cage full of cats with ears and noses that glowed every time they passed under an ultraviolet lamp.

So far, it looked the trophy wall of a madman.

'Cells have been modified with a gene that produces coral fluorescent proteins. It's a tracker trial,' Rajid offered, watching me.

Hazily, I recalled the fluorescent animal I'd spotted many months before in the genetic rubbish heap of the Prolet world. Had it been rejected for possessing a faulty tracker system? All at once I felt new empathy for these feline creations; cats were natural trackers in the outside forest.

We passed through an aviary infection screen into the primate section, and I deliberately avoided their gaze. These bigger animals were harder to pass by. Every type of small and large monkey was housed here, and although dozens of eyes swung our way, not one natural sound broke the ominous silence.

I glanced at Max, knowing he was feeling the same silent rage that we were powerless, just now, to help them.

At last Rajid drew to a halt in a corner housing a waist-height glass cage fortified with thick steel bars. I stepped up next to him, unsure whether to be anxious or relieved, and looked down warily.

A small creature looked back up at me, and for a moment I struggled to identify it – and then I understood. I wasn't meant to.

'It has at least two sets of genetically different cells,' Rajid whispered. 'One type of animal cell is fused with the eggs of another … or maybe more.'

'It's named after the …

'Chimera,' I finished, the word clinging to the air, as though it knew it belonged here.

I looked into Rajid's schooled face, which was as unreadable as ever.

'An ancient creature from mythology – comprising a fire-breathing lion, with a goat's body and the tail of a serpent,' I finished quietly.

I pressed my fingers into my leather rations bag containing Aelia's torn page from the Book of Arafel. Could it be a coincidence? Or was this part of what Aelia had been trying to tell me? To warn me?

'Perfect,' Rajid muttered, with a curious smile.

I gazed down at the pensive little creature sitting in the corner of its tank. With the head of a small ape, the body of what looked to be a wild leopard and thick tail of a salamander, it was a jarring sight. I swallowed. It was still a living creature, I told myself, though not a creature of any natural design. Max stepped up beside me.

'For the love of Arafel, is that thing real?'

As if it heard, the fluffy black-faced creature released a whining

148

cry before bounding around the reinforced tank. For a second it almost looked endearing, and then Max whistled softly, the way he might call one of the village dogs in Arafel. The animal paused in wonder, before looking up and slowly pulling back its tiny black lips to display a complete set of full-sized ugly canines. In a second burst of energy, it flew at Max's hovering fingers, impacting the tank lid with some force and releasing a stream of fresh, oozing saliva in a fit of rabid fury.

Max snatched his hand away, despite the solid glass walls; just like Octavia's piranha monkeys, nothing in this place was ever what it seemed. I glanced at Rajid, who was watching silently.

'Intelligence, speed, strength,' Max observed. 'It's a clever combination.'

'It's a travesty!' I snapped. 'It's the most unnatural ... creature I've ever set eyes on.'

'And yet, the ancient Greeks and Romans thought up far worse.' Rajid's eyes glittered.

'*Thought* up far worse,' I defended, 'but the chimera of mythology never really drew breath ...'

Did it?

I was pretty sure I hadn't spoken my doubt aloud as my head started to pound, recalling snatches of Aelia and August's Voynich revelations. I'd just about accepted that creatures of mythology had once graced the earth, but a chimera? Surely that wasn't even biologically possible?

Rajid stared at me, before leaning in so closely I could see his inked Cerberus pulsing with aortic blood.

'The Voynich,' he breathed. 'Aelia knows its oldest secret.'

'What secret? What else does the Voynich hide?' I rattled back, beads of cold sweat breaking out across the back of my neck. My head felt woolly. Surely medieval coding for mythological creatures was enough of a secret for anyone?

Rajid shook his head.

'Cassius and Thomas, your ancestor, stumbled across something else buried deep within the text of the Voynich. A legendary curse, so old even Octavia didn't know of its existence,' he whispered excitedly. 'So, when Thomas worked out the cipher and ran, he also took the medieval coding for a legend that only he and Cassius had shared. Then, of course, he went on to hide his research in the—'

'The time! Rajid!' I interrupted, preventing him from divulging the Book of Arafel's secret.

My brain rattled. Could the Voynich be hiding something more? His new revelation made so much sense. Cassius's fury, his interest in the young Prolet insurgents and Aelia's hastily torn-out note.

Rajid nodded, his panther eyes narrowing. I glanced at Max, feeling like I was sliding down a mountain of ice, towards an inevitability.

Cassius knew, Aelia knew, Rajid knew.

And yet I was carrying Arafel's responsibility alone. How did it make any logical sense, not to balance the circle of knowledge out? I clenched my fists; if only Grandpa hadn't made me promise, things would be so much easier.

'Is this a ... chimera laboratory then?' Max asked, turning to stare into the endless cages and tanks around us.

'Something like that,' Rajid responded, his voice suddenly whimsical again, 'but with Cassius, you can never be sure you have seen the whole.'

Silence hung in the sterile corridor, chased swiftly by a shrill bleeping noise.

'We need to go,' I urged.

I shot a look at Max, the air bleeding with new tension.

'Fifteen minutes,' Rajid confirmed with an odd smile. 'Just time for one last thing ...'

He spun on his heel and slipped through to an inner room that was darker than the rest, holding the door open after him.

'Fourteen and a half?' he updated, patiently.

We dived into the inner room without uttering a word. And as soon as Rajid closed the door, it closed in like a giant clamp. The room was too cocooned, too warm and cloaked in a darkness that had nothing to do with the lack of light. I shivered despite the clammy temperature. There was a feeling in this room that was different from the rest. It was malevolent and knowing, almost as though it had a consciousness of its own.

I swung my gaze around, trying to work out why Rajid had dragged us in here despite the risk of being caught. The room was huge and lined with banks of tanks; attached to yet more whirring, flashing technology. An intermittent red light flashing above a third tier of long screens caught my attention. It was lit with familiar images.

As I stared, pieces of an ancient puzzle materialized and connected before my eyes. There were cryptic words in faded writing, alongside columns of letters that were merging and changing all the time. Cold fear spidered from my neck to my toes, as I recognized the ancient nonsense script from Thomas's research. It was text from the Voynich Manuscript.

'This is Voynich work. The computers … they're trying to work out Thomas's cipher,' I hissed.

'That among other things,' Rajid responded cryptically. 'Not that he's managed it. At least not yet. He needs more … information.'

Rajid was scrutinizing me with such intensity, I could feel my cheeks starting to burn.

I longed to challenge him there and then.

But there was Max to consider. I dropped my eyes in frustration, thinking of the carefully drawn-out cipher I'd stored with the Book of Arafel; the Book Aelia had stolen from Arafel. Did Cassius have it by now? He had the cipher, but surely he still needed the keyword to make it work.

'Why are we here, Rajid?' Max demanded, peering into one of the medium-sized tanks intently.

I gritted my teeth. We had to be approaching ten minutes. Why didn't he just say it, instead of being so mysterious-painted-man all the time?

'OK, this has gone on long enough, Rajid!' I rounded on him. 'Why don't you just tell …'

'Tal, come here!'

The alarm in Max's voice stopped me mid-track. And as I stepped towards him, to stare through the darkened glass, I felt my world slip sideways. This was it, the moment Rajid had been leading up to – the raw reality he couldn't explain and needed us to see. I inhaled deeply, trying to think straight, but it felt as though someone was driving a miniature spoke between every individual nerve.

Then the air was broken by another shriller alarm, and this time Rajid nodded.

Without hesitation, we bolted from the room and past the chimera tank. It looked up, only mildly distracted from its foraging, and the eerie hush seemed almost ironic. How could a Biotechnology Programme with the potential to reap such a devastating effect, be so quiet? I wanted to scream.

Rajid was fast. But Max and I were Arafel tree-runners. We sprinted back to the entrance, and descended swiftly into the heart of the laboratory. The whole area was gradually illuminating, and nausea rose in my throat as we sprinted towards the side laboratory. We couldn't be caught here, not again.

I hardly dared breathe as we dived through the infection screen and towards the grey, metal unit. This time, the confined space didn't even register, and I was inside and sliding back down the frayed rope ladder before Rajid had finished pulling the metal door across.

The faint, low voice of a Pantheonite filtered through the air, and although the rock floor beneath my feet was hard and reassuring, I was filled with a sickening suspicion that I'd glimpsed the eye of a new storm. And it was right above my head.

'Hey … you OK?' Max's whisper reached through my haze.

Impulsively I reached up and hugged him. He froze for a second, still not quite sure if he was ready to let our recent conflict go, and then he wrapped me up in the tightest, warmest embrace.

Somatic-cell nuclear transfer.

The words blew around my head like poppy seeds on a breeze. They hadn't meant much until I'd looked into the tank, and seen the tiny curled-up semi-gelatinous creature, still attached to an umbilical cord. And then the scientific words had slowly drained of their mystery. There had been a clipboard hanging next to it, filled with notes and ticks and scribbles. But the topmost line had been clear enough.

Voynich Genome Trial A: Gene characteristic isolated: Independent choice 2209 01/12

Pantheon had progressed from a vaccine that suppressed free will, to identifying and removing the gene altogether. And the most frightening part of all had been the endless rows of identical tanks stretching as far as the eye could see – in a room that looked nearly the size of Arafel.

August's words echoed through my head: '*My original DNA was enhanced with Octavia's signature coding – plus a little cocktail of two-thousand-year-old Roman DNA – and* non vos! *A new Equite was born.*'

But this wasn't as simple as enhancing existing DNA. This was creating whole new underclass designed to do just one thing: Cassius's bidding.

I closed my eyes. If Cassius was capable of producing an ever-ready army of obedient Prolets, their lives would bear even less value than they did already.

Max's arms tightened, the implications of what we'd just seen beginning to register.

'I don't need to know the science to understand the aim,' he muttered into my hair. 'We'll find Aelia and put a stop to this. Once and for all.'

153

Rajid cleared his throat pointedly. 'Touching though this moment is, we need to move. These tunnels are checked periodically, and Ludi is our last chance to rescue Aelia.'

***

We waited in Rajid's depressing cell until he said it was time. Sliding down on the threadbare blanket, I tried not to stare suspiciously at the eccentric man who'd somehow managed to evade the entire Pantheonite guard, while the rest of his hardworking population had been incarcerated.

'*Just what is it that makes you so special?*'

His words still haunted me, and I longed to demand what he meant, but it was impossible with Max around.

Rajid withdrew his white-handled curved blade from a dirty old waistcoat, and began sharpening it on a small piece of quartz. The sound was both unnerving and comforting, reminding me a little of the sound of the treehouse building in Arafel. Only in Arafel, there were always so many other more familiar village noises too: builders hammering, chickens clucking, lemurs calling to one another and the forest, always whispering.

Here though, it was the only sound in a small space, and it reverberated around the room like a saw.

'Why didn't you just tell us?' Max quizzed angrily. 'Why go to all the effort of actually taking us to the laboratories?'

'Would you have believed it … just so?' Rajid returned, his head crooked to one side.

He had a point.

'How could such a thing even be possible?' I asked after a beat. 'Surely genetics relates to physical characteristics, not will or choice.'

'Not necessarily,' he responded, not even looking up from his rhythmic paring. 'Genetic research has linked genes with key behaviours for many years. The first trials were with Prolet animal species, with varying degrees of success. But the genetic modifications hinder speech as well as free will, which made testing difficult.'

My thoughts flew to gentle, kind Pan and I knew in a breath he was one of those same creatures, born to fulfil a duty to Pantheon. No wonder he'd always appeared so bound and faithful to Lake, Pantheon had created him without a will of his own to choose.

What effort had it taken for him to accompany Lake in the escape from Pantheon?

And his sacrifice in Isca Prolet – had it been a final act of servitude or an escape? An uncomfortable silence descended.

'Why do you carry the mark of the Cerberus?' I ventured after a few minutes, watching his blade glint every time he ran it against the stone.

'Cerberus is the Hound of Hades, the offspring of two monsters,' he returned slowly. 'He watches at the gates, neither in nor out of Hades. And he guards with eyes that flash, like sparks from a blacksmith's forge. All who pass into Hades are welcome, but those who try to escape, Cerberus tears limb from limb.'

I stared as Rajid continued sharpening his blade, waiting for some kind of conclusion. There was none. Max raised his eyebrows.

'A friendly critter then,' he muttered, after a beat.

Chapter 13

'And now we take one of these,' Rajid instructed, as though we were learning to weave our first willow ladder.

He pressed a filthy yellow jar, suspended on a piece of thin string, into my hand. I swallowed as the creatures inside shuffled around, but I was grateful. It was substantially later, and every now and then a faint roar reached through the walls.

It was quietly terrifying.

'Ludi,' Rajid pronounced, as though it was the answer to life itself.

'OK, which means what exactly?' Max asked with a deep breath.

Rajid threw him a look of disdain. 'Ludi Pantheonares, like the infamous Ludi Apollinares. Held by the ancients in honour of the God Apollo!'

Rajid stepped up closer to Max, his face a curious mix of revulsion and excitement.

'The legend claims that during their first celebratory Ludi Games, the Romans were invaded. They took up their arms, released a deadly barrage of arrows upon their enemy, and then returned, victorious and undeterred, to their sport.'

I couldn't tell whether Rajid was intending to horrify or entertain.

Max scowled, holding his lantern up high so we could inspect the exit tunnel.

'Which only proves,' he scathed, 'that the Romans were a barbaric lot I wouldn't share my breakfast with any day of the week!'

I held my tongue. He was talking about one Roman in particular, of course. And I didn't know what I thought of him any more. Except he'd deserted everyone when they needed him most.

I forced myself across the dirt floor to the ventilation chimney and gazed upwards. My nerve evaporated instantly. It was endless. Max levelled a look of real concern in my direction, but there wasn't time for discussion. The plan was an ambush when Aelia was brought out of the Flavium dungeons. And the best observation point, Rajid swore, was only accessible via the tunnel.

'I show you Ludi, so you understand the game we play, huh?' His top lip curled as though he were enjoying a private joke.

'Why don't you wait here? Let me go with Rajid, scope it out?' Max offered.

I took one look at our unlikely guide, his Hades tale still echoing in my ears, and shook my head. We needed to stick together, and once we were close enough, take our chance.

Securing my jar to my leather rations bag, I reached out for the first rung of the ladder.

'Hanging around is for sloths!' I threw, before forcing myself up into the narrow gloom.

The climb was as claustrophobic as I anticipated, and if it wasn't for Max's steady pace behind me, I may well have given in to the storm brewing inside within the first few seconds. I tried to fade out my surroundings, to imagine I was shinnying up the Great Oak at the edge of the forest with nothing but wide-open space around me. *Hand over hand, foot after foot.* It was an exercise in sheer grit over instinct. And when at last the confined air chimney opened out onto a wider rectangular space, I crawled out with a sob of real gratitude.

For a few moments, I lay with my cheek on the dusty stone floor, filling my grateful lungs with fresher air, and waiting for Max and Rajid to emerge. Then I summoned the courage to lift my head and look round. And any fragile hopes spiralled away.

We were stuck in yet another stone box, just big enough to sit up in and lie out at a full stretch. I swung my gaze around the new confining walls, fighting a real wave of suffocating anxiety.

How could this be a good observation point for anything, let alone rescuing Aelia?

I shot a look at Rajid, sitting cross-legged and apparently unaffected. His face looked sallow in the low light, and as the ugliest suspicion began to rise like a monster from the depths of my mind, the long wall opposite broke into a series of vertical slats, each about a metre long. They moved in unison, letting in an unmistakable chorus of Pantheonite cheering. I froze as the sudden baying and flickering arena lights engulfed the small chamber. The effect was dazzling and disorientating.

As I tried to peer closer, a vice-like grip closed around my shoulder.

'Watch … like the Cerberus,' Rajid hissed.

I scowled and shrugged him off. We'd come here for Lake, Aelia and the Book of Arafel, but there were turning out to be so many more reasons to be wary of Isca Pantheon. Pan's gentle smile flickered through my head, together with his last words 'Prot-ect Lake'. The fire in my belly flared. I was going to do everything I could to make his sacrifice worthwhile.

We waited, the air thick with tension, until the air vents swung open again. And this time they stayed open for longer. I drank my fill of the new view, and tried to control my racing pulse. Rajid's wormhole had somehow bypassed the Prolet commercial trading world, and brought us right up inside one of the stone archways encircling Octavia's Flavium.

Now I was seated directly above one of the dark entrances I'd once faced as a combatant. But our narrow, elongated view couldn't be more different from the one I remembered. Another thunderous cheer filled the air before the ventilation slats closed, and I shot a look of angry bewilderment at Rajid. He shrugged almost sheepishly. He was clear he needed us to see it, that there were few words to describe the challenge Cassius had designed for his pleasure.

I dragged my gaze back to the floor, and our new enemy. The dusty Flavium floor was now completely concealed by a huge, black, grilled cage, that rose as high as the topmost tiered seating. I guessed instantly that those forced to enter weren't average laboratory rats.

'Prolets?' I whispered.

Rajid nodded, his eyes clouding, and for the first time I was doubtful. Anyone would close down emotionally under these circumstances. Was this how he'd survived, by detaching himself? Had I been reading the symptoms rather than the condition?

Silently, I wondered how many of his Prolet friends he'd watched succumb to Cassius's warped interpretation of the ancient Roman's Ludi Games.

'Strix?' I muttered next, the reason for their absence from the tunnels suddenly becoming crystal clear. The word hung in the box-room, like the stench they created.

He nodded again, his lips tightening.

'But the Prolets are his workforce!' I protested.

It made no sense from a practical viewpoint for Cassius to kill off his underclass, no matter how furious he was.

'He believes they know where the young ones are.' Rajid scowled. 'And has sworn to send one Prolet a day into the Ludi Labyrinth until one of them … sees sense.'

'But they can't possibly know!' Max added. 'There's a network of tunnels beneath the Dead City. It will have taken the young Prolets days, if not weeks, of wandering before they found the old baths …'

'For the love of Arafel, why?! Why are the young ones so

important,' I interjected, 'that he would sacrifice the lives of the older Prolets? It doesn't make any sense!'

I shot Max a warning glance. I wasn't comfortable with anyone knowing where the young ones were hiding, let alone crazy Rajid.

Rajid only stared at me, but he might as well have spoken aloud. The penny dropped, and this one fell with the toll of a smelting hammer.

The semi-gelatinous creature suspended at the end of an umbilical cord was as clear as if I was staring straight at it, and I knew. Of course, I knew. Cassius's existing workforce was disposable, because he was creating his own. He was cloning a Prolet underclass that would ask no questions, desire no life beyond what they were given, and work until they day they dropped. If he succeeded, Prolet life would be entirely meaningless. And expendable.

And yet, there was still a problem.

'But if he can replace them,' I muttered, suddenly recalling Atticus's great satisfaction in chewing off a raw rat ear, 'why are the children important at all?'

My question was drowned as the air vents groaned open again, releasing a fresh burst of noise into our small space. I stared out, feeling my spirits spiral further away. This time I could see smart Pantheonites milling around the arena as comfortably as though they were attending an auction on market day.

A flame of revulsion flickered inside. Had they learned nothing? Did it take so little time for the new Senate to disintegrate, and for Octavia's programme to reverse? August's face flashed through my head. *Or had the will never been there to begin with?*

Just then, the centre of the cage began to move.

'What's happening?' I whispered, feeling sick with apprehension.

And then I saw her. It was only her side profile, but I would know her elfin features and athletic limbs anywhere.

'Aelia!' I whispered in horror.

She was standing tall and proud, but her face was covered in dark bruises and she looked as though she hadn't slept in days. Worse than that, she was also incarcerated within a tight wire mesh ball, and was being slowly pulled up through the centre of the dense cage itself.

'You said we could ambush from here!' I seethed. 'But how do we get to her from there?'

Rajid leaned forward, his face contorted, beads of sweat breaking out across his forehead.

'Give it time.' He smiled. 'If she survives, she'll be given a pardon and taken to the Prolet garrison. I know a shortcut and then we make our move ... like the Cerberus.'

He growled softly as if to enforce his point, and I shot a look at Max. Was it me?

'It's the dawn of a new Roman era, or as Cassius calls it,' he continued in a conspiratorial whisper, 'the era of the black aquila.'

'Black aquila?' Max repeated, his ears pricking up. 'Black eagle?'

I knew exactly which direction his mind was taking. It was rewinding back to the moment the dark shadow had carried Lake away into the gunmetal sky.

'Rajid, what exactly did Aelia work out about the Voynich?' I demanded, painfully aware of her white pallor in the arena torch-light.

Just what is it that makes you so special?

His question seemed to echo between us as he stared.

'I don't know all the details,' he offered at last, 'but when August left, Cassius took over a wing of the laboratory, installing six of his most loyal Scientific Generals. There were whispers of new experiments. The Prolet gene-isolation work, and of course the ...'

'Chimera project?' I filled in, with a sense of impending doom.

He nodded, and stared back out at the Flavium arena, which was filled with milling people.

The thought that Cassius could actually be trying to genetically

161

engineer the mythical creature in the same way as the molossers, haga, manticore and strix, stretched even his murky boundaries.

I recalled a pencil etching of a fire-breathing hybrid monster from Grandpa's book of ancient mythology. How could such a creature even be capable of biological life in the first instance, and could there be anything in its supposed omen for disaster? It sounded like pure fantasy, and yet Pantheon had breathed life into so many already.

'You saw the experiment in the laboratory. But that's only the tiny tip of the iceberg,' he continued suddenly. 'Aelia spotted a reference in a small section of Thomas's research to a near-forgotten legend. It was cryptic, but Aelia being Aelia, well ... y'know.'

I nodded. Of course, I could believe anything of the small, feisty doctor.

'She always believed Thomas knew more and that, buried somewhere in the text of the Voynich, there was coded information about the legendary chimera beast ... with unknown speed, strength and agility.'

He paused to flex his fingers, eyeing me intensely.

'She believes it is a forgotten top predator,' he continued after a beat. 'One that would naturally rule the biological world. And that Cassius has known of its coded existence within the pages of the Voynich for a long time. Of course, without Thomas's cipher and the elusive keyword, he cannot perfect his trials. But that hasn't stopped his experiments.'

He paused to smile crookedly, his teeth even more jaundiced in the patchy light.

I recalled the flickering computer screens in the laboratory, and then the ripped page from the Book of Arafel stuffed into my leather rations bag.

'Which explains why Aelia took the Book of Arafel,' Max interjected.

I whipped around, my heart pounding.

162

'Thomas's research would give Cassius the coding information he needs to re-create this beast accurately,' he continued in a low voice. 'So, taking the Book would have two neat outcomes: it would bring you to Pantheon and give her real power to negotiate for the Prolet insurgents.'

I stared at Max's shadowed face. *He knew.* He shouldn't – Grandpa had stipulated no one should know. I was a complete failure, but I couldn't deny the relief flooding my veins all the same.

'How?' I whispered, though it was more confirmation than a question.

I imagined Grandpa's disappointment reaching out across our separation and scowled at my feet, trying to order my thoughts.

'I've known for a long while, Tal,' he answered with a curious, sad smile, 'and you never told me, no matter how much pressure I put on you. I guessed something was up, when Octavia made such a fuss over the Book. Then you hid it when we got back to Arafel, and it all slotted into place. I hoped you were going to trust me without all this. And before you think it, your grandpa wouldn't be disappointed. I've seen how far you'll go to protect Arafel. There is no doubt you were born to this … Old George would be proud.'

The honesty of his simple words burrowed into my chest with the speed of a hummingbird. He still had the power to undo me, even when I'd made up my mind I wasn't any good for him. I wasn't so sure Grandpa would be proud, but I was grateful for his conviction anyway.

I nodded, my eyes prickling with sudden heat, just as a triumphant blast split the air.

Our collective gaze shot back to the air vents, which were grinding open again enabling a new view of a slight figure dressed head to foot in purple Pantheonite regalia, a gold-edged cape draped from her left shoulder. She was making her way down the central aisle to rapturous applause, only pausing at

163

the bottom to smooth her raven-black hair, pulled back into a tight bun.

I felt my skin grow cold. She looked no older than me, but she had to be the wicked witch of Rome Aelia had mentioned. Livia? She sneered sharply, and I felt the twist inside my cramped limbs. How did they always know exactly how to screw up their faces? Cassius's gloating features leered at me from the recesses of my mind. I scowled. I should have let Unus finish him. He was worse than a monster, because he paraded himself as a hero, when nothing could be further from the truth.

Livia reached the central balcony, a more lavish, ornate structure than the one I'd scaled when Octavia was in charge, and threw her arms skywards as a huge, black haga-aquila dived from the full height of the domed ceiling.

There was a rush of excitement, swallowed by a thundering swoosh as it skimmed across the labyrinth, before gliding in beside her to perch on the balcony. It screeched loudly as it came to a flapping standstill, creating air ripples through the arena with its powerful, tapered wings. The crowd hushed, and I saw the whole balcony tremble beneath its powerful frame. It was clear this two-headed haga was bigger and sleeker than any of Octavia's creations. I stared suspiciously at its bright red flight feathers, and golden eyes the size of oranges, which took me back to the City of Dust instantly. Back to the voluminous night, and the figure of a child hanging limply. Was this the black aquila Cassius had dispatched to bring Lake back?

Livia pulled a dead rabbit from her white Diasord belt, but before she had chance to offer it, the bird's closest rapier beak dived in, making short shrift of the treat with one resounding snap. It lifted its wing and preened, as Livia threw an indulgent smile at the crowd, but it was clear to see the bird was no pet. I swallowed hard. So much for aquila, this creature was some kind of hybrid cross between a haga and mythical phoenix fire-bird.

164

'More chimera trials?' I shot at Rajid, as Livia turned her attention back to the crowd.

'Friends, it is my very great delight to welcome you here today for Ludi Pantheonares, on behalf of your Director General: Cassius. And even though he is working through today's special Ludi holiday, he sends his best wishes for a victorious celebration!'

She paused to allow for fresh cheering. Her voice was smooth and young, but there was something else too. Octavia always let it be known she was enjoying every painful moment, but this new adversary wore a mask of detachment, which gave nothing away.

The crowd roared their approval.

'Ludi is a salute to the glory days of our ancestors – the finest civilization this world has ever known,' she continued as the cheering died away. Her dark eyes gleamed.

'They were glory days built on our ancient values of honour, valour and allegiance! And yet, even recently we were in danger of forgetting these values, of forgetting all we have worked so hard for ...' she paused to eyeball the crowd '... thanks to the dangerous rhetoric of Commander General Augustus Aquila!'

She gave an authoritative nod, as the large screens around the arena lit up. And I could only watch, my world hollowing out, as August's regal face flickered into view once more.

'Of course, at first we listened, as any great democracy must,' she continued, 'but after our great Civitas descended into chaos after *only three weeks*, it was clear his ideas were both radical and treasonable.'

Her voice rose, provoking the crowd into a chorus of booing and hissing. I bit my lip; friend or foe, August was being played to perfection.

'This is an inaugural moment,' he proclaimed proudly over the crowd's jeers, 'for every man and woman in Isca Pantheon to own ... a moment when divisive barriers are finally removed, and a new Civitas is born. A Civitas born out of our peace and progression. Progression towards an outside life!'

I stared at the hope in his face, at the way his eyes darkened to sea-ink whenever they were alive with passion. I'd nearly forgotten that.

The crowd fell silent as the screens flickered to two Prolet youths sitting astride a well-dressed Pantheonite. One pressed a butcher's knife to the victim's white throat as the second rifled through his pockets.

The pregnant hush continued as the image changed again to the Pantheon civic centre.

A single-storey market building was engulfed in smoke and flames, while a group of blurred figures stood around, watching.

The crowd booed, and the screen changed again.

This time there was a poorly dressed Prolet man and well-coiffured Pantheonite woman standing together in the shadows of a flickering street lamp. A moment later I realized that they weren't standing together at all. I flushed and stole a swift look at Max who was staring stoically ahead. They could have symbolized hope in such a fractured society, but the crowd were booing already.

'Friends … we know …' Livia held up her hands as though to appease '… the violence and debauchery knew no limits. And, in the end, even Augustus Aquila had to concede his notions were little better than distorted fairy tales; ideas that were born out of a type of fevered lunacy.'

The screen flickered again, and we were back with August.

'The early integration analysis indicates a common stress symptom among the Prolet class, which may be a reaction to the existing vaccine to suppress independent will. Of course, the recent rioting cannot be tolerated,' he repeated, his traitorous voice echoing from every corner of the arena. 'Because of this, and the new investigation required, I would recommend a temporary suspension of all new Prolet privileges and reinstatement of the existing Pantheonite system.'

'But, at least he saw sense before we were all murdered in our beds,' Livia concluded with a dead smile.

I stared down at my interlaced fingers, watching my white flesh turn red. Each time I heard him uttering those words, it got worse. It was quite clear the old August was gone, if he'd ever existed at all. And for the first time since Grandpa had died, I felt vulnerable. It didn't make any sense, but then none of it had ever made any sense. I'd only known him a few days and August had hijacked every rational thought, twisted my feelings into knots, and my dreams into nightmares. And now it was scorchingly clear it was all for nothing.

'These last few weeks have seen recommitment to all our ancient values of honour, valour and allegiance!' Livia picked up as the screen faded. 'Especially allegiance! Allegiance to Isca Pantheon, and to the honest, hard-working individuals within our Civitas.'

A fresh round of cheering ensued.

'So much for being an enlightened civilization!' Max whispered fiercely. 'I'll take bare feet and never knowing where the next meal is coming from, any time of the day.'

'Now, it has come to our attention, that there are still some ill-advised Prolets who believe it is better *out there*,' Livia began again, a sour smile staining her face. 'So, let me be absolutely clear one more time: the wilderness outside is hostile, dangerous and can barely sustain itself, let alone a burgeoning population.

'While the young insurgents remain outside, they are not only endangering themselves, they are also betraying our ancient values and investment. Expensive investment. Now Cassius is patient, but he will not tolerate wilful disrespect!'

A roar broke out again across the stands.

'Which is why each and every member of the Prolet community has been invited to come forward and make amends by doing one … simple … thing. To save the lives of their ill-advised younger compatriots by sharing their location. Disappointingly, not one has chosen to do so, so far. I'm not sure if it's the vaccine that is at fault or just plain insubordination.'

Her voice rose excitedly, and I suppressed a shudder. Why did power always fall into the hands of those least qualified to hold it?

'But, if they will not return the same respect we have always afforded them, Cassius asks we remind them of our ancient values: honour … valour … allegiance!'

The crowd's cheering grew wilder with each of her chants, and I shot a glance at Max, knowing he was trying not to think about the last time we too stood in the arena.

'Friends, it is the fourth day of our celebratory Ludi Pantheonares and time to bring our celebrations to an exciting conclusion. So today, I give you one of the generals of the discredited PFF and a criminal against the state: Dr Aelia Vulpes.'

Livia's tone was calm again, but her eyes glittered. In a breath, I was back in Octavia's personal experimentation room. I swallowed so hard it hurt. Octavia, Cassius, Livia – their enjoyment of other people's pain and torture was too real and close.

'Her crimes, and there are many, include inciting a rebellion against the Civitas of Isca Pantheon; encouraging insubordination among the lower ranks, and more recently, withholding classified information … highly prized classified information!'

'That information was not yours or the Director Generals to steal! It belonged to Arafel; it belonged to the Outsiders!'

Aelia's voice rang out strong and rebellious, and a fresh murmur broke out across the crowd.

'Silence!' Livia cut across in a tone that sliced the air like a Diasord. 'The Director General decides what is state property, as is the law in Isca Pantheon. Or do you wish to add defamation to your list of misdemeanours?'

All eyes were on Livia, the vein in her thin white neck pulsing visibly, and for a moment I could have been watching Octavia herself.

'The criminal has chosen the voided Cyclops as her champion,' she continued smoothly, 'but, as he has a clear advantage over most, we've levelled the playing ground, a little. This should make our Ludi Pantheonares one of the most exciting yet! So, without any further preamble, I declare this historic finale of the Games open. And may the luck of the gods go with you!'

There was a feverish cheer as the archway opposite filled with a huge ponderous shape, shuffling slowly into view. For a minute, I was blind, too stupid to process the possibility that it could actually be him. And then his silhouette tightened into focus, and every muscle in my throat clenched tight.

Unus?

But any brief feeling of euphoria was swiftly replaced; his one pudgy eye was completely blindfolded, and his plate-like feet were shackled by a thick, heavy chain, shortening his stride by more than half. I shuffled forward as far as I dared, unwilling to watch, unable to drag my eyes away.

This time the cheering was punctuated by heavy foot stamping, and baying. The combination was almost deafening. Aelia straightened her back, and lifted her hand to Unus, only to lower it again when she, too, spotted his blindfold. And as she did so, I noticed several dark horizontal welts staining the back of her tunic.

'I also have a little something else for you, friends, a treat to coincide with the revered Emperor Nero Claudius Germanicus's Feast Day!'

I scowled, watching Aelia barely acknowledge Livia. She was formidable; even when injured and incarcerated inside a spherical cage. But the truth was we were also incarcerated and powerless to help while we stayed in here. Where was the fair trial and justice? Where was Pantheon's honour and valour now? I was done watching.

'We have to do something, Rajid!' I fired at him. 'We can't just wait here until …'

But what I was about to say was lost to a raw nerve-jangling, grating sound. Aelia shot a panicked look around as the giant cage around her came to life; slowly shuddering, rising and expanding around her spherical ball until finally, it rested, monstrous in its metamorphosis. A tense silence hung on the air as we stared straight into a vision of hell. A labyrinth, complete with a maze of mesh passages big enough for Prolets. This wasn't just a cage for insurgents, this was the Game … This was Ludi. I stared, my blood growing cold.

'And lastly, because we always like to save the best surprise until the end,' Livia gloated, as though her final announcement was giving her untold pleasure. 'Please do extend a warm welcome to your surprise bonus entertainment this afternoon, straight from the poisoned wilderness and without invitation … feral Outsiders!'

I was conscious only of Max's gasp, of the floor splitting beneath us, and of clouds of suffocating dust filling my lungs. Then there was a deafening, blinding blanket of nothing – like a fist closing around my throat. And as the toothless grin of the Flavium reared up to greet us, I found myself thinking only three words.

We were back.

Chapter 14

I was grimly aware that I wasn't caught up in one of my nightmares, no matter how much I wished it. In my nightmares, I couldn't feel anything, no matter how hard I pinched or dug myself. But right now, as the slow burn of reality returned, my body was in agony. I blinked my streaming eyes to clear the dust, and as my vision slowly returned I tried to assimilate the broken scene. There was a wide trapdoor clinging to one fragile hinge above me, scattered stone cladding all around, and the soft groan of pain.

Max! I shot a look across the floor, and tried to form his name. He was just a couple of metres away, crumpled up. The colour of dust. I opened my mouth, but only a feeble croak came out. We were surrounded, in the arena of death, with thousands of Pantheonite faces watching.

And then I spied Rajid, or rather parts of Rajid as the bulk of his body was concealed beneath a pile of heavy debris. Was he dead? Did it even matter? He had betrayed us. Hadn't he? I was vaguely aware of Max's hoarse whisper somewhere, and then it started.

It sounded like baying at first, but as my ears gradually adjusted, I realized it was a word.

171

'Maze! Maze! Maze!'

I tried to pull myself up, but it felt as though I'd drunk too much elderflower wine at harvest. Everything was slow and stupid. And then we were surrounded by a blaze of crimson, and stamping heavy boots that merged like the trees when I was running. Except I was lying stock still.

Large, rough hands clamped beneath my arms, and dragged me to my feet. They were hazy figures, shadowed by a blurred pack of muscular creatures standing shoulder-high. I struggled, sinking my teeth into a shoulder, and had the satisfaction of hearing a muttered Latin curse before the room finally shrank into focus.

Max and I were in front of the Ludi Labyrinth, which looked even bigger from the ground, surrounded by an arena full of livid, chanting faces. Livia's personal guard and a pack of the ugliest molossus hounds surrounded us in a tight formation, while Aelia stared down from above it all, an expression of shocked disbelief pinned to her face.

Disorientated, I jerked my aching head around. On the far side, beneath an archway engraved *L11* and surrounded by another pack of guards and molossus hounds, was my beloved Unus. Silent and completely ignorant to our arrival. My heart strained as I watched his great head jerk from side to side, bewildered by all the fresh commotion.

'You're a little late, but you always knew how to make an entrance!' Aelia yelled. Now I was closer, I could see her sunken eyes gleamed from hollow blue-black sockets. And my heart ached harder.

'*Silentium!*'

Livia's caustic tone reached above the roar of the crowd, and this time everyone hushed.

The guards backed off, leaving only Aelia, Max and I in the arena spotlight. The air was laced with raw anticipation, and my limbs tensed as though I was facing the biggest predator in the forest. And then, finally, I saw them. The lost Prolets, staring through a fortified panel of dirty glass, running the entire circumference of the arena.

'Max,' I whispered, nodding towards the lower boundary of the Flavium.

His gaze followed mine, and I heard his sharp intake of breath as he too spotted their white faces, their genetic differences paling in the shadow of their despair. There were so many too, adults and children; their faces pressed up against the glass, their silence conveying a thousand hopeless stories.

'*Cassius has sworn to send one Prolet a day into the Ludi Labyrinth, until one of them sees sense.*'

Rajid's whispered words filled my throbbing head.

Just how many friends and family had they already watched die here?

'Friends,' Livia's voice came, freshly thickened with excitement. 'I promised you a treat to mark this special Feast Day. And here it is: toxic ... feral ... Outsiders.'

The words rolled off her tongue as though she were savouring us.

'And, providentially, the very same intruders responsible for the near collapse of our great Civitas. Cassius has ordered we show them exactly what we think of trespassers, especially those who hold our Civitas in such low esteem. They are to play Ludi Pantheonares!'

'No! They are innocent! I have chosen my champion; Unus must play!' Aelia yelled, kicking and punching the wire ball like a caged tiger.

'Oh but I concur, Unus must play ... alongside the intruders!' Livia responded, playing the crowd expertly.

She nodded once, abruptly, before Diasords were pushed against the small of our backs, forcing us towards a tall metal door in the cage. I stared upwards at the oppressive structure, which loomed like a giant mechanical spider, woken from its slumber. Then a loud whirring noise filled the air, and Aelia's ball began to descend directly into the centre, taking her with it.

'The floor, Tal! Watch the …' she yelled frantically just as she disappeared from sight. A heavy metal lid ground closed, sealing her inside the labyrinth, and reality flared. I balked, digging my heels into the same dust floor that had seen too much death and violence already.

I might be back in the Flavium, but I wasn't the same girl who'd faced Octavia. This was different. Grandpa was gone, the Book was gone, and I knew what I was up against. Pantheon had already stolen so much from me and from Arafel. I wasn't afraid any more.

'Where … is … it … Livia?' I fired, imagining each word was a tiny poisoned dart burying itself in her austere face.

From the corner of my eye I saw Unus start and turn in my direction, despite his blindfold. A fresh blaze of emotion threatened to choke me.

'Unus!' I yelled, 'it's me … Tal!'

A thick, sweaty hand clamped over my mouth as Livia levelled her piercing gaze at me.

'Talia, isn't it? I remember you. How nice of you to pay us this little visit so we can remind you about respect for the Civitas. And you brought your Neanderthal too! Oh, I don't think I know his name … or is he a pet?' She paused to laugh at her own joke as Max threw me look of abject disgust.

'Seriously?' he muttered, unimpressed.

I bit the hand over my mouth, earning a temporary reprieve.

'There is no respect here, only the iron fist of torture!' I yelled. 'How can you do this? To the people who keep Pantheon working? How can you blame them for wanting something more than … slavery?'

'Where are Lake and the Book, Livia?' Max added defiantly. 'We've already brought this Civitas to its knees once. Don't force us to do it again!'

I raised my eyes to look at the rugged man standing beside me, at his golden skin and the cleft in his chin, and felt a rush of sudden heat through my sore limbs. I was so damned proud of him it hurt.

All eyes swung back to Livia, whose schooled expression momentarily betrayed her ugly thoughts.

'*Ludere!*'

Her command left the guards in no doubt, and as the grilled door groaned open, thick black walls simultaneously rose from the floor creating a black, uninviting solid cube. We resisted as much as we could, but it was futile, and seconds later a final solid door rose from the floor, sealing us inside.

We were alone, in the darkness. And the breathing silence.

At first, I thought the darkness was part of the game, but then the ceiling flickered and lit up with bright screens revealing an excited, clamouring crowd.

'Of all the sick, twisted …' Max swore unsteadily.

I stared upwards at the hysteria. How could people who'd witnessed the slaughter of so many of their own, only a year ago, sit and watch this depraved entertainment dressed as some celebratory game?

A hollow breath escaped me as I swung my gaze around. We were stuck inside a long metal tunnel lined with thick black metal mesh.

'We've already brought this Civitas to its knees once?' I scorned, taking out my fear on Max. 'What comic book did you lift that from? Arafel's library only has a handful!'

'Well at least I focused on why we're here!' Max shot back. 'You were so busy trying to save the world you forgot we tried that once already. They've had their chance. Now it's about rescuing ourselves, before we can be any damned help to anyone else!'

I scowled as a loud booming noise ricocheted through the structure, making the walls shake.

'Unus!' I exclaimed, turning and sprinting down the passageway in his rough direction, just as the floor caved in beneath me.

'Max!' I screamed, jumping and clinging to one side of the wire mesh, as he mirrored my move on the opposite side. I spread my weight to spare my arms. This had to be what Aelia was yelling as she disappeared. Then I made the mistake of looking down.

And the view dried my mouth faster than the sun ever could. No wonder the tunnels beneath Pantheon had been so quiet. The giant strix were right here, barely a tree-jump away, staring up at us. And there were hundreds of them.

I'd never seen them properly before, only glimpsed their profiles while running from the echo of their hooked claws. But now they were no more than five metres below me. And they were far bigger and uglier than I'd ever imagined.

I sucked in a tight breath. Each giant rat-owl had to be at least two metres tall with thick, oily black feathers, and powerful calcified beaks as long as my forearm. Their streaked, yellow eyes fixed upon us from the depths of their stinking pen, as one of them tipped its angular beak to deliver a raucous shriek to the air. By the vociferous response, it looked as though they hadn't been fed in a while either.

My stomach convulsed. Cassius must have had them rounded up purposely for Ludi; no wonder the tunnels had been so empty.

Then the leader tipped its head back again, and this time its ravenous cry was filled with purpose. I shot a terrified glance at Max.

'Fly!' he muttered hoarsely.

I nodded and scrambled along the frame like a spider monkey, Max mirroring me on the opposite side. I was vaguely conscious of something whirring behind us, of my fear welling up like black floodwater and then we were past the pit and above solid floor again. Or so it seemed. Just as another skin-peeling, shuddering noise filled the air.

'Max! The centre!' I gasped, looking through a succession of layered metal corridors towards the centre of the labyrinth. At Aelia. She was imprisoned in her wire mesh ball, yelling and banging within a second sealed cage. But we couldn't hear a thing.

I tried to sight-read but my fingers were growing numb and my grasp weakening.

'Tal, jump! Jump down!' Max shouted, reading Aelia's fear just in time.

I closed my eyes and we both leapt as the metal grill lining the corridor sparked with an intense blue light. Then I was conscious of Aelia being swallowed up again as the walls around her darkened.

'We're coming, Aelia!' I yelled, kicking the wire mesh and watching it spit and crackle as the last of her wire ball disappeared. I lifted my hand towards a few strands of my hair, caught by the mesh in my hasty descent. They were blackened and broken.

'Electric?' I growled, watching the floor with suspicion.

We used something similar as part of the outside forest warning system, but I had a feeling the surge running through this mesh was far stronger. I forced my gaze ahead into the darkness, focusing on the surreal light pools created by the flickering ceiling screens. The floor looked solid enough, while the shrieking and clawing was growing ever louder behind us. I sucked in a breath. There was only one way of telling for sure.

'Let's do it! Now!'

Somehow my feet fell into a sprint down the dark metal corridor, chased by the ceiling screens as we ran. And every image was the same – smiling, laughing Pantheonites watching our every move, cheering as though we were just sport. *Blood sport*. The little apricot monkey incarcerated in the laboratory cage flickered through my head, and I swallowed the hot bile burning my throat. We were just laboratory animals to them. Live game to be used, and manipulated, as they chose. How did it feel to have so much expendable life at the fingertips? To play creator? I shook with anger. They still didn't understand what it meant to be feral.

I skidded to a halt at the end of the black mesh corridor. It was a dead end.

'It goes nowhere!' I yelled at Max, glancing back down the black tunnel.

An ominous grating noise reached out through the black. Max yanked out his crossbow and started attaching his hunting rope swiftly as I scanned the walls. The strix were cawing in excitement and the grating noise was getting louder. Was the floor moving? I got my answer all too soon as the silhouette of their huge, calcified bony beaks suddenly became visible above the murky floor line.

'Max, the floor is rising; they'll be free any moment,' I gasped, just as he released an arrow through a hole above our heads.

It landed with a clatter, and he pulled until it stuck tight. Then he grabbed me, and forced me to take the rope.

'It's a game, remember?' he urged grimly. 'They want a show. We just need to stay one step ahead. And right now, that means playing by Cassius's rules, right up until we find his weak spot.'

I nodded, adrenaline sating my veins as I pulled myself up the rope, hand over hand. Then, with a couple of swift kicks I was through, and the ceiling lit up with a roaring crowd. I grimaced. Clearly, not everyone found the hole in the ceiling.

Max pulled himself up behind me easily, and unhooked his arrow from the second-floor mesh wall.

'Told you it would come in useful,' he breathed.

I raised my eyebrows, before gazing around cautiously. We were in another black, uninviting tunnel, but the screeching noises beneath us were getting louder. The strix were loose in the corridor below.

'Think those things can climb?' I asked.

'Let's not hang around to find out,' he muttered.

Steeling myself, I slid a foot forward into the darkness, and thankfully the floor seemed solid enough. But we'd only trodden a few more steps when the air was consumed by a fresh metallic groaning, and everything started to shake.

'It's moving,' I yelled. 'It's all moving!'

So, I threw my arms out and grabbed the only static thing there: Max.

For a few moments we clung together as the metallic monster incarcerating us shed its skin and morphed into something new. Then the floor fell away from beneath our feet, and we tumbled down into a newly created tunnel. There wasn't time to yell as the ceiling followed us at an abrupt speed, forcing us to crawl like animals along a narrow, claustrophobic pipe. Hysteria started climbing my throat, just as Max's warm hand closed around my calf. *Reassuring, always just behind.* I steadied my breathing, consoling myself with the thought that at least the new tunnel was too small for the strix to squeeze through.

But it was also too far from Aelia, and there were tiny scurrying noises all around. I'd never been afraid of the creatures that crept and scurried in the forest, but this was not Arafel, and we were trapped inside a small cramped space. As if on cue, Max cursed, and jolted behind me.

'Bastard thing bit me!' he cursed through gritted teeth. 'Argh! And another … Tal, for the love of Arafel, move!'

I willed myself to crawl, ignoring the way my hands and thinly covered knees pressed into the large segmented abdomens and thick scurrying legs of whatever was sharing our confined space. They were big – there was no denying that – with strong wings that fanned open without warning, carrying their jellied underbodies directly into my face. I squeezed my eyes and mouth closed, denying the prickling horror that was stealing across my skin, and concentrated on moving. *Hand over hand, knee after knee.*

Several times, I felt their incisive pincers sink in with blade-like ease, and had to stifle a yell in my throat, not wanting to give our spectators any more satisfaction. And I could tell Max was just as close to losing it as me. He needed me to be strong, as much as I needed him to be there, always just behind. And so I pushed forward, head down, willing there to be an end, willing myself in the bright open sunshine of Arafel's forest. And then, just ahead, there was a murky glimmer of light.

'Max!' I whispered, just as one of the creatures' spiky legs brushed my lip. The contact gave me the last bolt of energy I needed, and I barrelled through the rest of the confined tunnel, conscious of Max's intense stress behind me.

We sprawled out into the half-light of a regular-sized tunnel together, and I twisted, dragging myself away from the strange insects spilling out with us. I stared at our hybrid companions. They had to be at least thirty centimetres long, with dark bulbous eyes and cockroach top shells concealing white jellied bodies and thick, scurrying legs.

'Ugly pinching biters!' Max jumped up and started swiping himself down like a madman.

'Uh, you got one …' I started, pointing at his head.

'What! Where?' he responded, swatting every part of his rugged outdoor body, before he spotted my wry smile.

He shook his head, grinning, while my heart ached like it was being squeezed. Humour. We were facing our deaths and it was still the best I could do? The screens went quiet above my head as I threw them the most sardonic smile I could muster. It didn't matter what Pantheon threw at us. We were stronger. This much was true.

Then I spotted the timer. It was in the shape of an egg timer, and glowing red in the corner of the ceiling screen. It was also a quarter empty.

'A quarter of the time's gone!' I hissed, scrambling to my feet and looking up and down the tunnel, trying to get my bearings. 'We have to keep moving!'

I couldn't let myself think what might happen should the time run out before we got to Aelia, assuming that was the point of the game. Or perhaps it was just plain survival. Who knew what the rules were, or if there were any. Was Cassius watching?

Somehow, I knew he was, even if he wasn't in the Flavium, and the thought gave me the ugly fuel I needed.

A show Max said, well, he was going to get that, at least.

I led the way down he nearest tunnel, but had only managed a few paces before Max reached out.

'Tal! It's too quiet, which means this is exactly what they're expecting us to do!' he whispered. 'If it's a game, we should do the opposite!'

I bit my lip. He was right, of course; it made complete sense. We turned and started back towards the corner, just as a fresh grating noise echoed through the air. I hesitated, and in the next breath a black iron mesh dropped directly in front of my face. Dividing us.

For a second I only stared, refusing to accept we were actually, physically separated. Then the whites of Max's eyes confirmed it. And I kicked and yelled with every bit of hatred coursing my veins.

'No!' I yelled, my fury echoing through the shadowed corridors, rendering the screens above our heads dead silent.

'Cheat!' I screamed at the top of my lungs, not caring who or what else was in the cage in that moment. 'You son of a miserable, lowlife, bitching cheat!'

'Tal … Tal!' Max's hoarse whisper brought me back to the breathing darkness with a slam.

'Sssh! Don't … turn … around.'

It was then that I sensed the stakes had changed. And it wasn't his words, so much as the fear behind them.

He lifted his crossbow, and angled it through the wire mesh directly at me.

I stared, feeling my breath shorten. Max was never this serious – ever.

'When I say drop, drop,' he muttered, screwing up one eye in concentration, a bead of perspiration just visible at the top of his forehead.

And then I heard it. Behind me. Not close enough to touch, but enough to know it was big, snorting and angry by design.

I nodded, my mouth like arid soil. One, two, three seconds crawled past, and I could feel the crowd's hateful anticipation above my head. Watching and revelling. Some of them cowering behind their hands.

'Drop!'

Max's whisper echoed as loudly as a roar inside my head. I slammed down and spun to face whatever it was, just as Max released an arrow. And for a second, I couldn't breathe. Something told me this was what it was all about. *Ludi.*

It was huge, at least three metres tall and bulky with it, filling the entire width of the corridor. And its hairy body oscillated awkwardly, as though every breath cost it effort, but it was its thickened snorting head tapering into two colossal, twisted horns that held my terrified gaze.

'No,' I whispered, as though the word, if spoken aloud, would register on some divine barometer and force the mercury in another direction altogether.

It couldn't be, not this time. Not now.

The slim arrow slammed into its shoulder, and the beast screeched in fury, retreating back down the corridor into the darkness. Then there was a rough, ratcheting sound. It was the sort of noise no natural animal would make, and one that buried itself, like a beetle, beneath my skin.

'Run! There's a turning on the left. I'll go back around. We'll meet!'

Only a crack in his last whisper revealed his fear. I stared back into the eyes of the best friend I'd ever had.

'Don't be late,' I breathed, before sprinting into the darkness.

Blood pounded in my head as I rounded the corner Max had pointed out. Another long dark passage stretched out, but my only thought was to put as much distance between me and the towering creature, as possible.

I sank my teeth into my lip, releasing a drop of bitter red as I flew. How could I not guess this labyrinth would hold one of Cassius's prized creations? The strix and giant insects were clearly only the warm-up, and now we'd found the main attraction. And it was furious.

My sprinting steps echoed horribly without Max's solid pace behind me. My back felt exposed and the Ludi darkness even more terrifying, but more than that I suddenly and abruptly felt sadder than I ever had in my life. I shot a swift look around. The air looked misty blue in this part of the maze, and the screens above my head had taken on a muted, distant look too. My pace slowed as the fog of negativity and disbelief spread.

Why was I bothering? We were going to die anyway. And wouldn't that be easier than running, always running?

I shook my head, not understanding the sudden hopelessness that was swallowing my energy. My limbs felt wooden and heavy and all I could think of was lying down and giving in. The light was getting gradually bluer, and I was walking now. The beast was close again. I could feel it. I could sense its laboured breath. Perhaps it was right behind me, but I couldn't turn around.

It was all too much. They'd already taken Grandpa, the Book of Arafel, and Lake. And now we were trapped. There was no point. Fairy tales didn't exist. Dad was dead, Grandpa was dead, Pan was dead, Lake was probably dead. Pantheon was going to win. In the end.

'Tal!'

Max's voice was above my head, his strong hands were beneath my shoulders, and he was dragging me. Until the blue mist was gone.

The darkness was my friend, bringing reason. And suddenly hope. I shook my head, trying to sit up. It swam, and I swallowed to ease my fiery throat.

'Don't let them think they've won ... not for one second,' he forced, hoisting me onto my feet as the maze returned to mono-tone around us.

'Max!' I threw my arms around him.

It felt unbelievably good to have him next to me again, to feel his warmth seep into my cold wooden limbs.

'Where is it?' I whispered, looking back over my shoulder.

The blue mist was completely gone now, leaving only the breathing darkness in its place.

'I don't know, and I'm not hanging around to find out. This way.'

He dragged me into a run back in the direction from which he'd come, the screens going crazy with noise as I stumbled back to life.

'What happened back there?' he asked as we picked up our pace.

'Not sure! There's some kind of light mist that sucks the life out of you.' I grimaced. 'Either that, or I'm losing it completely.'

He threw me a wink. I scowled, trying to remember some of the science Dad taught us about the old world. He'd mentioned chemicals that could influence moods, something to do with natural circadian rhythms, and experiments with lights. He said they were used in scientific trials before the Great War. This had to be a new experimental line for Pantheon. Clearly, not all its monsters bore teeth and claws.

We turned a corner and pelted down the connecting tunnel and, within seconds, it had turned back on itself before turning left again. Then we glimpsed her, Aelia, imprisoned inside the spherical mesh orb that now appeared to be slowly lowering. My heart leapt higher than a new springbok. We were closer than I thought. And if we could reach her, we might just stand a chance.

'Aelia!' I yelled, injecting a spurt of speed.

She saw me right away and gripped the wire mesh of her ball, shouting, but the box was completely solid, muting any sound whatsoever.

'Mih … noo … taure?'

I read her lips, stringing the sounds together trying to work out what she was yelling. And then it made sense. I cursed softly, and exhaled as a prickling feeling tiptoed across the back of my neck.

'Minotaur,' I whispered, and as if it heard, there was a soft, low growl somewhere ahead in the tunnel. *It was waiting. It knew.*

We skidded to a halt, silently. Cassius was going to keep going until he'd used up all his cards, so why did I keep thinking it was OK? It was a game, his ugly little game. As Max said, we just needed to be stronger and faster.

And more feral. I grimaced as the tunnel started to shake, and the shadows merged to form the shape of a gargantuan, mytho-logical Minotaur. A raging one.

There was another deep snort that resonated down the tunnel in shock waves. We took a step back and it matched our stride deliberately, its muscles rippling and yellowed eyes gleaming, locked on us.

'What do we do?' Max whispered at my shoulder.

'We run,' I breathed, 'back through the mist.'

'Yes,' he whispered, understanding. 'Now.'

We spun in unison, and pelted back down the corridor as the beast crashed after us with a furious bellow.

'Minotaur?' Max asked in a strangled voice, as we rounded the corner a few seconds before the beast.

'Minotaurus,' I yelled, willing my legs to work harder and faster.

The screens above our heads were bright, affording us a first detailed view of the mythical beast on our tail. It was colossal, and the dim twilight all over its thick bull face made it look bruised with fury.

'What?' Max repeated, as we tore up the new tunnel.

'Minotaurus … is the Roman equivalent!' I yelled.

'Right … it's still a feckin' huge bull!' he ground out.

'Shield your eyes as best you can,' I returned, as we entered the blue-misted corridor, the ceiling alive with exhilarated faces.

I felt my pace slowing almost instantly, and reached out for Max's hand.

'Keep moving,' I forced through my numbing lips. 'Just keep moving.'

I could see the darkness up ahead where the mood mist finished, and I clenched my free hand, aware Max had slowed down. I twisted to see him. But it was hard, so hard.

'Not much further,' I pushed into the strange dead air.

'I … can't.' His words were like tiny leaden hammers, falling straight to the floor.

The screen was going crazy, and my feet were dragging abnormally against the mesh floor. Somehow, I managed to twist, and was filled with a strange disembodied sensation to glimpse the hulking Minotaur bellowing its drunken rage to the screens, its powerful legs buckling.

'It's workiiiiing …' I slurred.

Max's hand was becoming colder, more of a dead weight. And then I was aware of the floor getting closer, of a violent crash as Max lurched forward. I was on my knees, and the darkness was reaching out, just in front of us. I twisted one last difficult time. But the tunnel was completely empty. And my head was too exhausted to understand why.

Silence.

Hollow, laboured breathing.

I lifted my head. We were both down. My eyes glazed over the screens of Pantheonites going crazy – to my crumpled best friend, still inside the light.

My own legs, also beneath the light, were completely paralysed. And all I could hear was the slowing thump of my own heart, pulsing with fear, with blood, with Arafel. Before Grandpa's voice.

'*You have a feral heart, Talia, like the black leopard. Strong and free.*'

And somehow, with sheer gritted will, I pushed my elbows forward, and dragged my inert lower body into the darkness. Then I reached out and, wedging my numbed forearms beneath Max's shoulders, pulled until I thought my limbs might separate. My efforts were enough to drag his torso clear of the light, and slowly the colour returned to his face.

'Max,' I whispered, cradling his head, and watching the darkness around us.

My voice was hoarse with effort, but we were hardly out of danger yet.

He slowly eased an eye open.

'Think ... I might need ... CPR,' he croaked into my knee.

I hoisted him up to sitting, pulling his legs clear of any remaining light.

'You'll get more than that if you don't get your legs working right now,' I hissed.

It worked. He rolled over onto his knees and then staggered up onto his feet. The blue light had faded to a faint illumination, leaving us alone and exposed in the murky darkness.

'Didn't follow?' Max muttered, extending a hand and yanking me to my feet. Whatever the mood-affecting light mist was, it clearly didn't have a lasting effect once you were clear.

'It tried,' I corrected. 'Maybe it knew a better way.'

The thought had us scanning the darkness with fresh zeal.

'Which one?' I breathed, looking up and down the tunnel. One passage led back towards the giant flying insects tunnel; while the other probably led directly back towards the beast itself. And possibly Aelia.

We stared at one another; sometimes there were no words.

Chapter 15

We stole into the darkness. I led the way, with Max at my shoulder, his crossbow primed. We'd already injured and infuriated the animal which, in my experience, meant it would do one of two things: retreat or retaliate.

Somehow, I had the feeling a horned Minotaurus might not be the retreating type, although this part of the tunnel was empty, and it wasn't long before we reached another fork.

I glanced back at Max's strained face.

'Left?' I nodded briefly to the turning just ahead.

The egg timer in the corner of the screen was glowing bright red now, and I could see anticipation written all over the faces of the watching Pantheonites. Briefly I wondered what would happen if we hadn't reached the centre by the time the sand was through. I was pretty sure an honourable pardon wasn't in the game plan.

We crept forward as quickly and silently as we could, pausing every few steps to listen. The Pantheonites on the screens were revelling in our nightmare. And, ironically, their twisted delight quietened my own fear. We had to outplay them and that meant controlling everything we could.

At first there was nothing but us and the claustrophobic silence, but then slowly, there was something else. A presence more than breathing. It was close now. Up ahead. In the black. I pushed a hand out to stay Max, and we listened intently. The hairs on the backs of my arms rose as though caught by a rare northerly wind. He could feel it too. I could tell by the way he reached out to touch the small of my back.

I took another few careful paces forward, aware of a strange curtain hanging on the air. Afterwards I realized it was our adrenaline, as perceptible as a light mist. Then there was a pained, grating bellow, and I clenched every muscle I possessed.

'Now!' I hissed.

We sprinted forward towards the left turn with all the energy I had remaining. Releasing a furious howl, the creature also started forward, matching my pace with violent, thunderous leaps. And those few seconds running headlong into its path were a test of sheer guttural will over instinct.

As Max and I rounded the corner first, it released another vicious, angry bellow that caused my head to throb. It was the sort of sound you would expect a monster from hell to make, as though every pain it had ever endured was being poured into that one vibration. And then the terrific pounding was behind us, the entire cage shuddering, as though colossal weights were being thrown repetitively onto a metallic floor.

We sprinted as though our feet had grown tiny Apollo wings, down the new tunnel, which was long, black and contrast, completely uninviting.

'Maybe we should have turned back!' Max threw, as we pelted into the darkness.

'And trap ourselves until Cassius chose to make us scara-beetle fodder?' I scathed. 'Where's the fun in that?'

We were halfway down the corridor, the flickering ceiling screens chasing our flying feet, the crowds going crazy with excitement.

I gritted my teeth. We were not going to die here, not after

189

everything. It was not the final resting place for two Outsider hearts.

And then it was there. The faintest of lights, just ahead.

'Max!' I yelled, screwing up my eyes.

'Aelia!' Max panted simultaneously.

A shot of neat adrenaline doused my veins. It was the centre, finally, flickering with hope. And we were within touching distance. We could do it, we could reach her, I was sure of it.

Together, we flew towards the meshed ball cage, suspended at the end of the corridor, trying not to listen to the terrific pounding behind us. I gasped, as Aelia became clearer. We were so close, but for some reason I could only see the top half of her body. Then I understood. Her meshed ball cage was slowly disappearing into a black pit beneath her.

'Tal!' she yelled, her voice filled with unusual panic.

'We're coming,' I yelled. 'Hang on.'

And we were nearly there. Nearly. When it happened. A thick grill dropped just in front of her cage, sealing her off, leaving us in a dead end. With the Minotaur behind.

'No!' I screamed, running into the metallic curtain and throwing all my weight at it. The collision was so hard, I felt the entire left side of my body shudder, bruising instantly, but I didn't care.

She smiled, despite everything.

'You always were so wild!' she chastised, as though we were anywhere but here, facing our own gruesome deaths.

'Don't you dare!' I yelled, as Max also threw his shoulder into the thick metal, which vibrated but didn't budge at all.

'OK … I'm sorry then!' she yelled, climbing higher up the inside of her disappearing ball.

I nodded once, swallowing past the rock that had somehow lodged in my throat. Her iris-blue eyes were full, their mocking light finally gone as, together, we faced reality. Eyes that were so like her brother's. August's face swam in front of mine, and the

190

pain I'd buried for twelve whole months threatened to burst from my chest. This was it. I would never see him again. But it didn't matter; nothing mattered any more.

'Tal …'

The defeat in Max's whisper cut me like a knife as, slowly, I turned around. The Minotaurus now stood barely ten paces from us, its chiselled horns lowered, and dark blood matted around the shoulder wound Max had inflicted. Its eyes glowed with an amber hatred, and its heaving, muscular body was poised for charging. For killing. And we were trapped.

Max held up his crossbow and levelled it. It looked a pitiful defence now we were so close, and the beast tossed its snorting, hulking head as though it knew it too. It pawed the ground, playing with us, and the crowds in the screens above our heads fell silent, ready to witness a noble death. *A game well played,* they would say. *Worthy combatants.* Until the next.

How long had it taken for this world to descend into hell again? Was this the inevitability? That no matter how much time passed, and how advanced the human race considered itself, there remained, at its core, a primal roar for blood that would never evolve? Was that why August had walked away? Why he didn't come to find me?

My chest tightened with each emotional barb, infusing my veins with poison, as the Minotaurus threw its head back once more, celebrating its certain victory. The crowds watched in hushed awe, their faces shining with barely repressed excitement.

'Tal, you have to know …' Max began, taking my hand.

'No!' I shook him off violently. 'You don't say goodbye! Not now. Not ever!'

Quick as a flash, I grabbed a poison-tipped dart and loaded my tiny treehouse dart tube. It released within a gnat's breath, and the tiny arrow flew with perfect precision towards the beast's thigh.

But with one agile swing of its thick arm, the beast batted the tiny missile to one side. It fell to the floor with a clatter. A bizarre grimace twisted its thick, steaming, ringed nose before it snorted angrily, and started bearing down on us.

'Always so feckin' … angry!' Max seethed, firing another arrow from his crossbow.

It buried itself in its left foot, making the beast stare downwards in disbelief, before bellowing its fury to the ceiling, fracturing the glass of the screen. Then it broke into a violent lumbering run, directly at us.

'Now?' Max forced.

'No!' I yelled, channelling everything for one last fight.

'I'm … not … done!'

I flew into my own run. Straight towards the huge, terrifying creature. And just as it seemed we must collide, I leapt as though my life depended on it, catching the slim protruding edges of the fractured ceiling screens. My fingers curled around the thin rail, giving me just enough leverage to swing through and land the full force of my tree-running legs in the middle of the bull's forehead. It was enough unexpected impact to make the animal stagger on its plate-like feet. And then I dropped to my feet in front of it.

'It doesn't matter …' I yelled, conscious of a sea of aghast expressions through the shattered screens, '… how big … how ugly … or how warped!' I railed, reaching down to swipe the fallen dart lying on the floor, as the bull regained its balance and lowered its frenetic eyes to bellow in my face.

'Tal!'

I was only dimly aware of Max's terror as another of his arrows buried itself in the beast's right shoulder.

'Feral. Means. Free!'

And with my last yell I rammed the poisoned dart into the beast's powerful chest, as it simultaneously drove its chiselled horns down and forward in a brutal blow that stole my air.

I flew backwards as though I was falling, conscious of the

world in counter-motion; of the shocked faces of the crowd; of the bull being pulled away by another violent force; and finally of the pudgy, horrified face of an old friend. A gentle giant who gazed at me, before raining his full rage down on the Minotaurus.

And then finally I was conscious of Max, cradling me, as the world around us fell apart.

'Now?' he whispered.

There was such pain in his eyes, veiling them like the mist through the trees in Arafel. His forest-green eyes. Instant balm to the hurricane tearing up my chest. I tried to smile as it all shrank to a dot, no bigger than the wingspan of my distorted butterfly. It was like looking down my father's microscope, the one he'd kept in his study, salvaged from the old-world days. He called it his insect eye, a technological instrument to see the world as tiny life might.

'Nature and technology can have a healthy symbiotic relationship, Talia.'

His voice echoed as clearly as though it were him cradling me instead. I teetered at the edge, looking down into the black under-water tunnel. I always detested this bit. The dark before the light. I was conscious of his warm breath next to my cheek, whispering how the wild orchids were just in bloom; how the Arafel fields were gleaming gold and that the trees were whispering and waiting. Waiting and whispering.

'A harmonious balance can be struck, if science is a friend to nature.'

I exhaled, aware it was getting dark. That his words were fading, because that was in the before, when he was alive. When all I knew was the sweet lullaby of the breeze through the baobab leaves.

Chapter 16

'Keep it in the flame – it needs to be totally sterilized. And rip this up – I have to stem the bleeding ... OK, penetrating chest wound, thorax, fractured sternum, superficial and deep fascia, intercostal muscles ...'

I knew the voice, but it was so distant, like Arafel. I couldn't work out why. Then there was another.

'She was unstoppable, like wildfire! And she wouldn't ... let me ...'

There was a poignant pause, and then a wry chuckle.

'She does have spirit. And something more besides. Like all the forces of nature somehow got wrapped up in her small body.

'A real feral cat!'

There was a short, dry laugh.

'It was one of things that fascinated him. August always said there was intrinsic coding in Outsider DNA that the vaccine to suppress independent will had mostly eradicated. Free will or a feral instinct. Call it what you will. It's why we've had such problems motivating the older Prolets.'

'Don't say that name! If he'd kept his promise, we wouldn't have ended up inside Pantheon, inside that Ludi hell-cage in the first place! He's dead as far as I'm concerned, or will be if I ever see him again.'

There was a heavy silence, filled only with the distant harmony. Like the softest lullaby. Was I dying? Or already dead?

'I'm still his sister, Max … but as far as the feral thing goes, well, it's not every girl who will run headlong into combat against a Minotaurus. Can you pass me that tube? Did you clean it? And one of your arrow points, nothing you've laced with that bat poison. I need to find the second intercostal space mid-clavicular line. Then this needs to stay in until the air is released.

'Of course, the downside is she does have an annoying tendency to rush headlong into every situation like it's some personal crusade.'

'It is,' Max confirmed quietly. 'It couldn't be more personal for Tal. And she'd rather die fighting, than spend one moment doubting what being an Outsider represents. That's the real legacy she's protecting. As she said, feral means free.'

'And you'll always be there … at her back? If you can't be at her side?'

The voices faded.

∗∗∗

I was vaguely aware of the cavern walls, of the red-streaked rock, shiny with damp and blackened where the lanterns hung. The pungent scent was familiar, and a rumble filled the air occasionally. Then there was a sharp pain in my chest, followed by a cool hand.

'All done.'

It was the whisper of an angel in my feverish darkness, between the clattering echo of long-hooked claws. It was the same clattering from my nightmares, but I knew this pain-imbued hell didn't belong to the realm of dreams. Despite the snatches of distant harmonies. I knew that much. But as for the rest …

∗∗∗

It was tepid water that welcomed me back to the claustrophobic, underground world. And I wished immediately to leave it again.

My head pounded, while my chest felt as though the swarm of the giant, pincer-snapping insects were clawing to get out. Quite apart from the entire weight of a Cyclops balancing on top of it. Cyclops. I had to be slipping in and out of a fevered dream world again because there was a Cyclops staring down at me. Holding me. *Rocking me?*

'Unus?' I croaked in disbelief.

Surely, he should have disappeared now my lips had shaped his name, the way August used to fade from my dreams. Although once I had hung on long enough to glimpse a different outside reflected in his iris-blues. Two lives entwined in a parallel world. His skin next to mine every night, and a need so real it suffocated every logical thought.

'The whole damned world is waiting.'

His words were burned into my memory, as though he had engraved them with his own bare hands, but what use was a whole damned world stripped back to shadows?

'Because of this, and the new investigation required, I would recommend a temporary suspension of all new Prolet privileges and reinstatement of the existing Pantheonite system.'

My muscles tightened in protest, dragging me back to grim reality.

'Unus,' I tried again.

Even my voice sounded different, like an imposter had swallowed it.

I coughed and spluttered, and some of the liquid ran down my chin as I willed my eyelids to respond. There was a sliver of light, and I nearly choked again.

'Is that … really …?' I gasped, the irony of having passed through a painful death to find a mammoth pudgy Cyclops clutching me in the afterlife not entirely lost.

'Unus here. Unus friend.'

His stilted voice clarified the rhythmic swaying, and my shattered body filled with weak relief.

'Unus,' I managed again, brokenly.

I rested my heavy head against his warmth as fragmented memories, like falling snowflakes, threatened to make everything white again. A wave of grief welled up, and for a second struggled to spill over.

Had any of it been worth it?

'Max?' I struggled to force his name over my cracked lips. 'Ae-lia?'

'We're all here, Tal.' Max's low tone soothed.

I winced as I relaxed – the pain inside was still hot and raw.

'Well, all except the Minotaurus … You and Unus kind of ensured his was a one-off Ludi performance.'

Guilt and relief swelled my veins like flood water.

'How did we get here?' I asked, peeling my eyes back so I could make better sense of my surroundings.

We were moving down a tunnel. And there was no Minotaur, no Ludi Labyrinth – only Unus, Aelia, Max and me.

'How did we? What happened …?'

My chest felt like a hundred hot knives were being slowly inserted and twisted. Unus's ponderous walk, though his natural gait, was rhythmic agony to endure.

'Can … can I walk?' I gasped.

'No,' came Aelia's non-negotiable response, 'not yet anyway. We only just made it out. If Unus hadn't found us when he did, the Minotaurus would have finished what he started with the two of you, and I would have been a strix appetizer.

'As it is, Livia made her biggest Ludi mistake in putting you in there with us, didn't she, big man?'

I squinted up to see a shy grin spread across Unus's wide milky face.

'You should have seen it, Tal,' Max interjected in an awed voice. 'Unus used the Minotaurus as a battering ram against the iron door. We got to Aelia just after she dropped into the strix pit.'

'Yeah, that part was fun,' she quipped drily. 'Waiting for Boudica and her tribe to rescue my arse from a pack of hungry rat-owls!'

I scowled.

'But,' she teased, 'your timing was pretty good actually.'

'The grill gave way just as Aelia's cage touched down inside the strix pit,' Max explained. 'They surrounded her, but the keeping pen fell apart as Unus jumped in! I've never heard a crash like it. I thought the entire maze was going to collapse. And the strix couldn't shift fast enough. They'd been penned in, half-starved. Of course, they didn't dare take on Unus, even for fresh meat. They're now running amok through the maze of tunnels beneath the Flavium. It's enough to distract Cassius's guards for a while anyway.'

'And Livia?' I forced through my fog of pain.

'Livia couldn't get the labyrinth doors open quickly enough for the guards. She must be livid! She's not exactly used to losing,' Aelia scorned.

I didn't miss the hollow note in her voice, and wondered if she was thinking about the Book of Arafel. My head felt so woolly.

'Thankfully the chaos gave us time to find our way out through the Hypogeum. There's a network of old tunnels on two separate levels beneath the Flavium, and more than eighty vertical shafts so … a lot of dark corners to check.'

'And we had a little help from the Oceanids.'

'The Oceanids.' I stumbled over the new word, struggling to keep up.

'Sssh!' Aelia warned suddenly, pausing.

Everyone stopped, and my chest snapped like a Venus flytrap. I swallowed a groan, as a faint wooden beat became discernible. It was the heavy booted toll of pursuit.

'They've gained on us in the last hour,' Max muttered.

'They must have got past the strix now,' Aelia added. 'Unus, the Oceanids? Will they help us again do you think? How far 'til the Dead City? We have to get there before the molossers pick up our scent!'

Unus nodded gravely, before turning his head away and emitting a noise I'd not heard before. It wasn't the belly rumble he used to scatter the strix, but something far more muted, like a primitive call, from deep within his chest. I listened through my stupor, trying to focus on something other than the medieval torture taking place inside my own body.

The world stilled for a few seconds, but even I could feel the pressure of the ticking clock.

Was I slipping out of consciousness again? The cavern roof was flickering with the reflection of ghostly lights. Or at least that's how it looked. Not the reflection of real lanterns or old-world torches, just wild, dancing lights. Then there was the sound of water lapping. I struggled as much as my chest would allow, and finally Unus relented enough for me to crane my neck.

To my astonishment, we were standing beside a small, black water course that looked ice-cold and deep.

'What's with the water?' I managed weakly.

'We're inside one of the old Isca Dumnoniorum water tunnels, designed to bring fresh water directly into the heart of the old Roman city of Isca. Rajid discovered it. He was so passionate about the old city ...' She paused uncertainly, and I realized Max must have told her about our entrance into the Flavium with Rajid.

Had he trapped us? Or were Livia and Cassius tracking Rajid the way Octavia had tracked us when we first arrived in Pantheon? I thought back to his detached, erratic manner. Was it all an act?

'Just what makes you so special?'

The words rattled inside me like loose stones.

'He discovered the spring in a corner of the Hypogeum near the Spoliarium, where they strip the dead, but we couldn't spare the Prolet workers to explore it until recently,' she pushed on. 'We were going to announce it to the Senate – a project for the

199

new partnership – but things fell apart before we got the chance. So Rajid concealed the entrance with some rubble. It didn't take long for Unus to clear it back, and it worked in our favour to let the strix follow us.

'Furious though Livia and Cassius must be, there isn't a guard in Pantheon who would risk passing a starving strix, so they must have either rounded them up or fed them. That's good news for us.'

Unus lifted his head again, and the same soft, ancient sound filled the tunnel. This time it was so haunting it made me shiver. And much to my incredible surprise it was echoed a few seconds later. An octave higher.

I'd learned enough about Pantheon to know when something wasn't simply a distortion of the thick walls around us. The echo was such a pure sound, almost as though the water itself was sharing its song. And then the dancing lights dimmed momentarily.

I watched, entranced. It was a sound of nature, of the elements harmonizing. The cold cavernous ceiling was coming to life, and I could almost believe I was lying in the lush grass of Arafel beside Max, watching the fireflies dance around our heads.

And then there was a ripple. And a voice. Or rather a cacophony of sounds. They filled the tunnel although I still couldn't be sure they were real.

The water rippled again and, on the edge of my vision, a dark shape broke the surface. I opened my mouth, but my voice refused to come out.

The shape separated into two and then three, and then it turned towards us. It had a face, three of them. They glimmered in the murky light, like the glimpse of scales beneath water, while their hair writhed like sea anemones all the while. I held my scant breath. With black ovoid eyes, glistening skin and pulsing slatted gills, these creatures were different to any others I'd ever seen.

The only question was, to which world did they belong?

Unus emitted another soft noise, indicating behind us with one of his club hands. And through a haze of pain, my chest throbbed for the simple giant who, time after time, had proven such an ally. I leaned my head back and listened to the slow, slightly irregular beat of his heart, like chasing thunder. It gave me the strength I needed to absorb the new arrivals.

Their large eyes possessed the entirety of their eye sockets. It gave them a ghoulish appearance, but undoubtedly equipped them well for the lightless water. And rather than swim, they appeared to float on the water, as though they weighed nothing more than sea spray.

Grandpa's voice reached through the haze. I was twelve years old, listening to him read a page from Arafel's book of mythology aloud. A page about ancient water goddesses.

'They're called Oceanids,' he'd enunciated carefully, 'or sea nymphs, fabled to have once lived in the earth's springs, rivers, seas, lakes and ponds.'

I was fascinated even back then. A human torso combined with a long, muscular tail sounded Gothic and tantalizing. But although the Oceanids had appeared magical through my childish eyes, there was nothing fairy-tale about the creatures staring back from the water now. They were pure, ancient myth.

'Clymene, Asia, Electra, we need your help,' Aelia said quickly and softly. 'We are being pursued by Cassius's guard and their molossers. We understand your allegiance is to none and you've helped us once already. But you may not be aware we carry an injured Outsider. One of whom you may have heard … Talia Hanway, descendant of Thomas Hanway, and last guardian of the Book of Arafel.'

The silver faces inclined briefly, as though in recognition of new information.

'We need protection and the shortest route to the Dead City,' Aelia concluded, glancing over her shoulder. 'And we've no time to lose.'

I frowned, despite the energy it cost. Why would the Oceanids have heard of a girl from the outside?

There was a moment of silence, before an unnatural noise filled the cavernous space. It was much like the sound I'd heard before, only less distorted by the water. Unus jerked his great head forward, as the silent three slid back beneath the inky water. Then he started forward again, his one eye flitting between the rock path and the water that occasionally gleamed with eerie light. I gazed upwards at the contours of his face, and as reality receded, I wondered what other ancient secrets they protected.

'We need to pick up the pace,' Max urged from behind us.

No one argued.

'Aelia … Lake? The Book?' I muttered, feeling my eyelids sink as though under the weight of a thousand fathoms.

'Later.'

The word danced, as oblivion carried me out of reach.

Chapter 17

'She was always the most stubborn girl, never could be told anything. I should never have stayed behind when she went to see the tower with Atticus!'

There were swift fingers, signing, somewhere to my right.

'I knew she was waiting for her moment to try for Pantheon. At least if I'd been there, she might not be half-dead from wrestling a Minotaurus for a start!'

Eli's stress coaxed me back from my retreat of shadows and underwater voices. He sounded really worried, and more than a little annoyed.

'You would have been no help at all,' I muttered shakily. 'An irate Minotaurus would have tested even your talents.'

The homely scent of warm broth suddenly assailed me, and I breathed it in, savouring the moment and trying to hold on to the new dream. It was a good one. The air was so much fresher here than the stifling atmosphere of the tunnels. I could almost believe I was home. I forced my other eye fully open and the room spun like a spider's web. The dream wasn't disappearing; the air really was fresher here.

My head began to pound, and the oddly familiar surroundings chased away the remainder of my sleep. I was in a circular stone room, on a makeshift bed, with large bronzed bells suspended above my head. Had we made it back to the tower?

Carefully I craned my neck, relieved to see the faces of the young Prolets scattered around the large bell room, playing and chatting. It seemed such a naive, vulnerable scene after Ludi. They couldn't be less aware of the interest they had stirred up in Isca Pantheon. Or of the collective danger they were still in.

I forced myself up onto my elbow, ignoring the shooting pain down my left side. At least it was bearable now.

'What's happening? How long have I been out? Eli? Max!' I croaked.

'Hang on, sleeping beauty, let me check your bandages before you start throwing those badass moves again!'

I hadn't noticed Aelia sitting up beyond my head, resting against the cavern wall. Her small elfin features were twisted up into an ironic grin, but there was no missing the dark circles beneath her eyes.

She slid around and, lifting a thin blanket, peeked through a long incision in my tunic. Only once she was satisfied the bandages, which looked a lot like Max's trouser bindings, weren't seeping did she look back at me.

'You've been out a couple of days. Nothing major,' she confirmed with a perfunctory smile. 'A couple of broken ribs, thought one had punctured your right lung to begin with, but turned out to have narrowly missed. You managed to form a tension pneumothorax, but we released the air.'

I nodded. That had to explain the sharp pain among the haze.

'You lost a lot of blood though, and I had to sew you up using a sterilized bone from the Armamentarium – and some sheet thread. Thought maybe you were getting an infection but your fever broke last night so … I think you'll do.'

After another swift inspection, she closed my tunic and pressed her small hand to my forehead. I closed my eyes and recognized the familiar pressure. She clearly hadn't left my side at all.

'Unus?'

I gazed around warily, recalling the Oceanids.

'He's keeping watch at the bottom of the tower. The Oceanids led us through the water tunnels to the old bathhouse where the kids were sheltering before they moved up here.'

I nodded. There was something prophetic about sheltering in the blackened ruin of a Roman city, with a two thousand-year-old bathhouse beneath our feet. Wherever we went, a shadow of the ancient civilization followed.

'He volunteered,' Aelia continued, eyeballing me carefully, 'just in case any ravenous, wanderlust-filled strix tailed us this far. We spent the first night hiding in a Hypogeum cave, then the strix got so close Unus had to carry you. Max and I ran a few of the outlying tunnels beneath the Flavium, which should help to confuse the molossers.

'We got lost a few times, before Unus summoned the Oceanids, but once we had a guide we made it here in a couple of hours. Just as well. That wound needs time to knit.'

Aelia's exhausted tone said everything about how close a call it had been, and I managed a small nod. I knew anyway. I could still feel the shadow close by. And I wanted to ask so many questions – about August, about the Prolets, about exactly why she stole the Book. The questions crowded my dazed mind, competing for attention.

I glanced around the large, stone room. It was dark outside, and there was no way of telling the time, but it didn't matter because I could see the stars, and the shy night sky. And in that moment, it was one of the most reparative sights I'd ever seen.

I scanned the room carefully. Most of the young Prolets were exactly as we left them – pale, thin but in good spirits. Leaving Max. Who was seated at a small, round table, adjusting the settings of his crossbow. Ignoring me.

A wave of dormant guilt welled up as the Ludi maze returned in raw detail. He'd been there in my shadow, saved me countless times, and yet when we'd faced our final moment together I'd still stopped him from saying what he most needed to say. Our coiled bodies flashed through my head, and suddenly I wanted nothing more than for him to hold me, to whisper my name like he had that night. To feel that closeness and trust. I stared, needing to say so many things, and understanding none of them as a persistent tug on my sleeve dragged my gaze back.

'So, what's a brother got to do to get some attention around here?' Eli signed.

He leaned forward, and dropped the lightest of kisses on top of my head.

'Welcome back, most stubborn of girls,' he signed, scanning my face intently.

'Just so you know, when you're all healed up, I intend to be very annoyed with you.'

'Just so you know,' I retorted, 'when I'm all healed up, I intend to avoid ungrateful brothers!'

'How is your leg now?' I added pointedly.

'OK.' He smiled as I threw another glance at Max, who stared down at his crossbow stubbornly. My fragile hope crumbled. He didn't understand I couldn't say goodbye, not to him. It would be like saying goodbye to myself. So maybe this was it, maybe he would pull away now, and I would be the one left hurting. Maybe that was no more than a ghost girl deserved anyway.

'Aelia … Lake? The Book? Why did you take it? Where is it now?' I rushed, the words sticking at the back of my dry throat.

There was a pregnant silence while Aelia contemplated her hands, her pulse just visible in her neck.

'Cassius has Lake and the Book. Along with the rest of the Prolets. You must have seen them, imprisoned, forced to watch their friends and family run the Ludi Labyrinth one by one. No one has survived it before us. I'm so sorry, Talia.' Her quiet words came in a rush. 'Rajid and I thought we could trade the Book of Arafel for the Prolets' freedom. And reassure them enough to try for the outside. But with the price Cassius has placed on your head ... Well, you've become a little legendary yourself.'

I frowned, watching her dry lips move. I knew Cassius must hate me for escaping his clutches and yet there was always this hint of something else. A piece of the jigsaw missing.

'When I returned to Isca Prolet, Cassius had rounded up every man, woman and child and thrown them into the Flavium dungeons for Ludi Pantheonares,' she continued. 'He was always unpleasant when Octavia was in charge. But Livia – she's fanning his psychosis ... and now ... now he's turning out to be worse than Octavia!'

I thought back to when he'd nearly forced himself on me, and fought the stir of nausea inside.

'He's not worse,' I corrected. 'He's always been a monster.'

I could feel Eli's hawk-like gaze on me. He knew how I felt about Cassius, and I could sense the control he was exerting over his anger. He was hardly likely to let me out of his sight ever again. I shot him a covert glance. His mouth was set, his lips thin. I'd pushed him with my latest escapade. If only he could see it was because I wanted to protect the Book, the Prolets, Arafel and everyone who lived there. Because I wanted to protect him.

Aelia lifted a cup of water to my lips, and I took it with effort.

'Heal the body, heal the mind, Talia.'

I'd heard Mum say it so many times, I could even hear the little inflections in her voice. I inhaled deeply. Cassius and his menagerie were searching for us, and it was only a matter of time before we were discovered. Thinking myself better had to start right now.

'The Prolet trials, Aelia.' I grimaced. 'The embryonic workforce in laboratory tanks, their independent will suppressed so they are more obedient. It's ... obscene! Did you know about it?'

She looked at me carefully before gesticulating discreetly at the young Prolets in the room.

'They're the product of the first, unsuccessful round of the same scientific trials.' Her voice was low and serious. 'It's genetic modification work Octavia's team started in secret, before Cassius took over and made it an official part of the ongoing Biotechnology Programme. Somehow, after August left, Cassius pushed the proposal through the Senate – the new Senate comprising only Pantheonite members.'

'It's the worst kind of scientific intrusion!' I exclaimed heatedly. 'Free will makes us who we are. Without it the Prolets will be nothing but obedient clones, genetically modified workhorses until they drop!'

I coughed, and a racking pain claimed my right side.

She paused, regarding me quietly.

'You think I don't know that? These are my people, Talia. No one hates that laboratory more than me. When Rajid discovered it, I didn't believe him. I thought even Cassius couldn't be responsible for that level of insanity. So he took me there, and yes, it's like the worst nightmare you've ever had. But getting angry doesn't make it go away. We have to be smarter than that.'

'And Rajid has,' I interjected drily.

She stared at me, clearly struggling with the idea that Rajid could be a traitor.

'Rajid was always so passionate, I can't … Look, I've been wondering, maybe Cassius was tracking him once the Prolets were rounded up? Using him as bait, knowing you would come?'

I drew a breath. I'd wondered the same myself, hadn't I? So why didn't I believe it? 'The drawing?' I pushed on. 'Why tear a page out of the Book of Arafel and hide it?'

My mind whirled with too many unanswered questions, before settling momentarily on the tiny hybrid creature in the laboratory.

'Was it to do with the chimera work?' I whispered croakily, shifting to pull myself up against the wall. 'We saw something …'

She hesitated before nodding. 'The multi-genus work has been going on for some time … You might have seen evidence before

208

in Isca Prolet? We were trying to challenge it in the Senate before August left.'

She threw a swift glance around before returning her attention to us.

'The new night watch moved in a couple of days before I got back from Arafel. The *Rhinolophus ferrumequinum*?'

I grimaced, recalling the vampiric bats that had swarmed Max, Pan and me.

'I was careful, but the guards arrived so swiftly,' she went on. 'I knew of the new biotechnological work installing monitoring software into animal retinas, just not that Cassius was trialling it.'

I frowned. So that confirmed how he knew of our arrival anyway.

'I had no time to leave a note to warn you about the bats. And by the time the guards arrived, I knew Cassius was intending to take the Book. So, I ripped out the page of Thomas's research that I believe is linked to the oldest secret of the Voynich.

'Look, my conscience isn't clear, I know that. I ... I took the Book knowing it would make you listen. That it would bring you to Pantheon before it was too late. But ... that page ... Cassius should never own it.'

I shot a look at Eli who was lip-reading earnestly, looking perplexed. He still didn't know about the Book of Arafel containing Thomas's research, but I didn't want to stop Aelia. Not now she was finally opening up.

'I've suspected there was much more to the Voynich than Octavia knew for quite a while.' She stared down at her restless hands. 'She revered it as a medieval genetic blueprint for mythical creatures. But Cassius and Thomas had access to the Voynich archives way before the Great War. They were scientists employed to study the Voynich together. They kept aspects of their research secret from Octavia, who was only a junior scientist at the time.

'It was only when I was studying the few pages of Thomas's

research I kept in the cave, that I first found the reference to an older legend. It was buried within the dense cryptic text, and so vague I didn't give it credit for a long while. So, when I finally got a glimpse inside your village book …'

'I knew it!' Eli signed furiously, derailing Aelia instantly.

I caught hold of one of his hands, and pulled it down, trying not to let my frustration show. I shot a look at Aelia anxiously. Had the moment gone already?

'The Book of Arafel is my responsibility, and I've already let Grandpa down enough. Please … no one else can know,' I signed with effort.

First Aelia and August, next Max, and now Eli. The circle was widening, and I wasn't supposed to have told anyone. But something in my exhausted face must have persuaded him I was deadly serious. He gripped me back and nodded, just once, but with Eli that was all that was ever needed.

'We're like opposite sides of the same person anyway.' He winked, signing with his free hand. 'Fire and water, storm and calm …'

I pulled a face.

'Does Max know?' he added, his face darkening.

I nodded hesitantly.

'He guessed,' I added guiltily, 'but no one else can. Right now, our priorities are rescuing Lake, retrieving the Book and putting a stop to Cassius once and for all. Somehow. Life in Arafel won't ever be the same, until we do.'

Come what may nature finds a way. The wisdom hung in the heavy air, or I might have whispered the words.

I looked back at Aelia. She seemed a million miles away now, and I needed to finish. I needed to know how an older legend buried within the text of the Voynich could relate to a torn picture of a classical chimera.

And why I felt the biggest jigsaw piece of all was still out there, just out of reach.

'Just what is it that makes you so special? ... With the price Cassius has placed on your head ... well, you've become a little legendary.'

The mysteries danced through my head, taunting me. *What was missing?*

'Pan?' Eli interjected, interrupting my thoughts.

I shook my head, biting my lip.

'He traded his life for a chance of saving Lake,' I added in a hollow voice, staring across the floor at Faro playing pick-up sticks with a boy with tiny blue, pulsing gills.

The colour reminded me of my veins. Twisted and blue. The same colour as my thoughts.

'August?' Eli asked next, his voice oddly strained.

I shot a look at my sensitive twin. He was staring at me, visible pain in his gentle eyes, and in that moment I glimpsed the answer to the question that had been eluding me for so long. My heart swelled.

How long had he known? How could I have not seen this before? And where did it leave us? Twins. Bound by love for each other – and divided by love for another?

For a moment neither of us said anything, but I could tell he knew I'd read it. The truth. And the hopelessness. Right there and then. And that he cared for my acceptance more than anything in the world.

I gazed up into his gentle grey-blue eyes, at my thoughtful twin who had always stood back and waited. And finally, it all made so much sense. How hard had the last year been for him – silently watching me, reading my thoughts, guessing at the tangled web I was weaving with Max and being unable to say what he was feeling? Somehow his pain made August's fall from grace doubly hard.

I placed my hand over his and squeezed, feeling new strength flush my veins. What did it matter anyway? August might as well be dead! I'd spent twelve months holding on to something that didn't exist. I'd isolated myself, hurt my best friend, tuned out my twin's feelings and all for what? A genetically modified man who professed himself to be a Knight of the Old Order? A Roman Equite who'd sworn allegiance to a set of ancient principles that might as well be ash too!

The kiss outside the Flavium rose like a taunt from the depths of my mind, despite my attempts to bury it. I knew who he really was now, and yet my twisted mind kept torturing me with that one defining moment when anything had seemed possible.

'You're the most obstinate, self-opinionated, frustrating little feral cat.'

We hadn't made any promises, but how could he forget the promises he'd made to Pantheon? A promise to change it all, and bring about a society that valued Outsider ideals. And freedom. My chest ached, and I longed for solitude so I could give in to the throb that had nothing to do with my injury. But there was no chance of that. And no time.

Eli was still staring at me. *Still waiting.* And so I did the only thing I could do, and smiled. And he smiled back. A real smile that said all the words. And that stretched all the way back to when we were children, locked inside our twin fortress. *We were OK.*

Which left Max. My eyes wandered back to the table where he was still engrossed in his crossbow. His skin glowed in the lantern light, but I could see the faint discolouration of bruises, and two new bloodstained bandages around his left forearm. Our exit from Ludi Pantheonares had obviously been rough, and he'd had my back, as always. But this was a Max I didn't recognize, withdrawn and guarded. What had I done?

'You're flushing again.' Aelia frowned, pressing her hand against my forehead.

'I thought you were getting an infection a couple of days ago,' she continued, 'but it was just a scare. No need to develop anything new though, please? I don't have access to Tullius's surgery, and a sterilized bone will only do so much!'

I nodded. She was back in full doctor mode. Had the moment gone? I drew a breath. I had to find out.

'The Voynich's older legend?' I urged.

She frowned. 'Well, you don't have a fever, which is good.'

She was stalling. But I wasn't giving up – not now.

I fumbled inside my leather rations bag lying beside me, and pulled out the crumpled piece of paper. It was already yellowed with age and my screwing it up in a hurry hadn't helped its appearance.

Eli stared curiously as I smoothed out Thomas's annotated diagram on my tatty threadbare blanket, and turned it around to face her.

And then I saw it. I stared intently.

Was it a trick of the light? A smudge? Something to do with lack of sleep and an incapacitated state?

I stole a look at Aelia. Had she noticed too? Did it mean anything?

Despite her exhaustion, she was drawn to the page, and I could understand why. Even to my untrained eye, the chimera drawing was clearly something different. Thomas's research had been full of the Voynich's nonsense wording and drawings, but this page was denser than the rest, as though he'd spent a significant amount of time on it. And there was a detail in the pencil sketch that now jarred like hail on a summer's day.

Was this one of the reasons Thomas had originally run to the forest? Because he'd discovered coding for an ancient legend buried within the text of the Voynich? One that would eclipse the rest?

I only knew what I'd read in Arafel's library: that the mythological chimera was supposed to be a monstrous fire-breathing hybrid creature. And Thomas's rough sketch had all the classical description from Homer's *Iliad* – *the front half of a lion, the tail of a snake, a goat's body* – snorting out a terrifying flame of bright fire. But it wasn't any of those features that held my gaze. It was something tiny, detailed, and instantly recognizable.

'Yes,' Aelia breathed softly, relieved she didn't need any words.

I scrutinized the page again, willing it to be a trick of my imagination. A fever-fuelled hallucination even. The writing was all upside down, the REQ as faint and scrawled as before. But the more I stared, the clearer the detail became.

We were staring at coding Cassius desperately needed to reinvent one of the oldest myths known to mankind. It was perfect, if terrifying, trading material. I thought of the screens full of flickering coding, Rajid's insistence we saw the chimera laboratory, and finally, Lake's disappearance.

And I still couldn't drag my eyes from the tiny detail that Thomas's swift pencil strokes had recorded as a clue. Just what was this myth capable of that Thomas had hidden it behind a classical sketch of a chimera?

Beads of cold sweat broke out across my forehead. By now Cassius had to realize Aelia had torn out the specific page he was looking for, and that it had slipped out of his grasp when we escaped Livia in Ludi Pantheonares.

I sat bolt upright, ignoring the bite in my chest. It could only be a matter of hours until his ugly menagerie tracked us all down. We were holding the blueprint to an ancient chimera in our hands, and the tiny detail in the drawing left me in no doubt he was close. It was all so terrifyingly clear. The real reason he was hunting us.

'We have to make a plan,' I panted painfully. 'Cassius is coming.'

Chapter 18

Everyone was asleep. A fragile starlight danced across the silent bells, but my head was too full of Thomas's drawing to appreciate anything.

I'd managed to swallow some pigeon stew, which was infinitely more appetizing than the rat's tail Atticus had insisted on chewing. And while my chest still throbbed, the sharp twists of pain were lessening.

We'd also agreed a homeward plan of sorts. At daybreak, the entire party was to try for the north of the Dead City and a circuitous route back to Arafel, taking a large detour around Scorpion Plain. Atticus offered to go ahead, to scout out a path, but Eli was adamant we stayed together now. He said our strength was diluted the moment we split the party, and I could tell he didn't trust Atticus, not completely.

The decision to try for Arafel as soon as possible was unanimous. Even Atticus conceded, or perhaps it was the thought of the alternative – of remaining behind in an empty tower with only the vultures and rats for company.

And what may happen afterwards.

No one was under any illusion that Cassius wouldn't pursue us. And no one stated the obvious, although it was staring all of us all squarely in the face – we were sitting ducks where we were. Max said little except to stress we should move as soon as we could. It was clear he thought we stood a much better chance on the ground now, using the broken buildings as we would the trees at home. And despite my fragility, I agreed with him.

Eli had evacuated the young Prolets to the tower before we arrived, and it was tempting to believe the stone walls could offer protection; but the truth was we were completely isolated, and no amount of high walls would protect against Cassius's flying armoury. Aelia protested I needed a couple of days' bed rest at least, but it was obvious we didn't have the luxury of time, and I wouldn't hear of anybody remaining with me while the others went ahead.

I felt strong, I said. *I lied.*

Slowly, I scanned the dimly lit bell tower. Atticus was sitting paring arrows with a penknife, though his attempt to look tough was softened by Faro, curled in to him fast asleep.

I stared at his swarthy face and dark eyes. There was no doubt his youth and pluckiness had got the Prolets this far. They owed him their survival, but he was also stubborn, which made him unpredictable – and a little dangerous. I shook off my suspicion as best I could. He seemed to be stewing, but I knew his mood was probably more to do with Lake's disappearance, than Max's confiscation of his rusty weapons. He and Lake had been close, no matter how much he tried to protest his independence from everyone around him.

Lake. Her double-lidded eyes spun into focus and a barrage of conflicting thoughts crowded my head.

I craned my neck to look across the floor. Everyone was asleep or resting, and Aelia had ordered bed rest for as long as we were in the tower. Max had barely spoken two words to me since I'd come round, and Eli was acting as though every movement might be my last. It all added up to a feeling of claustrophobia I couldn't handle. And I had an overwhelming urge to see my anti-hero cyclopean friend who'd saved my life more times than I could count.

Slipping my legs out from beneath my blanket, I pushed myself up and cursed as a rush of blood made the cavern slip sideways. I shot a hand out to grip the cool stone wall, and slowly the room stabilized again.

After a couple of minutes, I felt strong enough to rock my weight forward. Every bone in my body protested, but I gritted my teeth, and before long I was teetering on the balls of my leather-clad feet. It hurt more to walk flat-footed so, using the wall as a support, I tiptoed towards the dark stairwell leading from the room and started down the murky stone passageway.

The steps were hewn into the rock in sections, and there were flickering lanterns placed at sporadic intervals. Their dancing light took me back to the dusk fireflies in Arafel, and I was suddenly beset with a wave of overwhelming homesickness.

I knew it was weakness, but it was a weakness I couldn't afford to have. Not now. I descended the eight separate flights as swiftly as my chest would allow, and exhaled audibly when I rounded onto the floor and spotted Unus's bulky mass silhouetted in the passageway. He was seated on a blanket with only a lantern and wooden club for company, his head resting back against the wall and his one eye gazing out of a window, over the moonlit ruin.

My heart lurched unevenly. He was always alone, whether through choice or design, and yet we all owed him so much. I owed him so much.

'Unus?' I muttered gently.

He started and turned his head swiftly, his white face breaking into a delighted childlike grin when he spotted me.

'Tal all fixed!' he exclaimed, as I stepped into his pool of light. 'Tal not fixed,' he remonstrated as soon as I got close enough for him to scrutinize me. 'Tal sit.'

He shifted his bulk up the blanket that was keeping the ground chill at bay, leaving a cosy spot for me. I accepted with real gratitude, and slid down the wall, marvelling at how much more comfortable his huge muscular body was compared with the wooden door on which I'd been lying.

For a few brief moments we sat like that, drawing comfort from each other's proximity, and listening to the rhythmic drip of water somewhere in the overgrown ruin outside.

'Tal torn,' he pronounced after a minute.

'Yes.' I scowled, recalling the moment the steam-blowing Minotaurus had ripped into me, and I thought it was all over.

'The Minotaurus...'

'No, not Bull-man ... Tal heart torn,' he corrected.

I nodded, lost for words. 'How do you know?' I whispered dully.

'Unus watch, Unus know,' he answered, patting my knee.

His simple kindness stripped away any remaining layers, and I let my head roll against him, as I might have with Grandpa.

'Unus, what happened ... with August?' I asked, my voice sounding hollow.

His face wrinkled up like a giant sea-weathered shell, as he lowered his great eye to look at me.

'He leave. Prolets die ... Unus try stop. Livia put Unus ... in Ludi. Lia say bring Tal ... then Cassius listen.'

He paused to draw breath; the effort of so many words costing him.

'But ... all too... late.'

I stared. There was so much truth in what he said, but why would my presence make Cassius do anything? It was so much worse than I'd realized. August's abandonment had reached so much deeper than throwing Isca Pantheon into chaos, and giving Cassius what he wanted. It had snuffed out the tiny flame of hope the Prolets had nursed, leaving them only with pain and a dull acceptance that their destiny was servitude or torture in the Flavium.

I blinked rapidly, willing my burning eyes not to betray me.

218

Not now. I'd wanted to believe everyone had got August so wrong, that there had been one terrible misunderstanding, but I trusted Unus more than I trusted anyone else in Isca Pantheon. And even he believed August had abandoned everything he stood for, and everyone else with it.

'Sometimes heart see different … to eye,' Unus offered, his inky eye sunk beneath the folds of a heavy frown.

I nodded, still blinking. He was a creature of so few words, and yet those he chose were uncannily appropriate.

'Yes.' I nodded. 'My grandpa always said the heart chooses what it wants to see. But for happiness, heart and head must agree.'

He nodded. 'Cyclops heart big, head small. Agree a lot.'

I grinned up at him. He was like a giant hot brick and I was the warmest I'd felt since leaving Arafel.

'Do you think they're close, Unus?' I asked staring out towards the ruined cathedral nave, feeling oddly calm.

He patted my knee again.

'Unus block tunnel … twice. Tunnel maze. Will take time … Oceanids help. They sing … Dogs and strix stupid. Go all ways.'

My ears pricked up.

'The Oceanids' singing confuses them?' I asked wonderingly, recalling all the fables I'd read about mermaids enticing sailing ships onto rocks with their seductive singing. Their black, ovoid, lashless eyes gleamed from my hazy memory and a shudder passed through me. They were the most unnatural of all creatures. A curious Gothic hybrid, lurking somewhere between reality and fantasy.

Unus nodded. 'Sometimes old tales … hold truth,' he commented.

'And they live in the tunnels? In the water?'

I couldn't imagine a life immersed in the black water of the disused Roman tunnels, a life without light.

He nodded again. 'Used to … Then follow river. Swim far. To outside.'

'But then, why haven't they told the Prolets about the outside?

219

Encouraged them to do the same?' I protested. 'If the Oceanids have made it to the sea, that should surely persuade the Prolets to see the outside world is thriving.'

'Oceanids not ... Prolets. They loyal only to ... Oceanids. Prolets respect Oceanids ... but no trust.'

'But they helped us, or you?' I frowned.

'Oceanids free. Like Outsiders. Oceanids helped you.'

I stared back. It was there again. That insinuation.

Just what makes you so special? ... With the price Cassius has placed on your head ... you've become a little legendary.

I was so conscious that the tangled web looped and spiralled far more than I ever knew. My quiet life was slipping further from my grasp every second, and it was clear Grandpa intended our halcyon days to be my body armour when it came to protecting Arafel's legacy.

I stood up awkwardly, aware of the glimmer of dawn through the window, and that Aelia might miss me soon. Although I hadn't inspected the wound, I could feel the stair exercise had eased the stiffness in my chest. One of the lanterns towards the end of the passageway guttered, and all at once I knew what I wanted to do.

I held up my right hand to indicate five minutes before moving swiftly towards the entrance, ignoring Unus's grunts of disapproval. He must have sensed my need because he didn't follow. My legs felt stronger with each step down the narrow passageway we'd explored only a few days before. Although it felt more like months now.

Carefully, I reached up and fetched down one of the small lanterns, but I didn't need it when I stood at the top of the stone steps. A dawn-fused sky greeted me, and I stumbled down the steps, suddenly desperate to be outside, even if I was standing in the Dead City. And as I made my way through the broken nave, I felt as though the milky balm was reaching right through my raw flesh and easing the anguish there.

I reached the arched entrance, and turned to look up at the ruined cathedral. Even though half its walls were missing, it still looked regal in its pale silken drape, as though I'd intruded while it was dressing.

'Excuse me,' I whispered, before stepping carefully up the shelled nave.

It wasn't the forest, but this skeletal church had a unique beauty. And as I followed the light dancing across the floor, like a shy moonlit nymph, I filled my lungs with the sweetest air I'd tasted in a long time.

There had been little breeze underground, which always made me feel half-suffocated, and claustrophobic. But here, despite the fact I'd narrowly escaped death, I felt more alive than I had for a long time, and I wandered through the ruined grandeur savouring the way the fragments of stone and determined grass felt beneath my feet.

A few moments later, my wandering gaze picked out a frag-mented stained-glass window, on the western side of the nave. A faded man in blue looked out, although some of the frame had been claimed by the war, leaving him clinging to this world rather precariously. I made my way up the side aisle, picking over the scattered debris, until I stood opposite him.

'Le-o-fric,' I picked out with difficulty from the old English lettering at his feet.

The breeze lifted my hair, and somewhere in the distance there was the faint hiss of a vulture.

'So, what did you do that was so special, it got you immortal-ized?' I muttered.

The vulture hissed again, and this time I could tell the strange birds weren't that far away. Perhaps on the rooftops across the street. Well, they would have a wait if they expected this body to provide a meal any time soon.

'He took a church and turned it into a cathedral. Isca's cathe-dral. He had a vision … for something better.'

The voice was low and familiar, reaching deep inside and jarring the memories buried there. *Shaking them, waking them, making them hurt.* The world inverted momentarily, and every muscle tightened. Was I feverish again?

I stared at Leofric, feeling a strange burn eat into my veins, my world tilting. Because it had come from behind me.

Hadn't it? Because ghosts didn't exist.

The voice had lived nowhere but my subconscious for twelve long months. It had to be some kind of hallucination; and yet some macabre thread was still willing it to be real, willing the voice to be attached to a breathing body. Willing its blood to be as red as my own. Willing it not just to be another nightmare, another trick, another heartache.

So somehow I turned, and everything stopped.

He was there. Silhouetted on the ledge of an ancient stone window, like an immortal hero clothed in full Roman military regalia.

His tall, arresting figure was so familiar, and yet so blurred by my reaction that I couldn't, really, believe it was him. Was it even possible? Could a feverish mind conjure up such detail, when a sound one had struggled so much these past few months?

He regarded me as though he'd seen a ghost himself, his swarthy face hard and unsmiling, his once honourable uniform tarnished and unkempt. The air was still, and he was so close I could see his cool breath hanging on the air. And yet I still couldn't believe it. He was a million miles away from this ivy-clad ruin full of whispered suspicions and broken promises.

I tried to steady my breathing though words were collecting, like mountains, at the base of my throat. The breeze lifted my hair, and just as I convinced myself he was pure manifestation, his hoarse whisper reached across the empty space.

'For the love of Nero, Tal … say something.'

Chapter 19

It was the vultures' hissing cry that pulled me back. That and his breath on my cheek. Surely visions, even fever-fuelled, didn't breathe?

I hadn't fainted, but my weakened limbs had given in to the sudden bolt of adrenaline, and much to my disgust, I'd buckled.

And now I could see he wasn't alone.

Eight more Knights of the Order of the Aquila, their standard emblazoned on their thick red capes, were standing around the moonlit ruin. Their military armour looked stained and dishevelled, and a new ragged scar ran across August's left cheekbone. His face was only centimetres away, gazing with the same fiery intent that always burned my bones while giving nothing away.

And for the tiniest of moments, for the smallest fragment of time that could possibly exist, the impulse to throw myself forward very nearly overpowered me. Nearly. And then his words ran through my head like a delirium.

'*The early integration analysis indicates a common stress symptom among the Prolet class, which may be a reaction to the existing vaccine to suppress independent will. Of course, the recent rioting cannot be tolerated.*

'*Because of this, and the new investigation required, I would recommend a temporary suspension of all new Prolet privileges and reinstatement of the existing Pantheonite system.'*

I shrank back as reality sharpened.

'You're a traitor and a liar!' I threw out, despite the energy it cost.

My anger spilled into the cold air like I was expelling that part of me that had ever been hypnotized. The terrified ringside Prolets ran through my head in tandem with August's traitorous words.

His exhausted face creased up into a heavy scowl.

'I don't know who you are!' I scathed, ignoring the pain fire-balling inside, and clambering to my feet.

His gorse-bush eyebrows flew together as he also stood up warily.

'You're hurt!' he exclaimed after a beat, and a flicker of emotion passed swiftly across his face. Like caring. *Not caring. Lying, lying eyes.*

He reached out and I stepped back, conscious I was in no fit state to run even if my fury hadn't demanded more. Lives had been lost, promises shattered, hopes destroyed – and all that besides twelve months of my life crushed into little more than the ashes, like this godforsaken city.

'How could you?' I forced out through gritted teeth. 'You claimed you were a Knight of the Old Order, that you believed in the free world, in Arafel … And I believed you. The same way I believed you hated Octavia, and everything Pantheon stood for, with every cell of your genetically modified body! And yet, as soon as the first opportunity arises to abandon everything and everyone, you skulk away like one of Octavia's dogs!'

August's face grew darker and stormier as he listened to my breathless tirade, a small vein in his neck pulsing swiftly.

'Commander General, Sir!?' one of his men interrupted, from the east side of the cathedral.

'And the Voynich!' I continued scathingly, ignoring him. 'You said you wanted to burn it yourself … stack the pyre high and

224

put Octavia at the top! Weren't those your exact words? But that was never the truth was it?

'What was the truth? Do you even know yourself? How can anyone who claims to love his people abandon them to a life of slavery and torture; and their children to living like scavenging rats beneath this crumbling wreck of a city!'

I was shouting now, but didn't care. My accusations echoed through the shattered building while August regarded me with an unfathomable expression, his hand gripping his empty Diasord belt until the whites of his knuckles gleamed.

'Commander!' one of the men called again.

He was standing in the centre of an empty stone window frame, opposite us, a black scowl pinned to his face.

'Silence, Grey!' August barked. 'The young ones got away? Where are they? Are they here?'

He fired the questions rapidly, his voice strained and fatigue etched into every line on his shadowed face. But he wasn't going to deceive me, not again.

'Give me one good reason why I should tell you!' I bit back.

'Commander!' the one called Grey interrupted again, this time much more urgently.

August spun on his feet in one violent move, his face contorted with fury and raven-black hair dishevelled. I struggled to steady my own raspy breathing as I fumbled with my leather rations bag. I was light-headed, sick and so disorientated, but I still had a few darts. He might have his personal guard, but I had my pride. And my temper.

'The sky! Commander General, Sir!' Grey said ominously.

And there was enough in his tone for everyone to understand that there was no time left for waiting. We all swivelled our gazes to stare up through the broken nave and into the endless beyond. It looked innocent enough, with the occasional twinkle through the awakening haze. But then the horizon started to disappear behind the shadow of something archaic, predatory and huge.

'Tal!' My name broke the sudden intense silence, but the voice didn't belong to August.

I shot a look back down the nave of the medieval church, and saw three people staring my way. Even at my distance, I could read their distinct expressions: anxious, disbelieving, accusing.

'August?' Aelia called, her voice cracking under the strain of her confusion, as Eli broke into a limping run. Strained, abrupt tones filled the air as August strode out to the central aisle.

'Grey, run an ammunition check! Harlo, Dent … cover the rear, the rest of you stay – stay with me. And wait for my command!!'

'Talia! I couldn't find you! Are you OK? Where did he come from?' Eli signed frantically as he limped towards me.

I nodded, searching the church for Max, and scowling when I finally found him, silhouetted beneath in the darkest part of the nave. He'd levelled his crossbow and was advancing purposefully, towards August.

'Don't waste your time! He's not worth it, Max!' I yelled frantically, recalling his threat.

'If he'd kept his promise, we wouldn't have ended up inside Pantheon, inside that cage! He's dead as far as I'm concerned, or will be if I ever see him again.'

Max didn't even acknowledge me. His eyes were locked on August, his expression thick with grim hatred. And I understood why. He knew what August's disloyalty had cost – the Prolets, Pan, Arafel … But most of all, he understood the cost to us. In just a few short months, August had forced a wedge between the tightest childhood bond and changed me. Max knew it and understood that he couldn't undo it, no matter how hard either of us tried. In a parallel universe, my heart would be whole and his. And he cared.

'Max!' I yelled again, ignoring the pain ratcheting up inside.

'Let him come,' August snapped, signalling to his loyal men. 'I have nothing to hide.'

'Oh yes, let him come. I do so enjoy heroic displays.'

226

Everything stopped as the familiar, languorous voice cut through the air like a dirty blade. And as I dragged my gaze around, the hairs on the side of my neck and face prickled with revulsion. Instinctively, I groped for my catapult.

He couldn't be. Not here, right now. Could he?

But it seemed he could. And no matter how much I denied it, the view didn't change. At the top of the nave, his death-adder eyes boring into mine, was the man responsible for everything.

Tonight, he was dressed as a conquering hero with a long black military greatcoat over his Roman regalia, and what appeared to be a battalion of griffin-mounted guards swooping in behind him. And yet there couldn't be anything less heroic about this man. This hate-fuelled cacodemon of a man.

Cassius.

With a new cavalry. The new cold-eyed griffins appeared less creatures of legend, and more sketches of cruelty. Bigger and sleeker, they still had the hindquarter of lion, and the majestic head of an eagle. But unlike the griffin Eli tamed, their bodies were the colour of old blood, and there was a coal-black streak down their gullets. Their wings were free, and there was one pure black, riderless griffin just behind Cassius, cawing its importance to the disappearing stars.

I scowled. Cassius hadn't wasted any time in putting Octavia's laboratories to good use.

And then I spied *him*, lurking in the shadows just behind Cassius – the reason for our discovery in the Flavium, for our incarceration in Ludi, and the reason we very nearly lost our lives in the most brutal way possible. He looked bruised, and uneasy, but it was definitely him. My eyes narrowed to slits.

'Rajid!' Aelia exclaimed in disbelief. 'What's happening?'

He shrugged in discomfort, limping away. He'd clearly experienced his share of Cassius's temper. But I had no sympathy. A fresh loathing blazed through me as I recalled Max's slip about the Prolets' hiding place while we were incarcerated.

Whether Rajid had started a traitor, he'd certainly ended one.

I'd stifled my suspicions because of Aelia, because I needed to believe there were some good people in Isca Prolet. Arafel kind of people. But he'd nearly killed Max and me. And now he'd led Cassius straight here. For the young Prolets.

I closed my hand around my catapult, barely registering as Eli slipped out of the church into the shadows.

'Well, isn't this delightful? A reunion! The cave-man and the crusader, so maligned and misunderstood,' Cassius jeered venomously, stepping across the top of the broken stone altar.

'How does it feel, oh great Commander General, to return to a homeland that knows you to be the coward and traitor you truly are? A homeland that scorns you?'

August turned to face Cassius, every aspect of his proud body exuding contempt.

'I don't know, Cassius, why don't you tell me? After all, your brother very nearly destroyed your reputation when he abandoned you for the outside – didn't he?'

A slow, frigid smile grew across August's face as he spoke, his unexpected words hanging oddly on the dead air. Suddenly it felt as though I was shrinking, that the world around me had grown extraordinarily large, with every sound accentuated. I held my breath, despite the looming silence.

'As we seem to be sharing, why don't we explore that? The fact that your very own brother didn't trust you enough to share the most important scientific discovery of the century? That he chose to seek out rank Outsiders, people he'd never met before and forge a brand-new beginning, rather than trust it … with you?'

Spider fingers scuttled down my spine, and I fought to clear my muddled head, to retain the power of logical thought.

I glanced around for Eli, for the person who would make it right, explain it even, but all I could see was a white-faced Aelia standing between the back rows of the pews.

Looking as frozen as I felt.

'And he took the precious research you and Octavia had been slaving away on, and disappeared,' August jibed, 'leaving his little brother to pick up *all* the pieces. Because the truth was … you weren't nearly as talented as Thomas. Were you?'

Cassius threw his head back and filled the hollow space with an ugly, scathing laugh that jarred every nerve in my body.

'It's quite a story, isn't it? He cracked the Voynich code,' August went on, 'but instead of sharing his discovery with you – his only remaining bloodline and official scientific partner – the big brother you looked up to left you with only a psychotic dictator for company. And now her number one protégé is shaping up to be a real black seed, rotten to its pithy core … aren't you, Cassius? Octavia would be so proud.'

The cathedral floor suddenly darkened as the large ominous shadow passed slowly overhead once more. Cassius glanced skywards, signalling his guards to form a tight pack around his central altar. They obeyed instantly, while August stalked towards Cassius, like a panther cornering its prey.

My heart started to pound. August had a quarter of the guard Cassius had surrounding him, and I shouldn't care. *But I did.*

'Poor Cassius,' he continued, unfazed by Cassius's clear advantage, 'left to ponder how his big brother worked it *all* out, while playing lapdog to Octavia. And it's a shackle you just can't throw off, isn't it? Which is why you brought in Octavia's toxic niece. A girl barely out of military training, to do your dirty work while you hide behind your precious programme.

'But the truth is, it doesn't matter how many laboratories and scientists you have at your disposal, or how many times you mix up the DNA and invent a new hybrid, because the one thing you desire most of all … *your brother's approval* … is dust. Just like him.'

'*Silentium!*' Cassius roared, pulling his Diasord from his belt and jumping down into the aisle. His griffin swiftly followed, throwing its magenta head back with a rapacious crow.

I glanced around for Eli again, desperate to know if he was reeling like me.

Cassius was Thomas's younger brother? It couldn't be true. *Could it?*

It was so improbable, it made no sense, and yet simultaneously … all the sense in the world.

I forced myself to think, my head racing with August's revelations. I already knew Cassius was one of the few original scientists from the time the domes were created; and that he, Octavia and Thomas had been part of the same team working on the Voynich at the time of the Great War. But now I was to believe they were actually related? A shiver stole down my spine.

How could I be staring at Cassius, flesh and blood, with Thomas all but dust in the ground?

And if Cassius and Thomas shared a blood tie, and Thomas was my ancestor, didn't that mean Cassius, Eli and I must also share a blood tie?

Bile started to crawl up my throat. The idea that Cassius was related to me was repugnant to the core, and yet every cell of my body felt shadowed with the truth. Perhaps it was the part of me that also found it hard to deny August. *Dark to dark.* I shuddered.

'And now you know he chose best. He took a chance, didn't he? A chance on a real life between the red earth and blue sky.'

August was in full combat mode as he prowled across the large grey flagstones. I dug my nails into the fleshy parts of my hands, not wanting to watch and yet unable to drag my eyes away.

'And everything since – the experiments, the games, the Prolet trials, the hunt for the chimera code, the disowning of your own son … it's all been about your jealousy… Jealousy of the brother, who even in his grave bequeathed a far greater legacy than you could ever dream of.'

I stared as August's convoluted revelations grew more tangled by the second.

'*The disowning of your own son?*'

More mystery underpinned by another nagging truth that had been there all the time. I inhaled sharply.

Cassius lunged before August had even finished, his Diasord gleaming in the pale dawn light, and sending up a spiral of smoke as it struck the stone floor. August whipped out an ugly-looking metal blade, but I could tell it was no match for the weapon Cassius was brandishing.

Cassius smiled caustically.

'Did Pantheon's disgraced son lose his Diasord on his pointless crusade? But this makes it all too easy!'

He lunged again, and this time caught August's forearm. A scent of burning flesh filled the air and two of August's battalion started forward. I sucked my breath in, and suppressed the urge to run in.

He wasn't who I thought he was. Perhaps he deserved this.

'Stay!' August yelled to his soldiers, readying himself again.

This time his lunge struck Cassius powerfully across the shoulder, sending him staggering across the floor. He crashed into a stone pillar before steadying himself and looking back with a menacing scowl.

'Kill them ... But not Augustus – I have a more useful end in mind for him,' he hissed, his voice making a long, sibilant sound around the cold space.

'No!'

Aelia's cry split the air as she pelted down the aisle to join her brother.

'Get back, Lia!' August roared, just as one of the mounted guards reared, his Diasord outstretched.

For a second the whole world drained to black and white as she flew towards August, blind to the teetering griffin until it crashed with a victorious crow, her slight body receiving the full impact of its serrated beak. A thick scream ricocheted through the cold air. It was a scream that stripped my bones faster than any hungry predator could.

'Aelia!' I yelled, flying up the left of the nave, only dimly away of Max by my side.

I skidded to a halt near Leofric as August's soldiers closed in the centre, forming a defensive group around their Commander General and Aelia's small, heaped body. My breath came short and jagged. Although August's soldiers were seasoned gladiators, I could see how exhausted and poorly equipped they were opposite Cassius's mounted guard. And Aelia wasn't moving.

The griffins started closing in, their interest caught by the scent of freshly seared meat that lingered, and their thick lion paws making light work of the broken pillars and decaying pews.

I caught my breath, fighting to think rationally.

I didn't care about him; he was a traitor. Wasn't he?

But Aelia was in there.

'This is not Aelia's fight, Cassius!' August bellowed, white with fury. 'She has not been convicted of any crime and you need her. Pantheon needs her!'

'Crime? What an interesting word!' Cassius ridiculed.

'What about the crime of withholding highly classified information? State information, punishable by death? Or perhaps the crime of inciting a crowd to rebellion? Or then again, how about enlisting the help of an outside community to destroy the Civitas that has nurtured and supported her work! Now, surely that is a crime deserving the very worst traitor's death? On the contrary, Commander, I think Dr Aelia Vulpes is right where she deserves to be.'

I tried to swallow, but my mouth was so dry and my head spun with a million conflicting thoughts. Why, despite everything, did I still want to rush in and be the one brandishing a Diasord by August's side?

He and his battalion stood protectively around Aelia, their weapons levelled, and his strained Equite face as stony as the bomb-blasted sculptures around us. I flashed back to the Flavium just twelve months before.

'*I stand for the Cyclops!*' he'd raged.

And now he was taking on Octavia's successor. Which didn't make any sense, unless ...

I was suddenly aware of Max, pulling me back into the shadows. At my back. Protecting me. Despite everything.

'Stay out of sight,' he whispered urgently. 'You're injured. I'll find Unus.'

My stomach lurched as though I'd swallowed a bowlful of raw shellfish. I threw a glance up at the tower, and caught a glimpse of a pale face through the narrow, arrow-slit windows. The young Prolets were marooned in the tower, awaiting judgement by Cassius and his band of executioners. Aelia, the rebel doctor I never thought I'd like, was fast turning out to be the closest thing to a sister I'd ever had – and then there was that damned racking ache in my chest, nowhere near the actual Minotaurus wound. It was enough.

'We have to help them,' I ground out.

And there was the truth. I would rather die trying, than let the doubt consume me any more. The relief was as fresh as an Arafel breeze.

Max scowled, his protest tangible. Before he sighed.

'Feral and free,' he whispered, leaning forward to gently kiss my forehead.

And it felt such a ray of peaceful light in the eye of a storm.

'Tell me now?' I whispered, not trusting myself to look at him.

'No,' he said vehemently before pulling me to him in the tightest embrace. 'When we get home and it's just you, me and the fireflies,' he breathed.

And for the briefest second, I was right there.

And then the air was filled with the angry clash of Diasord and metal. My veins were flooded with purpose, and pulling away, I nodded towards the intact tower.

'Why run when you can fly?' I challenged.

He winked, just as though I'd thrown him an apricot.

'Just like at home,' he added, as we started at a sprint towards the tower.

The shout went up immediately, but our tree-running limbs covered the ground swiftly, reaching the tower long before they guessed what we were intending. And then we were climbing, scaling the medieval stone walls of the tower like we were tree-running for real, using the uneven stones as we might the knotted branches and forks in the forest.

And although my wound scorched with every push, there was a cathartic therapy to leaving the ground behind, to scaling a fortress of prayer. We had a peace hut at the top of the valley in Arafel, but there was something about the solid construct of this tower that reached out and supported us back. I could feel people had been strong here, had stood for something other than a world of control and carnage.

We reached the tower's topmost windows, just as the first barrage of laser fire came. It ricocheted off the grey dusty walls around us as we pushed through neighbouring stone windows. I was the first to collapse onto the wooden floor inside, taking only a couple of seconds to realize Max wasn't with me. My world went white.

'Max!' I yelled in a half-strangled voice, pulling myself up to the next window just as a bloodied hand reached in. Atticus and I grabbed and hauled, as another barrage of crossfire deflected off the thick stone walls.

'You're hurt?' I demanded, as he slid in a heap at our feet.

My chest throbbed as I leaned over him, barely concealing my own agony.

'Pot kettle black!' he panted, pushing himself up to inspect his left bicep, which oozed a steady trickle of blood.

It was only a flesh wound, but Therry found some cloth among Lake's meagre provisions store, and I bound it swiftly.

When no one was watching, I also grabbed some extra cloths and pushed them in against my own chest wound, which was beginning to seep. It wasn't a good sign, I knew, but there were bigger things to worry about.

We took up posts by the windows. Now we were out of sight, the guards had returned their attention to Augustus; and from this vantage I could see he and his gladiators were outnumbered by at least four to one. The odds were terrifying.

'So, whose side are we actually on?' Max breathed, his eyebrows arching.

'Ours!' I shot back.

I lifted my dart tube to my lips and took careful aim.

'More darts!' I yelled, releasing my first.

It struck one of Cassius's guards in the neck and he fell from his griffin with a thud at August's feet. August threw a look up at the tower, but I couldn't tell if he was grateful or furious with our intervention. His lips were taut, his expression grim. It didn't matter, I told myself, I was doing this for Aelia, for the Prolets, for the outside.

'Use the weapons, use anything you can!' I yelled to the terrified Prolets.

The eldest took up positions at the narrow windows beside ours, and for the next few minutes we rained down fury, using Atticus's stockpile as missiles. It seemed fitting somehow, to deploy debris from the old world against debris from the new.

A number of Cassius's guards were instantly ordered to return our barrage, dragging their attention from the battalion on the floor to our narrow windows instead, which was precisely the plan.

'Aaergh!'

The thin scream merged with the deafening Diasord laser fire. I turned just as Faro's thin body slumped to the stone floor, her pigtails askew and freckles paling. Atticus was at her side in a heartbeat, gently pressing his fingers into her neck. His profile was masked, but a muscle in his cheek throbbed violently, and for the first time I ached for him. He didn't need to look up for me to know Faro wasn't coming to Arafel.

I turned back to my window, trying to ignore the pain darkening the inside of my broken ribcage.

'*Are we going to die here?*'

Her question returned like a ghost. And I'd let her believe she wasn't. Why was it always the ones who deserved it least? Why wasn't it me?

I stared at the violence and carnage below us, my thoughts caught up like a storm. August's soldiers were fighting like lions and the floor was littered with Cassius's soldiers, but they were still hideously outnumbered. The griffins were moving in like a pack of vultures, ready to make a meal out of those who'd so recently commanded them, Aelia was still heaped in the middle, and I was just too far away.

My breath was ripped and uneven, and my thoughts were growing uglier by the second. Bodies were strewn everywhere, like the Flavium, dirty and broken. *Black to black. Dust to dust*. No matter what I did, everyone I loved got hurt. Grandpa, Pan, Lake, Aelia and now Faro. I scanned the floor feeling my emotions drain away like my blood – *drop by drop*.

One of August's exhausted gladiators collapsed directly in front of Aelia's body. August swung around, trying to widen his ground but she was still too exposed. Two more of Cassius's cavalry wasted no time in dismounting and moving in, their purpose as vicious as their raised Diasords. And I couldn't breathe. Aelia's elfin face flashed before my eyes, her rebellious voice ringing in my ears:

'*Kiss my Prolet arse!*'

I knew what I had to do.

'Kiss mine,' I whispered.

'Cassius!' I yelled in the next breath, my voice sounding raw and rebellious.

Boudica, Aelia said. My lip curled and I leapt, poising on the stone window like one of the forest animals from home. There was a shout from the floor and several guards, including the ones

236

close to Aelia, levelled their Diasords. I combed the territory, assessing it as I would in a tree-running trial. There was a crumbling wall to my right, and roughly a ten-metre drop. It wouldn't be too far in the forest. But here, and with a pierced chest? I closed my eyes. And leapt like a cat.

Max's shout rang in my ears as I flew, landing on top of the crumbling, ivy-clad wall with a jolt. I felt the impact right up through my neck and shoulders, and struggled to keep my balance as something warm and wet gushed through my chest bandage. But I knew better than to hesitate. I'd learned that from the animals in the forest.

'*To hesitate is to lose, Talia.*'

I caught hold of the crumbling wall edge, and swung down onto solid ground with a leap that only just skirted the Diasord fire. Then I sprinted across the high back of a pew towards the centre of the nave, leaping and diving through the chasing laser fire. Until he raised a black arm and the fire ceased. I fixed my gritty stare on his, willing myself past the pain and weakness blazing inside.

'Ahh, I wondered how long it would take for the wildcat to join us,' Cassius drawled. 'But of course, the errant knight is in danger, and no matter what has passed, the wildcat will lurk, waiting for a moment to pounce and trade all her pointless little lives at once. But for what exactly? When the armour has lost its gleam?'

Silently, I leapt from the back of the pew directly into the centre of the aisle. Facing him. I was now fully exposed, less than ten metres from the man I detested with every bone in my body. My bandage was leaking badly, but something else was flaring through my veins, keeping my limbs moving. I gripped my tree-house dart tube in one hand, and one of my last remaining darts in the other. And forced a smile.

'I guess you could say I'd choose an aquila over a death adder any day.'

My words emptied slowly, and I had the satisfaction of watching his mouth twitch.

'Truth is, it wasn't quite as easy to acquire my pointless little life as you thought, was it? When it was just you and me?'

I advanced with the best prowl the volcano inside would allow.

'You'd have thought a strong Roman Equite like yourself would have the upper hand against this … wildcat … wouldn't you? But I wasn't the one who ended up trussed like a chicken for the plucking.'

I smiled as Cassius glowered.

'For the love of Nero, get out of here, Tal!' August threw out, his voice thick with fatigue. 'This isn't your battle; you've other priorities!'

His face was stained with blood, his soldiers were failing, but his eyes flashed with grit and pride.

Why? Why had he done it?

'Ahh yes, the insurgent Prolet children!' Cassius mocked. 'How civilized that you should round them up for us, ready to escort back to Pantheon for investigation … and perhaps a fresh round of vaccinations? We've had better success with the latest round.'

I recalled the pale-faced Prolets incarcerated beneath the Flavium, and ground my teeth. The vaccine was such a violation of free will. It flew directly in the face of everything Grandpa stood for. Everything I'd inherited.

'Yes, when faced with anarchy, eradicate free will!' I returned. 'Yet I don't recall any other great leader in history needing to genetically manufacture his own army. Just where is the Book of Arafel?' I fired. 'And Lake … where is the child?'

Cassius's face contorted into a sly smile. 'Where is the page, Talia? And what interest do *you* have in a child of Pantheon?'

'The same interest as you … Father.'

I spun around in the direction of the young, familiar voice to find Max, Atticus and Unus bridging the bottom of the nave like a wall. My eyes flew to Atticus's face.

He was Cassius's son?

I knew it, of course. I just hadn't been able to admit that the connection was there. And it wasn't because they bore a resemblance, though Atticus was leaner and taller. The proof was there, in Atticus's bearing, in his condescension. In his guilt.

And his sinister address sent fresh nerves haring through my body.

'Atticus!' Cassius scorned violently. 'You are no son of mine! Do not expect any special dispensation for this act of disobedience and rebellion. You will be treated exactly the same as the other insubordinates. You will …'

'… unlike his father, be the finest son of Pantheon its people have ever seen!' August roared, his voice echoing through the church like a prophecy.

And then he was sprinting, tackling Cassius before he could react, crashing him down from the stone altar as his black griffin reared. It emitted a throaty caw as it leapt into the top of the aisle, skidding into the brawling men. I was running before they halted, aware the air was thickening with hissing threats. The hairs on the back of my neck prickled in recognition. They were the cries of the natural world, *challenging the unnatural.* I shot a look back and my unique, one-in-a-million twin was standing inside the old stone entranceway, flanked by the flock of ravenous cinereous vultures.

'He brought the vultures,' I whispered to myself wonderingly.

And then pandemonium enveloped us all.

Eli waved the flock forward, and there had to be at least twenty of them now. They were smaller than the griffins by half, but far more experienced at the hunt. They were also territorial. I could tell by the look on their ugly, ravined faces that they weren't intending to leave hungry. The vultures took to the air with easy precision, creating a black tunnel of wind as they soared down towards the griffins.

The griffins responded immediately, rearing to the unexpected challenge, and shaking free their mounts.

'Tal, move!' Max yelled, approaching at a run with Unus lumbering behind him.

I scanned the guards. There was no order any more. Every inch of the stone floor was a writhing mess of giant birds and soldiers, Diasord meeting Diasord, beaks tearing flesh. Anguished screams and crows merging with the stench of blood, until it was impossible to tell who was who.

Come what may nature finds a way. The words were in my head and heart, as I bent low and ran right into the heart of the mayhem.

The encroaching dawn poured a mist over the chaos as I searched, as if to fade the violence. But at last I found what I was looking for: a small limp body right in the centre.

Aelia was white and unmoving, although there was a large wound at the base of her neck, where the griffin had buried its beak. She'd also lost a lot of blood, which was congealing around her head, and as I dropped to my knees beside her, I was vaguely aware of Max also skidding in beside me. I pushed the tips of my fingers into her neck, and could just feel her strength and fire, hanging on by a thread. I threw Max a terrified glance. He nodded and leaning forward, scooped her up as gently as though she were newborn.

He stood up, cradling her.

'Run!' I yelled furiously. 'I've got your back!'

I lifted my slingshot and fired at a guard running directly towards Max's broad shoulders. My small stone hit him square in the forehead, stunning him long enough for Max to start sprinting, through the frenzy, towards the tower. We both knew Aelia's own meagre first-aid stores were probably her last chance. *If there was one.*

And he ran as though his tree-running pride depended on it, dodging griffins and laser fire, despite his unconscious load. I kept my slingshot trained, firing and reloading repetitively, and he was nearly there, nearly at the tower.

Then I saw it. A single lone arrow, flying straight down the aisle, as though caught up in a time warp. So, it was both slow enough to watch, and too fast to stop, all at once. It was following Max and Aelia. Too closely. Until everything fell into some sort of disordered, distorted motion.

Because it couldn't happen. Not now. Not while I had his back. Not doing something I'd instigated. Unquestioningly. For me.

But it did.

It found him. Buried itself at the top of his spine. And he paused, as though he couldn't quite believe it himself. Indignant. Before collapsing. First onto his knees, and then sideways into a heavy sprawl, his shoulder bearing the brunt of both their bodies. *Being the hero. Always.*

And my world slowly fragmented, like a jigsaw being pulled apart by a cyclone. All at once we were back at the waterfall, the only moment in our lives Max had ever been vulnerable. The only moment Eli and I had ever needed to rescue him.

My gaze swung back, fuelled by denial, towards the source of the attack. Cassius. Lowering a short bow he had picked up from a fallen guard, a triumphant grin infecting his face.

And although it was my hand that grabbed the Roman dagger on the floor, it didn't feel like my legs that flew across the chaotic floor towards him. Towards the man who might as well have fired the arrow at me. Towards the man I loathed with more intensity I ever thought possible.

Towards my own black blood.

As a single word penetrated my fog.

'Please!'

Atticus. And there was just enough desperation in his voice for me to deflect the blade, and smash the butt-end of the dagger across Cassius's temple instead. He staggered backwards, and sprawled to the floor as Atticus skidded to his side, grabbing his father's fallen Diasord. He turned it back up towards me, his black eyes terrified and pleading, asking me to understand. But it didn't touch me – nothing could.

'He's still my father,' he said hoarsely, panting.

Cassius was muttering, dazed by my blow, and I had the satisfaction of watching a dark welt of skin split around his left eye socket. I gripped the dagger and held it high. I could let its own weight drive it downwards into his neck and, even if Atticus used the Diasord on me, it would all be over. A life for a murderous life. It was a good trade, wasn't it?

'Hunt to survive, Talia, nothing more.'

Grandpa's voice. As strong and loudly as though he were standing next to me.

I resisted. I needed this. But he was there, staying my arm. Letting the death adder slither away. I inhaled painfully.

'Talia, please?' Atticus lowered his Diasord, pleading with me. To be humane. To choose life. Didn't he know it was past that?

'Hunt to survive, Talia, nothing more.'

I dropped the dagger with a clatter and backed away, letting the fog take my thoughts. Just as Unus lumbered up behind me, his pudgy face white with exertion. He struck out at two large griffins rearing in Cassius's defence. They fell away, stunned.

'Tal?' he rumbled.

The room was awash only with blood and vulturic interest.

'Tal …?' he tried again, gently placing his huge boulder-hand on my shoulder.

I looked up at him and breathed out the only thought in my head.

'… *Max* …'

And Unus understood, as he always did. Turning with a rumbling roar, he started batting a line directly through the chaos, knocking soldiers aside as though they were rotten tomatoes spoiling a harvest.

And we were halfway down the aisle when a riderless griffin struck out in a frenzied panic, the violence of its attack bringing a vulture to a tumbling crash in front of us. The griffin recovered first, driving its beak down through the vulture's sparse tail feathers as Unus reached out and, lifting them as though they were river stones, scattered them down the middle pew. Clearing the aisle. Until finally there were only two inert bodies before us. Still and lifeless on the cold stone floor.

'Max …' my voice cracked as I sagged to my knees beside him, barely noticing as Unus deflected another looming guard.

I slid an arm under Max's head and lifted, despite the eruption of pain the manoeuvre cost me.

'Max!' I whispered dully. 'Please … you can say it …'

I was only dimly aware of the chaos around me, of Unus continuing to protect me as I cradled Max's heavy head.

'Talia?' My name hung on the air, but it wasn't Max's teasing voice.

It was an altogether deeper, harder tone, although right now it was also unrecognizably gentle.

'Max?' was all I could whisper, conscious too of Aelia's inert state.

If there had been a time we could help, surely that had passed. August dropped down beside his sister, and rolled her over. Her warm skin had taken on a pallid, waxen look, while creeping blue veins were reaching out beneath her glassy eyes. I looked away, not wanting to see her hold ebbing away.

'We have to move, Sir … the Prolets, Sir!' Grey interrupted, pointing beyond our heads.

I glanced up and caught my breath. A stream of terrified Prolet children were emptying out of the tower, and into the waste ground outside the cathedral. And as if it heard, the air grew suddenly dark as the huge, dark creature circled back, closing the awakening sky with its oppressive shadow. I shot a look back into August's drained face. The Prolets must have realized Unus was no longer protecting the stairwell, and made their escape before Cassius sent his guards inside. But out there they were even more exposed and vulnerable. I tried, really tried to think. But for once, the fire was out. What was the point any more? *It was hopeless.*

Cradling Max's head, I reached around and snapped off the exposed arrow length. The wood felt tapered and smooth, and when I withdrew it, it lay in the palm of my hand as innocently as the day it grew. It was partially stained, which was a curious irony. It too had been green and full of life, and now it too lay in pieces, bloodied and still in my hands.

Then an iron-clamp grip beneath my arms dragged me to my feet.

'No!' I screamed hoarsely, writhing and kicking back hard. 'I'm staying!'

A rough hand seized my face, forcing it up. It was August, and for a second I thought I detected empathy and real pain in the contours of his dust-stained face. He'd lost Aelia.

But what did he really know of either me or Max?

'Grey is a medic. He can help … and Unus will stay, to protect them,' he said in a low voice.

Unus nodded, and shuffled closer as if to convince me of his loyalty. As though I needed it.

August's proud Equite insignia was masked with thick congealing blood, as Grey dropped beside Max and Aelia, two more guards standing by.

'There are still the Prolets. Max would want you to help them. To live. For everyone's sake,' August urged, needing me to trust him.

I pulled back. I didn't and I couldn't leave Max; it was impossible.

This time August reached out and grabbed my shoulders.

'I thought you understood!' he seethed, as though he'd been suppressing the words for a long time. 'Don't you understand how important you are? The price on your own damned feral head?'

One of Cassius's guards careered into our circle. There was a momentary clash as Unus reached forward, then a sickening crack before he dropped him to the floor, motionless. I looked up at the fury creasing his gentle face, and closed my eyes. This war wouldn't be done until it had made monsters of us all.

An unnatural cry punctuated the sky. I gritted my teeth. It was closing in.

'Now,' August ground out, grabbing my hand, and somehow, my feet fell into step beside him, stumbling towards the stone archway that led outside.

We reached the ruined doorway and paused as mayhem rose to greet us. Prolets, scattered all over the grassy scrubland outside the cathedral, lost and vulnerable without Atticus to lead them. My body filled with an emotion, but I was too exhausted to identify it. Was it fear? Or denial? I only knew the ground was staining black, as the shadow approached like a brewing storm.

I'd lost Max. My chest felt like it was on fire, and I was struggling to take a full breath. But it still wasn't over. I threw my gaze skywards. It was the same creature I'd seen when Lake had been taken. I was sure of it. Cassius's mythical haga-phoenix.

The era of the black aquila.

Rajid's traitorous words spun out of nowhere. I blinked and was back in the Flavium again, staring at Livia's contemptuous profile as a huge, double-headed angel of death soared down to adorn her balcony, while the terrified Prolets awaited their fate.

I closed my gritty eyes. *I could still help.*

'Find somewhere to hide!' August growled. 'I'll round them up.'

I nodded, but he knew better of course. And as I stumbled instead towards the dispersed Prolets, I caught the faint echo of another sound. I exhaled harshly, aware my limbs felt detached and spent.

Cassius's hounds below ground, and an angel of death above.

'Molossers!' I yelled, converting all my emotion into one last burst of adrenaline. 'For the love of Arafel, move!'

245

Chapter 20

Chaos split the night. Terrified Prolets were scattering in every direction, and the nerve-shredding baying was getting louder every second. I wheezed as I ran, conscious the molossers' powerful legs would make short work of the tunnels beneath the ruined cathedral. And suddenly, I was intensely aware that I hadn't seen Eli since his release of the vultures.

A single-armed satyr ran in front of me, chasing the AWOL miniature griffin. I scooped both up, searching for a safe corner, and exhaled with relief as I caught sight of my twin, protecting a small group of Prolets beneath a broken stone lintel.

Surging across the waste ground, I deposited both with Eli before scanning the ground again, ignoring his entreaties. August had found Therry trying to follow the pig-dog down the tunnel steps behind the fallen gargoyle, while the rest of the young satyrs were still scattering in all directions. I ran out in the direction of a young satyr, acutely aware of fresh attention from the sky.

The black aquila was circling lower, its amber eyes in full hunting mode, as it suddenly power-dived, its coarse cry raking the air. I paused momentarily. It was a breathtaking sight. Its blood-red flight feathers gleaming in the encroaching dawn, its heads low and angled for the hunt. This creature wasn't born out of scientific curiosity for a lost era, it was the signature of something different. Something experimental, savage and archaic all at once. And it had a nature of its own that felt brutal and uncompromising. My lip curled. Hadn't it heard about the Minotaur?

I pelted towards the small satyr who was frozen to the spot, and pushed him as hard as I could. He went sprawling towards Eli, and I shot a twisted, satisfied smile to the sky. The creature wasted no time in proclaiming its fury, while adjusting its direction. And it was a most magnificent, arresting sight all at once: the creature diving directly at me, its four eyes gleaming and beaks open, displaying an ugly array of carnivorous teeth.

And I did feel the momentary impulse to run.

But then he was there, inside me, always when I needed him most. His voice guiding as clearly as though I was kneeling by his chair in his study.

'There is no freedom without sacrifice, Talia.'

I yanked out my last poison-tipped dart and nodded to the heavens.

'You always were right, Grandpa,' I whispered.

Its shadow loomed large, enveloping the wasteland and pushing back the dawn. As I prepared myself for impact I was vaguely aware of the sound of running feet, of a rough voice yelling behind me.

'Of all the most obstinate … stubborn … most frustrating feral … cats.'

Then the hurricane wind enveloped every other sound, just as a pair of strong arms pulled me forcibly to the ground. There was a deafening cry and, as I used what was left of my strength to dispatch the dart directly into the monster's black breast, the iron clutch of a claw designed only to maim and kill closed around both of us.

The ground fell away as though we were falling, not rising, while the pressure around my chest felt as though it would shatter

247

my ribcage at any second. But as I watched the cathedral ruin recede into the rest of the sprawled Dead City, I was engulfed by an odd sense of calm.

And it was only when the bird let out a drunken cry of euphoria, that I recalled I wasn't the only one clutched in its macabre, sharp claws. And it felt oddly consistent. That it was the two of us. Again. Like consistent fractures in the same story. The feral and the fettered somehow winding an adrenaline-fuelled dance. *Burning, always burning.*

A hand closed over mine, and I gripped back. Even from my twisted position, I could feel his exposed flesh and a blood-soaked tunic. It was too late now. And in a way it was the most freeing knowledge. Then there was another cry. I managed a jubilant gasp as its violence reached right through me. It was a cry of defeat as the dart finally took control of the beast, and paralysis set in.

It could have been worse. The talons holding us prisoner could have seized together as it plummeted towards the ground in a death spin. But instead the creature released its final prize, letting us fall like stones towards the unforgiving streets of the Dead City. *Dust to dust.* Somehow, through it all, we managed to stay entwined. And as I gazed across into the pink stain of a new day, I mumbled the words that had always felt like a prayer anyway.

'*Why run when you can fly?*'

Then there was the hollow splash of deep water, the slow suffocation of bitter cold, and finally, black.

Chapter 21

The hands and harmonies soothed as I passed through biting cold into the vacuum that stole reality. For the first time in days, the violent pain in my chest eased. And I wasn't furious or terrified or sad. I simply was.

If I could have stayed in that emotional and physical void, I'd have no hesitation. It felt like an intoxicating peace away from reality, and ignorant to its agony. So I let the hands take me to the darkness, and replace the suffering with dreams.

Until a choking breath split the still. Drawing me back to the cold air, and the silhouette of the Dead City, reaching up out of a glass river.

I sat up, disorientated, and looked around at my peaceful riverside surroundings, fumbling for my own wrist. There was the beat, regular and strong. Confused, I stared downwards at my fresh clean tunic. There was neat stitching up the front, just as though my mother had sewn it. I yanked it open, and the slim vertical scar snaking up my abdomen looked months old.

I inhaled audibly, willing the sweet spring air to help me remember.

Pale light was stealing up the river. I was seated on a grassy bank, and there was someone next to me. The contour of a tall, familiar gladiator reached through my semi-conscious delirium.

'August?' I spoke in wonder, his presence corroborating neither my life or death.

He rolled towards me, his olive skin glistening with fresh dew, and opened his eyes lazily, as though from a long, deep sleep. They fixed on me, softened by a light that had nothing to do with the honey blur of dawn.

Somewhere overhead a skylark warbled. It was a fresh song full of seafaring adventures, deep seas and of the creatures that swam there. Like Oceanids. The healing hands of the Oceanids reaching out to support me, *to save me.*

His hand was stroking my cheek, his warm lips searching for mine, stirring twelve months of repressed desire. His skin was intoxicatingly warm, his hands caressing and the only thing that mattered was quenching a need so real it almost hurt. Our bodies coiled instinctively, like snakes, around the most precious prize. There was no past, no future. Just this endless, satin moment, inside each other's kiss, suffocating all thoughts and questions. About the water. About the black aquila. About Aelia and Max.

MAX!

With a gargantuan effort I pushed August off. He groaned as if drunk while dragging himself to sitting. Whatever intoxication had cocooned us was ebbing away fast now, leaving nothing but a cold, ruined reality.

I was on my feet in a heartbeat. Conscious of how close I'd come to giving in to the worst impulse in my life – and how I was probably the most unworthy human being left on the face of the planet.

'Talia?' August was behind me, his hands on my waist, his deep whisper in my ear. It was mellow with need, and the sweetest, most divine torture. But he was a traitor. And Max and Aelia were dead.

I spun around to face him, my hurt welling up like river in a storm. Unstoppable and fierce.

'He's gone,' I whispered, staring up into his perfect face.

250

Where had the scar gone? All the battle bruises and fatigue? How dare he stand there, shining in the new morning sun when Max was likely filling the bellies of the scavenging griffins. Aelia too, and who knew how many of the young Prolets? Eli! Panic burned up my throat. He was alive when I left him, but now?

My heart flooded with memories, as heavy as molten metal, as the battle returned in minute detail.

How long had we been gone? And how had we survived? Let alone washed up here in this parallel universe beside a river as flat as glass? Perhaps this was some sort of purgatory, in which case I'd probably just failed my last test. *What did it matter, this ghost girl belonged in Hades anyway.*

'I don't know who you are.'

I backed off, aware of the early morning sun on the back of my neck, of the way I felt good, nurtured and healthy. And of how it was all so terribly wrong.

'How … how can this have happened?' I added in despair.

August was staring down at his bronzed arms, turning them over in awe, as though he had only just realized that he too was all fixed up, gleaming like a precious gem.

'Where are we?'

I swung my gaze about frantically, filled with a sense of grim recognition. We were still in the Dead City, the charred remains of a railway bridge and ruined buildings confirmed that much. And it looked as though the riverbank was a small oasis in the middle of the otherwise grey landscape. I looked back at the river; it was a black crystal snake glinting with secrets.

Closing my eyes, I forced myself to remember. The pain came first, then the violent clamp of suffocation, before the hands. Cold, healing hands that found me hanging by a thread. And breathed life back into my veins.

'Thank you,' I whispered, as though they could hear.

I fancied the smallest ripple on the glass surface.

'Are the Oceanids … healers?' I muttered, trying to rein in my

251

tumultuous thoughts. Trying to remember everything from before the river.

'There are legends, mythical tales that the Oceanids would abduct sailors near death and drag them down to hidden depths to heal them. In the stories they went on to live an undersea life of dreams and … debauchery,' August responded, his eyes narrowing.

The way he said debauchery made me flush, in spite of it all. I looked at my feet, nearly buried in the long healthy grass, as he inspected his hands.

'But despite their existence, I'd never believed the myths possible,' he added. 'Until now.'

I raised my eyes, my thoughts hardening. I had so many questions, but I had to think about Max and Aelia. And Eli. For the love of Arafel, where was Eli?

'How long have we been out?' I agonized, running towards the river, searching for any sign of life. There was no movement beneath the silent surface at all.

'I've no idea, and my Identifier was stolen in Europa … by bandits.'

I stared at him. Aelia had mentioned his dispatch to Europa, but nothing about bandits. It would certainly explain his knights' tarnished uniforms and lack of weaponry in the cathedral.

'We have to move! If any of them are alive … We're wasting precious time!'

'Tal, wait!'

I hesitated as August stepped up close, inside my space. I sucked in a breath. He always moved so damned fast. And his proximity still cross-wired everything. But right now, there was something else too.

'I've … missed you … so much,' he whispered with difficulty.

I exhaled, a rough breath that hurt so damned much. *Why now?* I wanted to scream. Words I'd spent so long wanting to hear they were almost tattooed on the inside of my brain. But it didn't matter. He was a traitor, Max and Aelia were probably dead, and I had no idea where Eli and the young Prolets were.

Unus too. They could all be dead. It was a thought that crushed so hard, I could only keep it from destroying me by running. There were no trees here, but the ground felt good beneath my leather-clad feet, and I was doing something.

'Why did you desert them?' I fired as he fell into step with me after a couple of minutes. 'When they needed you so much?'

'Is that how little you think of me? That I would abandon every principle I've ever held close, let alone my oath as an Equite?'

His voice was stony, and when I glanced at him his eyes were clouded.

Tendrils of doubt started to creep through my veins.

'What makes you think I deserted them at all?'

'But I saw you! The moving images in Isca Prolet ... Cassius ...'

My head crowded with all the accusations that had been festering for days; accusations that suddenly began to blur and dissipate.

'Think what Cassius is capable of, Talia!' August remonstrated. 'For the love of Nero, he can re-create pretty much anything!'

We were running beside the river. It must have been lovely here once: the glass water one side and the long green bank the other. But every so often the view was scarred with the blackened remains of a burned-out building, lest we forget. Nature and science; love and war; life and death.

I swallowed painfully. Why hadn't I thought of it before? The embryos in the bottle, the rows of laboratory tanks, the capability to re-create human life, only with a little extra signature coding.

'He ... re-created *you*?' I forced out.

He flashed me a tight-lipped frown.

'He would have, if it were the old Pantheon days. Octavia used to clone her Equites at birth. But it's far more efficient to use technology now. Remember all the screens and propaganda in Pantheon? The Senate has access to media tech beyond your wildest dreams. Why waste precious resources cloning anyone when they can have the same effect virtually?'

I swallowed, trying to align his response with all the questions in my head.

'So, the August I watched in Isca Prolet, and then in the Flavium was a … computer … image?'

I struggled to find a term for what he was suggesting.

His face was strained. 'It's a specialist area of simulated reality … but yes, sort of.'

Suddenly, I felt nothing more than a frightened forest rabbit, caught in the spotlight of some new Pantheonite toy.

'So how do I know it's the real you right now?' I whispered.

Without warning, he reached out and pulled me in beneath the crumbling canopy of an old shop. It was dark and dingy, and smelled of years of neglect. Then he drove me back until I could feel the rigid, cold stone against my back, his warmth moulding into my front.

I lifted my face to look at him. Really look, and this time I saw it all. Iris-blues, wide open and unguarded, his lips so close I could feel their warmth reaching for mine. At last he was there, the man I'd left on Octavia's balcony, the one who'd made all the promises.

'I think you know it's the real me,' he whispered intently.

And he was right – I did. Yet every cell of my disloyal body wanted to prove it. I stained to the roots of my sandy hair follicles. It was too much. How could I even think about August in this way when I'd already shared so much with Max? Promised him everything? Would August know? Could he sense I wasn't the same girl he left?

'But it doesn't stop at the images does it?' I whispered. 'Cassius is actually designing a Prolet army with one purpose: to serve him! And I saw the chimera in the laboratory,' I added, too conscious of the way our bodies were touching. 'It's … a time bomb.'

August frowned down at me. 'That little animal is the least of our troubles.'

'I know,' I breathed.

The frown deepened.

'Lake,' I whispered, watching the muscle in his cheek flex.

'What do you know of the child?' he demanded.

I thought of Thomas's classical chimera drawing and then Lake's distinctive, double-lidded eyes.

'I guess you could say I have an eye for a serpent.'

August stared at me, his thick brows drawn together. It was one of the old looks, one that took everything and gave nothing back. But this wasn't a time for secrets. I shook my head and, for the first time, he broke first, running his fingers through his raven hair as he shifted his weight back.

'I left Pantheon for two reasons. I'd lost support in the Senate. There were integration issues with the Prolet population ...'

'You found out they had minds of their own?' I shot back.

'Yes ... No! Look, there were issues, all predictable, but for which the Senate had little tolerance. Despite my repeated requests for time! Cassius recovered, and still had a lot of friends among the older Pantheonites. He made promises and gained authority as only Cassius can. Then, once he had support from two-thirds of the Senate he passed a resolution to unfreeze the Biotechnology Programme – in the interests of natural retirement and developing a fresh workforce for Isca Pantheon, so it was claimed.

'But it was all about gaining enough authority to restart the classified Prolet and chimera trials, which I only found out about through Rajid's surveillance.'

My shoulders tensed.

'I knew then it was only going to be a matter of time before he started developing the code for the Voynich's *Hominum chimera*,' August continued, 'as Thomas detailed in his research ...'

'*Hominum?*' I whispered, my head spinning until finally it arrived at the only translation that fitted.

Human.

And there it was. I stared up into August's face with the shadow of something stark and dystopian slowly staining every thought. I'd guessed at Lake's true identity in a way, but *human chimera*? It sounded so fantastical, even for Pantheon, even now.

'I played along with the Senate's recommendation that we return Isca Pantheon to its former order, but I'd already made up my mind, to find somewhere new. A fresh location in which to start again, with every last creature willing to come with me. But *Hominum chimera* … She's unstable … a different type of challenge altogether,' he muttered.

I thought of the small chimera animal hidden away in the laboratory, of its speed, agility and aggression. Lake seemed so innocent by comparison. Could she really be the human face of the Voynich's last secret?

'The Senate needed a high-ranking official to lead the mission for new locations. And Cassius wanted rid of me. He delighted in making it impossible for me to refuse after the Prolet riots, without losing all credibility.

'And then I had an idea. Very little real information existed at all about *Hominum chimera*, except for myths about its extreme volatility. A mission would give me the perfect cover to visit the birthplace of it all; to uncover any ancient stories about *Hominum chimera*'s abilities … and find out whether any DNA remains.'

'And does it?' I asked breathlessly.

August stared at me, picking his words with great care. 'We knew very little before we set out. The most famous story being that of *Hominum chimera*'s imprisonment beneath the Colosseum, within the real labyrinth of Rome.

'She was barely ever allowed above ground, because of her extreme strength and aggression. And yet on one celebratory public occasion, Emperor Augustus ordered her appearance. She was heavily shackled, with his strongest gladiators in attendance, but it wasn't enough.

'When she got there, she unleashed all her anger at being incarcerated for so long by snapping her chains and …'

'And?' I prompted.

'… devouring the spectators,' August finished bluntly.

I thought of Lake's serpentine eyes, and a shiver slid along my spine.

'In Pantheon, it was always assumed to be nothing more than a story, an old Roman fireside tale, if you like. But when we arrived in Rome's ruined Colosseum, we found a caved-in entrance to an ancient Hypogeum. Once we were inside, we found perfectly preserved catacombs with mythological frescos and engravings. One particular tomb depicted the same legendary story about *Hominum chimera* … told in exactly the same way.'

I swallowed to ease my dry mouth. *A story repeated had its roots in fact.* It was something Grandpa used to say.

'I took samples, and recorded images before we left, enough to share our findings and warn Isca Pantheon about the final destructive potential of *Hominum chimera*. Enough to lead a revolt against its re-creation, and discredit Cassius's renewed Biotechnology Programme. But we were ambushed on our way back, our evidence destroyed, and of course Cassius lost no time in sabotaging my name while I was away.'

I looked up at August's bitter expression and felt my guilt swell. It all made so much sense.

'It happened while we were sleeping,' he forced out. 'We never identified them, but …'

I nodded.

'They cut the throats of most of my soldiers while we were sleeping. They didn't realize a small party of us had left early to hunt. It was like returning to a battlefield. We weren't expected to return to Pantheon.'

I dropped my gaze to my feet, feeling like someone had just righted the world's axis. Finally. He'd lost some of his best friends, come close to death himself, and I'd done nothing but treat him like a deserter.

257

I lifted my hand to touch his cheek. He turned towards my fingers, pressing his lips against them.

'Lake's capabilities?' I whispered, knowing already what this was all leading to: power.

What sort of weapon was she?

There was silence, while the rotten guttering rattled above us.

'The tomb of *Hominum chimera* had a complete mosaic ceiling,' he responded after a beat, 'depicting the fabled chimera glowing like the sun. Like some kind of ancient Roman god describing *The Requiem*.'

'The Requiem?' I repeated, my words sounding oddly brittle.

'The Mass for the Dead.'

His eyes blazed even in the shadows, and I knew this was it, the real reason August had agreed to the mission in the first place. The only reason he'd risked leaving Aelia, the Prolets, perhaps even me, because of a bigger threat to us all.

'It's a myth we'd only heard whisper of before, that *Hominum chimera* can ... is capable of triggering a sequence of natural disasters, culminating in the eternal fire of damnation. In other words, the end of civilization as we know it.'

'Didn't we do that bit already?' I whispered, my brain reeling. 'What makes *her* so different?'

He smiled, pushing a stray hair back from my eyes.

'Now that's where it gets really Roman. *Hominum chimera* was believed to be the mother of all mythological beasts, the one hybrid capable of being stronger, faster and more agile than her only existing counterpart.'

I looked up at August, a strange acknowledgement sating my veins, as though the answer had been inside me all the time.

'Which is?' I asked, my voice sounding tight and odd.

He hesitated momentarily, iris-blues fading to ink, narrow and assessing. Then he leaned close, letting his lips brush my cheek as he whispered words that gleamed with a timeworn truth.

'Nature herself.'

258

Chapter 22

We slipped out of the dark building. The sun was higher now and the birds in full chorus. It seemed ironic that any creature would choose to live here.

'So re-creating *Hominum chimera* was always Cassius's aim?' I asked. 'Even in Octavia's time? He must have been scheming to overthrow her for years. The fact that Lake already exists ...'

August looked at me, a blaze of anger in his eyes.

'Yes,' he answered shortly. 'After Thomas left, Cassius was left with a clear choice: follow his brother or become Octavia's lapdog. There were always rumours about an illegitimate son, hidden away somewhere in Isca Pantheon, but Lake ... He told no one about her.

'It wasn't until Rajid came to me with tales of a honey-eyed serpent child, that I put it together with stories of *Hominum chimera*. I knew the scant stories we had weren't enough. I needed old-world evidence and knowledge, enough to warrant an official Senate investigation at least.'

There was a moment's silence while we paused to check our progress against the sun's position.

'Where are we even going anyway?' August frowned. 'You don't know these streets.'

'I'm navigating,' I muttered, squinting at the sky, 'the feral way.'

I was cutting an easterly direction across the city, having recalled Max saying something about the river running in a south-westerly direction. My initial target was the ruined cathedral, and from there I was hoping to pick up a trail. I couldn't think about any alternative.

Suspiciously, I scanned our surroundings, listening and watching as I might in the forest. We were moving down a medium-sized old road, approaching some sort of overgrown crossroad. The remains of a rusted sign caught my eye, its lettering just clear enough to make out a mottled *Exe Str**t*. It felt poignant and, briefly, I wondered about the bustle of life it once watched. A direct contrast to this dusty vacuum.

I scanned the rest of our surroundings. On my left was a succession of crumbling, bombed-out buildings, while to my right there was what must have once been a green park, although it now resembled more of a small forest. Directly ahead, at the end of the street, there was an old iron bridge that looked intact.

'It looks quiet enough,' August muttered.

I closed my eyes and let my senses tune in to the concrete jungle around me, though it felt so lonely without Max. *Without Max.* My chest flared as though the Minotaur was ramming its twisted horns into me all over again. He couldn't be dead. He just couldn't. I launched into a fresh sprint.

'Why didn't you detour to Arafel? We could have helped!' I fired as August caught up with me beneath the ornate bridge, and paused for breath.

He scowled as I assessed our next best route. His golden face gleamed with health. As though he had stepped straight from a wheatfield in Arafel. The thought only fanned my anger.

'And do what? Bring the entire Prolet population with me? So we could completely upset the balance of a precious Outsider community? The only one we know about in these parts?'

I looked up sharply.

'The only one you know about in these parts?' I repeated. 'You mean there are more?'

In all my years in Arafel, there had only ever been them and us – the Insiders and the Outsiders, the last of the real human race. But the question about other survivors had haunted my father. He'd spent so many evenings poring over old-world maps and hypothesizing where oases, like ours, could have sprung up.

And it was a possibility discussed at great length by Thomas's Council. I'd seen pages of minutes recorded in the Book of Arafel. But it was one emergency plan that had never needed to be dusted off, and as the years went on, most of us had drawn the lonely conclusion that Arafel was unique.

But right now, my pulse began to gallop.

'Where? Where are the others?'

Together, we would stand a chance. A chance against Cassius and his programme.

But August had no chance to answer. The north sky was suddenly awash with a fine magenta mist, followed by a roll of thunder that made the ground tremble.

I made a grab for one of the bridge's green supports, and shot an anxious look at August.

'And so it begins,' he offered cryptically, staring upwards.

'North-east, sporadic spread,' I analysed swiftly. 'What is it?'

He drew a breath. 'If I'm not mistaken, Cassius has unleashed his alpha weapon.'

And as though she heard, a poignant cry cut across the wind. It was so different to anything I'd heard before. A sound that raked through history, with a coarse and rusted voice.

We were running before the cry merged with its own echo, my heart beating with fresh hope. These streets were as decaying and abandoned as the rest, but if Cassius had seen fit to unleash his chimera, there had to be good reason.

This time I didn't care who saw me. The blood sky was our guide and the north-east direction fitted with the path I would expect the task force to take if they'd survived somehow. *Somehow.* My heart leapt.

'Talia! *Hominum chimera* is one of the most volatile creatures of the ancient mythical world,' August called, struggling to keep up. 'If it's her, or a form of her, it's unlikely she'll remember you. There's a lack of conscious awareness between morphing forms.'

I thought of the small child who'd looked so innocent, and yet different in a way I couldn't quite identify. She always appeared wise beyond her years, earning her friendships in unlikely places as well as the devotion of a wise silenus.

Pan had clearly known. No doubt he'd been charged with her guardianship and protection as a dutiful Prolet. A ball of emotion rose up my throat and I ran faster to beat it. It was a duty he'd fulfilled to his death.

'Why do you think Atticus and Lake took off together with the young Prolets?' I asked, leaping the remains of a large metal pipe protruding from the road.

'Did Atticus know what she was? Perhaps he saw her potential to defeat his own father? Why else would he free her?'

August shrugged, white-lipped.

'From what I've learned of mythical *Hominum chimera*, she wasn't a creature capable of friendship or loyalty. In that way, Lake already confounds expectations. But she is Cassius's handiwork, and a creature of Pantheon,' he added grimly. 'She and Atticus must have befriended each other while in isolation. It was no secret that Cassius bore little love for his son, that he was the result of an illicit Prolet liaison. Atticus must have made a few underground friends, and broken Lake out for revenge when they decided to try for Arafel.'

'Hell hath no fury like a son of Rome scorned,' I quipped.

August looked at me.

Just as I recalled the page of chimera coding torn out from Thomas's research. Panicking, I fumbled in my leather rations bag and, much to my amazement, pulled out the crumpled piece of paper. It was just how I remembered it. Somehow it had survived the river and the Oceanids, and I already knew better than to ask how. I smiled, before realizing there was something missing.

'My slingshot!' I exclaimed, double-checking my tunic pockets. They were empty.

I knew a single slingshot wasn't going to be much use against the mythical beast of beasts, but it meant so much more than that. It had belonged to my father, and my grandfather before him. It was the only weapon I used in the forest, and I felt naked without it.

August frowned.

'If the Oceanids kept one of your personal possessions it's a good sign. It means they consider you worthy. They usually only keep personal effects they intend to trade in the future. It's a compliment of sorts. Like a calling card.' After a pause he added, 'They didn't take your new dart tube though. The one shaped like a tiny treehouse.'

I looked down, and saw Max's gift still resting against my chest. And in a flash, I was back in Arafel, accepting his gift, making him promises. It was chased swiftly by memories of the night we shared, lying together and watching the dawn creep through the living canopy above our heads. Max had pulled me to him and called me his girl.

Guilt clawed up my throat. I was the most disloyal human being alive, I deserved my world to be ripped apart. And there were so many things written in August's face. Curiosity, sympathy, understanding, *jealousy*. My eyes fell to the ground. What use was any of it? How could this ghost girl ever be whole again?

As if he could sense my despair, August lifted his hands and placing four fingers against his lips, released a piercing whistle into the full glare of the morning sun.

I started. 'What are you doing? You'll bring it right here.'

'I might, but if the others have made it across the city, they may need the distraction. Besides, now we have a lead it's a risk worth taking. We lost most of our horses in the raid ... so we hid the last few in a small copse on the north side of the cathedral. We apprehended one of the raiders; it's how I know Cassius sent them. Anyway, he mentioned the Prolet escape and I hazarded a guess they might make their way to the old ruined cathedral. Atticus was fascinated by the ruins as a young boy, and it's the obvious landmark.'

He pulled me back into the shadows of a large building, fronted by a series of tall, rusted frames.

'But we don't have time to wait ...'

My protest was interrupted by the sound of beating, not the striking of a drum or the peal of war. This was something different. It was the approach of an animal. Of hooves. Heading our way.

Fascinated, I watched the dust billow up, automatically predicting the animal's size and species. It was a skill I'd learned while hunting, assessing the depression of a branch, or displacement of water in order to better know my adversary – or friend.

'About the size of a horse,' I muttered, just as the most breathtaking white stallion rounded the bottom of the overgrown street, and throwing its head high, galloped directly towards us.

With its bare back and white mane flying, I could have almost persuaded myself I was standing at the edge of the outside forest, looking out onto the scraggy moorland that stretched out from the wood. Herds of cross-breeds ran there, wild horses with thick coats and ever thicker manes. Outsiders had tried to catch and tame them many times, but no one had had much luck. Before Eli. My eyes swam momentarily, and I forced myself to blink back the pain. To bury the doubt.

As the stallion approached, I recognized it as the same animal that carried August into the Flavium all those months before – and without a saddle I could see it didn't have typical equine physiology at all.

'Wings?' I muttered, only half surprised.

August grinned, as it slowed to a trot.

'Ornamental only. One of the weaknesses of Pegasus's genetic coding. The wingspan to body weight ratio isn't quite right … is it, Bellerophon?

'Hey boy, easy now … easy,' he crooned as the impressive animal slowed to canter up and nuzzle right in to his chest.

'Bellerophon …?' I grimaced, dimly recalling an ancient myth about a chimera being defeated by a hero with the same name. 'Guess it had to be, really.'

I reached up to smooth the damp flank of the panting horse. He really was a beautiful animal, standing at least nineteen hands high, with large white wings folded down against his snowy back.

He whinnied as though in confirmation, as August leaned to whisper into its twitching ear.

'You speak to him?' I asked, eyebrows high.

'Yes … mostly about a certain feral cat. Bored him stupid around Europa.'

As if in agreement, Bellerophon whinnied and stamped his feet. August cupped his hands, and I stepped in to them without hesitation. I was astride Bellerophon's steaming back in a second, his wings folded protectively over my knees. I was surprised by how secure they made me feel.

Remembering Eli's riding instructions, I leaned forward to reassure him by rubbing between his ears. He whinnied softly in response.

'Don't believe the rumours, Bellerophon,' I muttered, as August leapt up behind me.

Then leaning in to his full thick mane, the three of us flew through the soulless city together, Bellerophon's swift hooves the only sound of life on the cold broken road.

Twice I thought I heard the hiss of a vulture reaching through the rhythmic lull of his stride. I clenched my eyes, the massacre in the ruined cathedral replaying in relentless detail. I could see the gleam of moonlight reflected in pools of blood, and Max's body crumpling as Cassius's arrow buried itself in his back.

Where were they all? Had any of them made it? Had Eli watched the black aquila take us? Or had he assumed I'd abandoned him and run for my life? Could they both be gone?

The thought raked the inside of my chest until it ached anew. I concentrated harder than ever before, but couldn't feel him at all.

'Eli,' I whispered, and felt August's hand tighten over my own momentarily as we galloped through the wilderness of streets.

Another unrecognizable cry cut through the haze of the morning sun. It was closer now, although the higher, intact buildings in this part of the city precluded a view. It didn't matter. If they weren't there waiting, let her eat me, I pleaded. Like the Roman spectators.

Which was exactly the moment Bellerophon reared in panic, and the crumbling buildings tipped sideways. I was aware of August cursing profanely, before the world righted itself in a blur. Then the broken grey merged with a small ball of black and white, before separating itself again. I blinked, and then blinked again. But it was still there, a beautiful ball of flecked fur, cowering among the smouldered remains of an upturned vehicle, and a tall street lantern, snapped in half.

'Jas!' I exclaimed in a strangled voice.

I yanked my leg back over Bellerophon's steaming back, as she let out a yowl of recognition, padding up to me as though it was the most natural thing in the world for her to be here. A snow leopard, stranded, in the middle of the Dead City's concrete jungle. I threw myself to my knees and buried my face in her warm thick fur. She smelled of our treehouse, of Arafel. *Of home.*

'She must have found her way here all by herself,' I babbled at August, who was towering over us, an incredulous expression pinned to his face.

A bubble of intense emotion reached up my throat, and I inhaled rapidly to stop the heat from spilling over into my eyes. Did this mean I dare hope Eli was still alive? Why else would Jas have come all this way? What had he said to the griffin in the forest?

'I'll tell you the same thing I told my wilful, beautiful Jas. If I'm not back in three days' time, feel free to come and rescue me.'

His words rang sketchily through my head. Her presence wasn't proof, but Jas was highly intuitive and the fact she was here made me so dizzy with painful hope, I could barely breathe.

'Where is he, girl?' I asked, as she nuzzled her thick, broad face into mine. I rubbed her flanks the way she always loved, and found handfuls of matted hair and burrs.

'And what have you been through to get here?' I scolded gently. 'How did you get through the mountains and scorpions all by yourself?'

'She found a way. And a reason. Hope will lead a new army, when the white-faced tiger rises from the dust.'

August's words were barely discernible, as though he was telling himself rather than anyone else.

I frowned up at him.

'When a black aquila falls from the golden sky, it will spark a winter of a thousand fires,' I responded.

We stared at one another, conscious of the parallels. Of two lives lived so separately, and yet beneath a cloud of silent expectation.

And hadn't we just witnessed both? We'd plunged into the river in the clutches of a black aquila. And now, Jas was here, like a message from the ancient gods herself.

As if they heard my thoughts, a cluster of trees a little distance away suddenly mushroomed into bright, scorching flames.

A deep shudder passed through me: *The Book of Arafel, The Voynich, Cassius, the Ludi Labyrinth, classical sketches, tumbling aquilas and white-faced tigers.* Prophecies were drawing breath all around us. And at the centre of it all was the mother of all mythological beasts, Lake, the *Hominum chimera*. It all felt pre-ordained. Out of control. And terrifying.

Was this what it was all about? The training and the teaching? Had Grandpa known that one day the old prophecies would likely come true? Had he known about *Hominum chimera*? I recalled his wise, smiling eyes. How much had he known about the real legacy of the Book of Arafel? And what part was I supposed to play in it?

Just what makes you so special? Don't you know the price on your own feral head?

And there was that damned feeling I was *still* missing something.

I gritted my teeth and, taking August's outstretched hand, swung up behind him.

White tigers and winters of a thousand fires. Whatever the myths meant, we weren't going to fulfil or defy them by sitting here, ignoring the signs. All the questions would have to wait, for now.

Another reptilian cry divided the air, and this time August let Bellerophon have her head. She tore up the road after Jas's sleek rhythm, through an overgrown crossroads and on again. And Jas seemed to know exactly where she was going, only occasionally rolling her head to one side as though to check we were keeping up.

She tore down a side street of ruined red stone buildings, leaping debris and fallen rubble as easily as though they were roots and fallen trees in the forest. And even the sight of her outside colours in this barren grey landscape gave me hope, a beacon of white leading us through the concrete maze.

A worn, rusted sign reading Nort*ernh*y G*rd**s protruded from a grassy verge, but Jas didn't stop, and with our heads bent low, we kept pace until we were finally cantering through overgrown forested ground. And although this wasn't my outside forest, it was clear this had once been an area of beautiful parkland, surrounding an ancient old-world wall.

'The Castle of Isca!' August exclaimed suddenly. 'Octavia talked of a fortress built into the northern corner of the Exeter Roman walls when I was a boy. Although it was already more than one thousand years old when the bombs fell, the Great War destroyed much of the existing ruin … Rougemont Castle I think she called it!'

Another reptilian cry sounded, and this time it made the leaves and trees quiver.

Could the Prolets and task force members have made it here? I couldn't face the possibility that we'd been chasing nothing but Cassius's nightmares.

'We're close!' I whispered, gripping August's belt and swinging down from Bellerophon mid-canter. I landed stealthily, like a falling cat, and Jas yowled her approval.

'Tal, what the …?!' August remonstrated.

'I'm faster in the trees,' I yelled, running towards a silver birch that stretched higher than most of the others in this forested area.

I started to climb. And the city slipped away. Here it was just me and the rustle of the trees, telling me who else was in the vicinity. Ears pricked, senses tuned. It was the same high alert I maintained while hunting. And with Jas just behind me, testing the whitened branches with her strong claws, I could almost have believed I was in the forest at home. Except for glimpses of a Roman knight, and the distant silhouette of the domes, stretching up like a huge, segmented insect. *Ready to ingest its next prey.*

I pulled my eyes away, and concentrated on my leaps and runs among the branches. There was life here too. Not large life, but life all the same. And it made me feel stronger. Feistier. Feral.

Until a glimpse stopped me in my tracks. Five monstrous chimneys brushing the skyline, and the hind part of a scaly tail trailing across them all.

My breath caught painfully, while Jas snarled, her flecked back arching with aggression. She could sense its unnatural air. I reached out to soothe her as I thought rapidly. There had to be a good reason Cassius had seen fit to unleash Lake in her most volatile form. I shinnied back down the tree to wait for August. He'd dismounted and was leading Bellerophon through the dense trees a little way behind.

'I've remembered something,' he offered in a low voice, when he grew close enough. 'I've been here before. Long ago, when I was a child.'

I stared back as he moved towards me, his Roman regalia so at odds with the forest surroundings.

'But you can't have,' I responded. 'No child ever left Isca Pantheon, no matter how privileged. You've said so yourself.'

'I know, but I've seen this place all the same,' he responded from the shadow of the trees. 'With Octavia.'

I nodded. My mind was racing.

'Lake … I think she's up ahead … and …'

It was August's turn to nod. 'I've seen the smoke – she's agitated,' he muttered, striding ahead.

And this time we stayed together, until we reached a high wall made of ancient mossy stones.

'Isca's original Roman wall,' August muttered.

He reached out to touch the reddish stone bricks, and for a brief second, I wondered how much of a difference his two-thousand-year-old Roman DNA signature coding really made.

There was a poignancy about it, the ancient world and the future connecting in the same time and space; both claiming advanced civilization and yet both pivoting about the same archaic savagery. Arafel couldn't be more different, or more precious.

'Think you can scale it? With a lift?' August gesticulated.

I smiled, turning back towards the grainy, timeworn wall, and was seated astride its top within a breath. Slowly, I scanned the landscape inside. It was so unexpected.

If there had been a castle here once, it was long gone leaving only a crumbling gatehouse fortified by a thick portcullis. But the long, white clinical buildings set inside the landscaped lawns were uncomfortably familiar. They had the same clean lines as Pantheon, and grew up out of the ground like a poisonous fungus. Somehow I knew, without setting even one step inside, whose handiwork I was staring at.

Jas leapt up beside me as I extended a hand to August. He scrambled up, in a most un-gladiatorial way, and gripped the front edge as though it might disappear into thin air.

'Not so great with heights,' he confessed.

I smiled tightly before returning my attention to the buildings inside the wall. They were in no way as big as Pantheon's domes, but looked to be made of the same thick impenetrable material.

'Satellite research centre,' August muttered in a suffocated voice.

I shot him a glance, and knew this was answering so many of his own questions.

'With Cassius you can never be sure you've seen the whole.'

Rajid's wisdom had never seemed more apt.

'Do you remember it?' I asked.

'I think so … bits of it anyway. I always suspected Octavia of having back-up facilities, but never anything this … big.'

A robin chirruped its bashful song somewhere behind us. The irony made me want to laugh out loud.

'Could they be here, do you think?' I asked.

Eli's athletic figure swam in front of my eyes, first as he advanced down the ruined cathedral nave with a pack of vultures flanking him, and then later as he sheltered the young Prolets. He'd changed so much over the past year. I thought of our shared affection for the man sitting with me now, and a surge of feeling blazed through my veins. It was all so complex, but he had everything to live for. And Max and Aelia? Were they here too? With the rest of the Prolets? I gritted my teeth. I was done with wondering.

'Talia, wait!' August shot out a hand, but he was too slow.

I was already on the ground, and a second later Jas was with me, clearly not content to let me out of her sight after her solo adventure. I turned to offer August a hand, only to find him scrabbling ungracefully down the wall, before dropping the last few feet.

'Don't be a little fool, Talia!' he hissed, recovering his balance. 'I've already lost Aelia and most of my men.'

I blinked as what he wasn't saying gleamed in the duplicitous sunshine.

'We stick together … Besides.' He nodded towards the top of the rectangular building, stretching out of which was some kind of fortified watchtower. 'Perimeter tower, for keeping intruders out, and everyone else in.'

'And Lake?' I asked breathlessly.

He held his finger to his lips, before propelling us both at sprint pace towards the end wall of the satellite facility.

The whole building was suspiciously silent, and as we got close I could see there were no guards standing sentry anywhere. I frowned at August as we reached the smooth white walls.

'Guess you need less security with an ancient, unstable myth-ological beast around.' He winked.

'You see her?' I whispered.

He nodded towards some smoking trees just visible at the front of the building. I swallowed hard.

Of course, she had to be close. Cassius wasn't going to rein her in until he had what he wanted.

'*Hominum chimera* is a morphing beast; needing careful handling and a guard she trusts. I can't imagine she has either right now.'

Pan's gentle silence had never seemed more noble. He'd been charged with the guardianship of the mother of all mythical beasts, a changeling with the ability to rouse and challenge the forces of nature. No wonder he had protected her so fiercely.

And then there was the pale, thin child herself, the one who'd shown me the sparse living arrangements in the tower, her double eyelids her only distinguishing feature. Even then, I'd assumed her to be just another discarded Pantheon experiment.

'It's her multi-genus DNA. From what I've read, no one species is completely dominant so, given a particular trigger, she morphs into the creature that best responds. And as she comprises three different sets of genetic coding, all competing for alpha position, she is highly unpredictable.'

'And her current form …' I asked, already knowing the answer from the glimpse of reptilian tail and smouldering trees.

'I'd say the draco,' August answered curtly. 'As far as I know she has multi-genus fused DNA from the draco – or dragon, the Nemean lion and the goat.'

'Yeah, waaaay too easy if she were the goat,' I breathed.

'Don't underestimate her in any form. Classical writers believed the chimera to be a metaphor for a volcano with good reason!'

There was silence while I digested the enormity of what we were facing.

'But what does it mean for her humanity?' I whispered finally. 'If it's overshadowed by so much other DNA? How much of it is Lake?'

It felt like a question far bigger than either of us, far bigger than this clinical white centre, and its unethical experimentation.

A ghost of a smile flickered across August's face. 'If a chimpanzee's helix is broken and human DNA inserted, is it animal or man? It's a point I've argued often in the Senate. Nature isn't always perfect either. Chimerism, although rare, can occur naturally. Original humans have been known to possess two sets of DNA … it's rare, but possible. So even a pure Outsider life isn't perfect. But perhaps that's the point.'

I stared at the Roman scientist, who was still such an enigma, in so many ways.

But any further conversation was lost in another bone-grating cry. She was only metres away now, at the front of the building.

I craned my neck to glimpse her, before recoiling in shock. She was unlike any beast of Pantheon I'd seen.

Lake, in chimera-draco form, had to reach at least five metres high. She was ash-grey with spiny, arrow-point scales, which stretched from the tip of her thrashing titian tail to her muscular neck, where a black band flickered with an intermittent light. Veins of regal purple stretched down her torso and into the top of her powerful forelegs. But it was her double-lidded honey eyes that were most unsettling. Eyes that didn't belong on such a vast, serpentine creature. Lake's eyes. Set inside a hideous creature designed with one thing in mind. And apart from the black metallic collar, she was shackle free.

I drew back to catch my breath.

'She's untethered,' I whispered. Panic welled up my throat as I sank my fingers into Jas's soft fur, trying to steel my nerve.

'She has a perimeter collar.' August nodded, pale-faced. 'The tower is sending out an electrical field that will channel a few thousand volts through her collar should she try to go beyond a certain perimeter … probably the Roman wall,' August added casting his gaze around swiftly, 'which means she's free to deter, but not to escape.'

'And, it's still her? In this form?'

He drew a breath. 'From what I've read about *Hominum chimera*, when she's in human form, she's human; when she's in draco form …'

I nodded.

Jas growled again, pawing the ground.

Somehow, I knew she could sense Eli, and the thought gave me the fire I needed.

'I'll draw her off; you get inside and see if you can find them.'

August spoke the words calmly, but I could tell it was costing him everything to suggest separate paths. It was likely suicide, for us both. But what was the use in living, if everyone who mattered was gone?

I slid my fingers into his, and he gripped back as though it was taking all his restraint not to pull me in there and then, the adrenaline of our semi-conscious dream beside the river not quite spent. Lifting our hands, he pressed his lips to the backs of my cold fingers, and I strained until I ached. Strained with the loss of so many lives, and a dream, of two people growing old together beneath Arafel's magenta sky.

'*Et in Arcadia Ego*,' he whispered briefly.

Then he was gone. And I was in chaos.

Chapter 23

There was a bellow of instant fury, and I clenched my teeth as I slid around the corner. Jas slunk low on my tail.

I spied August immediately, running alongside the far wall, with the draco's reptilian head thrown back in violent anger. But it had worked. And his swift action had already ensured the double entry doors into the facility were unguarded. Briefly.

Jas leapt into a graceful sprint towards the entrance, and I followed, my eyes trained on the draco's gleaming titian spine. She roared her anger skywards again, livid that anyone dare cross her territory. Then she started advancing on August, her weight reverberating through the ground, and serrated jaws projecting bright orange bursts of flames I could feel fifty metres away.

As I reached the double doors, I grabbed the handles and twisted downwards, my heart pounding. They swung open into a dark silent interior, and Jas sprinted inside. Then I stopped dead, the whites of my knuckles gleaming in the shadows. As far as I knew, August and I were the only ones left alive. What was I doing?

'To be courageous, is to act courageously, Talia.'

I set my mouth grimly. Grandpa's wisdom was always lurking.

'Hey, Lake!' I yelled irreverently, spinning on the spot, and for a second it felt as if the whole world paused.

The spiny, honey-eyed draco shifted slowly around, her head low, and jowls pulled back in a hideous grimace. Lake's trademark double lids hung low over her glare, offering no sign of recognition. Instead she threw her head back and released a scorching trail of flames to the sky. She was angry, and determined I should know it.

'Hey, it's me, Lake!' I tried, holding up my hands, 'Tal ... remember? The girl who gave you her last meal? In the tunnels?'

The draco's vast spiny head sunk lower, and she took three heavy steps forward, her nostrils flaring with steam, and exposed canines glinting in the sun. She was distracted enough to give August a chance.

'Talia!' he exploded, running out from where he'd been cornered. 'For the love of Nero, this isn't a game! Move!'

'I know that!' I returned, side-leaping another long, smoky volcanic flare. 'I just remembered ...'

'Just remembered what?'

August's tackle impacted before he finished, driving us both backwards through the open doorway at a crippling speed. I hit the sterile floor first, and braced myself as our tangle of limbs slid towards the bank of units fixed to the back wall.

'That in no part of the story, did Bellerophon get fried by the chimera,' I whispered when we stopped.

He rolled his eyes and enveloped me in a crush, just as one huge double-lidded eye levelled against a ground-floor window.

'Draco!' I croaked as the first burst of flames reached through the open doorway, charring the solid frame opal black in a single breath.

We were on our feet and running before she had time to try again, chasing the hind legs of a pining leopard up a circular flight of steps. A bank of cameras whirred and swung as we reached the top, and I couldn't help a sardonic smile.

'Not dead yet, Cassius,' I smirked, blowing a kiss as August dragged me past.

We were in a long white corridor, similar to those in Pantheon's laboratory, and the sickly formaldehyde hit me like a wall.

'Which way?' I asked, my momentary hope wavering.

There were endless doors leading off the clinical space. And, bleakly, I recalled the multitude of long clinical laboratory corridors in Pantheon, and the horror that lay behind each.

But I'd underestimated the best watch-cat in the world.

With a low yowl, she set off at a sprint towards the T-junction at the end. She rounded to the left without hesitation, her beautiful flecked coat a luxurious contrast to our surgical surroundings. August and I wasted no time in setting off in pursuit. We hadn't come this far to lose her now, and as we turned the corner, I glimpsed the tip of her tail disappearing inside the last door on the right.

I slowed down as we approached. The building had been suspiciously empty so far, and there was a distinct technical hum in the air. We crept forward softly, the sound of machinery burrowing beneath my skin, evoking memories of invasive tubing and a blue noxious liquid. Stealing life. *Stealing Grandpa.* I bit my lip. August and I had nothing but his knife and my dart tube between us, but for some reason I wasn't afraid.

I'd lost so much already, what was the point of losing more time to fear?

Which was exactly why I pushed open the door and walked in, my soft padding footsteps echoing oddly in the quiet space. I paused to scan our new surroundings. Two opposite walls of the huge chamber were lined with banks of screens that flashed and whirred with hundreds of changing numbers and images. The third wall was lined with countless vertical white tanks.

Occupied vertical white tanks.

And my small flame of hope finally guttered and expired. The tanks here were less the life-freezing canisters of Pantheon, and more the observation tanks of the chimera ward, but the faces staring out were still as wan and pale as the dead.

I broke into a run towards the tall oblong tank Jas had chosen, her flank sunk low in fierce protective mode. The solid lower half concealed what lay beneath, but there was a clear window into the face, and my world started to crumble as soon as I got too close for denial.

'Eli!'

My agony echoed pointlessly around the lifeless chamber, making nothing and no one look, except August. Jas lifted her large front paws, and stretching up the front of the canister, letting her beautiful feline face sink as close to the glass as she could. Now a fully grown adult snow leopard, she was taller than my brother, and had to incline her majestic head to see inside.

But her plaintive soft mew took me straight back to the icy winter he'd brought her home, a tiny bundle of white and grey flecked fur, tucked into a makeshift sling around his neck. She'd understood him like no other animal, and now I could tell she understood again.

I let my hand fall onto her muscular neck, and felt her warm skin quiver as I forced my eyes to his pallid face. He was staring out at me, his scalp attached to a plate of coloured tubing, and next to him was Aelia. Their skin was the colour of fire-ash, and their eyes tightly closed, but their chests were rising and depressing. My body flooded with a raw grief that threatened to choke every last thought. Were they dead? How had Cassius caught them? What had they suffered before being incarcerated in these coffins?

There was blood on my lips, and I was only dully aware of its bittersweet metallic taste. Of iron. Pungent and earthy. I ran my tongue around my mouth, painting it like a declaration of war, trying to think though it felt like the walls were closing in around me.

Every one of the uprights contained a pale-faced guard. It seemed even Cassius's own gladiators hadn't escaped. And each was wan and lifeless, aside from the synchronized lifting and depression of their chests. It was almost more terrifying than their colour, their collaborative rhythm. I scanned the tanks numbly; the young Prolets, Max and Unus were nowhere to be seen. They had to be here somewhere. Where else could they be?

'August, help me unhook all this stuff,' I demanded hoarsely. 'August?' I repeated, suddenly aware I hadn't heard him utter a sound for the past couple of minutes.

I spun around and spied him staring at a screen on the opposite side of the room. Cursing, I ran across and closed my fingers around his listless forearm, pulling insistently. Until I realized what he was staring at. His own face. Only much, much younger.

Citizen MMMDCCXCVIII to be exact, or so the moving screen said.

A toddling infant running across a manicured lawn, a brief glimpse of a sterile white building, and Octavia, watching. Waiting. Fast-forwarding to a golden-haired boy. Learning and excelling at gladiatorial training school, Equite division. Fast-forwarding again to a young knight's triumphant graduation, with combat trials and celebrated brilliance in the field of genetic modification and biotechnical engineering. Finally, his secondment to the Government's Scientific Programme and rapid escalation to the role of Commander General.

It all amounted to one clear thing: his clear preparation for a life as Octavia's Deputy Director General.

Then the screen flickered and switched. We were back in the Flavium on *that* day with August declaring a traitorous allegiance to feral Outsiders. There were slow shots of the mayhem: image after bloodied image of the carnage, until August's final emergence as Director General of Pantheon. He stood before the Senate, their new self-appointed leader. And it all looked so damned contrived.

I gazed up at August's side profile, the muscle in his cheek twitching uncontrollably, and then back at the screen.

The moving images had rolled on to the Prolet riots, focusing on August's inability to quell the revolt, Cassius's recovery and then the words I knew nearly by heart.

'*The early integration analysis indicates a common stress symptom among the Prolet class, which may be a reaction to the existing vaccine to suppress independent will. Of course, the recent rioting cannot be tolerated.*

'*Because of this, and the new investigation required, I would recommend a temporary suspension of all new Prolet privileges and reinstatement of the existing Pantheonite system.*'

I pulled at his arm again, knowing the intoxicating effect of this poison, but August was rooted to the spot.

'It's oddly unsettling to stare into your own face,' he whispered, sounding dazed, 'but it explains the memories I have of this place. Octavia must have brought me here. It seems she was always … preparing me.'

I squeezed his arm fiercely.

'You stood for something other than Octavia's rule,' I whispered. 'And the Equite on that screen is only half you. This is Pantheon's favourite game, remember: lies and deceit.'

Max's words suddenly came flooding back as clearly as though he were standing next to me.

'We just need to play it better,' I added, struggling to keep my voice even.

'Actually, it's not so much a game, as a simulated reality trial … There are problems with the technology, as there are problems with the Voynich experiments, until we translate it once and for all.'

I turned as though swallowed by a dream.

'On the whole though, the tech is much more successful than the last round. And if you hadn't got *Hominum chimera* all jumpy, we'd have been here before now – to welcome you properly.'

And she was there, standing before us in her Tyrian purple tunic, dark hair pulled back in a tight bun, and surrounded by guards.

'Livia!' August scorned.

'What's going on?' he added in an uglier tone, as one of the guard's hounds slunk back on its powerful hind legs and started to snarl.

'Don't make this any harder than it already is, Augustus,' she sighed, her features twisting into a curious smile.

Now we were closer, I could tell she was older than I first supposed her to be.

'You were created for a life of Pantheonite honour, a life that automatically gave you privilege. But I've had to find a way to the top of a system that rewarded no one who wasn't male or modified!'

I shot a look at August. He was transfixed. This had to be the first time he'd seen the real Livia.

'You were one of Octavia's prize projects,' she continued, clearly enjoying herself. 'Prolet DNA, mixed up with two-thousand-year-old Roman Equite signature coding. Not exactly unique, but still a little different. You wanted to please; you wanted to be everything Octavia wanted you to be. You still do.'

August's brow creased and darkened.

'You see the vaccine to suppress independent will wasn't just trialled on Prolet embryos – in the beginning.'

'No!' August denied, his eyes flaring.

'Oh, but yes. And she adored you too, didn't she? No matter what.'

I recoiled. She was digging deep, twisting the knife.

August's face grew tighter and harder as the enormity of Livia's suggestion sank in. My own mind whirled. I'd known of his strong allegiance to Octavia, despite everything, and always put it down to years of sworn duty. Nothing more. Nothing this … chemical. It was too horrifying, and yet so easy to believe of Pantheon.

'Of course, once the new Prolet trial is in delivery stage, we'll be able to void all previous test subjects … including you … And then, together with the Simulated Reality Project, we'll not only have an obedient workforce, we'll also be able to create who we like, when we like, for as long as we like. And although the technology isn't perfect,' she added breezily, 'there's every chance Emperors Constantine, Augustus and Nero will be helping us take the Civitas into the next millennium.'

'No! It's unethical, Livia! You backed me at the Senate!' August exploded, his face pinched with anger.

I could tell he was reeling with shock. The revelations about his own genetics had stirred up feelings that would be hard to quieten when all this was done. *If all this was ever done.*

'I did what I needed to make you think I was on your side. But I'm a scientist, like you, August. We trained on the same programme. Why wouldn't I choose a path of knowledge? Just think of how much prestige they could bring to Cassius's rule? Perhaps even more than deciphering the keyword to the Voynich.'

And that was it, I fumed silently. It still all came back to the Voynich.

'How do you undo these tanks!' I seethed, done listening. 'And where are Max, Unus and the Prolet children?'

'Ah, Talia…well let's see … the young Prolets are back where they belong, subject to another vaccination. Seems we had another rogue trial,' she sighed.

'Unus was a little bulky to take far, but he's safely garrisoned – and Max …' her eyebrows flew up in mock amusement '… let's just say he's joining a special investigation project, back at base.'

'No!' I ground out, launching at her, only to find myself caught fast by August, centimetres from a hound that looked suspiciously like Brutus. The molossus strained at me, his yellow eyes filled with cold aggression. This was no longer the same hound Eli had tamed.

Livia's cold, curious smile grew. 'Octavia began …'

'Well who gives a Roman toss what Octavia began?'

Every pair of eyes shot to the doorway, while the guards and molossers parted to let a malicious, cloaked figure through.

'Because Octavia is dead. Our simulated reality trials are excellent, and I'm closer than ever to owning all the secrets of the Voynich. In fact, some might say, these are the glory days indeed!'

I stared numbly at Cassius's hateful face, and felt a flicker of satisfaction at the white surgical patch stretched over his left eye. Then Max's teasing smile flickered through my head, and my pain flooded my body like a broken dam. I should have finished him while I had the chance.

'You're nothing but a yellow-bellied snake!' I hissed, my voice trembling. 'You'd shoot a man in the back rather than face him. You persecute the young and weak, and lock up anyone who even dares to think for themselves!'

My voice was pure acid, but I didn't care.

'And, you believe a few unethical experiments qualify you to own the most powerful secret known to ancient legend and myth?'

I shook my head contemptuously.

'It will burn you alive!'

Cassius's face darkened, as I dived back towards Eli's canister. Pantheon had already stolen my grandfather and Max. They weren't getting anyone else.

Jas pushed herself up, arching impressively before stalking forward to stand between me and Cassius, her beautiful jowls pulled back in her most menacing growl. Brutus, twice her size, responded by slinking low on his muscular haunches and filling the air with his throaty challenge. It was clear she was no match for such an animal.

I turned and ran my eye over the canister swiftly, but it was entirely smooth.

Cassius smirked, recovering himself.

'The trouble with Outsiders is that you always think you can change things. The truth is, our scientific processes are far beyond your comprehension. But in a way your brother is being useful, at least. We extract some DNA, create something new, and your kind isn't completely eradicated. Now there's some comfort to be had from that, isn't there? The same way as there's comfort to be drawn from your special sacrifice … Talia.'

His voice was silky-smooth, predatory, taking me straight back to his room when I was so vulnerable. And he knew it. I swallowed back the bile rising in my throat and threw a look at August, who was now flanked by two of Cassius's biggest guards. So this was it, all the innuendoes and hushed half-truths had all been leading up to this. The final moment of truth. *Well bring it on.*

'And what's that, Cassius?' I returned. 'What Outsider sacrifice can possibly be so special in your perfect Civitas?'

'Talia!' August interjected, his voice strained.

'Ah! Now now, August, she should know, don't you think? It's such an interesting part of the story. As it concerns the little red miracle that binds and defines us all.'

I fixed on him, a slow realization spreading through my veins.

'Yes, that's it … clever girl, Talia … keep thinking,' he crooned, his opal eyes glinting.

'You see, I'm going to let you into a little secret, Talia. *Hominum chimera* wasn't just my specialist project. Thomas was working on her too. And as much as Lake is my success, I do owe a little of her coding to him.'

I thought of Thomas's hand-drawn classical sketch of a chimera and knew this time Cassius was telling the truth, and revelling in every second.

'And I'm sure Augustus has filled you in on her … morphing nature?' he drawled.

'Thomas more than understood *Hominum chimera* would be volatile and unpredictable. Such is her intrinsic nature, and perhaps her destiny, some would argue. However, he realized that without a measure, no one would be able to control her, and what use is the best biological weapon in the world without control? And so, my dear inquisitive, solution-hungry older brother developed one. Of course, his motivation was far more altruistic than mine has ever been. A control to give the creature a period of stability, he thought. But the end result was the same.'

I stared, growing cold.

'He developed an antidote of sorts – not to her chimerism, but to her volatility. A complex protein that would give her owner final control over which of her mythical natures dominated. And he hid that information where no one could ever find it.'

My mind whirled and I thought of the Book of Arafel. Had he hidden it there among the dense pages of text?

Cassius sneered, his black eyes like hard coals, revelling in my confusion.

'Come come, Talia! The answer's so simple even an Outsider should be able to guess at it …'

There was a short theatrical silence and then he sighed.

'It's you, Talia! He hid the control inside his own bloodline.'

For a second the room was completely silent, my shock so tangible I could almost taste it.

And then, slowly, I swung my gaze to August, and his iris-blue eyes had never shone with more sadness. I swallowed to catch my breath. Why hadn't he told me? It explained so much: Grandpa's insistence I bore the legacy alone, August's frustration and insistence there was a price on my head, Rajid's curious suspicion, and Pan's deference. Perhaps even Lake herself had sensed the connection.

I looked back at Cassius, and drew myself up.

'If the proteins are in my blood, they're in yours too!' I burned. 'And what about Eli? Or is that the reason you're already draining him dry!'

'Ah well, that was the intention, I confess. But it turns out the proteins are time-sensitive, meaning they have a twenty-five-year lifespan inside any new Hanway embryo. That leaves you and your dear brother who, alas, doesn't possess the purest blood type at all. So, there you are in the spotlight, Talia, and I know you'll be obliging … the same way you would have been back in Pantheon, if we hadn't been so rudely interrupted.'

'Enough, Cassius!' August roared, shaking free of the guards and hurtling forward.

I saw Cassius had it then, The Book of Arafel, tucked tightly in the crook of his left arm. It was wrapped in a black cloth that had slipped, exposing a corner. The tatty brown, dog-eared village book took me back instantly. Back to a hunched old man shuffling through the Ring, back to the respect in which he was held, back to how much I'd let him down. It was the book I'd promised to defend until my dying breath. Dying. Dead. *What had August said? Mass of the Dead … REQ … REQUIEM?*

Rapidly I recalled the picture Aelia had torn from Thomas's research. The picture with three faded letters: *REQ*. Could they be an abbreviation for Mass of the Dead? *It would make so much sense.* I inhaled hoarsely, trying not to let the moment crack my mask. If I'd stumbled upon the last clue to the Voynich, Thomas's keyword, the correct translation of the ancient Voynich could finally be within reach.

Cassius's hooded eyes glinted. I'd let the Book slip through my hands, and I was about as far away from being able to protect its secrets as I could ever be. I'd let Grandpa down, I'd let Max down, I'd let Eli down, I'd let August down and most of all, I'd let myself down. But there was one thing left I could do to offset it all.

Grabbing a disinfectant-laden trolley, I sprinted towards the window at the back of the laboratory, and rammed with all my strength. It crashed against the fortified glass, which shuddered violently, before a single hairline fracture spread up and outwards like veins on a forest leaf. The tiny glass flakes paused before shattering, raining glass all over the floor.

'Lake …? Are you hungry?'

My voice reverberated through the still air. She had to have heard me. And sure enough, before I had time to call again, Lake's honey-coloured, double-lidded eyes rose into view, together with the rest of her brutal reptilian profile.

In the same moment, Jas sprang for Brutus. He reared to meet her, snapping his guard restraint, and instantly the room was in turmoil. I ran forward, only to be forced back by the sheer physicality of their combat. Razor-sharp claws pierced and raked, while Brutus's heavier jaw ripped and mauled. Jas was easily the faster animal, repeatedly sidestepping his powerful swipes, but it was clear she was no match for Brutus's violence. She traded blow for blow before leading Brutus from the room with a leap that made my heart swell with pride.

'Arrest them!'

Cassius's command rose above the baying molossers who'd formed a tight pack in front of Lake's head. And yet their protest, while vehement, seemed paltry against her savage design. I was so close I could see every marbled vein and the hot steam billowing from her thick nostrils.

'Lake?' I whispered and just for a second, there was a glimpse of recognition inside her liquid amber eyes. And then she bellowed her fury to the heavens.

'Tal! Move!'

August hurtled from nowhere as she opened her mouth, displaying enough teeth to shred a molossus in seconds. And just before the room disappeared inside a fireball of chemical heat and rage, I glimpsed those same distinctive eyelids lowering in vengeful satisfaction.

The screams resonated longer than the burning, and the room was filled with a thick black choking smog that scorched my skin without the need for flames. But somehow, August wedged us tightly between two of the canisters, and their impenetrable material protected us from the worst.

'Quick,' he wheezed, coughing. 'Get inside!'

He pulled opened an empty canister and pushed me in, quickly pulling the heavy door closed after us, so there was barely room left to breathe.

'Wait … Jas!' I implored, as he shoved a white mask against

288

my mouth. It smelled of the outside, of the forest, of home, and I inhaled deeply, letting its sweet intoxication carry me away.

'There is no time,' he whispered hoarsely.

Then he held me tight while all around us, Isca burned.

Chapter 24

When a black aquila falls from the golden sky, it will spark a winter of a thousand fires.

Cassius's black angel of death had dropped like a stone; but while *Hominum chimera*'s fire was intense, it alone was no winter of a thousand fires.

We picked our way over the smoking debris, looking for survivors. Although there were a few charred, unidentifiable bodies, it seemed as though the majority of Cassius's party had escaped. There was no sign of Jas or the draco either, although the fire had completely destroyed the tower perimeter. Side by side, we stared out at the early summer day, searching for a glimpse of either, but only a warbling bullfinch dared disturb the smoke shroud that hung over the research centre.

And when finally we turned back to the canisters, Eli, Aelia and the rest of the occupants were just as we had found them. We knew their comatose state left us with little choice. Leave them to Cassius's guard once news of the chimera's disappearance reached Isca Pantheon. Or let them go.

I stared through the glass into their familiar faces, not letting myself think about the absolute finality of the moment. All Aelia could do was glare back as though to say, *What are you even waiting for?*

As for Eli – gentle, gifted Eli who'd been a part of me since I began – he would never know I hadn't deserted him. And there were no words to explain the darkness that claimed every tiny heart capillary at the thought.

The hurt welled again, like an unstoppable wave, taking with it every whisper of comfort I could drag up. I couldn't let myself think where Max might be right at this moment, or what he might be going through. The thought of his teasing, Outsider face being any part of Pantheon's cruel programme was almost too much to bear. And it was that desperation that was responsible for the thought. A last, wild thought.

'Unus?' I whispered, turning to look up into August's sombre face.

He was staring at Aelia, saying nothing.

'Unus wouldn't have left Aelia to this! Livia said he was too bulky to take far. He has to be here somewhere,' I insisted.

I thought back to the chaos in the cathedral, to the last time I saw Unus. And then to Livia's words. What had she said? *That he was safely garrisoned somewhere closer?* Where would Livia put an irate Cyclops?

And then, a flash of inspiration.

'The old Norman guardhouse. Are there rooms there? Dungeons?' I asked swiftly.

August frowned. 'Yes, I think so, but you have to remember I came here a long time ago.'

It was enough.

We flew down the stairs, across the manicured grass and towards the old gatehouse built by William the Conqueror – or so the cracked plaque propped up beside the portcullis claimed.

It was so at odds with the rest of the satellite research centre, with its imperfect structure and old-world red stone. And I hesitated only briefly before ducking through the open doorway on the right-hand side of the portcullis. The room was dark, and I tried to ignore the stench of guano as our footsteps crunched over the shaly stone floor.

'Unus?' I ventured after a beat, figuring our odds would only be improved if my unique cyclopean friend also knew we were here.

There was no immediate answer, only a soft, distinctive clunking noise somewhere beneath the floor. I frowned, trying to identify it. August pulled an object from his pocket, and tapped it against the damp wall. Much to my surprise it flickered into life giving us enough light to search the space. I nodded. The science of the future had its moments. Then I spied thick black grill bars sunk into the stone floor.

'Unus?' I called cautiously, stepping forward.

Again, there was a strange clunking. Chains? Plus something else. A sloshing noise. *Water.* I grabbed August's light and held it over the grill, only to nearly drop it inside when a single large eye blinked back up at me.

'Unus!' My choking relief ricocheted around the dank mouldy walls as I absorbed his weakened state.

He was neck-deep in black water, chained and gagged.

A furious sob caught in my throat, as I gazed down at my bewildered giant friend. I had no doubt it had taken a small army to take him down, and that he'd done everything he could to defend those he loved.

'For the love of Nero ...' August's loss of words said it all.

We each took one edge of the iron grill, and pulled with all our strength. It must have taken four men to lift it into place but somehow our exhausted muscles managed to inch it out of its resting place and onto the stone floor. It dropped with a huge clatter, but I didn't care.

'And now I get to rescue you back,' I whispered, before jumping into the black water.

The sudden freezing water slammed every muscle of my body,

292

squeezing it like a million tiny vices, but I had years of pulling myself through Arafel's tunnel on my side, and I kicked back until my head broke through the surface.

'Unus!' I gasped. 'It's Tal.'

His freezing body had been wound tightly with thick chains, and a sodden cloth was bound around his huge pudgy face; although it didn't stop his belly from rumbling weakly as August and I dived to find the end of the heavy metal. Thankfully the chain was only weighted, and as August detached the huge anchor, I wrested the tight bandage from around his mouth. At first, he was so cold and quiet, I thought we were too late. And then I remembered.

'A cyclopean artery is particularly thick, meaning his heart rate can drop far lower than ours.'

Aelia had brought Unus back from the brink of death before. I had to hope his physiology was enough to save him without her skills this time.

'Unus, Unus?' I whispered into his cold face.

'He's free, move his arms,' August whispered.

Taking one thick trunk arm each, we began to move his limbs in a circular motion, until finally he blinked, and swung his huge milky head towards me.

'Tal ... find ... Unus?' he mumbled through blue lips.

'Yes,' I panted, 'sometimes the damsel rescues the cyclopean knight. But you have to help, because this water is freezing my brain!'

Minutes later we were all lying out on the cold stone, trying to regain our breath after a united Herculean effort to heave Unus out onto the gatehouse floor.

'We have to keep moving.' I shivered. 'Before Cassius's guard arrives.'

August nodded and somehow, between us, we got Unus on his feet. The soft warmth of the sunshine breathed new life into our near-frozen limbs, and slowly our strength returned as we made our way back across the green towards the satellite centre.

Unus lumbered painfully, his exposure to the cold taking longer to wear off, but by the time we reached the centre he looked much more my old friend.

'Tal... come for ... Unus?' he repeated unevenly, as though he still couldn't quite believe we'd found him.

I reached up to hug him, the reality of nearly losing him suddenly threatening to swamp me.

'It's what friends do for each other,' I whispered. 'They stand their ground, even when they're not feeling heroic. And they play the game, despite the stakes ... despite the crowd clamouring for blood.'

He nodded once, his great eye misting with understanding. He'd nearly given his life fighting for us in the Flavium, he'd rescued me from Cassius as well as the Minotaurus – and protected me through the tunnels beneath Pantheon countless times. The truth was, he was more a hero, in spite of his genetics, than anyone else I knew and, right now, I needed him. The embrace he returned broke nearly every bone in my body, but it said more than all the words in the world.

Then the three of us stood before the main entrance, the light summer breeze jarring with the task ahead. From here it was easy to see the entire western side of the building had been entirely destroyed in the blaze. I thought of the small, unassuming girl with serpent eyes. She was such an enigma and, if the omen were to be believed, a real threat to the natural world. Yet somehow, I found myself hoping she'd made it.

The wind whistled through the facility eerily, as we retraced our steps back to the burned-out wing. There was still no sign of Jas and when we reached the tank room I averted my gaze from the charred bodies; there was always a choice and mine was to believe a resourceful snow leopard, who'd found her way over the North Mountains, would also escape Cassius's monster hound.

And then it was time. August shouldered Eli's slumped body while I took Aelia. Once detached from the ventilation systems, their pulses seemed to fade until there was scarcely anything to distinguish them from those we would carry to Arafel's peace hut. But I still refused to believe this was over.

The price was just too high.

And if Bellerophon was surprised at the listless bodies he was forced to carry the short distance to the river, he didn't show it. We took the most direct route and reached the snaking glass water within fifteen minutes.

'How?' I turned to Unus breathlessly. 'How do we call them?'

He understood, of course. There was only a moment's silence, and then the air vibrated with the same ancient call I remembered from when he carried me through Isca Pantheon's tunnels. And it seemed as though the birds themselves stopped to listen. I watched the river like a hawk, but everything was still and devoid of life. *Nothing stirred.*

'But we just fell and they helped us?' I rounded on August, my chest shrinking with pain.

This had to work; it couldn't not work.

He shook his head once, his expression raw and broken.

'Oceanids are loyal only to those they choose,' August muttered. 'There are no rules. Except if they don't come to us, we can only let them find them ...' he added, staring down at his sister's limp body.

My heart strained as though it was being squeezed by Unus's fist, but there was a blue tinge around Eli's mouth and Aelia's skin had taken on a waxen sheen. *There was no more time left.*

So, we stood there, watching their lifeless bodies sink into the chasm of water, and I whispered a prayer, not to the heavens above but to the ovoid eyes and webbed hands living within the black. It was a prayer carried by the most fragile of wings. And as the day finally started to fade behind the grey ruins of Isca, we knew we were the only ones left.

***

The sunshine thinned as our small party crossed the trail of a Nemean lion in the North Mountains; a Roman gladiator of the Equite Order, a ponderous swaying Cyclops and a silent feral girl with only one thought driving her leather-clad feet forward.

The winter of a thousand fires had arrived, and she was burning.

Glossary of Terms

Armamentarium: Roman gladiatorial weapon store beneath the Colosseum.

Basiliscus (basilisk): mythological 'king of serpents', a giant reptilian creature famous for its ability to kill with a single glance (another version has rooster-like qualities). Both versions are mortal enemies of the weasel.

Bellerophon: mythological son of a mortal, hero and slayer of monsters (before the days of Heracles) whose greatest feat was killing the chimera.

Boudica: Queen of the British Celtic Iceni tribe who led an uprising against the occupying forces of the Roman Empire in AD 60 or 61, and died shortly after its failure, having supposedly poisoned herself. She is considered a British folk hero.

Chimera: mythological monstrous fire-breathing creature of Lycia in Asia Minor, composed of the parts of more than one animal, usually a lion, goat and snake. Homer's brief description in the *Iliad* is the earliest surviving literary reference: 'a thing of immortal make, not human, lion-fronted and snake behind, a goat in the middle, and snorting out the breath of the terrible flame of bright fire.'
Beyond mythology, the term 'chimera' is used in scientific research to explain an animal that contains more than one

set of genetic coding. This is a clear nod to the Greek monster, in that the monster itself is a combination of three different 'normal' animals.

Hominum chimera: Hominum (Latin for human), Hominum chimera: human chimera, a fictional concept, though real human chimeras can occur when a person's body contains two different sets of DNA; for example, the result of a bone transplant or when a fraternal twin embryo dies and the other embryo absorbs its twin's DNA.

Citizen MMMDCCXCVIII: Citizen 3798, Commander General Augustus Aquila's Citizen Number.

Civitas: In the history of Rome, the Civitas was the social body of the *cives* or citizens, united by law. It is the law that bound them together, giving them responsibilities on the one hand, and rights of citizenship on the other. The Civitas was not just the collective body of all the citizens, it was also the contract binding them all together, because each of them was a *civis*.

Clymene, Asia and Electra (Oceanids): mythological sea nymphs who were three of the three thousand daughters of the Titans Oceanus and Tethys. Clymene, Asia and Electra were closely associated with the Titan gods.

Draco: from Latin for dragon. A mythical creature depicted as a large horned serpent or a winged, fire-breathing reptile with magical or spiritual qualities.

Et in Arcadia Ego: *Even in Arcadia, here I am*. Arcadia was a rural region of Ancient Greece, whose inhabitants, chiefly shepherds and farmers, were seen as living a quiet, idyllic life away from the hustle and bustle of nearby Athens. The Latin motto *et in*

Arcadia ego, 'even in Arcadia, here I am,' comes from the title of a painting by the French Baroque artist Nicholas Poussin (1594–1665), which depicted four Arcadian shepherds attending the tomb of a local man. Precisely what Poussin meant the title to imply is hotly debated, but it's often interpreted as a reminder that no matter how good someone else's life appears to be compared to your own, we all eventually suffer the same fate – the 'I' in question is Death.

Flavium Arch L11: The Flavium's (Colosseum's) huge crowd capacity made it essential that the venue could be filled or evacuated quickly. The architects adopted solutions very similar to those used in modern stadiums to deal with the same problem. The amphitheatre was ringed by eighty entrances at ground level, seventy-six of which were used by ordinary spectators. Each entrance and exit was numbered, as was each staircase.

Hypogeum: The area beneath the Colosseum was called the Hypogeum (meaning underground). The Hypogeum consisted of a two-level subterranean network of tunnels and thirty-two animal pens. It had eighty vertical shafts that provided instant access to the arena for animals and scenery. There were thirty-six trapdoors in the arena, allowing for elaborate special effects. The atmosphere and smell beneath the Colosseum must have been terrible. The Hypogeum would have had little natural light, so lamps would have burned continuously. The heat in the Hypogeum must have been almost unbearable. The stench of animals, the excrement, blood and death would have filled every part of the Hypogeum – both above and beneath the Colosseum must have been 'hell on earth'.

Livia: Livia Drusilla, Empress of Rome (58 BC–AD 29) Long-lived, influential matriarchal figure in the early years of the

Roman principate. Held up as an example of womanly virtue and simplicity. She may have also been a murderer, and has been described as treacherous, avaricious, and power-hungry. Wife of the first Roman Emperor Augustus, mother of the second Tiberius and deified by her grandson, the Emperor Claudius.

Ludere!: from Latin meaning *Play!*

Ludi Apollinares: solemn games (*ludi*) held annually by the ancient Romans in honour of the god Apollo. The tradition goes that at the first celebration, the Romans were suddenly invaded by the enemy, and obliged to take to their arms. A cloud of darts and arrows fell upon their enemies, and the Romans then returned victorious to their sports.

Ludi Pantheonares: fictional version of Ludi Apollinares (above).

Nemean lion: a vicious monster in Greek mythology that lived at Nemea. It was eventually killed by Heracles, but could not be killed with mortal weapons because its golden fur was impervious to attack. Its claws were also sharper than mortal claws, and could cut through any armour.

Oceanids: see Clymene, Asia and Electra.

Rune: letter of an ancient Germanic alphabet, related to the Roman alphabet.

Silenus: (plural sileni) Greek woodland gods or spirits, closely connected to the satyrs. They were occasionally referred to as being half-man half-horse, instead of half-man half-goat. The sileni were portrayed as lechers and drunkards, bald-headed and pot-bellied, with thick lips and stub noses, and with the tails and ears of a horse. Playing the flute and lyre were their attributes. The sileni can often be found in the company of Dionysus.

Spoliarium: where the dead bodies of gladiators were stripped of armour and weaponry.

Vulpes: Aelia's family name and a genus of the Canidae, which also includes wolves, jackals and other members of the dog family. The members of this genus are colloquially referred to as 'true foxes'.

Acknowledgements

No book comes together without a dedicated team.

So, for all the support throughout *City of Dust's* journey, I'd like to extend my special thanks to:

My amazing HQ Editors Hannah Smith & Nia Beynon, for their perceptive insights, talent for spotting plot holes and all round editing wizardry. Hannah, I will miss your incredible enthusiasm and Nia, I can't wait to tackle Talia's final explosive chapter together.

The fabulous HQ Design team for yet another stunning cover. You guys rock!

Chloe Seager (Northbank Talent Management), who continues to be just brilliant writing inspiration, as well as my agent-extraordinaire and much valued friend.

Catherine Johnson (Author) & the Curtis Brown Creative Team, for the ongoing belief, support and words of wisdom.

The lovely Dr Sarah Parkin, for providing valuable medical advice, and never once questioning my mention of a Minotaurus.

My awesome writing group: The Scribblers, for the solidarity, retweets, and (virtual) hugs and doughnuts.

And finally,

my incredibly supportive parents, family and friends, who continue to put up with my rambling conversations, midnight marmite raids and gypsy-folk music crimes – and who never, ever, mention how late I am...

I couldn't do it without you.

The final book in this fantastical trilogy is coming in 2019 ...

If you enjoyed *City of Dust*, why not read on
for an extract from the first in Michelle
Kenney's fantastical trilogy, *Book of Fire*?

Prologue

In the old world, people foraged for food in bright cities the size of the forest, Grandpa said, and rode toxic boxes on wheels, instead of running with the sun.

Embellished truth or plain fiction, Grandpa's fireside myths were my favourite part of the day. And as my twin brother and I grew, the myths turned into stories from his own childhood, like the time he found a tattered advert for the Lifedome on a creeper-choked wall. When he pulled the foliage aside, it still bore the ripped, black lettering of its utopian dream.

It was only when Eli and I turned sixteen that, in keeping with village tradition, we learned the real story of Arafel's fore-fathers from the Council. We plagued Grandpa for the rest, and when he finally relented, there was something in his stark portrayal of our beginning that shadowed me, even on the brightest day.

The Lifedome was supposed to be a landmark scientific experiment, he told us, a microcosm to investigate how Genetic Modification could serve the technological world. The goal was the Nobel Prize, but global funding meant the Government had to make extravagant promises. Prime Minister Johnstone went one step further, claiming the Lifedome would provide emergency shelter should the tension between the East and West ever erupt into another Great Holy War.

That day arrived sooner than everyone expected, on 3rd November 2025.

They claimed it was a rogue test missile, that it wasn't intended to reach London, but the dust clouds enveloped most of the country, and their effect was cataclysmic. With cities in ruins and thousands of refugees left with nowhere to shelter, the Government's Scientific Team had to throw open the Lifedome doors, and provide what shelter they could.

Those who were still able took their families and fled towards the only safe haven in the West, clinging to its costly propaganda that it could withstand every bomb known to mankind. Others accepted a grateful ride from the Sweeper vehicles.

But there were whispers right from the start, whispers that grew with the silence, that things were very different, once you got inside.

Chapter 1

Feral. That's what they called us. Those who knew of us. It was ignorance bred from fear – fear of life on the outside, and fear of us. The Council said without it we would be far more vulnerable, that their fear was our greatest strength. I preferred a strength I could touch.

Sometimes I would climb to the top of the Great Oak – the one that had somehow survived the devastating effects of the biochemical warfare – and stare out at the impenetrable, domed expanse of bright white that climbed and dipped as far as the eye could see. They said there was a roof like the sky at the top. They said humans beneath it had developed differently; but no one could corroborate the myths because no one had been inside … and returned.

The stark contrast of lush forest before miles of deceptive brown dirt, culminating in a security fence four oak trees high, never failed to fascinate me. It represented the difference between us, in what our lives had become.

I leapt back down the tree, trusting the foot and fingerholds I knew with my eyes closed, and crouched in the soft grass beside my favourite water hole. It was one of the first the Outsiders had trusted in the early days, as its trickling source began high in the

311

hills of the craggy moorland mountains surrounding the only home I'd ever known.

At the time of the Great War, before nature was allowed to reclaim what was once a bustling city, the moorland forest had covered only a few square miles. Now it stretched as far as the eye could see, swallowing up eerie ruins as it grew. It was dwarfed only by the monolithic Lifedome rearing up to the skyline, and swallowing one bite of the moon every night.

Our ancestors had called this area Exeter, but now it was only wilderness, filled with every species of animal from every corner of the earth. In the old days, people kept them in treeless forests called zoos for other people to stare at, but that all changed when the cities were burned to the ground.

I stared into the crystal-clear pond and watched small darts of life ripple through my reflection, my impassive features oscillating on the water's surface. Large forest-green eyes stared back at me, at my sandy hair, clay-streaked skin, and lean limbs sculpted by a childhood spent moving and melting into trees. The elders said we'd developed a long way from the physical limitations of our ancestors, who had lived in endless rows of claustrophobic redbrick boxes. They said the charred bones of our ancestors still lay among the ruins, if you knew where to look. But that, like leaving the forest, was strictly forbidden.

I dipped my stained hand into the fresh, clear water, and watched a smear of dried clay dissolve, creating a momentary swirling dance. The rusty pigment darkened the water, and my naked, bronzed skin emerged slowly. Removal of camouflage was also forbidden outside the village. It made you vulnerable to their Sweepers and our numbers were precious few already.

As the water calmed, the reflection of a purple and black butterfly flickered across the delicate ripples. Each wing had been freshly decorated with perfect, concentric circles that disappeared into infinity. And yet something wasn't quite balanced. I looked up to watch my shy companion, who was investigating the wild orchids clustered around the pond.

Now I could see there was no water distortion at all, and that one wing was nearly twice the size of the other. The pretty insect corrected its defect by spreading half its weight on a lower leaf as it sought out the succulent nectar. I smiled. Its imperfection was a common by-product of life's recovery.

Come what may, nature finds a way. Grandpa's favourite motto rang in my ears as I rolled onto my back, bathing in the sunlight filtering through the canopy of leaves. There was something in this sweet spring afternoon that made me want to linger. I let my eyelids droop, and relaxed into the gentle light warming my skin. The forest's palette never failed to interest me, and I'd spent hours trying to locate exact shades for my drawings using berries, tree roots, soil, and leaves. They all offered something different, but there were certain shades that eluded me too, such as the first glimmer of dawn, and the warmth in my dad's eyes when he smiled.

My eyes flickered open. It was time for a snack. I reached into my small leather rations bag and withdrew a misshapen apricot. What it lacked in appearance it more than delivered in flavour, and I devoured the juicy flesh with relish until all that remained was a pitted stone. It was an intriguing stone: old and wizened, like it had lived a thousand lives already.

Care for the seed, and it will care for you. Grandpa's wisdom had guided and protected us all for as long as I could remember. I reached out for a large dock leaf, and rolled the hard stone up before stowing it safely in my rations bag. In the same moment, there was a rustle, about twenty metres away, among the willow and bamboo. My ears pricked. Something snapped, and then I was alert. The branch had been forced, which meant an animal. A big one.

I leapt to my feet, sprung into the branches of the nearest willow, and pressed myself into the nutty bark. The thick foliage concealed me, as I scanned the trees and bushes carefully. They looked quiet enough but I knew better than to trust my eyes. The Sweepers had become increasingly intuitive when looking for specimens in this neck of the woods.

Instinctively, I withdrew a catapult from the belt around my waist, and placed a small stone in the centre of the well-worn rubber. Stretching the rubber taut, I counted to five under my breath, a precaution my brother had instilled when we were barely out of village school. The forest held its breath for a second, and then I released. The tiny missile flew through the air, finding its target beneath an unsuspecting blackbird high among the jungle of trees.

'Sorry,' I mouthed and was rewarded with a sharp tweeting and flurry of feathers. But it was enough.

A large black feline emerged lazily from the thick branches, and surveyed the clearing with an arrogant scowl. She fixed her unblinking yellow glare in my direction. It was a formidable look so many of her prey must have encountered before me. She lowered her eyelids and slunk forward unhurriedly. I released my hold and slid down the tree, stepping slowly into her full view. She paused, just a few metres away from me.

On the ground she looked bigger, sleeker, and more foreboding; I could tell she wasn't a young animal still cutting her teeth. My breath slowed as I focused on her dark, brooding face. The blaze in her gold-flecked eyes left me in no doubt I was in her way, but I knew enough about big cats not to run or climb. That only made you the prey. For a few heart-pounding seconds we regarded each other in a combative stand-off.

'Hssss.'

I clenched my fists and pushed my shoulders forward as I made the first challenge, eyeballing her intently. Her ears twitched in recognition of my strength, and then stilled. Eye to eye, breath to breath, there was nothing else except our racing hearts beating fast and free. The forest echoed our pulses and the birds held their song, waiting for the drum roll to reach its peak.

She tilted forward. My legs tensed and her nose flinched momentarily. A cool breeze lifted my hair, and somewhere in the trees a lemur called its warning as the powerful animal sank back on her haunches. The moment had come. Adrenaline spiked my coiled muscles, propelling me upwards as she sprang. Her outstretched claws grazed my feet as I swung my light body up and over one of the overhanging branches. She landed lightly on a broken stump at the tree base and gave a disgruntled growl, not used to missing.

The entire forest was hushed, watching and waiting as she looked upwards, assessing my strength with a hunter's eyes. I stared back. Unflinching. Her ears twitched. She understood. We were just the same, her and I, two feral cats fighting for survival. Pulling her thick jowls back in silent acknowledgement, she turned and slunk back into the undergrowth.

I exhaled slowly. Such a beautiful animal should be more aware of the price on its head; she was a predator to us, but the Sweepers had a sinister interest in the bigger animals. Sometimes we heard their cries, echoing through the forest as they were hunted.

I lifted my nose, the breeze was fresher than earlier. It was time to move. I set off in the opposite direction, trying to shake off the darker mood creeping through my veins. Stories abounded about life on the inside, about the mysterious projects they undertook. All I knew for sure was that Sweepers left a trail of devastation in their wake, and always stole life from the forest.

Grandpa said the whispers began the moment the Lifedome started sending out collection committees. Those who'd considered the dome a safe haven began to suspect a scientific-military coup. And then there were suspicions of a new hierarchy based on age, health, intelligence, physical attributes, and more.

Fear spread like a disease, and Grandpa's Great-Grandfather Thomas was the first to take a group of dissenters into the forest. Many followed, setting up makeshift camps and villages on the fringe, but that only got the Insiders angry.

They claimed to respect the wishes of those who chose life on the outside; but it was all lies. Images on the Lifedome walls shamed deserters, alleging they were not part of the new world effort. Sweepers raided the crumbled ruins of the city, looking for anyone who'd tried to remain. And then they turned their attention to the forest. The Council told stories of a second apocalypse when an army of Sweepers mowed down entire camps, leaving behind nothing but mangled bodies, withered wildlife, and devastation.

That was when Thomas took matters into his own hands.

He gathered together a selection of surviving crops and wildlife, and offered a truce. The Outsiders would supply the Lifedome with occasional samples, in return for an amnesty from hunting us. He didn't ask what purpose the samples served, and the Insiders didn't offer any reason. There were always suspicions of scientific research, that the Insiders couldn't understand how life had survived at all. Yet our very existence was tantalizing proof, perhaps why they sometimes took us too. But no one ever talked about that.

As usual, I waited under the gnarled willow for Eli to appear, and just as the sun began to dissolve into the berry-stained horizon I felt a pair of gentle hands shield my eyes.

I grinned and spun to hug him fiercely. It was always such a relief to have Eli back within reach. I never liked splitting up, especially given his … differences, but we had little choice. Every man and woman had to take turns to forage and hunt in the outside forest; it was one of the village rules and the only way to supplement food.

We'd cultivated small farms and certain crops grew well, but the good soil was still thin. The forest, on the other hand, had been one of the first places to recover and offer up wild roots, vegetables, fruit, berries, and occasionally, a kill. I left the latter to Eli. For all his shy nature and affinity with animals, he was also profoundly practical when it came to surviving. Today he had a small dead boar strapped to his shoulders, which Joe would make last for a week.

'Grandpa will want to roast that one.' I nodded at it.

I received a wide grin in response, accompanied by a short flurry of fingers. Our improvised sign language had rescued him from a fortress of silence when we were tiny, and cemented our unique bond. When the other kids had teased, I'd protected him and slowly he'd became the voice of my conscience. Silent from birth, Eli's differences were lost among the countless impacts of the war, even now, generations on.

I watched Eli swing the boar from his shoulders, and tie its legs deftly with some braided twine, before we climbed up into the old bushy willow – the control tower for our infra-red security system. Thanks to Thomas's initiative, the Outsiders had foraged enough component equipment to build a basic first-alert system. The technology was rudimentary, but effective. I used my chiselled key lever to flip open the false bark door, and was relieved to see the familiar flashing red light.

Swiftly I flicked the switch upwards, and watched four meters drive straight lines across a small black panel, indicating a clear parameter of three miles. The system was designed to give those hunting and gathering the chance to access the hidden entrance to our valley in complete safety. If a Sweeper or human life was detected in the exclusion zone an alarm was triggered in the village, and those out hunting were not expected to try again until the zone was clear.

'C'mon, we're lit up like the 4th of July. Time to call it a day!'

I signed one of our dad's favourite expressions, before scrambling back down the knotty trunk. It was ironic that Dad's voice rang bright and clear in my memory, while his face faded a little every day. He had been the village schoolteacher; a quiet man who always made time to read to us beside the fire, but one winter he just kept coughing. Mum made chicken broth and told us he would get better, but by spring he was dead. Eli and I had just shared our ninth birthday, and it was the year I stopped trusting in anything outside of my own control.

We walked over to the familiar crossing stones, visible just beneath the rushing water. This was the trickiest part of the return journey, and timing was paramount. The river lowered twice a day, making the swirling water passable if you followed a specific route. Time it incorrectly, and the current would sweep you away and drop you over a fifty-foot waterfall. Eventually.

Eli went first, leaping nimbly from stone to stone, while I followed closely behind. We reached the other side without mishap, and ducked beneath a protruding rock. It concealed the entrance to a small cramped cave, which always looked so unremarkable at a glance. This was the beauty of our valley home, and its discovery was retold at special Council gatherings, as a rite of passage.

It was while Thomas had been hiding meagre food supplies that he made the chance discovery: a heavy metal disc concealing a slim dark tunnel and ice-cold water. Some believed it to be a disused mineshaft, others part of the old-world sewerage system. Either way, he glimpsed a stream of natural light, and desperate to protect his small following, climbed down into the icy water.

The Council said he likened his first discovery of our hidden world to waking in Eden. I could understand why. I hated the tunnel, but it made the emergence into the sudden light and sanctuary of our valley so special. He named the valley Arafel there and then – lest we forget, he said, the dust clouds we were leaving behind. A few called the Hebrew name spiritual protection, but I suspected it was the solid rock between ourselves and the Lifedome, we really needed to bless.

Taking one last look at the dusky forest behind me, I ducked into the cave to find Eli already sending his kill down the tunnel using our system of pulleys. Once the rope went slack, he pulled it taut three times, the general signal that all was clear, and stood aside to let me go first.

'Race you to dinner!' I threw back before dropping like an arrow into the freezing water. The temperature was always glacial, and hit my chest like a rock. I grabbed the guide line and followed it to the dark wall, before inhaling deeply and diving down into the blackness below.

This was the worst part for me, blindly gripping a line and pushing against constrictive tunnel walls that scraped at and dug into my cold skin. And it was always just as my suppressed panic threatened to burst, that the tunnel would rise sharply, spitting me ungracefully into a pool of water at the back of a much larger cave. I swallowed hard to ease my protesting ears, and gazed out at my favourite view in the whole world: Arafel.

The lazy afternoon sun was still bathing our woodland sanctuary, which was completely encircled by high, white peaks. The Great War had left its mark on our landscape, as well as the northern climate, and much of it was unrecognizable from before. Only an Insider Eagle aircraft could chance a glimpse of our village, but the Insiders dispatched them rarely, and it seemed the prospect of a descent through close, angular rock faces discouraged even their most skilled pilots. Thomas had made few rules, but the secrecy of Arafel's location was considered sacrosanct – something no one ever questioned.

Two sets of strong arms plunged in to pull me out as I reached the edge of the pool, and I smiled my thanks as I was thrust a woollen blanket. Wrapping it swiftly around my cold limbs, I gazed out at our small forest village. The maze of interconnected treehouses, just visible among the leafy foliage, reflected one of the pillar beliefs of our community, and the hum of ordinary village duties reached out like an old friend.

It looked as though evening chores were underway. Resisting chickens were being rounded up, a wooden coop was being mended, Jed was adjusting one of the rudimentary crop sprinklers and, judging by the noise, work was continuing on the drainage system.

In truth, we lived like kings compared to Thomas's time. When everyone else had abandoned their homes for the protection of the Lifedome, my ancestors had placed their faith in the natural world. And, despite its terrifying destruction and slow recovery, I couldn't be more grateful. Life was raw, we rarely knew where the next meal was coming from, and we had precious few expectations. But we were free.

I looked back, waiting for Eli to surface. He always did so with a smile on his face and didn't disappoint this time. I helped pull him from the black water, and passed him a dry woollen blanket from the stack in the corner.

'How on earth can you enjoy it?!' I signed, pulling a face.

He flicked water from his sandy hair, making me step back rapidly. His grey-blue eyes shone with silent laughter and I chuckled, feeling the last of my stress melt away.

'Hey, nice work, you two,' Raoul called from the mouth of the cave. Eli's catch was already attracting a small crowd. 'Sausages for breakfast, lunch, and dinner 'til Christmas!'

Laughter rippled through the evening air, as we grabbed our bags and made for the entrance.

'Don't forget the greens.' I winked, emptying the contents of my leather rations bag onto the homemade twig-and-twine platters, before walking away. My hoard comprised a wide selection of wild herbs, edible berries, field mushrooms, and my best find of the day: a whole branch of sweet, ripe apricots – Joe would definitely put those to good use.

'Great forage, Talia!' Raoul called, tossing back two of the apricots.

I spun to catch them deftly, before replacing them carefully in my rations bag. Grandpa never ceased to be amazed at the variety of fruit I foraged. He remembered when fruit didn't grow at all except in the most isolated, sheltered areas; and most of that was withered and spoiled. His generation had a real problem with scurvy. Nowadays, we had our pick of many different exotic fruits, which would never have found a home in the forest before – one of the benefits of catastrophic climate change, or so the Council Elders said.

With the excitement of fresh food supplies growing, we made our excuses and started for home – an old treehouse situated a little way into Arafel's forest. It was one of the first to be built, and Thomas's plans for the village were still etched out in charcoal on the living-space floor. Grandpa said it blessed our home, and reminded us how Thomas always trusted in the recovery of the natural world.

'Eli … Talia, is that you?' Daniel – one of Grandpa's friends – called out as we started for home through the trees. He shuffled across the leafy forest floor and, grasping Eli's hand, shook it profusely. My brother grinned from ear to ear as I rolled my eyes. Eli was going to be able to live off the boar glory for days at this rate.

Nodding politely, I widened my eyes at Eli. He understood. Mum worried so much when we were outside, and all I could think about was watching the colour return to her face when she saw us. We walked swiftly, but were only a few metres on when we were interrupted again.

'Apricots they said? It's not even June! You really are the craziest queen of foraging!'

This time, it was my turn to smile before peering through the trees in the direction of the teasing voice. Max was a couple years older than us. He was also a close friend, natural athlete, and one of the best treehouse builders in the village. He and his dad had designed the new open-air tree showers, and everyone was looking forward to washing without the complimentary mud footbath their predecessor had provided. Max, like Eli and a couple of his friends, were also gifted hunters, and willingly took extra shifts outside the village to boost meat stocks.

'I saved you one, but I want to trade!' I challenged, ignoring the faint frown on Eli's face.

Reaching into my leather pouch, I held the promised golden-yellow treat high, turning slowly on the spot so he could appreciate its unusually perfect, ripened form.

'Well, now I'm intrigued. What could the queen of foraging, teacher of … old stuff and OK, not half-bad tree-runner, possibly want from a lowly construction worker?'

My grin widened and I flexed my limbs. Tree-running was a skill our ancestors had developed as a way of improving our coordination within our new environment. Thomas had started a timed hunter's challenge around Arafel's forest, recognizing that if we were to survive in a new habitat we needed to move more like the animals within it.

'There's no need to be embarrassed about being beaten by a girl, Max,' I teased, craning my neck to peer through the thick undergrowth. 'Last week's new-moon trial was pretty fast, and I've a couple of new tricks I could show you … if you like?'

An excited chaffinch twittered its warning from the under-growth.

'C'mon, a couple of tricks and a juicy apricot in return for one hour of your time to help fix Grandpa's roof … What do you say?'

My ears pricked and the apricot was suddenly spun from my fingers, as a lithe figure sprang from the middle branches of a nearby tree. Instantly I darted for the fallen fruit, but just as my fingers closed around it, Max performed the perfect side-on tackle, knocking all the breath from my body.

'Cut it out!' I yelled, between gulps of laughter as we rolled, his fingers tickling me mercilessly for ownership of the precious fruit. For a couple of minutes I held out, using my runner's strength to keep him at bay while Eli watched from a fallen log. But I was no physical match for Max, and when he prised my fingers open I gave in, using his moment of victory to roll away and catch my breath.

'Where in the name of Arafel did you get this?' he questioned through mouthfuls of the apricot's sweet juicy flesh. 'This is definitely worth a bit of roof repair work – which you know I would have been happy to help with, apricot or not!'

He reached out a strong brown hand and pulled me to my feet, his hazelnut-green eyes twinkling between indignation and amusement. A length of his golden-brown hair had escaped during our tussle, and I watched as he deftly tucked it behind one ear.

He smiled and opened his mouth as though to speak, just as Eli stepped up beside me.

'Is it me or is it raining?' my brother signed with a flurry of fingers, and a brief smirk.

It was a reference to the time Eli and I had needed to rescue Max from a narrow ledge behind a forest waterfall. We'd managed to live off that one glory moment for years.

'Raining? You mean *pouring*!' I signed with an exaggerated flourish.

Max rolled his eyes, understanding perfectly.

'For the love of Arafel, we were seven years old!'

'Seven and eight to be precise,' I corrected, giving in to the gentle pressure of Eli's hand. 'Tomorrow evening for the repair work … After supper good for you?'

He nodded.

'Why don't you help me?' he threw out suddenly. 'Give you a break from teaching all that old, dead stuff?'

'All that old dead stuff is called history, and I happen to believe it's important to learn as much as we can about the past – mostly so we don't screw up the future! But I don't mind lending a hand … Fancy it, Eli?'

Eli's face brightened, and I stifled a frown. He seemed so edgy around Max these days.

'You should probably know,' Max called as I turned away. 'I strained my Achilles last Sunday.'

'Yes … Eli said … no excuse not to win the quarter moon then!' I responded, walking away.

'Oh, I intend to,' he responded, 'so you better get practising those tricks, crazy queen of foraging!'

I rolled my eyes before heading for home, unable to repress a small smile.

Dear Reader,

Thank you so much for taking the time to read this book – we hope you enjoyed it! If you did, we'd be so appreciative if you left a review.

Here at HQ Digital we are dedicated to publishing fiction that will keep you turning the pages into the early hours. We publish a variety of genres, from heartwarming romance, to thrilling crime and sweeping historical fiction.

To find out more about our books, enter competitions and discover exclusive content, please join our community of readers by following us at:

🐦 *@HQDigitalUK*

f *facebook.com/HQDigitalUK*

Are you a budding writer? We're also looking for authors to join the HQ Digital family! Please submit your manuscript to:

HQDigital@harpercollins.co.uk.

Hope to hear from you soon!

ONE PLACE. MANY STORIES

ONE PLACE. MANY STORIES

If you enjoyed *City of Dust*, then why not try another brilliant read from HQ Digital?